# THE SWORD

# OF WINTER

# Marta Randall

TIMESCAPE BOOKS
*Distributed by Simon and Schuster*
*New York*

*for*
*Richard Karl Bergstresser*
*with love*

# Acknowledgments

Special thanks are due to Debbie Notkin and Rebecca Kurland for helping me tie this all together. Thanks are also due to Harris Zimmerman for his encouragement and patience; Howard Cohen for the cold stuff; Richard Curtis, Henry Holmes, and David G. Hartwell for helping turn a manuscript into a book; and to the South Fork of the American River, for keeping me sane.

# Contents

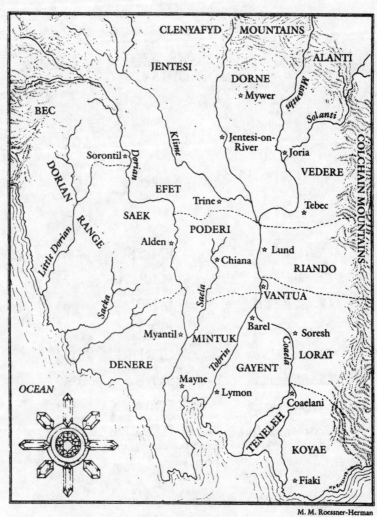

M. M. Roessner-Herman

CHEREK

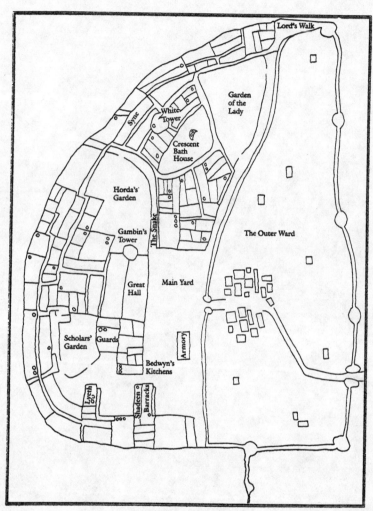

Lord's Walk

Garden
of the
Lady

Syne

White
Tower

Crescent
Bath
House

Horda's
Garden

The Snake

Gambin's
Tower

The Outer Ward

Great
Hall

Main Yard

Scholars'
Garden

Guards

Armory

Bedwyn's
Kitchens

Lyeth

Shadeen
Barracks

M. M. Roessner-Herman

# JENTESI CASTLE

# THE SWORD
# OF WINTER

# ONE

# EMRIS

I T was night by the time she drew near the village. She reined in
Darkness on the last shoulder of hill, leaning forward to pat his
shaggy neck while she surveyed the valley. In the light of the full
moon the river shone like tarnished silver, broken near the village
where the millrace kept the ice from forming. A few lights glowed in
the village itself, yellow against the pale snow. The large, brightly lit
building in the village center would be the inn, offering its last rites of
comradeship and hospitality before bedtime. Folk slept early in these
mountain villages and woke with the sun. Darkness turned his head
inquiringly. His breath puffed clouds in the cold.

She pulled the hood of her black talma over her brows and tucked
it around her throat, trying to remember the name of the village.
Darkness moved down the slope. She'd already visited Helsrest,
Marjoram, Three Crossings—this place would be the last, then back
to Jentesi Castle. She wondered if Lord Gambin was dead yet.

Someone must have seen her and given the alarm, for the inn was
quiet as she rode into the yard. She swung off the snowhorse as the
innkeeper hurried out, pulling the sleeves of a fleece jacket over his
arms. Lamplight spilled from the open door. Pelegorum, she
thought. They raise sheep here. The innkeeper tried to hide his worry
behind a large, patently false smile.

"Rider," he said, holding his hand for the reins. "Welcome, we are
honored. A cup of hot wine, of course, on such a night. Certainly,

assuredly. Welfred!" he bellowed over his shoulder. "Wine for the Rider and a place by the fire! Let me take your horse, go right in, there's plenty of—"

"I'm sure there is," she said amiably. The innkeeper froze, eyes wide. He must have borrowed the jacket; its collar hid the sides of his thin face and the sleeves kept falling over his hands. "Relax, innkeeper. I'd take my bags before you take my horse."

"Of course. Of course." His hands were unsteady on the reins. She lifted the saddlebags and slung them over her shoulder.

"See that he's rubbed and warm," she said as she walked to the open door. "He's worked harder than I this night."

The innkeeper didn't reply.

The public room was silent, the inn's patrons carefully disinterested, and the innkeeper's wife greeted her with a terrified smile and gestured toward a bench near the fire. She dropped her saddlebags by the door, confident that no one would touch them, and unclasped the talma. The careful disinterest increased. She hoped the farmers and shepherds wouldn't strain their eyes trying to look around their ears and paused with her hands on the clasps, about to swirl the talma dramatically from her shoulders, remembering Jandi's disapproval. Theatricality, he had written once. You are too angry, Lyeth. They do you no harm. Their fear harms me, she wrote back. Their hatred harms me. Jandi refused to argue and his next letter spoke only of the comings and goings at the Vantua guildhall. What did Jandi, coddled in the warmth and high regard of Cherek's capital, know of Jentesi Province? She thought a brief, hard curse against Lord Gambin and slid the talma gently from her shoulders, spreading it over the mantelpiece to dry. Water dripped from the edges of the hood where her breath had frozen on the black fur. The innkeeper's wife dipped a measure of mulled wine from the pot by the hearth and handed her a cup. She nodded her thanks and sat before the fire, stretching her legs. Her boots steamed faintly in the warmth.

"Something to eat, Rider?" A plain brown woman with a plain brown voice, barely audible in the room's quiet.

"In a moment, goodwife. I have to thaw my stomach before I know whether it's hungry or not."

The joke met with silence. Lyeth hid her grimace behind the winecup. The innkeeper came into the room, stamping his feet and beating his hands together.

"A cold night, most certainly a cold night," he said, his voice loud in the silence. "Welfred, you've not fed the Rider. What's come to you, woman? I say, what's come to you? Step sharply—some stew and good fresh bread." He came bravely up to the fire, still beating his hands. Behind him his goodwife clasped her hands and stepped nervously from foot to foot, caught between the innkeeper's orders and Lyeth's disregarded humor.

"Your goodwife offered," Lyeth said calmly. He met her glance for a moment before moving away. "I'll eat when I've given the news." She turned on the bench to look at him and beyond him to the inn's patrons. They stared back at her. Unquestionably mountain folk, dark hair and dark eyes, all wearing the same apprehensive expression.

"You're not just passing through, then?" The innkeeper's voice was almost comic with distress. "Not bound somewhere else?"

"I have business in Pelegorum," Lyeth replied. "Is your guildspeaker here?"

Amid the shuffling of feet an old woman rose and stood with her hand on the shoulder of the young man beside her.

"I'm Taela Weaver," she said. "I'm guildspeaker here. Is—is it a conscription, Rider?" She paused. "A warrant?"

Lyeth shook her head but no one looked relieved. She put her cup down on the bench by her thigh.

"Lord Gambin in Jentesi Castle is taken ill," she said, pitching her voice to fill the room. "He is not expected to live and may even be dead by now—I left Jentesi Castle two weeks ago and my news is old." She paused for the incredulous murmur to still. Gambin had been lord in Jentesi Province for forty-seven years, not a good lord but the only one most of these people knew. When the room was quiet again, she said, "A general council is called to confirm the new lord. You are required to send your guildspeaker or someone who can swear the oath for Pelegorum. The council meets four days from now in Jentesi-on-River. The penalty for nonattendance is suspension of trade for one season." She lifted her winecup. "That's all. Grandmother, your guilds had best elect a substitute. A midwinter's ride would sit hard on you."

Taela Weaver's grey brows drew together. "Must we send at all? We've always made reports and paid taxes by messenger, through Three Crossings down mountain. Can't we do that now?"

Lyeth shook her head. "No, Grandmother. The council elects and confirms the new lord and must swear the oath. You can't swear by some petty messenger."

A skinny man in the brown robes of a seminarian moved his shoulders unhappily. "We must pray for the lord," he said, distracted. "I think—I'm sure there's a service for a lord's passing." He looked doubtful. "Somewhere. Rider? To which God do we pray?"

"The House of Gambin is given to the Mother, seminarian. But Gambin himself worships the Father." The seminarian looked dreadfully confused. "Perhaps you'd best pray to both—or to all of them."

"To Death? We should pray to Death?"

"Who better?" Lyeth replied. The people looked at her nervously and the innkeeper's wife placed a bowl of stew and a slab of hot bread on the bench beside her. The stew smelled rich and looked to be thick with mutton.

"When must we let you know?" the guildspeaker said. "About the substitute."

"Me? Not at all. I merely come to bring the message and leave at dawn tomorrow."

"Without the speaker?" the innkeeper said with surprise.

"I go cross country," Lyeth said, the bowl halfway to her mouth. "It's not an easy journey, even for a Rider. Send your speaker through the pass to Three Crossings. If it doesn't snow it will be safe enough; I came through it yesterday. And the road from Three Crossings to the Water Road is clear." She brought the bowl to her lips. The stew tasted even better than it smelled.

"I'll go," said the young man beside the guildspeaker. He looked very eager and not too bright, and wore apprentice weaver's colors. "Let me go, Grams. I'm not afraid of any snow or the passes. Just let me go—I'll show them."

The old woman tugged his dark hair as she sat. "You'll stay with me," she said, and he looked crestfallen until she added, "I need you, lambkin. Couldn't manage without you." He smiled happily.

Lyeth bit into the bread as the innkeeper said, "Who's to go, then? Not me, I say, I can't, I'm far too old. Not young anymore. And who's to run the inn, eh? Who's to run it then?"

Lyeth finished her meal while the argument rose and fell behind her. She watched the play of firelight and lamplight on the inn's heavy wooden walls, smelled the aroma of stew and wine and damp wool, touched the worn, comfortable bench. A good place to spend a winter's evening, were it not in Jentesi Province, were she not a

Rider. Someone went out, someone else came in, the debate continued, and it seemed certain that the issue would not be quickly resolved. She wiped the bowl clean with the last of the bread and ate it, then refilled her winecup. When she turned to face the room again, the voices died.

"Will you hear the news?" she said. "Otherwise I want to go to bed."

"There's *more?*" the innkeeper said.

Lyeth smiled. "Pelegorum is a tiny village in Jentesi Province, and Jentesi only one province in Cherek. There's more."

"Of course, certainly, assuredly." The innkeeper felt for a bench at his back and sat, thin knees held primly together. "Well then, Rider? Well then?"

So, as was her duty, she told them the news. An outbreak of the dancing illness in Riando, soon quelled—but all Cherek remembered the Dancing Plague that swept the country almost a century before, killing half the population and leaving the provinces weak and on the borderline of famine. The villagers looked relieved when Lyeth told them the outbreak had been contained. She mentioned another episode in the long-standing feud between Saek and Denere over which province produced the better wines, and the news that the Captains Guild had launched another trading fleet, the largest one yet, headed for the barely imagined boundaries of the world known to Cherek. Clan marriages, the current prince of mutton and beef in Vantua, rumors from Vedere about possible new ore lodes. Trapper raids in Bec, quickly controlled and avenged by Lord Orlsky's shadeen. The folk widened their eyes at this and shifted in their seats. Lyeth hid her amusement. Pelegorum was a long way from the outlands border, and the white-haired Trappers were, to these people, more a frightening superstition than a real threat. Magical, mystical, able to ride the winds and steal the soul right out of your eyes—Riders, in comparison, were at least assumed to be human. She put her winecup down and talked about the province. The succession in Jentesi was by no means clear, and the folk listened avidly as she named Syne, Coreon, Maranta, and Culdyn, the four possible heirs to the sword, and spoke of who backed which candidate, and what the various guilds and seminarians had to say about it. She wondered how often the folk in Pelegorum heard news from the outside. Possibly once or twice during the summer months, when wool, weaving, and flocks were taken down mountain to market; probably not at all during the winter, with no telegraph lines up, the passes blocked, the valley sealed from the rest of Cherek as securely as if by walls of magic, or walls of time. A new lord might raise or lower taxes, border skirmishes might mean a visit from shadeen come for recruits to their guild. Saek's disputes with Denere would not affect them— the wine in her cup was of the good, common vintage of southern Dorne, not the fancy wine of the sealands. A new lode in Vedere might mean tools more cheaply come by; a rise in the price of mutton or wool in Vantua would bring the money necessary to buy those tools. When she finished some of her listeners asked questions, but she knew better than to expect a friendly gesture. She finished her wine, put the cup on the mantelpiece, and, gathering her talma and saddlebags, asked to be shown to a room. She followed the innkeeper up the narrow stairs, hearing subdued talk from the public room, but knew that it would not last. A Rider's presence guaranteed a drop in an innkeeper's earnings. The man opened the door of a room, wrung his hands under his apron until she indicated that it was acceptable, and hurried back down the stairs.

They'd given her the best room. The windows, heavily shuttered against the cold, faced the front of the inn, and the inner wall was formed of the huge stone chimney rising from the fireplaces in the kitchen and public room. They'd even managed to find fresh sheets for the bed. It creaked when she sat on it to remove her boots. A pitcher, washbasin, and chamberpot occupied a stand near the chimney, along with a clean, coarse towel. Lyeth put the towel around her neck and padded down the cold hallway to the common washroom, whistling silently. This evening had been, as such things went, almost pleasant, and tomorrow her mission was over and she'd be on her way to Jentesi Castle through what promised to be new country. Perhaps Jandi had finally arrived at the castle, ready to satisfy at first hand his usual curiosity about distant provinces. She hadn't seen him in over four years, since he had come with her up the Water Road to Jentesi Castle, accompanying his personal apprentice to her first post. He had been delighted that she was oathed not to some petty land-baron or eventual heir, but to the lord himself; for a little while she, too, had been delighted. Now she thought about Jandi lumbering about the endless, echoing hallways of Jentesi Castle, ignoring the effect his talma would have on the castle's denizens and asking endless questions. Her whistle became audible. The washroom door was locked; she tapped on it lightly with her knuckles.

"In a moment." The voice was young and irascible. Lyeth leaned against the wall, thinking about Jandi and absently inspecting her fingernails. They needed cleaning again. Dirty hands and lame horses—remembered in the grumbling tones of the guild's Master of Apprentices. She slid her dagger from its sheath and cleaned under her nails with its tip. The washroom door opened and a boy backed out, knotting a towel around his waist. Damp golden hair stuck to the back of his neck.

"There, it's all yours," he said, turning. Not a mountain face at all, not with all that bright hair and those hazel eyes. Lyeth nodded, waiting for him to move so that she could step into the room, but after his first jerk of surprise he stood his ground, looking up at her with hatred and not a shred of fear. He couldn't be more than ten years old, she thought. He should have run from her in terror.

"Rider," he said with contempt. She tilted one eyebrow, deliberately sheathed her dagger, and crossed her arms. "Who have you come to kill this time?"

"No one," she said. "Are you going to move, or shall I move you?"

"We put a basin and pot in your room. Why can't you—"

"Little boy, you annoy me. Get out of my way."

He glared at her a moment longer, then spat on the floor between her feet and bolted down the hallway. Lyeth stepped over the sputum and stalked into the washroom, slamming the door behind her. Too angry, Jandi? In what cold heaven, she thought, do I find the spirit to ignore that kind of hate? She stripped quickly and plunged her arms and head into a basin of cold water, gasping a little; the towel was rough against her skin. Her fingers touched the black and yellow guildmark tattooed on her right shoulder and she paused, remembering the faces in the room downstairs. If a ferret worked in Pelegorum, he or she would have been in that room, sipping wine with neighbors and listening, always listening. And, on occasion, reporting to a superior, probably in Three Crossings. Gambin's network of ferrets covered Jentesi from the bank of the Tobrin to the bank of the Klime, from the outlands border to the confluence of the two great rivers at the southern tip of Jentesi Province; an invisible plague of spies quietly listening, quietly watching, quietly reporting. A report might pass up the net to Gambin himself, and if he saw fit a Rider would move through the province, not to deliver news, or bring messages, or map the countryside, but to bring someone to Jentesi Castle, to the inquisitors, to death.

Lyeth touched the tattoo again, hating Gambin, hating his perversion of her guild, hating the ferrets, and hating the folk of the province who heaped their sullen animosity on the only visible symbol of the entire filthy thing—on the Riders. She thought of the boy's expression and wished she had her boots on so she could stomp on the floor. She pulled her shirt over her head and heard some commotion drifting up from the family quarters beside the kitchen. Probably the boy catching hell for insulting her. The family would spend the night stiffly sleepless, afraid of the doom she'd bring down on them for the boy's discourtesy. The thought made her feel better. She pulled on her pants and banged open the door. The inn silenced quickly and she smiled as she stalked down the deserted hallway to her room.

Something woke her hours later. She came out of sleep immediately and lay unmoving, her eyes closed. The room was silent, no soft breathing, no quiet footsteps. The hall, too, sounded empty. Wind muttered about the gables outside; wood creaked. She pulled the blanket close about her chin and the noise came again, a familiar, muffled whinny from the stable. She rolled from the bed, slid into her boots, and grabbed her clothes, struggling into them as she ran silently down the stairs and through the dark public room.

"Welfred?" the innkeeper's voice said sleepily from another room. Lyeth shot back the bolts on the door and let it slam loudly behind her. A dark figure darted from the stable door and ran toward the back of the inn. As Lyeth gave chase she heard Darkness whinny again, loud and angry. She lengthened her pace. The moon was down, but stars peppered the sky and shed a pale radiance over the innyard.

She caught him by the kitchen door, grabbing his shoulder and slamming him against the wall. He struggled silently until she rested her dagger against his throat.

"It's the discourteous little boy," she said with calm fury. The kitchen door opened and the innkeeper appeared in his nightshirt, holding a lantern. He stared at them, jaw hanging.

"Good," Lyeth said. She took the lantern with her free hand. "Go back to bed, innkeeper. Your son and I have words to speak together."

"I'm not his son," the boy muttered.

"You'll not—" the innkeeper began.

"I'll do as I please. I said, go to bed. Now."

The kitchen door shut hastily. Lyeth looked at the boy's defiant face in the lantern light and tapped his shoulder with the dagger's hilt.

"Into the stable. And you will show me precisely what you did to my horse."

"I didn't—"

She tapped him again and he moved reluctantly before her to the stable. The cold mud of the yard sucked at her unlaced boots.

Two horses, a mule, and a flock of chickens observed them suspiciously. Darkness occupied a large stall in the corner. He banged the hoof of his right foreleg against the wooden wall. When Lyeth called he looked over to her, snorted, and banged the stall again.

"What did you do to him?" she demanded.

The boy moved his shoulders defiantly. "Put a burr under his shoe."

"Put a—how did you get close enough? Did you drug him?"

"Of course not," he said, offended.

"Of course not," she mimicked. "Since you put it in, boykin, you can get it out again." She reached overhead to hang the lantern from a hook and pushed the boy toward the stall. Darkness reared and whinnied angrily. The boy jerked away from her hand. She followed him closely, ready to grab him; she wanted him frightened, not injured or dead. He stopped at the gate and said something in a low voice. Darkness quieted, eventually laying his nose in the boy's palm.

"I need your dagger," the boy said.

She hesitated, then gave it to him. He opened the stall door and knelt by the snowhorse's forelegs. She put her hand on Darkness' shaggy mane, afraid he would lash out, but the horse stood patiently on three legs while the boy worked at the hoof with the tip of the dagger. When he rocked back Lyeth put her hand out. He put the burr and the dagger in her palm and rose, patting the horse's neck and murmuring as he backed out and closed the gate. Lyeth sheathed the dagger and examined the burr. It was a nasty, professional-looking thing, a metal ball set with long, dull-edged spikes. She closed her fingers around it.

"You expected him to throw me?" she said.

"Yes."

"I see. Tomorrow morning in the innyard, with everyone watching. To make me look foolish?"

"With luck, to hurt you." He crossed his arms and looked up at her. She felt a surprising jolt of amusement temper her anger.

"A thoroughly nasty boykin," she said. "When did you make friends with my horse?"

"I didn't need to. I can handle horses."

"Ah. A thoroughly nasty boykin with an affinity for snowhorses." She leaned against Darkness' stall. The snowhorse put his nose on her shoulder. "The innkeeper's not your father? No, I can see that. Who is, then?"

"I don't have to answer your questions," he said sullenly. "What are you going to do to me?"

"And I don't have to answer yours," she said, unhooking the lantern. "Back to the inn, boykin. It's late and I'm quite willing to deal with you in the morning."

The innkeeper peered anxiously from the kitchen door. Welfred hovered behind him, wrapped in thick blankets. They backed rapidly as Lyeth came through the door and thrust the boy at them.

"If I don't see him in the morning, you'll answer for it," she told them, and went back to bed. More noise from the family quarters, silenced when she slammed the door of her room. She peeled off her clothes, dropped them over a chair, and crawled shivering under the quilt. The metal burr felt cold and hard between her fingers. She turned it over for a moment, wondering where the boy had found it. It looked Vedere made, or possibly from Alanti; not something easily come by in a sheepherders' village. She put it on the bedside table and was instantly asleep.

She came down just before dawn, to find the boy sitting in a far corner of the public room. His face looked puffed and bruised and he stared sullenly at his feet. Welfred brought a pot of tea, hot bread, a thick slab of fried mutton, butter porridge, and eggs. She put them all on the table and laid out a plate, mug, knife, and spoon. Lyeth pulled the bench close to the table, sat, and reached for the tea.

"Mistress," the innkeeper's wife whispered. Lyeth looked at her. The woman bit her lip anxiously. "He's only a child, mistress. Please don't be harsh with him."

"I'll treat him as he deserves," Lyeth said at normal volume, looking at the boy. "Has he eaten?"

"No, mistress."

"What's his name?"

"Emris," the boy said distinctly. "My name is Emris."

"Ah. Progress. Come here, Emris." She waited until he stood across the table from her. "Sit down. Eat."

"Why?"

"You'll need it." She cut a hunk from the fried meat and brought it to her lips. He stood a moment longer, sat, and reached for the porridge; his rough shirt was too small, baring his wrists. The innkeeper's wife brought him plate, cup, and utensils, and at Lyeth's gesture retreated to the kitchen. The inn was creakingly silent.

"Are you adopted?" she said suddenly. Emris looked up from his porridge and shook his head. "Then who speaks for you?"

"Trave Innkeeper, I suppose."

"No blood relatives?"

"Not anymore," he said bitterly. "Are you afraid of retribution?"

"Riders are untouchable save through Clan Court," she said. "You should know that. Finish your breakfast, boykin."

She swung her legs over the bench and took her tea mug with her into the kitchen. Trave Innkeeper and his goodwife stood by the door, conferring in whispers with some townsfolk. They didn't notice her at first, then they all stopped talking and looked at Lyeth apprehensively. She began to find the expression wearing.

"Emris is your stableboy?" she said.

"Yes, Rider." The innkeeper's hands flew under his apron and twisted about each other, rucking the smooth white cloth.

"Rider," Welfred said nervously, "he's not a bad boy, he's—"

"He's busy," Lyeth said. The innkeeper glared at his wife and nodded his head violently. "Saddle my horse. And saddle a second one. The grey, I think. It's not lame or sick, is it?"

"The mare? No, Rider," the innkeeper said unhappily. "A very fine horse, the grey. My best horse. My only good horse."

"I'm pleased to hear it. Saddle her. And you, goodwife, will pack Emris' winter gear. Enough for two saddlebags—no more. And clothes that fit, hear?" Welfred bit her lip. "You do have saddlebags?"

"Yes, mistress."

"See that they're good ones. Two water pouches for the grey, full, and fill mine. And a way-meal, enough for two." A wisp of smoke rose from an oven, bringing the scent of charred bread. Lyeth walked out of the kitchen.

Emris had finished his meal and sat with his elbows on the table, running his fingers distractedly through his tangled yellow hair.

"Use a comb," she advised.

He jerked around to face her. "Why don't you just get it over with?" he demanded. "You don't have to drag it out, you just do it to —to scare us."

"Thoroughly nasty, discourteous, and acute," she said, resting one booted foot on the bench. She picked up the last of the meat with her fingers and chewed it thoughtfully. Emris put his hands in his lap and looked at them.

"It hurts her," he muttered. "At least for her sake—she hasn't hurt you."

"Welfred, you mean? She's been kind to you?"

He refused to answer. Lyeth finished the meat, looking at him, then drained her tea mug and put it on the table.

"Wait for me here, boykin," she said, turning away. "It won't take long."

It took little time to repack. She checked the capacious pockets of the talma, settled it over her shoulders, and twisted her long brown hair into a knot at the nape of her neck, pinning it in place. The sky paled into full dawn and she pinched the candle out, thinking of Welfred's distress, the innkeeper's nervous hands, Emris' eyelashes, then cursed emphatically and swept open the holding seams of the talma. The myriad tiny hooks hissed as they came free of the dark fur lining; the talma spread around her, a cloud of black. Satisfied, she picked up her saddlebags and went downstairs.

The public room was crowded with townsfolk standing against the walls; they moved back as she came into the room, pressing against each other and watching her with wide eyes. A tall man behind Emris put his hand on the boy's head. She paused and stared at him, expressionless, and he licked his lips.

"Rider," he said softly. "Surely you can reconsider. He's just a child; children play pranks, innocently—unwisely, perhaps, but just child's play."

"He tried to cripple my horse," Lyeth replied frostily. "That's child's play?"

"No, of course not. But he didn't succeed, did he? He's learned his lesson, Rider." The tall man's brown eyes gleamed, beseeching understanding and something more. He jerked his head, flicking light brown hair from his eyes, and smiled suddenly. "We're rational adults, Rider. We can work something out."

"I have something worked out," she said. "Let him go."

The man dropped his other hand to the boy's shoulder. "Leave him to me, Rider. I'll see that he's adequately punished." He paused. "I know the rules," he said carefully. "You can trust me in this."

"I said, let him go. Or perhaps you wish to share his fate?"

"Rider—"

*"Now!"*

The man's hands flew away from the boy; a child wailed and buried her face against her father's jerkin. The seminarian's fingers moved in the sign against evil and Lyeth clamped down hard on her anger. She jerked her head at Emris, who took his saddlebags from Welfred and followed Lyeth into the yard. The corners of his mouth were white with tension, and the townsfolk followed cautiously after.

Darkness and the grey stood side by side, their reins in Trave Innkeeper's thin hands. Lyeth motioned the boy to mount the grey and swung up on Darkness' back, taking the reins for both horses from the innkeeper. He stood back hurriedly. The tall man now had his hands on Welfred's shoulders, staring over her brown head at Lyeth. The Rider ignored him, reaching into her talma.

"The boy comes with me," she said, her voice clear in the icy silence. "The horse also comes with me." She tossed a small bag to the innkeeper. "Buy yourself another mare and another stableboy, and mind that the new one has manners." The innkeeper's fingers were already busy counting coins through the cloth. "Welfred," Lyeth said suddenly.

The woman's shoulders went back, then she stepped away from the tall man and came to Lyeth's stirrup. The Rider bent down.

"I'll treat him as he deserves," she said quietly. "But he won't be harmed. I swear it to you."

Welfred looked deep into the Rider's eyes. "I believe you, mistress," she said, and backed away.

Lyeth stared at her a moment longer, then jerked the reins impatiently. Darkness moved out of the yard, the grey trailing obediently after. A collective, unhappy, quiet noise rose from the yard and she pulled the hood low over her eyes and paced through Pelegorum's one street, thinking dark thoughts. The mill stood silent, waterwheel still; the water in the millrace had frozen solid overnight. By now, she thought, even the wide Tobrin would be locked tight. The road took them over a low bridge. To the right the ice was smooth and undisturbed save for the tracks of skates; to the left it lay rucked and twisted above stones. The hills rose again after a few acres of farmland. The white sky of dawn darkened marginally to a cold, pure blue, fringed on the horizon with white snowfields and black trees. She waited until the village dropped from sight before stopping the horses and turning to look at the boy.

"Is this how we took your parents?"

He looked startled. "No, not in daytime. How—how did you know?"

"An educated guess." She tugged at the talma, tucking and pressing it into a more manageable shape for riding. The tiny hooks sank into the fur as the cloak shaped itself to her body. "You can't go back to Pelegorum, you know," she remarked as she worked. "You know the penalty for harboring a fugitive, and so do they. The nearest town is fifty kils from here, over the mountains. You won't make it in one day, and without me you won't make it at all." She threw the grey's reins to him. "Does that thing have a name?"

Emris wrapped the reins around his gloved hand. "Myla."

Lyeth nodded and Darkness moved up the slope. A moment later Emris came up behind her and settled the grey in Darkness' tracks, a dozen paces behind. She bit her lip, frowning, and didn't look back. She'd take him to the edge of the valley and let him go; it would be sufficient.

At noon she pulled cheese and dried meat from a saddlebag and handed half to him. They ate while the horses picked their way through snow-covered scrublands. Finished, he pulled his gloves on again but did not drop behind. She took another bite of meat.

"Did you come for me?" He didn't look at her. "Specially, I mean."

She shook her head and swallowed. "No. Why should I?"

"Riders came for my parents."

"That hardly matters. Children aren't taxed for their parents' sins." He looked ahead stubbornly, the reins clenched in his fist. "Come now, you're not a baby. You don't think Riders come if you don't finish your supper, do you?"

He glared at her. She finished her cheese and shook crumbs from her hands before pulling on her gloves. Myla slowed to let Darkness take the lead.

By midafternoon they approached the far end of the valley, and she glanced over her shoulder at him. He stared back at her defiantly, and she pressed her lips together. A ride to the valley's end was not, apparently, sufficient. Another two hours until sundown—

she'd send him home the next morning. She resisted the urge to look again at the boy. Too stubborn, Jandi called her. She thought the boy was probably as stubborn as she. The light forest thinned and the track widened; Emris came to ride beside her again.

"Why did you take me, then?" he demanded.

"You annoyed me."

"That doesn't make sense. If I really annoy you, you'd have left me back in Pelegorum."

She didn't reply. A winter hawk circled overhead, barely visible against the pale blue sky.

"Rider?"

"Boykin?"

He hesitated before saying quickly, "What are you going to do to me?"

She briefly considered the truth, and discarded it. "I've not decided yet." He looked at her quickly, frightened beneath his bluster. "Riders don't kill, Emris," she said. "We're not executioners."

His expression was heavy with disbelief. She gestured sharply. "We're messengers. We bear the news and warrants, and when necessary we call people to justice. We only fight in self-defense." His mouth twisted. She said, before he could speak, "We worship the Mother, Emris. We're not shadeen, to worship the Father. Or Trappers, to worship Death."

She couldn't read his expression. His hand dove into the folds of his jacket. He fumbled for a moment, paused, and brought his hand into the light. Cradled in his palm, fastened to a chain around his neck, was a token. Lyeth bent to look at it. He gave her time for only a quick glimpse before secreting the token in his clothes again, but she had seen the heavy upright crowned with thorns, the circle of fire, the mace and the sword. She sat back and let the reins hang loose between her fingers.

"Where did you get that?"

"It was my father's," Emris said defiantly.

Lyeth thought about that while Darkness picked his way along the snow-covered track. No simple amulet, that; not the sort of thing passed from father to son. Never given at all without the bond, the pledge, the promise, the initiation. If the token had indeed belonged to Emris' father, it should not have been hidden in the boy's jacket but fastened around a dead man's neck.

"Do you know what it is?" she said.

"Do you?"

When she didn't answer, he said unhappily, "Part of it's the Father symbol, and part is protection. I don't know the rest."

Lyeth took a deep breath; cold air touched the back of her throat. "It's a shadi's token," she told him. "Your father must have been one."

He shook his head, bewildered. "I don't remember my father fighting. I don't— How could he . . ." His voice trailed off. Lyeth shrugged and flicked the reins. Darkness moved ahead. The image of the token danced before her and she repressed a shudder. Why would Riders take shadeen?

Soon after, the sun touched the distant peaks and the small light of dusk filled the mountains. The land rose again while Lyeth searched for a place to spend the night. They crested a rise and she turned to the boy; he shivered in the saddle, his lips blue and his jaw clenched hard. He hadn't said a word about being cold. Stubborn, yes. She made him stop while she rummaged in a saddlebag and produced a spare talma.

"I d-don't need it," he said through clenched teeth.

"Liar," she replied. "Survival is the first law. Take what you can." She threw the talma over his shoulders. He shuddered at the touch of the black fur but drew it around himself and fastened it beneath his chin. It fell well past his heels and trailed over Myla's rump. He looked, she thought, like a bundle of laundry half-full and propped on a horse; she kept forgetting how small he was. She turned to look over the shallow valley before them.

"Emris, what's this?"

"Su-summer pasture. F-for the sheep."

The stutter worried her. "Good. There should be a shepherd's hut. Do you know where?"

He urged Myla forward and she followed him down the slope of the hill. The hut was boarded closed for the winter. She pried boards away from the entrance while he tended the horses, and by the time he finished she had a fire built near the door of the hut. Smoke rose straight up in the still air.

"It will be cold tonight," she said. He hesitated at the entrance, came around the fire, and sat on the far side. "Are you hungry?"

He nodded. Her largest pot hung over the fire; when the water in it began to boil she made cups of tea. She took dried meat from her bag and sliced it with her dagger, added it to the pot, and tossed in some dried vegetables. A pinch of salt and spices followed, and the hut filled slowly with the scent of soup.

"Who will they send, do you think?" she said companionably, leaning forward to stir the soup. "To Jentesi-on-River, I mean."

He shrugged. The hood slid down to his shoulders; his lips were pink again. "Not Taela—she's too old. And Trave Innkeeper won't go, he's too lazy. They'll probably send Cerdic." His tone changed when he said the name.

"Was he there last night?"

"Yes, and this morning, too." Emris hesitated. "He's the one who talked to you."

"Ah." Lyeth rocked back and looked at Emris. Hero-worship, she thought. For a tall, strong-looking man with suspiciously gentle eyes. "Think he'll make it?" she said blandly.

"You said the pass was clear."

"So it was. But a clear pass means nothing if the traveler is an idiot."

"Cerdic's not an idiot," Emris said hotly. "He's the best shepherd in Pelegorum—in all the mountains. He can climb anything and he always knows where everything is. He's the best."

"Is he, now? Did he tell you so?"

"He doesn't need to tell anybody anything." Emris' jaw thrust forward. "He's taken me with him sometimes; I can see what he does. Nobody's better than Cerdic."

"Um," she said noncommittally. She dug out another pot, poured half the soup into it, and passed it over. "So Pelegorum is to be represented by an intrepid sheepherder, probably full of strong opinions about the price of mutton and smelling of lanolin. I'm not surprised."

Emris glared. "Just because he doesn't spend his time running around in black capes scaring people, just because he's kind and gentle and comes from the mountains and not some dumb city—"

"Emris, shut up," she said sharply. "Not all of us come from the cities."

"I'll bet you wish you did," he retorted, glaring through the steam of his soup.

She cursed and went outside, taking the last of her soup with her. Stubborn, ill-tempered, sharp-tongued brat—if she let him go tomorrow, she thought sourly, he'd probably see it as a victory. She finished her soup and tossed the pot inside the hut as she stumped through the snow to the makeshift corral. Emris had hobbled the horses in a circle of bare trees and bushes mounded with snow, relatively protected from any wind that might come. The animals bent their heads to the feed he'd given them. She put her hand out and called. Darkness snorted at her and returned to his meal, and she walked into the valley. The night was still and cloudless, the cold striking straight down from the stars. She watched the valley, her breath forming ice clouds that clung to the edges of her hood. Her eyes felt sandy. Sleep, yes, unbroken by night alarms, and the next morning she'd send him back to Pelegorum. Sharp-tongued brat. A shadi cub. Clan policy moved the families of criminals from their hometowns or villages; she wondered where he originally came from. Cold bathed her throat when she yawned.

When she returned to the hut the pots had been cleaned and put aside, embers glowed in the firepit, and the boy slept in the folds of the talma, his golden head cradled on his arms. She looked at him a moment, shook her head, and knelt to make sure the front seam of the talma was sealed. She pressed the bottom hems together, creating a warm bag for his sleep. He mumbled but did not waken. She'd have to hunt tomorrow—their rations would not last without some supplement and it was a good two days to Jentesi Castle, perhaps more now that she traveled with the boy. She shook her head sharply, correcting herself. But even if she sent him home in the morning, she'd need more food for herself. Weary and bemused, she made a bag of her own talma, pulled the hood well over her head, and resolutely thought about catching rabbits until she fell asleep.

Behind the shepherd's hut, past where the horses paced restlessly in their makeshift corral, the woods thickened and broke against the banks of a stream. Frozen water twisted through tree roots and smoothed over the occasional pools. Lyeth followed the stream until she found a pool that pleased her, deep enough to carry running water below the surface ice and surrounded by snow-heavy bushes, their bent branches forming hollow runs along the ground. An indistinct trail led through the trees to the stream; ice, decorated with droppings, gleamed darkly in the pale light before dawn. She moved upwind of the pool and waited motionless, dagger ready.

Catching rabbits by hand was a trick she'd learned from her father, back before Cherek had reclaimed her and the guild had given her a home. The other apprentices had thought it magic, some deep and mysterious Trapper enchantment; bereft and furious in her loneliness, she had not disabused them, leaving Jandi to lumber furiously through the Vantua guildhall, tracking the rumors of his ward's dark ways. She was, eventually, unmasked and punished, not for catching rabbits but for fostering the deception. Jandi sonorously made the punishment fit the crime, forbidding her the hunt; she merely stopped practicing the trick in public, and years later when he again caught her with rabbit in hand, he merely bellowed his despair and let the matter drop.

The trick looked far more simple than it was. When a rabbit finally appeared, peering about the pool nearsightedly and twitching its nose, Lyeth remained still. The rabbit moseyed over the ice, found the spot Lyeth had known it would choose, and began thumping its hind legs on the thin, splintered surface. Before it had thumped thrice, Lyeth had it by the hind legs and slit its throat. It jerked convulsively between her hands. She pressed a handful of snow against its throat, staunching the blood, and left the woods, pausing at the treeline to drain, skin, and gut the animal. The sky brightened although the sun was not yet over the eastern mountains, and she loped down the slope to the hut, swinging the rabbit in time with her easy strides.

Emris had seen to the horses, saddling both and strapping his own bags in place. The fire burned warmly; a pot of tea steamed on a stone. Lyeth dropped the rabbit next to the teapot and stamped her feet, brushing snow from the folds of her talma.

"Can you spit it?" she said.

Emris took the rabbit silently. She packed the remainder of her gear and cleaned her dagger; by the time she finished the rabbit turned above the embers, dripping juice. It was tough and skinny, but flavorful. They ate most of it and, while Emris boarded the hut, Lyeth wrapped what remained into two packets and put one in Emris' saddlebags. When he came up to her she tossed his reins to him.

"Okay, boykin. Back you go."

He looked at her blankly. "Back?"

"Back home. To Pelegorum. To your fearless Cerdic and pinchpenny Trave and all those sheep. Go on, I have a long way to go yet."

Emris, adopting his stubborn expression, clenched the reins tightly in his fists. "I don't want to go back," he said.

"You don't—boykin, have you lost your mind? You hate Riders, remember? I'm going to take you into the high passes and eat you for lunch, remember? Go on, stop wasting my time." She put her foot to the stirrup.

"I'll follow you."

She took her foot out of the stirrup, turned around, leaned against the horse, and stared at him with exasperated puzzlement, but before she could speak Emris reached out suddenly and laid his hand on her arm.

"Rider, listen," he said urgently. "First, you took me and I'm your responsibility now and it wouldn't be very responsible of you to take me this far and just leave me in the mountains, would it?"

"You grew up here. You have the wonderful Cerdic as an example. You can find your way back; there's plenty of daylight for it."

"And I don't want to go back. I told you."

"Too bad."

"And besides," he added, "they're not my people. I'm just Trave's ward—someone sold me to him, just like you bought me from him. So I'm your ward now."

"I didn't buy you, damn it." She shook his hand away. "I paid Trave for a room at his inn and the use of his horse for a day. He'll find that out when he counts the coins. What in the Holy Mother's name would I want to buy you for? And why, for Her sake, do you want to come with me?"

Emris put his hand under his jacket, fingering the token. "I want to find my family," he mumbled.

"What?"

"I want to find my family!" He raised his chin. "There has to be someone somewhere, maybe an aunt, or a grandmother, or somebody. You have a family. Everybody has a family. I don't see what's so terrible about me wanting to find my own family." He paused. "And you did so pay Trave Innkeeper for me. That bag was heavier than just a night at an inn and renting a horse. That was enough to buy the horse, and enough to buy me, too. And if you don't want me," he concluded, rushing, "then when we get to the city you can sell me to someone else, or apprentice me, and they can pay you back for me. Or if you want to wait, I'll pay you back when I have money."

She stared at him. He breathed deeply, his hand clenched under his jacket.

"Why," she said finally, "is being sold to someone in the city, or apprenticed in the city, any different from staying in Pelegorum? You don't even know what the city is like."

"I can't find my family in Pelegorum," Emris said. His voice wasn't as steady now.

Lyeth looked away from him, through the trees toward the small valley.

"You know about Lord Gambin," she said finally. "Does anyone in Pelegorum like him very much?" When Emris didn't answer she looked back at him. "Do they?"

He shook his head.

"Emris, I'm Lord Gambin's personal Rider. I've oathed to him." She paused. "Do you still want to come with me?"

This time Emris hesitated. "You said Riders don't kill people," he said finally. "And . . . and I don't have a choice. If I can't go with you, I'll never go with anyone at all."

"Never is a long time, boykin." She looked away again. You're going to regret this, she told herself while the voices of Jandi and Joleda, in the back of her head, agreed fervently. This is a mistake. This is absolutely not the right thing to do.

"Get on your horse." She swung herself aboard Darkness. "We have a pass to find and cross before sunset."

"You're going to do it?" Emris said, astonished.

"Don't press your luck." The boy mounted hurriedly. "And Emris. Just remember that you're unwanted baggage now."

The boy set his shoulders back and, when she was satisfied with the quality of his glare, she flicked Darkness' reins and they moved off as the sun cleared the peaks and bathed the valley in light. The thin forest snapped with the cold. *Everybody has a family.* I don't. She pushed the thoughts away, pulled a map from one of the talma's many pockets, and scribbled occasional notes as she rode. How many maps, she wondered, had Jandi put together over the years from the scribbled notes and rough sketches she sent him from Jentesi Province? The one she now held, reason for this circuitous route back to Jentesi Castle, would be reborn under Jandi's fingers, the vaguely noted pass on it transformed into specific detail. She envisioned a time when all of Cherek would lie disclosed, precise and plain, in the vasty maprooms of the Vantua Riders guildhall, and the thought, as always, displeased her. But there were lands beyond Cherek, the alps of the Trapper country where, four years ago, Jandi had forbidden her to go. That distant argument still rankled. Other Riders were sent into the outlands to explore and furnish the genesis of maps; who better than Lyeth who knew the language, knew the customs, had some tenuous claim to a tribal connection beyond Cherek's borders? But Jandi had refused, sending her instead to Jentesi's despotic, Riderless lord—afraid, she thought, that if she rode north she would not ride back again. Afraid of losing her. She snorted and wrote something crude on the map's margin, and her attention snapped around when she heard Myla stop. But Emris had only dropped from the saddle and stepped into the woods to relieve himself. He remounted, his expression wary, and she let the silence continue as she urged Darkness up the slope.

Here the wind had scoured snow from plates of rock, leaving it piled in high drifts on the lee side of outcroppings and huge boulders. The stillness of the valley gave way to strong gusts which tugged and whipped at the talmas, but in the sunlight and under the clean, washed blue sky, it was warm. Lyeth consulted the map, made a note, and changed their heading slightly so they moved to the southeast. Within a few kils the rocky slope ended at the foot of a towering granite scarp, its base heavy with shattered rock. The wind rose. She rewrapped her talma, sealing it to her gloves and the tops of her boots, and did the same for the boy, fastening hooks until nothing showed of his face save his eyes, deep in the hood's shadows. He flinched from her touch and when she called his name he turned his face away, sulking. He had what he wanted, she thought impatiently. What cause did he have for sullenness?

But his silence could not survive the view awaiting them as they came through a tumbled pass in the scarp. Before them the land dropped precipitously, falling into the darkness of an immense fissure; mountains soared beyond, peak upon peak of grey rock and white snowfield gradually purpling with distance, the farthest peaks backed by the darker grey and white of storm clouds. Emris gasped, his eyes wide, and Lyeth felt an exultation and a familiar ache.

"If for nothing else," she said over the yelling wind, "this makes it worthwhile."

The boy's hood jerked as he looked at her. "Why?"

"Isn't it obvious?"

"Yes," he said, his voice muffled by cloth and distant in the wind. "I didn't think you could see it."

To her surprise, the remark hurt. She turned from him, looking south down the ravine where the ledge narrowed to a shelf just wide enough for one horse; overhead the rock leaned forward, forming a grey roof. Darkness picked his way along the shelf and Myla put her head down and followed his trail. At the overhang's deepest point the wind abated. Lyeth reined in and dismounted. Emris tethered the horses while she dug out the flask of cold tea left over from breakfast. Some dried and brittle twigs against the far wall provided enough fire to warm their hands. They sat near the lip of the cliff, watching winter hawks circling below them through the liquid air, looking like dark spots dancing an infinity away. Lyeth breathed deeply, remembering other places. The tea was strong and chill.

"It looks like the outlands north of Alanti," she said after a while. "Canyons like this, but deeper. Tall straight mountains with clouds around their tops, falling all the way down to their roots and coming up again. Sometimes you find meadows high up in the mountains, so cold and distant that only goats and eagles live there. Or valleys so deep that the sun shines only at noon, and the rest of the time it's either night or twilight."

Emris looked at her curiously. "Higher than Pelegorum?"

She laughed. "High enough to make you dizzy just thinking about them. Higher than we are now."

"That's Trapper country," he said dubiously. "You were there?"

"Yes. A long time ago."

"You saw Trappers?" He turned to her, eyes bright. "Real ones?"

"Yes, real ones." She leaned back against the rock. "Pale folk, most of them. The ones with Cherek ancestors are a bit darker, but not by much. Most of Constain's people intermarried—you know about him?"

"Sure. He was a tyrant and a murderer and he tried to conquer all of Cherek but he was defeated and kicked out and he escaped to the Trappers before he could be killed. He wasn't a very nice man," Emris concluded piously.

Lyeth laughed again. "That's a fair enough assessment. And sometimes other folk come up from Cherek to become Trappers, so they're not all pale." She took another swallow from the flask. "They live on horses, traveling from one meadow to another, one valley to another, putting up tents made of goatskins and gathering whatever comes up ripe. And trapping for furs—you've never seen such furs, Emris. Dark ones, deep and warm, and pale ones so white they make your eyes hurt. Sometimes they sew them together in bright patterns you can see from kils away, and sometimes they sew them into things you can't see, they blend with the snow and mountains so well. Can't see them until you blunder right into them, and even then sometimes it's hard to tell they're there." She smiled, touching the deep fur lining of her talma. "These are Trapper furs. The guild buys all the black ones the Trappers can provide."

Emris put his fingers through the fur of his own talma. "They use magic," he said. "They can make themselves invisible."

Lyeth shook her head. "No."

"They do so," Emris retorted. "And they have white hair and red eyes. A man came up from Three Crossings once and told us so. They're evil."

"He was lying—didn't you listen to me? The pure-blooded Trappers have white hair, yes, but most of them have blue eyes, pale blue. Or brown. And the ones with Cherek blood—some look a lot like me, Emris. Some even look a lot like you."

"No, they don't," he muttered. "I don't look like any stinking Trapper."

She stopped smiling. "How do you know, boykin?"

"Everybody knows what Trappers look like. Besides, they worship Death, and they like to kill people, and they steal babies and use them to make magic." Emris looked at her smugly. "Our seminarian said so."

"Your seminarian is an ass," she said inelegantly and jerked the last of the rabbit from her saddlebag.

"He is not." Emris took part of the rabbit from her. "Were you there a long time? Did you kill any of them?"

"Shut up and eat," she muttered fiercely, taking a bite of rabbit. He moved to the other side of the fire, eyeing her warily. Serves me right, she thought. Hell, it's not the boy's fault; he speaks what he's been taught. She glanced at him. He made a rude gesture and turned away, and she decided not to apologize after all. Taking the map from her talma, she spread it over her knees and made notes with one hand, a leg of rabbit clenched in the other. Emris watched her, sucking on his fingers, until his curiosity got the better of him.

"What's that?"

"A map." She hesitated before moving her arm so that he could see. He cautiously came a bit closer. A smear of rabbit fat graced the tip of his nose. "We're right about here, I think," she said, pointing. "Somewhere over here there should be a break in the ridge and a narrow pass through to the mountains above the Tobrin Valley. My guess is that the pass is part of this scarp, and this ledge should lead us to it."

"And if it doesn't? Or the pass is blocked?"

"We turn around and go back through Pelegorum and Three Crossings until we hit the Water Road, and from there to Jentesi Castle."

His finger traced lines on the map. "Why are you writing on it?"

"Making notes for our master mapmaker. The Riders Guild has always provided Cherek's maps. It's one of our duties."

He rocked back and looked at her, the hood of his talma thrown back. Bright hair tumbled in the wind. "That's why we came this way? To explore the pass?"

She nodded. "What did you think, boykin? That Riders are so nasty they can't take regular roads, and have to creep about the backcountry like wolves?"

He looked at her dubiously, but leaned forward to put his finger over the mark for Jentesi Castle.

"That's where we're going?"

"Yes. Once Lord Gambin dies, I'm to ride to Vantua with the news."

He considered this. "They'll know already, won't they? By the telegraph?"

"Probably, if the lines aren't down." She rolled the map and replaced it in her pocket. "But it's a tradition, Emris. A Rider has always delivered the Deathnote, and they won't enter it in the Vantua records until I get there." She handed him her handkerchief. "Here, you've got grease on your nose."

He frowned, rubbing at his face with the cloth. "Will you ride all the way there?"

"Not likely. Darkness is a snowhorse, not a speeder. I'll take the Water Road."

"I remember that," the boy said slowly. "The iceboats with big sails all different colors, and the runners. I wasn't allowed onto the Water Road because of the runners."

"Makes sense," she said, picking the last of the meat from the bone. "Where was this?"

"I don't know. Before I came to Pelegorum." His face hardened into an expressionless mask and he let the handkerchief drop on the stone beside her.

Before the Riders, Lyeth thought. He's as resentful as I was. She wiped her hands, pulled on her gloves, and rehooked the hood. When she reached to do the same for Emris he jerked away and fastened the hooks himself, his hands clumsy on the tiny catches. Lyeth left him to it while she fetched the horses.

She almost missed the mouth of the pass, hidden as it was between boulders and a monstrous drift of snow. She eyed the drift unhappily; if the pass didn't lead all the way through, if the snow mass fell while they were within, if an avalanche blocked the pass— The walls of the pass leaned toward each other at the top, eating daylight over the narrow canyon. A tunnel, almost, of rock and snow. Her heartbeat quickened; she deliberately pushed her ancient fear away. The horses picked their way through the thin gap. The pass plunged between two soaring angles of mountain, a steep ravine whose walls were marked by the rush of water. Dry now, but not a pass to try during the season of the melt. Thick falls of snow blanketed the slopes overhead and Lyeth watched them suspiciously. A vicious wind filled the pass. Darkness and Myla lowered their heads, plodding forward over rock and brittle ice, and Lyeth fumbled in a bag for the goggles. She slipped one set over her wrist and turned to Emris. Wind tore the words from her lips but he stopped and sat quietly while she slid the goggle straps through the eyelets on his hood, settled the goggles, and rehooked the cloth. Now he looked like a pile of windwhipped laundry with bulbous eyes. She grinned and turned, lifting her own goggles, and a gust of wind laden with sharp particles of ice slapped her face, filling her eyes before she could blink. She gasped and clapped her hands to her face. Her eyes stung and burned and her tears froze, cementing her lashes together and locking in the pain. It hurt so much she could barely breathe.

Hands tugged at her wrists. Emris shouted. She jerked away but he clung to her tenaciously.

"Stop that," the boy yelled. "Rider, stop that. Let me help you." She forced herself to sit still. Emris pulled her head forward and his mouth covered her left eye. Ice melted from her lashes. He clapped a dry cloth over the eye and moved his mouth to her right eye, and when both eyes were bandaged she felt him fumble for her goggles.

"I can do it," she muttered. If he heard, he ignored her. He tightened the goggles over the bandages and put her hands on her hood. She fastened the hooks with shaking fingers; it took all her will

power not to claw at her eyes. When Darkness moved forward she
clung helplessly to the pommel, listening to the shriek of the wind. It
dropped to a howl. Darkness stopped; Emris tugged on her boot. She
slid uncertainly from the horse and stood, her hands on the shaggy
mane. Emris took her elbow and pulled, and the wind's howl became
a whine as she stumbled after him.

"It's a cave," he said. "Sit down. Here—there's a big rock."

"No fire," she said, thinking of the snowshelf overhead. "We can't
have a fire."

"Of course not." He sounded exasperated. She loosened her goggles and pulled them off, and Emris helped her take the bandages
away. She raised her lids. Tears ran freely and her eyes stung; the
pain lessened marginally but the world blurred into shapeless
patches of dark and light. Emris blotted her tears with the cloth. She
took it from him and wiped her eyes, cursing.

"We can't stay here," she said. "It's late, we couldn't make it
through the night. That snowshelf could fall, block us in—" The
ancient fear rose again; her pulse thudded. "We have to go back.
Now."

"I think it's too far," Emris said. "I saw the map. Even if we went
back we couldn't find a good camp before nightfall and I don't want
to follow that ledge in the dark." His high young voice sounded
authoritative.

"I suppose," she said nastily, "you think you know what you're
doing."

"I've traveled with Cerdic," he replied. "I'll lead the horses and
you ride Darkness. Are you still crying?"

"I'm not crying," she retorted. "My eyes are tearing, there's a
difference." The crazy beating of her heart steadied. "What makes
you think you can lead us out of this?"

"You certainly can't," he said evenly. "You'll just have to trust me,
Rider."

Lyeth realized unhappily that he was right. She wiped her eyes
again, breathing deeply to calm the pain and the fear. "The map
shows a plateau at the far end, but doesn't show what's between here
and there, or what kind of plateau it is." She hesitated, then stuffed
the bandage around the edges of the goggles, leaving her lids free,
unwilling to ride in total darkness. She pulled the goggles and bandages over her head. "All right, Emris."

He took her arm. She pulled the hood far over her face and let him lead her out of the cave. Once mounted, she took Myla's reins from the boy's hand and felt Emris take Darkness' head. The wind boomed and what she could see of the pass swam and blurred maddeningly around her. Darkness moved slowly. It grew colder and darker; she imagined the cliffs leaning together, burying them. The cold hurt her lungs, numbing her cheeks and lips; she hadn't felt this helpless since they'd bound her and taken her from her father's body. Darkness stopped and started again, unwilling to move forward; she heard indistinct words as the boy spoke to the horse. It's my eyes, she thought. I wouldn't be afraid if I could see, if I could only see. Myla followed unerringly; Lyeth gripped the reins and moved her lips in soundless prayers.

After an eternity the darkness lifted slightly; the wind fell. She raised her head, rubbing frost from her goggles. Her eyes stung miserably and a headache pounded at her forehead, but she could see, albeit poorly. Sunlight glowed beyond the indistinct form of Darkness' head. The horses' steps quickened. The pass opened overhead, the wind dropped, and they were out on a broad plateau. Lyeth blinked, trying to ignore the pain, and squinted.

"Look," Emris said.

She frowned down at the tiny, dark figure at Darkness' head, then followed the swing of his arm. The Tobrin river valley lay below them, purple with evening shadows; dark shapes moved where iceboats skimmed along the frozen river called the Water Road. Far up the valley, the lights of Jentesi-on-River colored a lightly clouded sky. The horses blew and trembled and she slid to the ground. Emris handed her Darkness' reins. She put them in her left hand and reached her right to him. He looked at it blankly.

"Hello," she said and coughed to clear her throat of coldness. "Hello. My name is Lyeth."

He looked into her face. After a moment he extended his own hand and, very briefly, touched hers.

# TWO

# JOLEDA

THEY camped near the pass that night, in a small clearing amid towering rocks. She sat hunched near the fire, touching her face gingerly, while Emris prepared a meal, fed the horses, and generally bustled about efficiently. More lore from his blessed Cerdic, she supposed; he seemed to have the basics of camp-making and cooking in his grasp and only had to ask a few questions. She answered monosyllabically. The pain in her right eye diminished and her vision improved, but her left eye still ached and teared. She tried to make a patch for it; after a few fumbling minutes Emris took the cloth from her fingers, folding and tucking it into shape. She thanked him with a grunt and, tying the patch in place, put her goggles on and slept. Her dreams were uneasy with double images, an uncomfortable duplicity of selves through which she watched herself move in a sightless world which she both saw and did not see. She woke early and lay in the warm sack of her talma, trying to believe that her fears were groundless. A hawk skimmed low over the camp and wheeled away through the pale dawn sky. Darkness snickered quietly and Emris moved about their slapdash firepit; soon the scent of tea drifted to her. She sat, opening the front of the talma, and touched the goggles. They hurt her when she moved them, and she winced and left them alone. Bandor, who kept the guildhouse in Sorontil, was blind. She thought about him moving through the heavy stone building, efficiently ordering his truncated domain and listening to the sighted

Riders coming and going. Locked forever within the walls of a city, within the walls of a guildhouse, within the walls of his own darkness. She shuddered and kicked at the bottom of the talma, stood, and marched off behind the rocks to relieve herself. With one eye patched closed her depth perception disappeared and she banged her thighs twice against stones. It didn't improve her spirits.

"Can you hunt?" she demanded when she returned.

Emris gave her a cup of tea and shook his head. "Not very well."

"What, the saintly Cerdic was lax about that?" The tea burned her lips. Emris merely shrugged and turned back to the fire. She mentally reviewed their supplies; enough, she thought, for one good meal or two skimpy ones, but they should reach the Tobrin by nightfall and could find food there. With luck they'd be in the city tomorrow night. Her headache threatened to return and her thighs hurt.

"We eat at noon," she said, rising. Emris silently replaced the uneaten supplies and collected their gear.

The foothills sloped easily into the valley, pasturelands smooth and serene under a white mantle. The terrain presented no major obstacle but Lyeth and the boy made poor time, camping that night well away from the Water Road. Emris found a stream, broke the ice, and refilled their water pouches. Lyeth sourly listened to him settle the horses and prepare their meager supper, either ignored his questions or responded to them with barbed sarcasms. She felt a mean satisfaction when he stopped talking entirely and kept the fire between them. Eventually he closed up his talma and fell asleep. Lyeth sat by the fire, poking at the embers and listening to the boy's breathing. Jandi could fix her eye, if he'd reached Jentesi Castle. Otherwise she'd see Joleda, whom she trusted more than Gambin's stiff, pompous doctor. She wondered if she could stay in the guild, one-eyed. She wondered if she could fake it. Jandi would fix her, or Joleda; this was just a temporary problem, nothing to agonize about. Unconvinced, she closed her talma and huddled within it. Now her stomach hurt, too.

She woke to a sound so familiar that for a moment she thought she was back in the apprentice dorms at Vantua. She lay still, listening to Emris' muffled weeping. Homesick, probably, for that petty tyrant of an innkeeper and his quiet wife, for the country inn and the provincial village and valley it served. She pressed her lips together. She'd never cried—at least not where she could be overheard. She couldn't make him out in the darkness and cursed the impulse that had made

her take him in the first place, and the second impulse that let her
agree to bring him along. Yes, he'd helped when she hurt her eyes,
but if he hadn't been there she wouldn't have been distracted and it
wouldn't have happened in the first place. This fine train of logic did
nothing to comfort her. She pulled the hood tight about her ears but
could still hear his crying.

"Oh, shut up and go to sleep," she said crossly. The crying ceased.
She turned onto her side, drew her legs up, and put her arms around
her stomach. Joleda would take him; the innkeeper always needed a
few extra hands. Or if he really annoyed her, she'd give him to his
blessed Cerdic, who should certainly be in the city by now. Send the
brat home to his damned village, and to hell with his quest. Other
people had lost families; he should be grateful, she thought savagely,
that he hadn't seen his parents slaughtered in front of him. She had.
She heard another smothered sob, cursed under her breath, and tried
to get back to sleep. Give him to Cerdic; that would do it. Ice
cracked distantly and her stomach ached.

She woke meaning to tell him of her decision but her eye hurt, her
vision betrayed her, and he had already packed things away and
prepared for the day's ride, events which plunged her back into her
foul mood. Flaunting his eyesight, she decided, knowing the thought
as stupid and unworthy and holding to it regardless. Her right eye
improved, only tearing occasionally, but the left one burned and
ached continuously. The hills flattened to grazing land and these in
turn to croplands, wood and stone fences marching through the
snow. A wind sprang up from the south as they rode beside a line of
tall evergreens; the trees perfumed the crisp air, boughs and limbs
and needles black against the snow. A bough cracked in the cold,
Myla whuffed, and Emris said, "Oh, look." She raised her head and
together they looked out over the frozen Tobrin.

Along the distant Dorne bank, a mass of dark evergreens and pale
snow marched eastward from the cliffs to the river's edge, where ice
lay rucked over stones. The river's main channel was clear and
smooth, kept so by the daily hotboats that moved slowly along it,
melting the top ice and reforming it into a silky expanse which the
iceboats ridged during the day and the cold buckled at night. Iceboats decorated the river, dipping and turning under taut, brightly
colored wings of sail, their seasoned hardwood runners throwing
plumes of shaved ice against the sharp blue sky. A goods barge
labored near the Jentesi bank, pulled by teams of stocky snowhorses

along the towpath. The barge flew all its canvas, taking advantage of the wind, but the horses strained in their traces. Lyeth blinked and tried to make out the barge's registry; her right eye teared and the world blurred; she blinked again and the world came clear, but she still couldn't read the registry lines. The barge probably came from Vantua or Lund, overloaded with goods and bound for the city, ready to take advantage of the uncertainty and fear of changing times. Power teetered, folk bought at a madcap pace and hoarded against expected scarcity, and the Merchants Guild, cleverly promoting the panic, made fat profits. That was not unexpected, though; the Merchants Guild seemed to have its collective fingers in everything in Cherek, from the Teneleh sailing ships to the burgeoning inventiveness of the Smiths Guild, and the Merchants gained from all of it. These profits had led, Lyeth heard, to uneasy mutterings in Vantua Council. Now she rubbed her goggles, cursed, and wished the barge and all aboard it bad luck. The landroad ran just above the towpath, at the edge of a small bluff. Darkness started down the road toward the city and Myla trailed behind. Emris stared at the river.

"Look familiar?" Lyeth demanded.

The boy, buried in the dark talma, didn't answer.

The road grew crowded as they neared the city. Hovels lined it, mean shacks with thin lines of smoke rising from chimneys and dirty children playing in dirty snow by the front doors. Lyeth paused at one of the shacks and negotiated with the tenant for some bread and cheese. The woman was too terrified by Lyeth's talma to accept coins, and eventually Lyeth flung them into the snow at the woman's feet and turned Darkness away, muttering. The coins might stay there forever, tainted by her fingers. She threw some of the food to Emris and they ate while they rode. The sun dipped toward the horizon and the land rose, farms giving way to stone hills and these to high, precipitous fingers of rock reaching inland, Jentesi-on-River cradled between them like a bright jewel in a crabbed, forbidding hand.

One of those forbidding fingers stretched to the river's edge and the landroad turned away from the water, seeking the pass in the natural barrier. Emris twisted in his saddle to watch the river until it was out of sight.

"Keep close," Lyeth said curtly.

He looked at the increasing press of people and brought the grey up to ride a pace behind Darkness' rump. The road narrowed and ran between high cliffs, ending in a stout gate. Sentries paced the wall overhead and folk crowded below, eager to get into the city before night came and the gate closed. They fell away from Lyeth's talma, making a narrow path; she wiped her goggles and ignored the quick hand-gestures against evil. Emris, seeing them, retreated into the darkness of his hood. The city shadi at the gate thrust his arm forward, barring the way without looking up.

"Business in the city," he said, loud and bored. "Hurry it up, state your business."

Lyeth took the folded papers from her pocket and tapped his wrist with them. He glanced at the stylized stirrups and dagger of the Riders Guild embossed on the wrapper, and the wax stamp bearing the Gambini arms, straightened immediately, and gave Lyeth a brisk salute.

"Your pardon, Rider. It's been a busy day."

She looked at him through her goggles without replying. He pulled open the cloth wrapper and paged through the papers.

"The boy is with you? The pass is for one Rider only."

"He's in ward," she said calmly. He hastily slapped her papers into order, scrawled his mark on the top one, and handed them back, looking at the boy sympathetically. Emris followed her silently through the gate and into Jentesi-on-River.

A broad plaza opened behind the gate, its center crowded with goods wagons and the pitched tents of wandering merchants, its periphery lined with the stone fronts of stables, inns, foodshops, and taverns. Normally winter travelers to Jentesi-on-River were few, but the lord's dying had brought more than just guildspeakers and land-barons to the city: merchants, gamblers, whores, the curious elbowed together in Palisade Square. The noise was a constant, chattering roar; somewhere in the maze of tents a group of musicians thumped and banged away at their protesting instruments and a few dogs bayed accompaniment. Animals grunted, squawked, called, gibbered; voices howled; wood and metal beat against each other and against themselves. A boy ran from the tents and ducked in front of Lyeth's horse, clutching the bulging front of his shirt. A woman caught him, dragged the stolen chicken from his clothes, and boxed his ears. The boy yelled and the chicken squawked indignantly as the woman held it by its feet and disappeared through the tents. Banners glimmered in the slanting evening light; Lyeth tugged at her goggles and peered, seeing the red and green of peddlers, the rust-colored flags of tinkers, the warm brown of spice merchants, and the gaudy, multicolored banners of the fortune-tellers and minstrels. The scents of a hundred different dinners competed with the stench of animal dung. A caged bird shrieked. It could have been summer and fair-time, it could have been harvest festival. It was all familiar and more than familiar; Lyeth remembered the view from the ledge, mountains falling and soaring in clear detail, Emris beside her and a clean wind blowing. She put the thought away. City urchins congregated near Palisade Gate, hustling the incoming crowds. They shied away from the black talmas as Lyeth guided the horses around the eastern edge of the square and into the city. The reek and confusion of Palisade Square dropped behind them.

The sun sat low on the city's granite barriers; long shadows reached from tall stone buildings at one side of the broad street to tall stone buildings on the other side. A few folk passed quickly and made the gesture against evil, fingers crossed and hand passed swiftly across the chest. Lyeth's left eye ached dully behind the patch and her right eye watered, the underside of its lid painfully gritty. She stopped Darkness and waited for the boy to come up beside her.

"It's too late to reach the castle," she told him. "This street leads to a market but before we reach it we'll pass an inn, the Dagger and Plow. Tell me when we get there. I can barely see." Emris was silent. She squinted, trying to read his expression in the gathering dark. "Think you can do that, or didn't your blessed Cerdic teach you how?"

"I can do it," Emris said.

Her vision cleared momentarily. His eyes were wide and tired, mouth turned down at the corners. She was briefly sorry for her cruelty. Emris flicked the reins and rode beside her down the empty street. A murmur in the distance became the sound of busy public rooms, the banging of doors, whuffing and shuffling of snowhorses, the discordant twang of music and voices. Emris moved closer until they rode almost knee to knee.

The Dagger and Plow was, as usual, relatively quiet. A stableboy came for the horses but Emris glared at him and clenched the two pairs of reins in his fist. Lyeth took their saddlebags into the public room and dumped them near the mantel, adding her talma to the cloaks already spread to dry. Her entrance caused an unexpected lull in the conversation; usually Riders were a common sight in this inn, but Joleda undoubtedly had her share of provincial visitors, too.

Lyeth didn't much care. Joleda came from the kitchen, her wooden leg making sharp, staccato sounds on the stone floor. She put her tray down, saw Lyeth, and came over, wiping her hands on her apron.

"So you made it," Joleda said. "I thought you were supposed to be back yesterday."

"I had some trouble. Gambin?"

"Still alive, but—"

"I need a room, and room for my boy."

"A boy?" Joleda rocked back. "You've come up in the world. What did you do to your eye?"

"Hurt it. Do you have room, or do I get the horses and go elsewhere?"

"Who else would have you?"

"Interesting question," someone said. Joleda turned inquiringly and Lyeth saw Petras, captain of Gambin's personal guard, standing at ease behind the innkeeper. One hand held an earthenware cup, the other rested on his hip. He gestured with the cup, taking in her travel-stained clothing, the saddlebags, the patch over her eye. "Looks like you had an entertaining trip."

"A hard one," Lyeth said shortly. "And long. You're not in uniform."

His smile was open and friendly. "No need. I'm not in the city on business."

Lyeth, her expression neutral, didn't believe him. Petras looked like a child's stuffed animal, round and comfortable and friendly, never standing on ceremony save in fulfilling his lord's orders, fond of jokes and stories and hopelessly sentimental songs. He never spoke of his origins but Lyeth thought he probably came from one of the plains provinces, Poderi perhaps, or Mintuk, where the long, repetitive seasons drove the impatient and ambitious from the fields and into distant occupations. A high proportion of them took work with the various non-guild mercenary companies thinly scattered throughout Cherek. The guilds, and particularly the Shadeen Guild, looked upon the mercenaries as upstarts: chaotic and, because they were not controlled through Vantua or the guild city of Lymon, dangerous. Cherek's lords, though, remembered the Guild Wars after Constain's defeat and were ever mindful of the guilds' increasing power; the nobility, phlegmatic about the mercenary companies, hired them at will. Petras smoothed his moustache with a forefinger and looked at her benignly. Lyeth repressed a shudder. The Dagger and Plow was not one of Petras' usual drinking places.

"I'm surprised you're not up castle," she said.

Brown curls danced on Petras' forehead as he shook his head.

"I should be, of course," he said, smiling. "But the innkeeper's wine punch is a great inducement to forgetfulness." The smile widened playfully. "And I will admit to ulterior motives. I'd like to talk with you."

"We have nothing to discuss," Lyeth said rudely.

The captain's smile ebbed. "But we do, Rider. You've been away for a while; a lot of things have changed." He tilted his head to one side engagingly. "Will you join me for dinner?"

"No." Lyeth turned to Joleda, who stood with her arms crossed and her eyebrows raised. "Is there room for me?" She barely waited for the innkeeper's nod. "Captain," she said, and followed Joleda up the stairs, followed in turn by a maid carrying the saddlebags. She put her hand to the wall of the narrow stairwell, so tired she felt dizzy. Joleda shook her grey head.

"Will you never learn civility?" she said.

Lyeth bit her lip. Gambin sent her out with Notes of Justice, but it was into Petras' hands that she delivered the ferrets' victims. And, since this information came to her as a private communication from her master, she could no more break that secrecy than she could desert her post. She had, once, on Gambin's orders, observed Petras oversee an inquisition. The memory sometimes haunted her sleep.

"I'm too tired," she muttered, following Joleda into a tiny room. One small, shuttered window decorated the wall, across from a large bed covered with clean, worn blankets. Lyeth sat on it while Joleda issued instructions to the maid. The girl ran out. Joleda put her hands to the goggles and Lyeth jerked her head away.

"Stop that." Joleda took a hank of the Rider's dirty hair and tugged it. "You're not a baby, except when it comes to being polite. Be still."

Lyeth clenched her teeth. The straps tangled in her hair; dirt and tears adhered the patch and bandages to her skin. Joleda loosened them with quick, competent fingers.

"If you'd keep your hair short you wouldn't have this mess," she muttered. "Holy Mother, did you take a bath in a blizzard?"

"Got a faceful of ice crossing above the Tobrin. Jandi wants new maps."

"Jandi's an ass."

The maid came back, holding a bowl of water and a small box. Emris entered after her, carrying Lyeth's talma. Joleda looked at him while she took the bowl and box, then turned back to the bed.

The water burned Lyeth's skin. She tucked her lower lip between her teeth and gripped the mattress. The bandages came away slowly and Joleda snipped hair from the goggle straps. Lyeth blinked and her left eye watered. Joleda put her loupe to her eye, squinted to hold it in place, then pulled at Lyeth's upper lid, pushed at the lower one, and flashed a bright light into Lyeth's eye that made it hurt worse.

"You've scratched the cornea some, but it will heal," Joleda said, letting the loupe drop into her palm. "Fine time to damage yourself."

"What's that supposed to mean?"

"Later."

Lyeth lay back and put her arm over her eyes while Joleda issued more instructions to the maid. The door opened and closed again.

"You're the Rider's boy," Joleda said. "Your name?"

"Emris, mistress."

"Um. When did this happen?"

Lyeth contemplated the darkness behind her lids while Emris told Joleda about the accident and what he had done. Her muscles felt slow and heavy, her eyes stung, her stomach hurt, the thought of Petras in the same inn did not please her, and the voices above her were distant, irritating whines. Her sleeve, trailing over her nose, smelled of horses and sweat.

"Good," Joleda said at last. "You did well. Who taught you?"

Emris didn't answer. The door opened and Joleda conferred with the maid, and after a moment the bed shook again as she sat, pried Lyeth's arm away from her face, and dropped something into her eyes so quickly that the Rider had no time to protest. Lyeth cursed and tried to move away but Joleda pinned her to the bed, hands pressing on her shoulders.

"How does that feel?"

"Horrible." Lyeth hesitated. "Better." The sting faded and the salve felt cool and soothing.

"Hungry?"

"No." Joleda released her. Lyeth put her arm over her eyes again. "Not with Petras downstairs. I want to sleep. What do you mean, a fine time to damage myself?"

"Later," Joleda said again. She pulled Lyeth's arm away and put a new, clean-smelling patch over her eye. "Don't take it off. You'll have to wear it for a week, maybe two." The bed jiggled as Joleda packed things away. "I'll leave the salve. Use it twice a day. Both eyes." She paused, the bed still. "You want to explain this animosity toward the captain, or are you just keeping in practice?"

Lyeth groaned. "I can't tell you. Mother, Joleda, just take my word for it, will you? Captain Petras is not a pleasant man."

Joleda rose and the bed bounced again. "Your oath?"

Lyeth nodded. "Has Jandi come?"

"Yesterday. He didn't bother to stop by. Supper's in an hour."

"Not interested."

"Huh." Joleda's uneven footsteps moved out of the room and down the stairwell; the door closed. The bed moved again and Lyeth squinted through the haze of salve to see Emris at the foot of the bed, unlacing her boots.

"I only said you were my servant," she said with weary impatience. "You don't have to act like one."

He ignored her, hands busy with knots. "Who was that woman?"

"Joleda." Lyeth yawned hugely. "She owns the inn."

"Oh." He pulled her boot off. Lyeth dropped her arm to cover her face again. "Is she a friend of yours?"

"Um. She was a Rider before she lost her leg."

Emris paused. "In Jentesi?"

"I don't know; she doesn't talk about it." She yawned again. Emris resumed unlacing the second boot. It came off and she wriggled her toes. The bed warmed.

"Have to share the bed," she muttered. "Don't kick in your sleep."

Emris moved about the room, dragging saddlebags. Her eyes stopped stinging entirely. She turned on her side and put one arm under the pillow, holding it close to her face and breathing the scents of clean linen and medicine. She'd have to bathe tomorrow, if Joleda's plumbing cooperated. Horses galloped by outside, hooves sharp on the stone pavement.

"Did you mean it?" Emris said quietly. "What you said to the shadi?"

"Wha' shadi?"

"At the gate. That I'm in ward."

"Had t'tell him something. Go get dinner."

"But . . ." He hesitated, then said in a rush, "But you gave Trave Innkeeper money for me."

She groaned. "I paid for a horse. He didn't sell you and I didn't buy you. I don't buy children."

"But you told the shadi—"

"I lied. Go 'way." She pulled the pillow closer and fell asleep.

She woke to pale bars of dawn light falling through the shutters, and the early morning bustle of the city. Someone had undressed her and put her under the covers, and she idly wondered who as she yawned and stretched and turned onto her back. Emris was a warm lump against her side; he snored delicately as she swung her legs from the bed and groped for her talma. The common washroom was empty and, an added blessing, Joleda's recalcitrant plumbing coughed up enough hot water for a quick bath. The pipes groaned and shouted; whoever slept in the room next door banged on the walls, demanding quiet. Lyeth touched her hair, decided it could wait to be washed, and gathered it up in sticky handfuls, pinning it to the top of her head. Back in the room she found the salve and sat at the corner of the bed. Her eyelids kept clamping shut and by the time she successfully dosed herself, her cheeks were slick with medicine. She wiped them while searching the room for her clothes. Emris mumbled and twisted to sprawl diagonally across the bed.

Salve clung to her lashes and blurred the vision in her right eye. She put her hand to the stair wall as she walked down, feeling the warmth of wood overlying the solidity of stone. The shutters were open in the public room and sunlight flooded the tables and benches. Lyeth stopped at the bottom of the stairs and squinted. The floor gleamed where someone stood, pants legs rolled to the knee, sloshing a damp mop across the stone. Someone else knelt by the fireplace, a bundle of aromatic wood nearby. Flames danced in the dark recess. A child skipped through the kitchen doorway and began hanging tankards on the wall racks. The floor scrubber, looking up, saw Lyeth.

"Joleda! She's up."

"Lyeth?" Joleda called. "In the kitchen."

She rubbed at her eyelashes with the hem of her tunic. The salve fog cleared as she picked her way across the floor, nodding to the young woman before the fireplace and the young man with the mop. The kitchen was a riot of sunlight, voices, scents, and varying temperatures; cooks and cleaners scampered about waving pots and rags, a fire roared under the huge water tank, someone in the pantry sang a song with remarkably dirty lyrics. Fresh breads filled the cooling racks and a spitted sheep turned above a fire, fat dripping to hiss on the coals. Lyeth's mouth watered.

"You look better." Joleda picked up a teapot; morning light revealed the network of fine wrinkles on her face. "Hungry?"

"Starving. Is Petras here?"

"Left an hour ago."

A small knot between her shoulder blades relaxed. She slid onto a bench at the long table and put her hands out for the teacup. Joleda pushed a jar of honey across the table. While Lyeth spooned some into her cup, a scullion put a plate before her; temporarily forgetting the tea, she speared a piece of meat with her dagger and stuck it into her mouth. It was hot enough to burn her tongue but she ate it anyway.

"Your manners are as elegant as ever," Joleda said, sitting opposite her. "You slept well?"

Lyeth nodded and swallowed. "You put me to bed?"

"Both of you. I'm going to have to boil those sheets. Don't the villages have bathhouses?"

"You know as well as I do that—"

Joleda gestured, unconvinced. "The boy fell asleep before dinner. Libit," she called. "Go waken the Rider's boy."

"No, don't bother," Lyeth said around another bite. "He'll come down when he's hungry." She reached for the teacup. "I'm the only Rider here?" The same scullion brought her a plate of eggs scrambled with onions and garlic, and a thick wedge of new bread. She pushed the teacup away again.

"At the inn? Yes. How did you know?"

"No other talmas on the mantel. I may have been tired, but I'm not blind. Or not entirely. Since when? Jentesi should be crawling with them."

Joleda handed her a jam pot. "Since you left. As far as I can tell, you're the only Rider in the city, or up castle."

"Except for Jandi."

Joleda snorted inelegantly. "Jandi doesn't qualify. Jandi's a—"

"That's what you meant last night?" Lyeth interrupted. "About a fine time to hurt myself?"

"I didn't think you'd remember."

"I'm not deaf, either. What's it mean?"

"I was rather hoping you knew." Joleda reached across the table and took a bite of Lyeth's eggs. "Hebert! Not enough pepper! How many times do I have to tell you?"

"Tastes okay to me," Hebert replied sullenly, not turning.

Joleda rolled her eyes. "It's not normal, Lyeth. I don't like it one bit; it worries me. I think it should worry you, too."

"The pepper?" Lyeth raised her eyebrows, but Joleda didn't smile. "All right. I don't see what's so ominous about it, but I'll ask around up castle. It shouldn't affect me."

"Idiot. Something or someone is keeping every Rider away from Jentesi-on-River but you, and you don't think it should bother you? Maybe your cornea isn't the only thing you damaged."

Lyeth shrugged, speared another piece of meat, and asked about Gambin. He was no better and no worse, Joleda said, and the council had been postponed. Lyeth looked up.

"Why? They can elect a new lord before the old bastard's dead."

"Not easily. He still hasn't said who he favors."

Lyeth grimaced, not surprised. Culdyn, Joleda reported, was lying low up castle; Coreon had been wining and dining every district delegate he could find, and all the whores in Jentesi had been busy for the past week at his expense. And Syne had come up from Vantua a week ago, moved into Jentesi Castle, and was not seen much in public. Rumor had it that a constant stream of visitors moved through her rooms, not all of them by day.

"So one rumor has it that she's seducing anyone who might help her to the sword," Lyeth said, "and the other is she's sending out spies and plotting madly. Yes?"

"You've been in Jentesi too long, Lyeth."

"So have you."

"Yes. But you weren't born here." Joleda wrapped her hands around her cup. "Coreon has paid guest visits on Syne and Culdyn. He's the only one to bother."

Lyeth shrugged, refilling her cup. "At least he observes the formalities. And the Guard?"

"I haven't heard much. They're mercenaries, after all, and their service expires when Gambin dies."

"Like mine." Lyeth spooned honey into her tea. "Did you ever meet her? Syne, I mean?"

Joleda leaned back, frowning. "Years ago. She hated her father, her brother, the Rock, and everyone on it. It wasn't her idea to represent Jentesi in Vantua but when the opportunity came she snatched it." Her frown deepened. "She hasn't been in Jentesi in twenty years. I don't know if she's changed."

"You don't like her," Lyeth said.

"I don't know her," Joleda said sharply. Her frown cleared and she laughed. "And the Lady Maranta, for the edification of the masses, has sponsored a clockworks exhibition at City House. She's also brought two astrologers and her divination machine."

"Her what?"

"She calls it the Circles of Infinity," Joleda said gravely. One corner of her mouth twitched. "I won't try to describe it; you wouldn't believe me anyway. She's got it up castle, and four days ago she announced that it announced that the true heir to the sword—let's see." Joleda squinted thoughtfully. " 'Rides water to Jentesi and is of Gambini blood but not of Gambin's body.' "

"Great Mother! That's as self-serving as anything Culdyn would say. What's been the response?"

"Nothing. I suspect the others were laughing too hard to talk. On the other hand, Lady Maranta came overland to the Rock."

"She'd have had to cross water to the Rock, though." Lyeth smiled briefly. "Bad luck to all four of them. And the ferrets?"

"Lying low. Gambin *is* dying and they don't want to offend whoever might be the next lord." Lyeth opened her mouth, angry, but Joleda forestalled her with a raised hand. "Lying low, but not gone entirely," she said calmly. "It's amazing you've survived in Jentesi this long, and it's not over yet."

"They should be rounded up and killed, them and their master," Lyeth whispered.

"Child, shut up. The council's full," Joleda continued placidly. "I've an inn full of guildspeakers and so does everyone else. Lady Mother, you're not going to cut that?"

Lyeth put the meat back on the plate and began cutting it into smaller pieces. "Between you and Jandi, I'll never be an adult, will I? Any problems yet?"

"What you'd expect. The shadeen are keeping things under control." Joleda put her hands in her lap and massaged her stump. "The land-barons and a bunch of provincial lords, or their representatives, are all up castle, muttering about seating arrangements and getting in the way. The guilds are all represented, too. I don't know how

Jandi got himself appointed, but he came in yesterday by icerunner."
The corners of Joleda's thin lips turned down.

"He's no fonder of you than you are of him." Lyeth refilled their
cups. "He's up castle?"

Joleda nodded as a commotion erupted across the kitchen. She
turned quickly, encompassed the situation, and shouted. The woman
by the ovens planted floured hands on her hips and shouted back;
Joleda's wooden leg made angry sounds on the stone floors as she
stalked across the room. Lyeth watched her affectionately. She and
Jandi had been feuding since Jandi brought Lyeth to Jentesi Castle
for her first oathing, the mapmaker angry that Joleda had not stayed
in the guild after her accident, the innkeeper convinced that Jandi
was an idiot full of dangerously outdated opinions. Lyeth suspected
Jandi of starting the hostilities, but Joleda's disposition was not a
forgiving one and she held up her end of the feud enthusiastically.
And, once Lyeth began to discover the constraints and horrors of
Jentesi Province, Joleda served as her anchor, guide, companion,
advisor, surrogate parent. Without the sharp-tongued old woman,
Lyeth knew she'd have broken or disappeared the way Gambin's
previous Rider disappeared, riding into a winter storm and never
riding out. In his forty-seven years in power, Lord Gambin had gone
through twenty-six Riders; Lyeth felt a stab of pleasure at the knowledge that she would be the last. She stuck her finger in the honey jar,
twirled it around, and put it in her mouth.

"Speaking of rumors," Joleda said, returning to the table victorious from the battlefield by the ovens, "I heard a good one recently.
Seems that some Rider came into one of the mountain towns, took a
dislike to the innkeeper's son, roughed him up some, took him with
her into the mountains, and killed him. The rumor doesn't say
whether she ate him or not."

"Horseshit," Lyeth said. "He's not the innkeeper's son, he's a
fosterling. And he tried to damage my horse."

"Darkness? What did he do?"

"Put a burr under a shoe." Lyeth dug it out of her pocket and
handed it across the table. "I caught him in time."

Joleda turned the burr over in her fingers. "Alanti work, by the
look of it. Do you know where he got it?" Lyeth shook her head.
Joleda handed the burr back. "For that you brought him along?
You're not the parental type, Lyeth. If I hadn't seen the boy, I'd have
believed the rumors."

"He asked to come." Lyeth pocketed the burr. "I was only going to take him a day out, then send him back. But . . . he says that Riders took his parents."

"Both of them?"

Lyeth shrugged. "He says. And he wants to find his family. He'd have a better chance to do that here."

"Oh, Lyeth. Does he have any idea how impossible that is? Do you?"

"There are records," Lyeth said stubbornly. "It's not impossible, just difficult."

"Unless some unlikely friendship has blossomed between yourself and Master Durn, it's impossible. Send him home, child. He has no place in the city or on the Rock, and certainly no family."

"I don't know. There's something about him. . . ." She gestured uncertainly. "Whatever made me take him in the first place, I guess. He's a deep one, Joleda. He's . . . self-contained. He just didn't seem to fit in Pelegorum."

"That," Joleda said, rising, "is not your concern, is it? You want anything more to eat?"

Lyeth shook her head but put her hands around the teapot. The yard door opened and Emris came in, stamping his feet to shake away the mud and snow. He looked around the kitchen, saw Lyeth and Joleda, and came over to them.

"I thought somebody was supposed to curry the horses," he said angrily. "I left instructions, but nobody's touched them since I settled them last night."

"We've been busy," Joleda said.

Emris wiped his hands on the seat of his pants and glared. "Your stablehand promised me they'd be curried this morning. If you're that busy, you could tell your hands not to make promises they can't keep."

Lyeth hid her smile in her cup. Emris' curls stood out wildly from his head, sparkling with drops of water, and his hazel eyes were dark with fury. Joleda looked down at the boy with faint surprise.

"Very well, Master Emris. I'll send someone to do it now."

"Don't bother. I've taken care of it." He turned to Lyeth. "Do I eat in the kitchen, mistress?" he said with minimal politeness.

"No, go into the public room. I'll pack. We have to leave soon."

"I've already packed my gear, and most of yours." He pushed stiff-shouldered through the door. Lyeth let her grin blossom.

"Now, don't tell me he wouldn't be wasted in Pelegorum," she said, rising.

"Because he has a quick temper and a sharp tongue?" Joleda picked up the teapot. "And you'd best figure out what he is, Lyeth, and what you want of him. Servant, apprentice? Toy?" She shook her head. "You're too old for those, Lyeth, and he's not one. You probably haven't thought once about what he thinks of all this, or what you're doing to him. Your world, child, stops right here." She touched Lyeth's nose and Lyeth jerked her head away. "Always has."

The Rider banged her cup down. "How much do I owe you?"

"I'll tell you when Master Emris finishes breakfast," Joleda said over her shoulder, stumping across the floor.

Lyeth pressed her lips together and went into the public room. Emris sat on a windowsill, bent over a plate of eggs and sausages. His bright hair glowed in the morning light but the tilt of his mouth was still angry. Around him guildspeakers filled the room: weavers, potters, herders, saddlers, farmers, porters, foresters, the brown folk of the mountains and the blonder folk of the Tobrin Valley. Dialects clashed and melted, hangovers and wounds were displayed and remarked on, jokes and boasts and speculation accompanied sausages, eggs, hot bread, ale. Lyeth, anonymous in her plain breeches and shirt, helped herself to a mug of ale and perched on the windowsill beside Emris. The guildspeakers ignored her and Emris shoveled in his breakfast as though he hadn't eaten in the past three days. Which, she thought wryly, was close to the truth. He swallowed the last bite of sausage and helped himself to a sip from her mug.

"You'd think she could afford a decent stablemaster," he said, putting the mug down. "She must make a fortune from this place."

"She does well enough."

"Well enough! Trave Innkeeper would go wild if he had this many people in his inn."

Near the fireplace, a tinker and a riverman joyfully entered into dispute about the value, as far as Lyeth could tell, of steam engines over sails. She leaned her head against the embrasure, watching the room.

"It's not always this crowded, Emris. And it's not every day that a lord dies. These folk have come to swear the oath to the new lord, once there is one. All guildspeakers or representatives, like your blessed Cerdic. They'll listen to speakers from the various factions, and they'll go through a charade about elections, and they'll swear the oath, and they'll all go home feeling important and inflated, and they'll never be fit to live with again."

"Like my blessed Cerdic?" He grinned. "What charade? They don't vote on the new lord, do they? Just like a guildspeaker?"

"They think they do. The folk in your village elected that old woman—"

"Taela Weaver."

"Whatever. She's supposed to meet four times a year with the other guildspeakers, and they advise their land-baron and he advises the lord. Presumably. But Taela Weaver also votes with the other weavers within a ten-kil and they elect a small master for the guild in the barony, and the small masters meet with the other provincial small masters and elect a province master, and that master goes to Vantua and gets to live in the big guildhall and eat outrageously and drink too much."

"They do not," Emris said. "That's not what the seminarian said. They sit on the council and they help elect a guildmaster, and the guildmaster sits on Vantua Council and advises the triumvirate. And the triumvirate," he concluded, screwing his eyes closed in concentration, "is the lord first speaker, and the guild first speaker, and the Vantua city lord." He opened his eyes again. "They do teach us some things in Pelegorum."

"I'm speechless," Lyeth said. "And what does the triumvirate do?"

"Everything," the boy said grandly. "They fix taxes and decide who gets paid what and when, and how much the guilds pay in rent to the land-barons and how much the land-barons pay for mutton and wool and stuff like porters, and what the lords' fees are, and all of that."

"A sage and scholarly disquisition," Lyeth said. "Have some more beer. No? And how long have things run this way?"

"For two hundred years."

"And what happened two hundred years ago?"

Emris shook his head. "Something to do with Constain. The guilds helped push him out and the Lords Council let them in. Sort of like a reward, I guess."

"You don't believe that?"

"It sounds . . . well . . ." He hopped down from the embrasure, plate in hand. "People don't usually do things just because it's generous, do they?"

Lyeth watched him thread his way through the crowded tables, cadge more food from a servant, and come back. She held his plate while he climbed onto the windowsill again.

"And what about the lords?" she said.

He paused, a handful of sausage halfway to his mouth. "They just happen. I mean, a lord dies and then a son or daughter takes the sword, and everyone swears to them, and that's that."

"Sounds a bit too simple, doesn't it? You remember we talked about Constain? When he started tearing up the countryside, the Lords Council in Vantua squeaked a lot and did nothing, and he came right down from Dorne, burning towns and chopping up people and doing pretty much whatever he wanted to, until he crossed the Klime into Poderi. And then the Lands Guilds there, and in Mintuk down river, decided to put a stop to it. And they did, with scythes and hoes and pitchforks. Constain and his shadeen had never seen it before—people making fast raids at night against their camps, and popping out of bushes unexpectedly, and generally just not behaving the way reasonable warriors were supposed to do. They pushed him right up to the banks of the Tobrin, where the guilds in Lund burned the city rather than let Constain capture it, and went out to join the Lands Guilds. They all chased him through Riando, and Vedere's miners defended Tebec, and then Vedere's lord threw his support and his shadeen behind the guilds. It almost gave the Lords Council a collective heart attack—I don't think one of them had thought that sensibly in centuries. So then they all did it, and pushed Constain right out of Cherek where he got tangled up with the Trappers, but it never did him much good. So you see, the guilds didn't help push Constain out, the guilds *did* push Constain out, with the lords dithering and drooling behind them."

The argument by the fireplace had grown to encompass tinker, riverman, two herders, and a cook. Joleda came in from the kitchen to silence it before heads were broken. Emris paid no attention to it, his brow creased.

"So the guilds did it. And then—no, let me think. And then I'll bet the lords wanted to say thanks a lot and send them all back home." He looked at her and she nodded. "And—and then . . ."

"You're the Poderi Herders Guild," Lyeth said. "And you've just tossed Constain out of the country. You've got people behind you armed with everything you can imagine, and you've just fought a war, and you're feeling like you own the world, right? And then the Lords Council tries to send you home, tries to put things back just the way they were before. Which wasn't all that good to begin with, and you'd just as soon see things change, maybe see things favor you for once. So what do you do?"

"You make the lords change things the way you want them."

"And if they won't?"

"Oh. The Guild Wars." He looked as though a door had opened. "The seminarian told us about that, but he didn't tell us—I thought it was over land fees or something boring like that."

"Perceptive boykin," she said, smiling, and came off the sill. "Come on, it's getting late."

He jumped off the sill after her. "But you still didn't explain about the charade."

"And I won't, not in here."

He followed her up the stairs and sat on the bed while she packed the last of her gear. "In here?" he said.

"It's nothing much, Emris. The lords haven't changed. The guild-speakers are supposed to elect a lord, but all they really do is confirm whatever choice the land-barons have already made. And the land-barons can choose anyone, but they usually choose someone of the blood. So all those people down there will hear about it when Lord Gambin dies, and then the heir, only one of them, will make a big speech in one of the squares, and they'll all holler approvingly and make the oath and go home." She tightened a cinch and swung the bags over her shoulder. "Are you coming or not?"

He scrambled off the bed, grabbed his own saddlebags, and led the way downstairs. He had packed the second talma and wore his own jacket, a worn, patched sheepskin far too big for him; the sleeves fell over his hands as he held the reins. Joleda came out, a bill in her hand, and gave it to Lyeth.

"Send him home," she said as Lyeth counted out coins.

Lyeth dropped the coins in Joleda's palm and swung into the saddle. "I'll do as I think best," she said curtly.

"Hah." The innkeeper put her hand on Lyeth's knee. "There is something suspicious going on," she said quietly. "Be careful, child."

Lyeth grimaced and wheeled Darkness from the yard.

Folk filled the market, despite the closed stalls and booths. The porch of the seminarians' temple bristled with people who looked as though their heads hurt, come to beg forgiveness of their disparate gods for getting drunk the night before. Arguments rose and fell as Lyeth and the boy picked their way along the edge of the square; the notice board had disappeared behind bundled torsos and waving arms. Shadeen stood in twos and threes on corners, leaning against their spears and watching the crowd with hooded eyes; she saw shadeen in Jentesi Castle's blue and russet supplementing the darker blue and grey of the city troops. The two groups observed a traditional, friendly rivalry, and both despised the members of Gambin's personal Guard as outsiders and arrogant besides. The red and grey of the Guard, to Lyeth's relief, was not in evidence. The castle shadeen were in dress uniform, starched blue collars and short russet cloaks slit to reveal sword hilts, russet woolen leggings, and heavy brown boots. The hoods of their cloaks lay in folds on their shoulders. She recognized one of the captains and guided the horses toward him. He dipped his spear in informal salute and she leaned down to talk.

"It gets worse toward noon," he said, "when the sluggards get out of bed. At least there shouldn't be much trouble tonight. They've called an informal meeting, pre-council, mandatory."

"I hadn't heard. Expecting any trouble from it?"

He shrugged. "We always expect trouble. Headed up castle? Here, drop this off at the second gate, would you? I can't spare a messenger and Ilen gets pissed if he doesn't get his blessed reports on time."

Lyeth took the folded paper and put it into one of her pockets. "Any good rumors?"

"Take your pick." The captain grinned suddenly, revealing large yellow teeth. "Lady Maranta's got this machine to predict things—a regular wonder it is, too, with bells and buzzers and clockwork gimcracks, and I hear tell it's all gold and silver and jewels. She says it says the sword will pass in blood and blizzard. Hah!" he said emphatically. "There's always a blizzard come winter, and only a bloody fool wouldn't believe that, is what I say."

Lyeth smiled. "Anything else?"

"Nothing important. Gambin lasted the night, though."

"And the succession?"

"Is not discussed. It's not a healthy topic, up castle." He looked around casually. "They say the ferrets are gone. Don't believe it."

She nodded her thanks and rode down the avenue, Emris close behind. Shadeen traditionally policed their own and therefore had little to fear from Lyeth or the ferrets, for which she was duly grateful; what friends she had up castle were mostly members of the castle shadeen. The streets, like the market, were full; leafless trees reared against the pale morning sky, all the way to the wharf at the avenue's foot. People moved reluctantly aside before them, caught between the press of the crowd and the desire to avoid Lyeth's talma; a flat ferry at the wharf's end, already stuffed with people and supplies, rested under luffing sails. One castle shadi recognized Lyeth and gestured her forward, but another caught the grey's reins and held Emris back. Lyeth turned in the saddle, frowning.

"He's with me," she said. "Let him go."

"Pardon, Rider." The second shadi braced his feet. "We have orders—authorized travelers only."

A third shadi came for her papers. She handed them down without taking her gaze from the one by Myla's head.

"That boy is in ward to me," she said coldly. "He's part of me until I see fit to send him away. You know the rules as well as I do."

The shadi tightened his jaw. "My orders, Rider—"

"And I claim Rider's Passage on that scow," she continued. "If I go, it goes. If I don't go, it doesn't go. And if the boy doesn't come with me, we can sit here and be polite until Master Durn comes to inquire. As he will."

A sergeant emerged from the guard booth, holding Lyeth's papers flat against a tally board. He heard her last words and came to stand by her stirrup. "If you will sign a statement, Rider, of responsibility . . ."

She took the paper, read it, and signed it. The sergeant initialed her papers and handed them back, and the shadi dropped Myla's reins and stepped away. The gesture he made was not one against evil.

The grey balked at the foot of the gangplank but Emris urged her aboard and into the corral. The ferrymen hauled in the plank and cast off; wind caught in the sails, snapping them full, and the ferry moved away from Jentesi-on-River and across the frozen Tobrin. Wooden runners hissed against ice; the rigging creaked. Lyeth leaned against the rail, watching the city recede. After a little silence she glanced at Emris.

"That paper," she said conversationally, "states that if you do anything wrong up castle, I'm liable for it. I'm not fond of punishment and especially not fond of punishment for the sins of others. If you step out of line at all, I'll beat you bloody. Understand?"

Emris' lips twitched, then he nodded. She wondered what he wanted to say.

"Come with me." She led him around to the bow. Wind cut sharply at their faces and Emris buttoned his jacket all the way up, its collar hiding his ears.

"That island is Jentesi Rock." Lyeth pointed. "The castle's around the other side."

The sun climbed the eastern sky and the island was a dark, featureless peak rising from the white of the river. Emris went back to the concession stand and returned with two mugs of steaming cider. The other passengers moved away as they leaned against the rail, sipping. Lyeth rested her hip against a bale of parchment, watching the forested Dorne bank race toward them.

"It doesn't look like much," Emris said.

"What doesn't? The Rock? Wait, we'll move downstream and come up on it."

He licked cider from his lips. "The stablemaster at the inn, the old one? She said that when Gambin dies, Culdyn's going to take the castle and hold it until he's confirmed as next lord."

"Culdyn? Culdyn couldn't hold his—never mind. Joleda's stablemaster has a thick head and a loose tongue. Don't believe rumors, Emris. And for the Mother's sake, don't talk about any of it up castle."

He looked at her. "That's stepping out of line?"

"Folk have disappeared for speaking rumors." She turned her back to the railing and looked at him. "Does it interest you? The succession?"

He nodded.

"All right. This is fact—the rumors come later." She started to tell him about Gambin, the lines of succession, the maneuvering since the old man sickened, pitching her voice for his ears only. She gave him an edited version, thinking about Gambin as she talked. She saw him often: a stocky, grey, powerful man with a weathered face and coal-black eyes with, it was said, no soul behind them because he'd sold it early on to Death and the Father and never felt its loss. Greedy for power, status, and wealth, earnestly hated by the people of Jentesi Province and fawned upon by the people of Jentesi Castle, he'd been thrice widowed and left with one daughter and one son who hated each other and their father with equal passion. Legitimate daughter and legitimate son, she amended wryly. Gambin's lasciviency was the stuff of legends, and rumor had it that Jentesi was peppered with his illegitimate offspring, none of whom he either supported or acknowledged, letting their miserable mothers bear the burden of their lord's lust, and its results. At least, she thought, Gambin's unacknowledged children were spared the dubious benefits of his attentions, unlike the two come to him through marriage. Hard to choose between the three of them: Gambin a tyrant; Culdyn a fop rife with petty cruelties; Syne withdrawn, mysterious, and therefore feared. Syne Gambini represented her province well in Lords Council in Vantua; her own provincial lands, administered through her steward Torwyn, seemed no worse than other lands in Jentesi Province. But the lady's protracted absence promoted speculation and, unable to know Syne herself, folk extrapolated from her father and brother and distrusted her all the more. And then Maranta, Lyeth thought, daughter of Gambin's murdered sister, and Coreon, Gambin's surviving cousin: the succession in Jentesi Province was a maze of rumor, intrigue, and unappetizing choices. A circus, and just the circus Gambin wanted. The old bastard, refusing to name his successor and watching the resultant chaos, was probably enjoying the show. She should have guessed he'd do something like that—it was so much in keeping.

The great sails moved as the ferry changed course for its final run up river to the Rock; she knew when Emris saw the castle because he stopped attending to her entirely. Looking at him, she remembered what Jentesi Castle had looked like to her, riding the Water Road to her first oathing. Four years ago, before she knew about Gambin, or what it felt like to ride into a small town at nightfall to serve a hated lord's hateful orders. She rubbed at the patch and turned to look at the castle over Emris' shoulder, surprised, as always, by its beauty.

The island was a quarter-sphere of dark rock, its round face looking north to northeast and its concave side facing down the Tobrin and across to Jentesi-on-River. Halfway up the concave side, Jentesi Castle occupied an immense ledge of rock, backed in turn by a huge crescent overhang. Built half of wood and half carved from native rock, it rose straight from the ledge, an austere grey stone wall topped with turrets, wall walks, and arrow loops. Behind this outer rampart rose another wall, and beyond that a maze of towers and barbicans, buttresses and steep roofs, marching in pale, glorious disorder into the darkness of the overhanging rock. Arches and covered passages connected the towers, walls, roofs, and balconies; light flashed from windows and caught the occasional roof tile, making a spot of intense color on the pale grey stone; white snow outlined the peaks and valleys of the ramparts and the crowded masonry behind them. The face of Jentesi Rock was bleak, hard, unforgiving, but behind the castle walls treetops loomed, bare, deciduous limbs stark against the dark green of conifers. To the far right, Lords Walk reached a tentative finger over soaring cliffs, tumbled with rock and footed in huge, frozen waves. This side of Jentesi Rock, in summer, was protected by a series of fierce rapids, white and seething; in the winter these froze to a treacherous jumble of ice and rock. No flags or banners flew from the turrets, as they had not flown since Gambin was taken ill, but along the outer curtain, about the gatehouse, guest flags flapped against stones. Lyeth saw them as a blur of colors; she hadn't expected so many. A single narrow road, plunging behind stone walls, leaping ravines on slender, arched bridges, led from the stone quay at water level to the castle; a few wagons moved along it, in and out of sight among the walls, and more congregated at its foot. The wagoneers stamped their feet against the cold. Sails rattled down, brakebeams hissed and groaned against the river ice, and the ferry slowed and swung against the quay. Lyeth tucked her talma close about her neck as she turned to the corral. Emris closed his mouth, looked at her awestruck, and went to help.

They came off the ferry first, leading the horses around the carts. Myla skittered and did not calm until her hooves touched the road-bed. They mounted and cantered past the staging area where the carts were set on the notched track paralleling the road. Their small, serrated inner wheels meshed with the notches, metal grips clamped to the thick, continuous, and continuously moving cable, and the carts climbed the face of Jentesi Rock, powered by the moving cable which was, in turn, powered by teams of snowhorses hitched to the immense winch at the lip of the ledge. Lyeth thought the arrangement ungainly but clever; Emris, overcome with admiration, chattered about it enthusiastically as they rode alongside. Behind them, bales and boxes were transferred from the ferry to the carts, amid shouted orders and shouted curses. Their horses took the gently stepped roadbed easily. A dozen iceboats skimmed the river; in Jentesi harbor a barge hooked onto the skate lines and was jockeyed up to a wharf; the city gleamed, white stone buildings offset by dark wooden towers, crabbed ramparts of rock softened by snow. Wind tugged at Lyeth's talma and Darkness quickened his pace, eager for the pleasures of his own stable.

Shadeen paced the ramparts, blue and russet in the crenellations and balistraria, spear tips poking above the merlons. The small wagon gate stood open beyond the upper staging area, where wagoneers and teams waited for the first carts. Guest flags slapped sharply above the closed ceremonial gate. The shadi on duty scrutinized Emris thoroughly, marked Lyeth's papers, and waved them through.

The outer ward sat well away from the stone overhang. Snow covered the terraced gardens and grazing fields, clung to the roofs of the square houses in the holders' village, was churned to mud in the stockyard. Arched, high-walled passages crossed overhead from the outer curtain to the inner, each one pierced by loops through which arrows, spears, and insults could be hurled at attackers; the passages themselves were engineered to collapse should the outer curtain be taken. But there had been no attackers on Jentesi Rock for five centuries, and the castle itself had never been seized. Farms, yards, and houses stood secure between stone boundaries, the village shops and inn prosperous, the holders healthy and fat. Should the castle be attacked they would be the first conscripted for dog-labor on the curtain walls, their houses and holdings the first to fall, but the prospect never seemed to cross their minds. Some half-bowed to Lyeth as she passed, others tried to hide their hands as they signed against evil. She glanced surreptitiously at Emris, but he was too busy gawking to notice.

The inner curtain soared from the strip of dead land at its foot, a smooth palisade of rock crenellated at its top. The masts above the barbican were empty but smaller flags still decorated the gatehouse doors, gaudy against the sturdy grey wood. The shadeen on duty lowered their spears; a third one came from the gatehouse and waved.

"Lyeth! You took your time getting here."

Lyeth shrugged. Crise, Commander Ilen's lover and second in command of the castle shadeen, stood by her stirrup and rested her hand on Lyeth's foot. "Didn't have much choice," Lyeth told her. "All's well here?"

"As well as can be expected." Crise's pale brown eyes surveyed Lyeth carefully. "Too many visitors. What happened to your eye?"

"Got a face full of ice, crossing above the Tobrin. Stupidity."

"It happens. And this one?"

Lyeth glanced at Emris. The boy stared intently at Myla's mane. "He's in ward," she said. Emris' mouth tightened.

"Truly? You'll have stories to tell. Come by tonight, if you're free. Ilen and I will both be off watch at the same time, for a wonder."

"If I can. Here, from the captain in the city."

Crise took the note and stepped back. The shadeen raised their spears and the light breeze died as Lyeth and Emris rode through the gate into the main yard. Lyeth shook her hood back; her hair tangled in the folds of the talma, brown on black, escaping from its pins. A clatter and roar rose from the armory; the ornate doors of the Great Hall were closed fast. Emris twisted and craned and gaped, trying to see everything at once. Beyond the main yard the land sloped upward to a smaller yard surrounded by the shadeen barracks and stable, the armory, and the kitchens. Servants rushed, busy on errands. Shadeen, lounging about the stable entrance, gossiped and cleaned their weapons. Lyeth saw the colors of Dorne, Riando, and Denere among those of Jentesi, and wondered if the outland honor guards were allowed to keep their weapons. Some of Gambin's guards stood by themselves, as usual, in a corner of the yard. Their barracks and mess lay in the small extension between the kitchens and Scholars Garden, over entrances to the ancient warrens beneath the castle which Lyeth had never seen and never wished to see. All that cold and buried stone . . . The guards never mingled casually with the castle shadeen, a state of affairs which pleased the shadeen considerably; now they leaned against the walls, laughing. Petras was not among them.

"There?" Emris pointed to the stables.

Lyeth shook her head. "Those are the shadeen stables, and their barracks. We go to the Lords Stables." She grinned at his look of surprise. "Riders are important folk, boykin."

The first of the provisions wagons came into the yard and stopped by the kitchen storerooms. Some of the shadeen came over to watch the unloading and, with luck, steal something to eat. Bedwyn Cook and his undercooks stormed from the kitchen, shouting and flapping their aprons angrily. The shadeen laughed. Lyeth led the way through the narrow, up-sloping passage called the Neck and into an exercise yard where snowhorses and summer horses were being groomed or exercised or simply admired. An equerry, busy near the stable doors, saw Lyeth and turned to shout inside. Lyeth and the boy dismounted as a thin woman strode into the yard, wiping her hands on her pants. She ran her palm over Darkness and peered at his mouth and eyes while Lyeth removed the saddlebags. The snowhorse rubbed his head against the thin woman's hair affectionately.

"He looks all right," the woman said. "What's this other one?"

"Myla, Emris' grey. Stable her with Darkness."

"My grey . . ." Emris looked at her, eyes wide.

"Of course. I don't need two horses." Lyeth slung her bags over her shoulder. Emris stared from Lyeth to the grey and the thin woman held the reins in her hands and watched him. The corners of her mouth twitched.

"I'll see if there's room," she said. "We have every horse in Cherek in there." Emris moved to follow as she led the horses away, but Lyeth put her hand on his shoulder.

"Not now, boykin. Daeni's no innkeeper's slouch, she'll take care of them properly."

"But—you *gave* me the horse? For myself?"

"Mother Above, I have a horse already. You expected me to eat the thing?" She turned abruptly, as surprised as Emris by the gift. He took up his own bags, eyes still on the dark entrance to the stable, and followed. Her boots were silent on the stone stairs and along the narrow portico; a corridor leading off the portico held torches unlit in their brackets and a single door. She opened it and dropped her bags on the floor, unclasping her talma and throwing it over them. Emris lingered at the door, looking uncertain.

"Come in." She moved to the tiled woodstove. "And close the door. It's cold enough in here already." Kindling and logs, slightly dusty, lay within the firebox. She struck a spark, nursed it to flame, and lit the kindling. When it caught she rocked back on her heels, holding her palms toward the small flames. "Are you hungry?"

He didn't reply and she looked over her shoulder at him. Emris stood with his back against the closed door, his saddlebags forgotten on his shoulder, and stared at the room. She followed his glance curiously. Thick woolen hangings on the walls, rugs over the stone floor, the shelves filled with books or equipment or the various ragtag things she had collected in the four years she'd lived in the castle. The delicate porcelain bowl Torwyn had given her two years ago, and the even more fragile glass sculpture he'd given her the past

spring. A few framed paintings, the inlaid tables and cushioned
chairs and benches, a messy pile of papers on the desk by the window, a couple of scattered braziers. One crystal lamp of which she
was inordinately proud; she'd forbidden Janya to clean it for fear of
breakage and as a result it went from one season to the next covered
with dust. The bones of the room, the heavy furniture, shelves flanking the mantelpiece, were all Gambin's, but the heart and spirit of
the room was hers. She'd not had time to tell Janya to pack before
that cold ride into the mountains but the woman could do it now, in
whatever time remained before the tyrant died. She glanced at the
room again, at the two curtained doorways leading to the other
rooms of the suite and, not seeing anything out of place, turned her
attention to the fire again.

"I'm hungry if you're not," she said. "Pull that rope there and put
your stuff in that room." She nodded toward the smaller, curtained
doorway.

"Are we—" Emris coughed to clear his throat. "Are we supposed
to be here?"

"Are we— Emris, these are my rooms. I live here. And, for the
time being, so do you."

He looked at her dubiously and cautiously crossed the room, lifted
one side of the yellow curtain, looked inside, and went through.
Lyeth shook her head and tugged on the bellpull, then knelt to add
another log to the fire.

Janya, her cap askew, came to stand in the doorway.

"Mistress, I didn't know you were coming. The rooms haven't
been aired."

"I noticed," Lyeth said dryly, dusting her hands on her thighs.
She rose and turned, stretching. "Sweet Lady, Janya, are you going
to carry that thing about forever?"

Janya put her hands over her bulging stomach. "Another two
weeks, mistress. It doesn't get in my way."

Lyeth snorted and gazed critically at Janya's belly, then crowed
suddenly. "I know whose it is," she said, grinning.

Janya's broad mouth twitched. "Do you, mistress?" she said
sweetly. She had refused to divulge the name of the child's father,
and Lyeth, sitting in a splash of late summer sunlight, had tapped
her fingers thoughtfully against her thigh. "If it's Gambin's, I'll have
your hide," she told the servant, and Janya's look of commingled
horror and disgust was enough to convince the Rider that the old

man, then still seemingly hale and fit to live forever, had nothing to do with Janya's bastard. Since then the two women had let the mysterious paternity become a joke between them, Lyeth proposing more and more farfetched candidates and Janya squealing or giggling as she saw fit. Now Lyeth gestured carelessly, the grin growing malicious.

"It's obvious. It's the size of a horse; we live by the stables; therefore—"

"Mistress!"

"No? Pity; it would have been an interesting addition. Find me something to eat, would you? And something for the boy. He's called Emris, he's in the other room, and he's not to go out without my express permission, understand? Good. And get someone to air this place out. Start packing things—no, not you, somebody without a belly to lug about."

Janya nodded and turned.

"And wine!" Lyeth called after her. Janya disappeared. Lyeth took her bags and talma through the brown velvet curtain into her bedroom. The room was clean and cold and musty. She emptied her saddlebags into the laundry basket, shoved her travel box onto the mantelpiece, and tossed her talma over the back of a chair. The shutters were closed over the window. She raised the heavy leaded glass and threw the shutters open. Cold, fresh air poured in; she leaned out, breathing deeply. The Tobrin glimmered in the distance and snow lay clean over the castle's roofs and walls, save atop the kitchen where the heat had melted it, and over the guards' quarters where kitchen smoke blackened it. It happened this way every winter and struck Lyeth as ridiculously apposite. Someone sat in a window in the shadeen quarters, playing a flute; its crisp music decorated the chill air. Lyeth leaned further out and looked to the left to see the bare limbs of trees in the Scholars Garden. It never failed to astonish her, this deep appreciation, almost love, for the beauty of Jentesi Castle, for its precipitous collection of roofs, the graceful symmetry of its gardens, the dark solidity of the stone surrounding the castle, part of it yet comfortably separate, protective. No question that she hated the place, hated its small souls and complicated lies, hated the tyranny of its master and the cowering submissiveness of that master's vassals (including, she thought honestly, her own); despite all, the castle caught at her throat, beguiling her, making her feel dangerously at home.

The flute music stopped suddenly and a brief hush fell over the wards. Lyeth shook her head sharply, returning to the moment, and looked toward the Neck in time to see a party of riders move into the yard. The man at their head slid from his horse and threw the reins impatiently; a fast-moving stablehand caught them before they touched the ground. The man turned, hands on hips, talking to his companions, and Lyeth recognized Culdyn Gambini, the lord's only son. She grimaced with distaste; his father's death would be the only thing that could draw Culdyn from his upriver pastimes and diversions. He'd probably spent the night in a gaming house in the city, returning to the Rock on his own boat; he stood as though tired and his gestures were wearily elegant. Fop. She remembered Gambin riding into the ward last winter, fresh from a hard, dawnlit game of ice-flying on the river. Lord Gambin took his sport swift and dangerous; the game of chase and capture played on skates among the quick-moving iceboats, exhilarated him, terrified his courtiers, and left boat-captains up and down the Tobrin quaking with fear of crushing their lord, while under his strict orders not to slow, not to avoid him, to do nothing to diminish the danger and the pleasure of his sport. Only Captain Petras rivaled him on the ice; the two set themselves against each other, hair and cloaks flying as they danced through the deadly paths of the iceboats' sharp runners. When the sun was fully up Gambin rode into the ward, demanding breakfast, discussing the finer points of that morning's sport in a loud, argumentative, authoritative voice. And, catching sight of Lyeth leaning from her window, would bellow, "Good morning, little bitch," before disappearing into the bulk of the Great Hall. Grey hair, powerful stocky body, gestures sharp and hard, black eyes alert and observant, not missing a thing. Now Culdyn Gambini's querulous voice floated in the cold air and Lyeth abruptly slammed the shutters closed. Janya, in the outer room, hummed to herself as she set out crockery, and Militent, her kitchen helper, scurried about, her cheeks pink and her big blue skirt swinging as she moved.

Emris had to be ordered to the meal and jumped whenever another servant came in. Lyeth finally demanded that he sit quiet and pay attention, and he poked at his food while she washed down cheese and meat with gulps of red wine.

"I have to report to Durn but I'll be back before supper. Don't leave these rooms. You're not known here, you don't have papers, and I don't want to spend the night digging you out of some holding cell. Give Janya your dirty stuff to wash—better yet, give her all your stuff. You can wear something of mine until the laundry's done." She reached for another wedge of cheese. "If you need anything use the bellpull, but don't pester the servants or they'll never get anything done. You can read my books if you want. Here." She gave him her Riders token. "If anyone asks, show them this and tell them you're mine. Is all that clear?"

"Yes, mistress," he said, subdued. "Rider? About my family . . ."

"Mother, Emris, I've got things to do." She stood, brushing crumbs from her tunic. "I'll see what I can do. Just don't get impatient."

"Yes, mistress," he said again.

Lyeth frowned with exasperation and went to splash water on her face and change her clothes.

# THREE

# JANDI

THE summer past, Master Durn, chamberlain to Lord Gambin, had imported a steam heating device from Tebec, in Vedere Province, and installed the thing in his council chamber. It stood before the disgraced fireplace, an ornate monster of iron rising a full seven feet from the parquetry floor and covered with brass and white enamel foolery, hissing and bubbling and threatening to erupt at any moment and scald everyone in the vicinity. Steam heaters were new to the colder provinces, another example of the Smith Guild's industry, and Durn made the most of his, running its decorated tentacles over the walls and floors, keeping it roaring and belching at all times, and only too willing to recite the details and cost of its purchase, transport, and installation to all who would listen. Lyeth thought it ugly, ostentatious, and unsafe, but had to agree that the thing worked impressively. Durn's council chamber, summer and winter, felt like a steam-heated anteroom to hell.

Master Durn pulled on his long, ribboned, white-streaked pigtail and frowned as Lyeth made her report. Marjoram, Helsrest, Three Crossings, Pelegorum; Durn deeply resented all the small, outlying villages of Jentesi where telegraph lines could not be run, or where they collapsed every winter in the heavy snows, or anything else in the province he could neither control nor conveniently spy upon. He glared at his immaculate desktop while Lyeth spoke, hiding her contempt and ignoring the crowd of courtiers, guild representatives, and land-barons in the overly furnished room. Servants scuttled through the press, balancing trays or lugging armloads of wood for the heater; the steady tapping of a telegraph came from a tiny room behind Durn's chair. When she finished she clasped her hands behind her back under the heavy folds of her talma. The nape of her neck felt damp with sweat.

"Is that all?" Durn said.

"No, sir." Her fingers tightened. "I would like to see the inquisition records, sir. As a personal favor."

The chamberlain sat back and stared at her silently for a while. She stared back as evenly as she could.

"Those records are sealed," he said eventually.

"Yes, sir. I know. But—"

"I see no reason to unseal them for you, Rider. I owe you no personal favors." He gave his pigtail one last, fierce tug and tossed it over his shoulder. "He wants to see you. Menwyn will take you there. If he's asleep, wait."

Lyeth bowed stiffly, concealing her anger, and followed Menwyn from the room. Durn was already busy with another petition, or report, or request. She tightened her lips.

Menwyn paced before her, the perfect pleats of his tabard rising and settling with the movements of his long legs. The arms of Jentesi glittered from the dark cloth, over the sigil of the House Gambini. He seemed always in a state of composed perfection; even his hair looked ironed. Lyeth hunched her shoulders, urging the front of her talma closed over the scuffs on her riding boots and the stain on the left breast of her tunic. Menwyn and his master could go to the mountain, and bad luck to them. She'd simply have to begin her inquiries elsewhere—with the castle shadeen, who might know of such things. She wondered why Gambin wanted to see her. The corridor was cold.

They followed the hallway behind the Great Hall and climbed the circular stairs of a tower. Banners and tapestries depicting battles hung from the walls; the hunting trophies of the Lords of Jentesi decorated the landings, a chronological progression beginning with Gambin's own trophies at the bottom level and ending, on the top landing, in a mouldering collection of stuffed heads, spears, and crossed swords caked with green and festooned, near the high, arched ceilings, with spiderwebs. Rumor said that these older trophy walls had once included the heads of human enemies, stuffed, mounted, and labeled in the thin script of the Scholars Guild. Lyeth didn't believe it: it exuded the same familiar stench as rumors about the Riders Guild. Menwyn ascended smoothly, the swing and sway of his tabard almost hypnotic against the dark grey walls. Lyeth's eye ached.

The topmost corridor looked hastily refurbished, cobwebs and dust swept clear and the walls hung with faded tapestries taken from one of the castle's myriad storerooms. Guards in red and grey stood immobile along the walls, spears bright and expressions stony; a servant scurried by, soft felt slippers shuffling against the cold floors, and otherwise the corridor was heavy with silence. Lyeth wondered why Gambin had been moved from his sunny rooms near the Great Hall to this inaccessible place. Perhaps it was a tradition among Jentesi's dying lords; perhaps the old tyrant was, finally and absurdly, afraid of assassination. She'd have to ask Torwyn; the name brought the memory of a face, a body, hands; laughter and a clean, warm scent. Her fingers curled. Guards, flanking the heavy wooden doors at the end of the corridor, dipped their spears and put their hands to the doors. They opened, groaning.

This antechamber, too, looked newly furnished. The furniture and hangings smelled musty and, despite the oppressive heat in the room, the walls were still damp with disuse. A fire roared threateningly under a mantel festooned with gargoyles and serpents; all the windows were closed. A gaggle of physicians stood in anxious consultation near the inner doors, and two seminarians, one in Mother's blue, the other in Father's scarlet, sat clutching their holy boxes and glaring at each other. Neither looked particularly clean. Couches and tables bore the detritus of the death watch, cups and plates holding half-consumed meals, scattered papers, a clutter of medical instruments and books, huddles of pillows and blankets. One bent servant moved desultorily through the mess, making vague gestures toward cleaning up. Tobi, Gambin's personal physician, stuck his grey head out of the medical huddle, frowned at Lyeth, and came over to her.

"Durn sent you. Good. He sleeps and wakens; you'll have to wait." He glared at Menwyn. "We don't need you here."

"My master instructed—"

"I don't care. You tell Durn that I'll send for him if he's needed. There are enough longnoses in there already. Scat."

Menwyn's shoulders stiffened and he left without bowing. Tobi rubbed his lined cheeks wearily with the heels of his hands; his eyes were decorated with red.

"You don't like him either," Lyeth said suddenly, surprising herself as much as the physician. Tobi put his hands down and looked at her, the corners of his mouth pinched. "Why not?"

"I don't like waste," he said curtly. "Yours or his. Do you want me to look at that?"

Lyeth resisted the urge to touch the patch, resisted the urge to snap back at him. "No. It's healing."

Tobi turned away abruptly, muttering under his breath, and disappeared into the battalion of his colleagues. Lyeth stared down the seminarians and glanced at the walls. The tapestries, ancient, patched, and tattered, showed in sequence the story of Death: his birth flaming from a volcano's maw, her harrowing of the lands, his banishment, after innumerable sins, by the Father and Mother, and, last, her kingdom under the volcano, complete with the Wheels of Judgment and the Flail of Truth. Two of the tapestries were out of place. Death, traditionally, was shown as a figure of surpassing beauty, now male and now female, a cunning and irresistible seducer melding both pain and transcendence into one fluid yet uneasy whole. A cheerful subject, Lyeth thought sourly, for such a room as this, and turned her back on it.

She cleared the window's embrasure of plates, cups, and a discarded wintercloak, hitched herself onto the stones, and stared out the window. The servant brought her a mug of watered ale. She nodded her thanks and loosened the collar of her talma. It was as hot here as in Durn's chamber, and she longed for a breath of clean winter air. Behind her the physicians mumbled and gestured; the seminarians grunted disharmonious chants. The window faced Jentesi-on-River and the southern run of the Tobrin. Far below, the inner ward bustled with activity. She cradled the mug in her palms, watching good barges and icerunners on the Tobrin. It could have been any sunny day in any winter, and she shook away the feeling that she watched her world from some other time and place entirely. Turning back to the dismal room, she sipped her ale and wished she were elsewhere.

One of the inner doors opened marginally and a page gestured. Tobi entered and disappeared into a crowd of death watchers. The physicians stood with their heads up, like dogs listening for a distant call. When the door opened again they and the seminarians started forward, but the page gestured them away and beckoned to Lyeth. She put her mug on the windowsill and followed him into the inner chamber.

The room was dense with heat and people and the constant murmur of hushed voices. Gambin's Guard, standing about the walls, looked impervious, and Torwyn, Syne's steward, nodded to her. The corners of his long mouth moved upward marginally. Lyeth met his eyes for a moment, her face expressionless, as she passed, but under the talma's folds her fingers curled again. The others, both familiar and strange, watched her with suspicious curiosity as she and the page popped through the edge of the crowd and paced across the empty half of the room, over the worn purple carpet of some ancient lord, and toward the curtained bed. The smell of sweat and damp wool faded as the stench of illness increased. Wooden posts rose from the bed's corners, carved with the figures of demons and nightmares; the heavy velvet curtains were patched with material that did not quite match the original color, and held open by new golden ropes. Petras stood at the foot of the bed and looked at Lyeth impassively; nothing about him, now, seemed at all round or comfortable or friendly. She nodded briefly and passed him by. Tobi stood near the pillows, his hands in his sleeves. The page bowed and retreated, and Lyeth came around to the head of the bed and dropped to one knee. Gambin looked down at her from the high mattress, his pallid skin stretched over the broad bones of his face, black eyes sharp. He looked like his own grandfather.

"Lyeth," he said, his voice rough and dry.

She rose. "My Lord."

His right hand rose fractionally and dropped on the coverlet. "Do you like what you see?"

"Yourself, Lord? No."

"You never have." He coughed sharply. Tobi rushed forward, his hands open, and Gambin waved him away impatiently. "Sick of your stink," he muttered. "Go away, leave us alone. Carrion crow. Give me that cup."

The silver goblet, decorated with serpents, stood beaded with condensation by the bed. Lyeth handed it to him, then had to sit on the bed and hold it to his lips as he drank. He lay back and closed his eyes briefly as she returned the goblet to its place and began to rise.

"No. Stay. You should be happy," he said, his eyes still closed. "Dance on my grave."

"No, Lord. I've hated you and I hate you still, but I take no joy in this."

He opened his eyes and tried to laugh. "My honest little bitch. Tobi says I have the lump disease, eating inside me. My prick is lumps, Rider. I piss blood."

Lyeth said nothing.

"Bitch," Gambin said again. "Kept you here. You hate me honestly."

She touched the edge of her talma. "Would you have released me if I flattered you?"

Gambin shook his head. Spittle gleamed at the corners of his mouth and Lyeth dabbed him clean with the sheet. "Too good a Rider, little bitch," he whispered. "You do as I tell you."

"No, Lord. I do as my guild instructs. I've never done anything for you against the rules of my guild."

"I've never forced you to," he said. Lyeth did not argue. His breath rasped when he tried to breathe too deeply. "Too good," he repeated. His sharp gaze held cruelty and amusement.

"What do you think of it, little bitch? What do you think of my circus?"

"I thought you might call it that, Lord." She rested her hands on her thighs, wondering how much she could get away with. "I think it's a crime, Lord. You should say your choice, before there is bloodshed. This . . . circus does you no good."

The old man grinned. "Ah. My confidential conscience. Should I listen to you?"

"You never have, Lord. You probably won't start now."

Gambin made a choking sound, a horrible remnant of his usual boisterous laugh, and patted Lyeth's knee with his shaking hand. She clenched her teeth.

"Little bitch, you've never broken my confidence, have you? You of them all, only you."

"My guild instructs, Lord."

"Convenient." He peered around and gestured to her, and she obediently leaned toward him. "I can't indicate my choice, oathkeeper. You know it—anyone I pick won't be confirmed. You know it, I know it, they know it." He leaned back against his pillows, grinning still. "Well?"

"It's the truth, Lord."

"Oh, you hide your satisfaction so well. You're a good Rider,

Lyeth. One of the best. And you'll stay after I'm dead. You'll stay for my son."

Lyeth's stomach went cold. "No, Lord." She stood. "I'll ride your death to Vantua and the guildmaster will send another in my place. I oathed to you, but will not oath to your son, whether he succeeds or not."

"He will," Gambin muttered. "He's an idiot, but he must. And you will help him."

"I will not. I'll ride to Vantua and not come back."

Gambin coughed and glared at her. She gave him more water and wiped his lips, and he lay back on the pillows.

"Shall we ask Maranta's device, Rider? Would you abide by what it says?"

"I pay no attention to nonsense, Lord," she said stiffly, rising.

"Rider!"

"My Lord?"

"You're oathed to obey me—"

"Not beyond your death."

"I'll have you taken."

"You have no grounds. My guild protects me, and Jentesi Clan Court would never support you."

Gambin's eyes gleamed with humor. "I can have you taken secretly. Tortured. Killed."

Lyeth shook her head, feeling the pins work loose in her hair. "What use am I dead? You're a bastard, Gambin, but you're not a fool. You know enough not to harm the guild, but Culdyn doesn't."

"Culdyn's a fool, you think? And you hate him."

"Even more than I hate you. He has the soul of a snake."

"He is my son!"

"Of course," Lyeth said, as her stomach knotted tighter. "Who, my Lord, could doubt it?"

His laugh became a fit of coughing and Tobi, coming forward quickly, brushed her aside. She looked over the physician's back to the rest of the room. Petras stared at her and she saw him smile quickly beneath the deep concealment of his beard; the death watchers behind him were avidly silent, staring at Gambin's shaking body. Lyeth's face tensed with disgust and she looked down. His twisting had pushed back the covers and a pale red stain spread over the sheet at his crotch. The watchers murmured and she turned her head aside. Gambin deserved an ugly death, she told herself, but a small tinge of pity invaded her thoughts. The coughing subsided. Servants whipped away the stained sheets and spread new ones, and Tobi came forward with a porcelain cup in his hands. Gambin breathed painfully and shallowly through his mouth.

"Go now," Tobi said to her.

"No." Gambin opened his eyes. "Get that away from me. I need to think—get it *away!*" Tobi retreated and Gambin gestured at the silver goblet. Lyeth bent over with it and he caught her hair, pulling her lower. His breath was foul.

"Rider. You'll stay for my son. You'll help my son." He tugged her hair. "Not a game. The guild can't touch a dead man. Or protect a dead Rider." Releasing her, he turned his face away.

She stood motionless until she could reassemble her expressionless mask, then stepped back from the bed and walked toward the doors. Petras nodded as she passed but the death watchers paid her no attention, busy with murmured speculation. She pushed through the tall doors and stood in the center of the anteroom, fists curled under her talma. The room, save for one servant, was deserted now, and she stared at Death's pale, beguiling eyes. Then Torwyn came from the death chamber and put his hand on her shoulder. She breathed deeply, moving her head so that her cheek grazed his fingers.

"It's not pretty," Torwyn said.

"No." She locked her thoughts away, stepping back. His hand dropped. "I've seen death before."

"Like this?"

She didn't answer. He touched her cheek gently. "What's wrong with your eye, Lyeth? Has it been seen to?"

"Yes." The hand spread along the side of her face and she shook her head. "I'm tired, Torwyn. I need to be alone. Let me be."

"Dine with me," he suggested. "It's been a long time."

She stepped back again, and he let his hand float between them for a moment before bringing it down smoothly to rest on his hip. "No. I rode in this morning and I want to bathe and sleep for three days."

"In three days Gambin might be dead."

"Or in three hours." She glanced at his dark blue eyes, recognizing their expression. "Ask me again tomorrow. Where's Syne?"

The steward's mouth twitched. "In her rooms. Waiting, like the rest of us. The four agreed to come to Gambin together or not at all."

"Trustful of them."

One corner of his mouth lifted in a half-smile. "You know the clans have sent representatives?"

"I saw the banners. Torwyn, I want to—"

"We have guild representatives here, too," he continued blandly. "Including three from the Merchants Guild."

"I—the Merchants Guild? Three?"

"One is their assistant guildmaster. Interesting, no?" He smiled again.

"But they're not a ranking guild—who asked them?"

"Nobody's taken credit for it, and they're certainly not talking." He bent his tall body toward her. "And I know what Gambin wants of you, Rider. I think I can help."

She stepped back angrily. "I thought better of you. You know my oath—"

"You don't have to tell me, Lyeth. I know already." He smiled at her glare. "Three merchants and Culdyn Gambini. The Crescent Bathhouse is lovely in winter, and so few people go there. I'm there most evenings. Come bathe with me." He nodded formally, still smiling, and went back to the bedchamber. The early afternoon light, slanting through the window, touched his copper-colored hair.

Lyeth clenched her teeth and stalked out, cursing Torwyn silently under the impassive gaze of guards and trophies. In the Great Hall a group of Clan visitors squatted by the huge fireplace, playing dice. Across from them a collection of guild representatives listened to Forne, Gambin's fat minstrel, and in a corner Coreon hunched over a dice bowl, arguing enthusiastically with a young, pale-haired shadi in Alanti blue. Jandi was not present and Lyeth didn't see the colors of the Merchants Guild, but in a far niche two shadeen in Maranta's colors stood guard over a glittering device. Lyeth hesitated in mid-stride, pivoted, and went over to them.

"Is that the machine?" she demanded.

They glanced at each other. "Yes, Rider," one said. He moved aside to let her see.

"That's where we are. I mean, that's our planet," the other said, nodding to the stone in the center. It hung suspended from wires so thin they were almost invisible, an unfamiliar, milky blue gem carved into strange shapes. "It's a Trapper stone," the shadi said, making the sign against evil. "The sphere around it is the first Circle of Heaven, then the second and third and fourth, and the sun and moon circling those."

Lyeth grunted, leaning closer. A thin lattice of golden wires connected constellations of rubies, sapphires, emeralds, diamonds, and a
fine mist of silver that, she assumed, represented the Scarf. By twisting her head she could see the star clusters in their individual
spheres: Mill, Bucket, Loom, Plow, and Wheel clustered near the
milky stone; Horse, Oxen, Tree, and Ice Palace in the second circle;
the Minstrel, the Scarf, and the Child in the third; and surrounding
them the sphere of the Lady and the Eye. Maranta and her crafters
had presented each of the fourteen houses of the Zodiac to glittering
and costly perfection; Lyeth reached one finger toward the constella-
tion of the Lady and the two shadeen stiffened. She leaned back.

"Those beryls there—those are the planets, and the sun and the
moon," the shadi said importantly. "They have their own circles.
And the colors—those are for the elements. Gold for earth, sapphires for air, rubies for fire, emeralds for water, and diamonds for
time. You should see it, Rider, when it's working and all the spheres
turn in their times and directions. It's very impressive." He blew an
invisible speck of dust from a star in the Eye.

"I'm sure it is," she said sourly. "But is it useful?"

"Useful!" The shadi looked outraged. "It predicted the time we
arrived here, didn't it? And this morning it said that that which is
unrevealed shall be known and the dead tree will bear a strange and
powerful fruit." He paused. "What do you think of that?"

"I think," Lyeth said deliberately, "that it's a load of ox shit."

The shadeen leaped between her and the device, hands on sword
hilts. Lyeth spun around, wishing them and their fellows to perdition, and stormed through the hall, her talma billowing behind her.
But most of these folk were out-province visitors and her talma did
not scare them. She opened a small door set in the enormous Ceremonial Door, closed it, and stood in the yard, breathing the cold air
gratefully. It was well past time for the noon meal, but her head
throbbed with questions, her eyes ached, her legs felt heavy with
fatigue, and she wasn't hungry at all. She leaned against the door,
waiting for her head and body to settle down. The shadeen on duty
at either side of the Ceremonial Door glanced at her and looked into
the yard again as a group of guards walked by in tight formation, one
after another, arms swinging and legs pacing in unison, looking
neither right nor left.

"Wonk wonk wonk," one of the shadeen honked under her breath,
staring after them. Geese, the shadeen called them, ridiculing their

formations and stiff-legged walk; these geese disappeared into the Snake, the alley running between the walls of Horda's Garden and the apartments of the nobility, at the far side of the Great Hall from the stables. Taking a deep breath, Lyeth left the Great Hall and followed the inner curtain to the base of the archers' stairs. She climbed quickly, ignoring the protest of her muscles, and paced along the wall walk until she came to another flight of stairs. The shadeen on duty glanced at her and saluted casually as she went by; the wind chilled her. She paused to seam the talma fully closed.

A few minutes later she stepped into a watch niche carved in the stone of Jentesi Rock, high above the castle and to the side. Jentesi-on-River shouldered up to its rock walls; behind it the snow-covered fields stretched for kils, broken by the dark lines of evergreen windbreaks. Mountains reared at the horizon, white and grey and purple under a pale sky. She stood for a moment looking over Gambin's domain before turning to the opening of the narrow tunnel. She hesitated, fists clenched, until her constant, irrational fear of the rock lessened, and walked swiftly into the tunnel before it had a chance to return. The sunlight disappeared as stone surrounded her, greedy and malicious, ready to freeze her within itself forever if she stopped for the barest fraction of a second within the dark, carnivorous rock. She forced herself to pace deliberately, one hand stretched before her, feeling the sides of the tunnel for turns and curves. Her chest grew tight and she remembered to breathe; her heart pounded and she slowed still more, refusing to be vanquished by her fear. The talma hissed against stone. Grey stained the darkness ahead and a little time later she walked out of the tunnel and stood on another small balcony, this one looking east over the forests of Dorne and north to where the Tobrin turned and twisted behind shoulders of mountains. She raised her face in gratitude to the sunlight.

Parts of the parapet had crumbled and fallen centuries ago, well after the last Dorne-Jentesi wars, and had never been replaced; the abandoned balcony had collected a thick layer of rock dust and the leavings of innumerable tiny falls. Lyeth, discovering it, had done only minimal cleaning, enough to remove the larger boulders from the tunnel and clear a space to sit on the watch niche itself. She sat there now, her legs dangling over the immense drop to the Tobrin and her arms folded along the top of the battered stone railing. She put her chin on her hands and closed her eyes.

You'll stay for my son. I've never done anything against the rules of my guild. You'll stay for Culdyn. I can have you killed.

Down the banks of the Tobrin, from Trine to Vantua and from Vantua to Coaelani, ran a ribbon of steel and wood which, in the summer months, bore the huffing, panting, belching machine the Smiths Guild had unveiled sixteen years ago. Behind the machine was a huge trough on wheels, carrying coal from Riando or wood from Dorne or Efet. And behind the trough, hitched together and rattling along, came flat platforms with low sides loaded with goods or produce or sometimes livestock, came houses with windows and chimneys and deeply upholstered seats where passengers could ride in comfort. The wood or coal fed fires in the black machine's belly; water in an internal tank turned to steam; steam turned the collection of gears and shafts and the like that propelled the Smiths' machine down the rich heartland of Cherek. A fast Rider on a swift horse could outpace the monster—for a time. Lyeth had heard rumors that the Smiths Guild planned to extend their steel ribbon up the Water Road to Jentesi-on-River and perhaps even across the passes to Mywyn, or Sorontil in Bec. During the fierce northern winters the machine traveled only in southern Cherek where the deep snow and ice did not block its path, but Lyeth didn't doubt that the Smiths would overcome this problem, too.

Every provincial capital, every major town or city, had a room like the one behind Durn's council chamber; a room filled with the clacking of a small machine, a desk, and someone scribbling messages or transmitting them. The wires ran from the small rooms to other small rooms, a thin, vulnerable web with Vantua, secure, at its center. The wires fell often in the winters or were blown down by summer storms, but year by year the Artisans Guild made the wires stronger, came up with new ways of protecting the web, and every spring legions of wire runners set out from the provinces and from Vantua, repairing the web. When Gambin died, if the web was unbroken from Jentesi Castle to Vantua, the Clan Council would know of it in minutes; if the wires were down, they'd know of it within hours, as soon as Riders from the nearest still-connected telegraph station rode into the city. The Historians would not note his death officially until Lyeth came into their halls, the scrolled Deathnote in her hands, but this would be mere formality—they would already *know.*

Certain guilds were, by tradition, expected observers of a lord's passing. The Artisans, Scholars, Captains, and others of the ranking guilds sent representatives from Vantua; the lower guilds were not expected to so send, and such sending would be unheard of, unsettling. And now three members of the Merchants Guild, a non-ranking guild, a trade guild on the same level as the Innkeepers, or the Peddlers, or the Rivermen, waited in Jentesi Castle on Lord Gambin's dying. Torwyn would not have lied to her. They must have come by invitation—whose?

Lyeth tugged her hood more closely around her cheeks and put her chin on her hands again. The rock's cold seeped through her gloves. It was rumored that the Merchants Guild was negotiating with the Artisans for telegraph connections of their own from one Merchant guildhall or warehouse to another across the length and breadth of Cherek. They'd get them; they had to get them. Over the past decade more and more of Cherek's economy rested in the hands of these traders and sellers, and in the hands of the non-ranking Smiths Guild. The Teneleh trade ships sailed at the Merchants' whim backed by the Merchants' money; the Smiths invented and built on the Merchants' financial backing. But it was also rumored that when the Smiths needed large quantities of iron, the Merchants Guild arranged the purchase with Vedere's lord; when the Artisans needed metal for their telegraph wires, the Merchants found it for them, using its contacts and its power to finance and enable the very projects it so enthusiastically promoted. It seemed to Lyeth now that the Merchants Guild stood at the eye of a hurricane of change and that those changes reached more deeply into the life of Cherek than the provincial lords, or even the Vantua Council, could imagine. Deathnotes and telegraphs, the power of Vantua threatened by the increasing influence of Lymon—Cherek's dependence on laggard tradition could not, and perhaps must not, last.

Some day, she thought unhappily, the Riders Guild would be an anachronism; would become, at best, a mapmaking guild, or a guild of explorers and guides. Or, at worst, a guild of enforcers, of those who brought evil news, who captured criminals and carried them to punishment. The guild could become, throughout Cherek, what it had already become in Jentesi. Any group without direction or place becomes a tool, she thought uneasily. Who, then, would wield the Riders Guild? To what purpose? And when?

Lyeth contemplated the image of future impotence, and it did not please her. Nor did Gambin's assumption that she could aid or hinder the succession in Jentesi. Riders lived within the rules of their guilds; those seconded to provincial lords served as messengers, no more, and the guild held no power save as one guild among the others in Vantua Council—at that, a small and increasingly anachronistic segment of the council. She wished she could think Gambin a fool, wished she knew what he believed could give the Riders Guild any more than the minimal power it held, but the thoughts skittered unmanageably through her mind, pursued by Gambin's whispery voice. You'll stay for Culdyn, Rider. I can have you killed.

The sun moved down the western curve of sky and the air chilled further; the knot in her stomach became hunger. She stood and stretched, her muscles creaking, before plunging through her enemy the stone. Emerging, Gambin's voice and her own endless speculations filled her head again. She made her way through the sunlit wall walks and passages of Jentesi Castle, listening to those maddening interior voices, barely seeing the world around her. And, putting her hand to the door of her room, froze, the interior monolog interrupted by the buzz of voices beyond the door. The high, eager voice belonged to Emris; the other was a deep, comfortable rumble with sharp undertones. Her heart jumped. She touched the collar of her talma, breathed deeply, refused to smile, and pushed the door open.

Jandi sat before the woodstove with Emris beside him. A map scroll covered their laps and fell to the floor on either side; Jandi's huge, booted feet rested on the stove's legs, his thighs and buttocks overflowing the chair seat. His hair, neatly braided, fell over his shoulders and one beaded braid-end twitched on the pile of his discarded talma as he turned toward the door, grumbling about interruptions. The grumbling faded and a huge smile took its place.

"Lyeth," he said warmly. "You look better with half your face hidden. Come in."

Emris peered around Jandi's paunch, saw Lyeth, and scrambled to his feet as she closed the door with her hip and tossed her talma over the cloakrack. She felt dangerously close either to laughter or tears, so looked around for something to yell at. Already the lower shelves were cleared, a couple of crates rested against one wall, and a bottle of her best apato stood open and half-consumed by Jandi's elbow. She glared at it.

"Did you ask, or did you just take it?" she demanded.

"I took it, of course." He caught her hair, pulled her down, and kissed her loudly. She blinked. "Would you like some?" he continued, releasing her. "Emris, fetch this bad-tempered person a cup. Sit down, my dear. The fire's warm and the apato's excellent." Jandi's pale eyes sparkled and three of his braids fell across his large belly.

"I know it is," she said rudely, taking Emris' chair. Emris looked flushed. Two of her best goblets rested by the bottle. "Sweet Mother, Jandi, you've been feeding him apato? He's only a child!"

"Just a sip." Jandi's intricately tattooed hand enveloped his cup. "And if I remember correctly, at his age you were belting down fermented goat's milk at a staggering rate."

"You forget where I was," she said sharply. "And it wasn't fermented goat's milk, it was krath. Don't exaggerate." Emris gave her a clean cup and a wide-eyed look, and retreated. She caught his sleeve and pulled him closer.

"Are you feeling all right?"

He nodded, his lips pressed tight. Lyeth let him go, shaking her head, and he sat abruptly on a stool by the stove, staring at the adults. It probably wouldn't hurt him, she decided finally, and let Jandi fill her cup.

"Here," she said, raising it. "To blue-skinned corrupters of youth. Damn, I'm glad to see you. What have you been telling my . . . boy?"

"The usual lies."

Emris grinned and said nothing, and Lyeth rubbed at her patch. "I'd have been here earlier, but Gambin wanted to see me."

"Ah? How is he? What did he say?"

"He's dying, and you know better than to ask. Emris, fetch my salve. It's beside the bed."

The boy stood, looked green, and sat again hastily.

"Just a sip, Jandi? Emris, do you need to vomit?"

He shook his head, stood carefully, and walked with great deliberation into her bedroom. Lyeth glared at Jandi.

"He's a handsome child," the fat man said approvingly.

"You keep your hands off him. He's only ten."

"So, my dear, were you. Let's take a look." He peeled away the patch and she gasped, cursing. Emris put the salve on the table and gaped at her. "Child, hold this." Jandi gave the boy a shielded candle, produced a loupe, and peered at Lyeth's eye, tilting her face this way and that and ignoring her stream of curses. He concluded by dropping salve into her eyes, patting her cheek paternally, and letting her go. She exhausted her supply of Cheran curses and switched, undaunted, to an older tongue.

"I know that one," Jandi said cheerfully. "I like the salve. Joleda's a hag, but she does mix a good potion. Put the candle down, child."

Lyeth shut her mouth and glared as Emris put the candle on a table and stood beside it uncertainly. She wiped her eyelashes, squinting at him. "What is it?"

"Can I stay down this time?"

She made a face. "Go lie down. Just don't vomit on the rugs, or I'll flay you."

"Put your head between your knees," Jandi advised. He took a handful of Lyeth's hair and forced her head back.

"Damn it, Jandi—"

"There, that's a girl. Hold still, now. Your hair's filthy."

She muttered and Emris giggled. Jandi tied the patch in place and pinched her cheek. Emris, on the rug by her feet, lifted his face and grinned at her, his golden hair fluffy.

"Just because this gutbag gets away with it," she told him sternly, "doesn't mean you can. Don't get any ideas."

The boy lowered his head, still grinning. Jandi refilled his cup and beamed, and Lyeth, giving up, shook her head affectionately.

"You've grown," he said. "You took forever getting here. Tell me about your trip."

She rested her booted feet on the stove's skirt and told him, gesturing with her cup. Jandi nodded and asked questions. When she told him about Pelegorum and Emris he frowned and looked down. The boy was asleep, head pillowed on crossed arms, face rosy with firelight and apato.

"I can see why you took him," Jandi said. "But I wonder if you do. Did you talk to Joleda about this?"

Lyeth moved her legs uncomfortably. "She thinks I think he's a toy. She wants me to send him home."

"And will you?"

"I don't know. He wants to find his family. I guess I want to help him." She turned the cup around in her fingers, watching the apato tilt and fall.

"Ask Maranta's machine," Jandi said, and giggled when she glared at him. "And if he doesn't have a family?"

"I don't know. He hates Riders. Did he tell you?"

"I had to convince him that I wouldn't eat him alive, and then he had to convince me. He has a sharp tongue for a child of ten." He reached for the poker and stirred the fire. It leaped and glittered in the firebox. "You told him about mapping the pass, yes? He remembered the entire thing, even to the distances. Mother, what a mapmaker he'd be. Or explorer. He can read."

"Mother," she mimicked. "What an explorer *I'd* have been."

"Lyeth—"

"I know: it's an old argument; let it drop. Let it drop." She shifted again, looking at Emris. "He's changed since we came up castle. This morning he seemed afraid, but I don't know why. Nothing frightened him in Pelegorum, or during the trip—and yes, Jentesi Castle should scare him, but he doesn't know enough yet, he hasn't learned what to be afraid of yet, so he shouldn't be—hell," she said suddenly, tangled in words, and moved her hands as though pushing them away. "Jandi? Did I do the right thing?"

Jandi stretched his eyes in assumed astonishment. "Mother Above! Either I'm losing my hearing or you're losing your mind. You're asking my approval for something?"

*"Jandi—"*

"Child," he said kindly. "First, you are an idiot. He's a fosterling without family, from a mountain village. You march in and change his entire life. I think he's afraid of you a little, yes? And I don't think he respects you very much."

"So?"

"So you drag him up and down the mountains, then bring him here. You leave your horse in the Lords Stables, you have servants to feed you and fetch for you, you live in this clutter—Hell, Emris probably thought you lived in a sewer and dined on infants nightly."

"That," she said firmly, "is crazy."

"And so, sweetling, are you. Before, he didn't know what he'd been dragged into. Now he does, and he probably couldn't even imagine it before. So he's frightened, and quiet, and uncertain. And that didn't stop him from letting me know precisely what he thought of me, and when I talked him out of it, it didn't stop him from inspecting that map and asking questions that you, child, didn't ask until you were a good deal older than he is now. Whew." Jandi refilled his glass. "So first, he's in a different world and he's lying low until he knows where all the wild things are. And second, I don't know if I approve or not. He's your morsel, not mine."

"He's not a morsel." She stood abruptly and, picking up Emris, carried him to his room. He put his face against her shoulder and muttered in his sleep; his eyelids flickered as she pulled his boots off, and he clutched the pillow and buried his head in it. Dining on infants indeed, Lyeth thought. She pulled the covers around him. Jandi looked at her expectantly as she stopped behind her chair and put her hands on its back. She breathed deeply and said quickly, before she could change her mind, "When Gambin dies, I'll go back to Vantua. I don't want to oath to another lord, Jandi. I want to join the explorers."

Jandi sighed, settling his massive shoulders more deeply into the chair. "You don't give up, do you?"

She gripped the chair tightly. "I won't oath again. I won't put my life, my mind, to work for someone like Gambin. I'll—I'll leave the guild first, Jandi, I swear it."

"Not every lord in Cherek is like Gambin," Jandi said reasonably. "And Gambin's not the first tyrant in Cherek and he won't be the last. Five centuries ago Boromil was selling his own serfs as slaves in the Vantua markets. And Constain—"

"I know that—"

"We survived Constain, and Boromil, and we'll survive Gambin, too. No, don't argue, just listen to me. You still see things in terms of absolutes, child, absolute good or absolute evil. Gambin's no more absolutely evil than I am."

"Don't tempt me to agree," she muttered, and Jandi ignored her.

"He reformed the Seminarians Guild and the Physicians Guild in Jentesi, he built the first telegraph net in the province, he promoted trade with Vantua, with Dorne and Efet. He stabilized the exchange rates in Jentesi-on-River."

"Sure, thirty years ago. He also created the ferrets, and the network, he lets his land-barons suck up all the taxes they want, and he pays lip service to the guilds when they complain, but he doesn't do anything about it. But what he's done to *us,* Jandi, that's the worst of all. What he's done to the Riders. He's turned us into deathbirds in this province, he's made us hated and feared and—"

"I don't see it," Jandi said.

"You're on the Rock! The place is full of outlanders or land-barons, and they're almost immune to the network." She came around the chair quickly. "Jandi, come riding with me in the city. Just one afternoon's ride, and then tell me what you think."

He shrugged. "That proves nothing. Besides, Gambin is dying. It will change when he's gone."

"But it won't," she said desperately. "Jandi, it was so easy for him to do this to us, and when others see that, when they see how easy—"

"I won't discuss it," he said flatly. "You're worked up, and you don't know what you're talking about. No," he said curtly as she started to protest. "No. This is a reunion, not a council meeting." And, leaning back, he smiled expansively and gestured toward his talma. "You haven't asked me my news yet."

Lyeth found herself, unhappily, employing the trick she'd used with Gambin all these years, putting the anger in one small mental room and slamming doors on it, one after another after another, until she could breathe smoothly, face calm, and deal with the moment. She had done it so often that it took only an instant to complete, and the fact that she did it so automatically now, with Jandi, made her ache. Obeying his gesture, she leaned to the talma and picked it up.

"What news? Let me guess. The price of apato's up, the Lords Council has banned dancing, the Seminarians—Lady Mother, Jandi," she said abruptly. "Where did you get this?" She stared at the insignia on the talma's collar.

"I came by it properly. Two weeks ago. I telegraphed, but you'd already left the Rock."

"You're Rider Guildmaster?"

"Why all this astonishment? You think I shouldn't be? I was elected fairly and easily—after the usual nonsense, of course. I was asked," he added proudly.

"Jandi, I'm—I'm speechless. Why didn't you tell me earlier?"

"Would you have treated me any different?" He laughed and hauled himself out of the chair. "I haven't changed, you know. I don't walk on air or talk intimately with the Triple Gods or any of that other superstitious nonsense. And if you start treating me respectfully, I'll probably die of the shock."

She draped the talma over his shoulders and he fastened it under his collection of chins. The red and gold emblem twinkled.

"Well?" he demanded.

"I don't know what to say," she confessed. "Did you tell Emris?" Jandi shook his head. "Thank the Mother. He'd have died of fright."

"Is that supposed to be funny?"

"No. Not at all. Mother, Jandi, if Riders are hated here, they'll think you're—you're Death's chamberlain—or Death herself."

"Nonsense," Jandi said coldly. "I'm treated with the respect due any guildmaster, or any lord, for that matter. I won't have you parroting that superstitious horseshit at me." He paused at the door to look down at her, then beyond her to the curtained doorway of Emris' room. "You don't respect me and he doesn't respect you. You two have a lot in common, Lyeth. You should think about that."

She tightened her lips and watched him leave the room. The door slapped shut and immediately reopened. Jandi stuck his head in, crossed his eyes, grinned, and went away. Lyeth heard his chuckle recede down the hallway. She picked up the empty apato bottle, then cradled it against her breasts and sat abruptly, resting her head against the chair back.

Jandi was right, of course. He was a guildmaster and guildmasters, like lords, were next to sacred in Cherek; they might hate and fear him, but it wouldn't show. At least not here on the Rock. I was asked, he had said. She nodded unhappily. Of course he'd been asked. Tovenet's faction pushing for change, for a restructuring of the guild to adapt to progress, while Hilbert's faction pushed with just as much energy for a return to the past, even to the point of demanding the destruction of the telegraph net and the Smiths' precious steam engines. Jandi would have been the perfect middle choice; affable, neither radical nor reactionary, and not terribly concerned with anything that could not fit neatly within the borders of a map. Lyeth looked down at the half-empty apato bottle ruefully. Mother Sun, I do love the old bastard, she thought. And Mother Sun, he's not the guildmaster we need.

Emris was still asleep by the time she finished eating. She called Janya to clear the table and went into the boy's room. He had burrowed deeply under the covers, only a swatch of golden hair decorating the pillow above the dark hem of quilt. Lyeth pulled the quilt down to his chin. A smudge of dirt covered his cheek, and he mumbled and pulled the quilt back over his ears. She went out, instructing Janya to heat water and make sure the boy bathed. Janya, her hands full of dishes, nodded and waddled from the room, and Lyeth pulled the talma around her shoulders as she walked onto the portico above the yard.

The sun sat low on the southwestern horizon. Across the Water Road the mountains behind Jentesi-on-River glowed pale pink in the failing light, and the Minstrel shone on the horizon, hands perpetually raised to strike the strings of his harp. Trappers called these stars the Gate and believed that if the Gate ever opened, the cold white fire of the River would spill through and bathe the earth in pale death. They looked forward to this event with considerable enthusiasm. In Cherek, the bright mist of stars was called the Scarf, a spanning gauze laid aside temporarily by the Minstrel as he prepared to play. Lyeth wasn't sure which version she liked more. The Scarf was invisible now, its thin lights unable to compete with the setting sun. Not a cloud in sight—it would be cold again tonight. She buried her hands in her pockets and went down the stairs, silent on stone, snow, and mud. The shadows of the yard took her. The Lords Stables were closed against the night, the Crescent Bathhouse far away, and besides, she thought impatiently, she'd had enough of arguments and intrigues today. Let Torwyn stew in bathwater all night, if he wished. She hunched her shoulders, restless and chill, and strode rapidly through the Neck to the shadeen barracks.

The barracks projected from the side of the stables to form one of the walls of the Neck; a few lights glowed in the sleeping quarters upstairs but the windows of the downstairs hall blazed. She pushed open the heavy wooden door and entered the cloakroom, peeling the talma from her shoulders. The wall hooks were dense with heavy winter gear, fur-lined cloaks, thick caps, woolen scarves steaming odoriferously in the warmth. She hung her black talma amid the russet cloaks of Jentesi, Alanti's blue, Dorne's brown, Efet's grey, the yellow of Bec, and, negotiating the paired litter of boots on the floor, went into the hall.

Shadeen filled the room, cleaning weapons, gambling, arguing, telling lies. She stood in the doorway warming her hands in her armpits and watching them. The barracks hall always felt good, especially after a ride through the hostile province; no one here looked at her with terror. Crise, in a tight knot of shadeen by one of the fireplaces, shouted her name and waved, and Lyeth picked her way across the room, nodding at people she knew. The Efet shadeen wore their hair cropped short about their ears; those from Alanti were small and lithe, and three had very pale hair. Trapper ancestors, she thought. They looked at her curiously as she nodded and moved on.

"I'll have nothing to do with it," Crise said grimly as Lyeth came up beside her. Her shadeen groaned loudly and the out-province shadeen nudged each other, looking expectant. "It's a piece of damned foolishness, it's senseless, it's dangerous—"

"Of course it is," Grims protested. "That's the whole point." Spiky hair, ungoverned and ungovernable, framed his small, eager face.

"What is it?" Lyeth demanded, reaching around Crise for the hot wine.

"These iceheads," Crise told her, "want to run forfeits. With the outlanders. Now. From Lords Walk to the barracks. Not giving a damn, I suppose, that it's dark, and winter, and icy, and Gambin's up tower dying."

"And has been," Grims said prosaically, "for the better part of a month. I suppose we're to die with him—of boredom, perhaps?"

"Ilen won't like it," Crise said.

"He will." Lyeth grinned. "If you come with us. Tell him that . . . that it's a good way of letting off steam. Keep the troops happy, in trim, out of mischief—"

"And warm," a Poderi shadi said with feeling, rubbing his hands against his arms. An Alanti shadi, pale hair and smile vaguely familiar, slapped his arm and called him a warm-weather nurseling, and their friends had to keep them apart.

Crise eyed Lyeth dubiously. "You'd come?"

Lyeth, shaking her shoulders back and shaking away the tension of the day, laughed. A smile tugged at the corner of Crise's mouth.

"I'm not explaining this to Ilen by myself," she said, and the shadeen, sensing victory, cheered. "Hush, we don't want to empty the place. All right, teams of two, from the tip of Lords Walk back here. Two hours. Who's running?"

"I am," Grims said immediately. "Lyeth, and you. We'll pick partners. Prena, you coming?"

"Are you kidding?" the shadi demanded. "I just got off duty. You're not getting me back out before tomorrow morning."

"Fine," Crise said. "You're duty officer and you can list the tokens." She straightened and glanced around the hall. Save for the group around her, the other shadeen paid her no attention. "Fine," she said again. "One of us, one outlander on each team. And no cheating, understand?"

The pale Alanti shadi, sliding between his friends, put his hand on

Lyeth's forearm. "I'll partner you," he said, hair silky and brown eyes gleaming. "Can you keep up with me?"

She looked at him, eyebrows raised. He couldn't be more than seventeen, and cocky with it. She opened her mouth to refuse him and remembered; she'd seen him playing dice with Coreon that morning, in the coolness of the Great Hall.

"I lead," she said sternly. "And you follow. Understood?"

"Of course!" He gestured extravagantly. "Laret of Korth. Of Joria."

"Lyeth of the Riders Guild." She pushed him toward the door. "Keep up with *you,* stripling?"

"I'm very fast," he assured her as they walked quickly and quietly through the ward. "And I'm very good." Moonlight illuminated his engaging grin. "Would you like to find out?"

"No. How's your luck at gambling?"

Laret looked abashed. "This morning, not very good. But tomorrow will be different, very different. Lord Coreon will be sorry he played dice with *me.*"

"Um. How much did you lose?"

Laret shrugged. "Nothing much. Something my father gave me. I'll get it back. When do we start, Rider?"

"Soon." She quickened her pace to catch up with Crise and Laret trotted behind.

Lords Walk, on the far side of the castle, was cold and deserted, its crumbling parapets and uneven pavement gleaming with ice. Where the Walk loomed above the frozen rapids, the stone paving blocks reared jagged and large, as though some huge and careless hand had crumpled and discarded them. Lyeth balanced on the balls of her feet, the short cloak Crise had loaned her brushing her thighs, and watched the other teams critically while Laret peppered her with questions.

"We run the whole course," she said, waving to shut him up. "Without being caught, as silently as possible. First team back declares forfeits for the others—that's the second-best part."

"And the first-best part?" Laret demanded.

"The run, the run," Lyeth said. "And stealing. Prena's made a list. We have to get back to the barracks before anyone else *and* with everything on the list, or we lose."

"Stealing," Laret repeated. "I like it. Do we get to keep what we take?"

"No." She bent and straightened, stretching her legs. "Korth. That's near the border, isn't it?"

"Just south of it," Laret said, and added, "But I come from Joria now."

"Indeed." She was right, then; there but for an accident of geography stood a Trapper. She grinned at him and was about to speak when chubby Horten, looking puffed with his own importance, coughed to get their attention, raised his lantern, and read the list for them in its shielded glow.

" 'A rose, a ring, a rock, a rhyme.' " His high voice skittered through the night. " 'A toad, a king, a dog, a chime.' *Now!*"

Lyeth tapped Laret, spun, and raced over the slick, jumbled rocks of Lords Walk, leaping from stone to stone, the wind cold in her hair. Laret caught up with her as she reached the high white parapet surrounding the Garden of the Lady, and she glanced at him approvingly.

"Maybe you can keep up," she said, not breaking stride. The balusters to their left gleamed.

"Moraine," Laret said, keeping pace. "You've done it too, haven't you?" He laughed, not waiting for her reply. "Rider, a *rose?*"

" 'A ring, a rock, a rhyme,' " she said, breathless. " 'A toad, a king, a dog, a chime.' The rose and the toad are the easy parts." And, in a burst of speed, drew ahead of him.

The parapet veered sharply left and opened onto the broad plaza before the Crescent Bathhouse. A shadi in Lord Torwyn's colors, looking cold and unhappy, stood watch by the doors. Lyeth ran silently along the blank wall behind the bathhouse, judged her moment, and dove for the overhang above the servants' entrance. She put her hand up, covering Laret's mouth just as he started to speak.

"The others will try for the chimes first," she whispered. "If we're not caught, we have two, maybe three minutes on them."

"And if we're caught," he said, lips on her palm. She dropped her hand.

"With Gambin dying and intrigue in the air? They'll kill us first, my highland friend, and mourn us later." She grinned amiably.

"Danger," Laret whispered excitedly. "Now I understand why you run this race. And now?"

"And now," she said, looking at him strangely, "we hope that you're not afraid of snakes." She opened the door quickly.

A gust of hot, damp air and the smell of animals enveloped them.

She closed the door and glanced around the dimly lit space. Gambin's menagerie keeper stored his more delicate charges here, away from winter's cold, just as Gambin's head gardener kept his fragile wards in this high, warm room. She strode quickly to a potted jungle, slipping her dagger from its sheath. After a second of rustling she tossed something to Laret.

"Rock-rose," she whispered. "That's two together." Something else flew at him; he caught it and almost dropped it, making a soft, disgusted noise. Lyeth, skipping back from a pool, glanced at him. "They do have toads in Alanti," she said. "I know it for a fact. Put it in a safe pocket—we don't want the darling to freeze." She opened a cage door deftly, reached within, and, opening her tunic, dropped this latest theft against her skin. Laret, busy with his toad, didn't see her.

Grims did, however, a bare minute later, flying up the stairs from the Garden of the Lady with his Dorne partner close behind; she jumped across the narrow walk between bathhouse and stairs before he had a chance to alert Torwyn's shadi, and led Laret between the high white walls of the nobles' apartments and around the White Tower's lower balcony.

"Half-done," she said as they rested for a moment at a corridor's mouth, waiting for distant footsteps to recede. The steps and walk behind them were empty.

"We only have three," Laret said.

"Four, highlander. Four." Before he could question her she was off down the corridor, boots silent on the stone. Just as silently, he followed.

The corridor passed Master Durn's storerooms, but Durn's shadeen, retreating from the cold, kept watch inside and did not see them flash by. As they rounded a corner, Laret, grinning, picked up a loose rock and skittered it back down the hallway. Shouts and the clatter of metal erupted from the storeroom.

"Dark Mother," Lyeth said. She grabbed a handful of the silky hair and dragged Laret, choking with laughter, up another flight of stairs, dark and worn. The noise receded behind them.

"Do you want to get us killed?" she whispered, shaking him.

"Let me go," he said, still laughing. "The others can't come that way now, can they?"

She released him. "Laret of Joria, you're a prime fool," she said, and grinned in spite of herself. The stairs twisted and they ran onto a portico half-opened to the night, then over the high, covered walkway above Horda's Garden, the night crisp and bright around them and Crise, below, rummaging with a Bec shadi for the small winter roses that lived, bright and chilly, under the mantle of snow. Lyeth scooped a handful of snow from one embrasure and, as she passed the next, aimed and let fly. Crise's smothered yelp followed them off the walkway. Laret giggled behind her; she turned right and right again into a narrow canyon between stone walls. The canyon ended at an abrupt drop. Lyeth saw one window lit below them, put a cautionary fingertip to her lips, and went over the side. She landed running; Laret landed hard, grunting, and hurried after her as the one lit window was flung open and an irritable voice demanded to know what was going on. Laret did likewise, *sotto voce*, when he caught up with her.

"A chime, a rhyme, a ring, a king," she said, working her dagger between a pair of shutters. The latch slid open and she dove inside, searched quickly amid a wonderland of gears and shafts and bells, and emerged, waving a small box.

"Chime?"

"Chime," she agreed, stuffing it into her belt pouch. Laret closed the shutters. "And king—it's got enamelwork on the back. Six."

"Five," he said, but she was already down the walk. He scurried to keep up, running silently behind her.

A flight of exterior steps, curving, icy, worn, and precipitous, led down to the roof of the great Hall. Lyeth swiftly touched her pockets and tunic, making sure her thievings were well stowed.

"Rider?" Laret said uncertainly.

She grinned, sat on the top step, and pushed off, careening down the stair, fending off the walls with her boots and gloved hands, the short cloak pulling at her neck and shoulders. The bumps smoothed as her speed increased, wind shrieked at her ears, and all the world went away save for speed, night, the sharp stars glittering beyond the overhang. She quelled the urge to shout just as Laret, above and behind her, punctured the night with a cry, high and sweeping and chillingly familiar. She reached the bottom of the stair, tucking in her shoulders, and somersaulted to land on her feet in time to snag Laret as he shot past. They went down together in a tangle of limbs and cloaks, leaving Lyeth, not by accident, on top and holding Laret pinned to the cold stones.

"Korth, *south* of the border?" she whispered furiously. "You damned fool, you'll get us both killed."

Laret, catching his breath, smiled at her. "I'm sorry," he said, gasping. "I'll be quiet."

"See that you do, snowbrother," she said in the Trapper tongue, releasing him. "If the others learn what you are, you'll die whether you're quiet or not." She started to rise but Laret came to his knees and grabbed her forearms.

"How did you know?" he said in the same language. "Are you—"

"No." She broke the hold and stood quickly. "Come on, stripling," she said in Cheran. "We have a race to win." She ran her hands down her tunic and breeches, making sure her tokens were intact, and ran. As usual, Laret made no noise as he followed.

She held up her arm for silence at the stairs leading to the Scholars Garden, crept to the edge of the walk, and peered over the balusters. Grims and a Riando shadi were busy at work, stealing one of the metal rings from the exercise bars in the children's section. Cursing, Lyeth retreated; she had planned to do the same thing herself.

"But you speak—" Laret said.

"Hush." She raced over the walkway, through a door, down a dark hallway, and through the interlocking rooms of the castle's school, taking a brief stop in a closet while an unsuspecting laundry maid, basket piled with clean linen, padded by.

"Where did you learn to—"

She popped through the arras, sped to the corridors in the scholars' apartments, and stopped again. "A ring, a rhyme," she said, pinning her hair into place. "If you ask one more question, particularly in that language, I'll kill you myself."

"But—"

She glared. "Any shadi who's fought on the borders knows that cry."

"Just so! Just because I know it doesn't mean that I'm a—"

"Of course." She put her fists on her hips. "But you know the tongue, and you run silently, and you look like a winter sprite. You'll have to tell me," she said, twitching his cloak into place, "how you lied your way into the Alanti shadeen. Not now, stripling, later is sufficient." Her glare melted into an expression of bemused exasperation. "Can you behave yourself for more than two minutes at a stretch?"

In reply, he executed a sweeping, courtly bow. "At your most humble service," he proclaimed. Lyeth rolled her eyes, adopted a serious expression, and knocked on a door.

The Poderi shadeen, she explained to Elot of the Scholars Guild as he sat slightly baffled before his fire, claimed that Guld of Chiana was twice, if not three times, the poet that Elot would ever be. Naturally, the Jentesi shadeen objected and Lyeth, hoping to avert a bloodbath, had come to beg Elot to accompany her to the shadeen barracks and favor all present with a recitation of the Hordiad, after which the Poderi shadeen were sure to retreat in shame. As would Guld, when he heard about it. In addition, she added, a great deal of money rode on the outcome, and Elot might see some of it find its way into his own pockets. Behind her, Laret choked and she kicked him swiftly.

The poet needed no further persuasion. He hauled out his manuscript and grabbed for his cloak, and while his back was turned Lyeth calmly reached into his wardrobe, secured his wide, crownless scholar's cap, and stuffed it into her tunic. Laret choked again.

Elot, in a fever to maintain his reputation and increase his wealth, scurried through the yard ahead of them, preceded by his belly and followed by his braids. Laret touched Lyeth's shoulder urgently.

"The dog, Rider! Where do we get the dog?"

"Peace, stripling," she said comfortingly. "We come with victory assured."

His frown deepened, settled, and cleared instantly. "You stole something while I wasn't looking," he said triumphantly.

"Dark Mother," Lyeth said, and clapped her hand over his mouth. He kissed her palm.

The barracks doors were crowded and the shadeen cheered as Lyeth, partner, and poet strode in.

"First team!" Prena said. Laret crowed.

"Where are these Poderi illiterates?" Elot demanded through the uproar. Ilen, appearing behind Prena, looked at him and blanched.

"Lyeth. You didn't."

Lyeth, smiling blandly, doffed her cloak and asked for a cup of wine. Crise came in as she took it, yelled contemptuously at the Rider, and unwrapped a very miserable dog from her cloak. Her Bec partner leaned against the wall, panting as miserably as the dog. When Grims appeared at the door he surveyed the other teams, snorted, and pushed his way into the hall. His partner followed, trying not to laugh.

"Tokens!" Prena demanded, clearing people away from one long table. "First in, second in, third in."

Laret bounced on the balls of his feet and Lyeth smiled around her winecup. "A rose, a rock," she declaimed. Laret pulled the bruised rock-rose from his pouch and put it on the table.

"Cheat!" Grims yelled.

"Is this a joke?" Elot demanded.

"Allowed," Prena said. Crise put a bud of winter rose on the table, and a pebble. Lyeth snorted. At Grims' gesture, his partner produced a hunk of pavement from Lords Walk and a piece of cloth which, unfurled, proved to be a woman's shift, delicately embroidered with flowers.

"Not fair!" Crise said. "That's only a representation of a rose."

"And that," Grims said loftily, pointing to Lyeth's offering, "is only a reference to a rock."

"Agreed," Lyeth said. "I won't challenge it."

"Accepted," Prena said. The shadeen shouted and cheered.

"You shouldn't give in so easily," Laret whispered. "You'll give it all away."

"Hush, stripling." She raised her voice. "A ring." And producing Elot's hat, stuck her arm through its empty center and spun it. The poet bellowed, grabbed it away, and stuck it firmly on his head, where the collection of paws and tails swung erratically around his face. Grims' partner threw the metal exercise ring on the table and Crise, looking smug, held up a chaplet of silver mesh instantly recognizable as Forne the Minstrel's most cherished possession. The cheers were deafening.

"Who's winning?" Laret demanded. "And why isn't it us?"

"Oh, it's not just getting in first," Lyeth said. "And it's not just having all the tokens. It depends on how difficult those tokens are to find, and how far you can interpret the clues without being disallowed. We're even: I won the rock, Grims the rose, and Crise the ring." She emptied her cup.

"This," Elot said indignantly, "is a disgrace."

Lyeth clapped her hand over his shoulder, stilling him. "A rhyme," she cried. "Master Elot, would you start now?"

Elot gave a mighty shake to his head, sending paws and tails lashing, and launched into the plodding, double-rhymed, interminable saga of Horda, on which he had worked diligently for the past twenty years. Once started, nothing known to shadeen or Rider could stop him. Ilen, before putting his face in his hands, mouthed silent imprecations at Lyeth, who stuck her tongue out at him.

Crise produced a love poem written, according to the inscription, to the eyes of Mistress Livia, the seductive and very fickle daughter of Bedwyn Cook, and signed by Durn's page Menwyn. It was a very dirty poem, as was the one Grims had made up during the race and now recited, to Elot's fury; but Master Elot took the prize by simple acclaim.

Lyeth's toad was accepted, Crise's stone toad from the storerooms of the White Tower appreciated, and Grims' toad absent. Whatever explanation he tried to give was shouted down; Lyeth won the round and Grims, cursing extravagantly, was out of the race. Laret bounced with excitement.

"A king," Lyeth said, holding the clock aloft. Carefully enameled on its back was a portrait of the Vernal King, extravagantly male, done in green and gold and gaudy enough, Prena said approvingly, for a whorehouse. "And a chime," Lyeth called. The clock hand touched the hour and a cascade of bells rang counterpoint to Elot's recitation. Lyeth, feeling smug, drank another cup of wine. Grims sulked.

Her king was preferred to Crise's king, a doll filched from the playrooms, but her chime took second place to the shimmering windchimes produced by Crise's partner and stolen from the grave-trees in the Garden of the Lady. Laret grew positively dangerous with excitement, arms waving and fair hair a nimbus around his face. And Lyeth, working on her third cup of wine, maintained a serene silence.

"Aha!" Crise shouted triumphantly, unmuzzling the bedraggled kitchen dog. "The dog, Rider! Show your dog or forfeit!"

Laret groaned but Lyeth, still smug, opened the neck of her tunic. Warmed by her body, protected through the long run, a flat-faced dog snake stuck its head into the light, flicked its tongue, and proceeded to curl around Lyeth's neck and across her shoulders. Laret fainted.

"I call forfeit!" Lyeth yelled across the shouting and laughter. The voices tumbled into a relative quiet, during which Lyeth looked fondly at Elot. The poet stood, eyes closed, one hand waving in inexorable cadence, and Crise glanced from Lyeth to the poet and back again.

"You don't mean it," she said. "Rider, you can't possibly mean it."

Lyeth's grin lacked the least trace of pity. "Every. Last. Stanza. Unless, of course, you can persuade him to stop."

At which Elot grabbed a stave and leaped onto a table, from which he protected honor with recitation, and person with an artful blend of jabs and thrusts against a wave of yelling shadeen. Lyeth, weak with laughter, leaned against a wall and allowed Prena to deprive her of her tokens.

"I should have you thrashed," Ilen said. "All of you."

"It wasn't my idea," Lyeth said. "Go thrash the loser."

Crise came up to lean against the wall by Ilen, her arm around his waist. "Your partner is reviving," she told Lyeth. "You didn't tell him about the snake, did you?"

"No." She couldn't see Laret, and yawned.

"I heard a rumor," Ilen told her, "that you fought your way through a blizzard on a glacier, stole a kid, murdered a cottager, robbed an innkeeper, and offered to poleax a couple of city shadeen at the ferry dock. Any of that true?"

Lyeth laughed. "Not a word of it. I was sold a rude brat in Pelegorum, got an eyeful of ice crossing above the Tobrin, and had to argue with the ferry shadeen. Damn, I'm tired."

"Me too," Ilen agreed. "Matter of fact, Crise and I haven't been off watch together in three days. Let's go to bed." He leered at his second and prepared to drag her off, but Lyeth, remembering something, stood away from the wall.

"Ilen? One question?"

He looked over his shoulder at her. "A short one."

She bit her lip. "Can you think of any reason for Riders to take a shadi?"

They both turned to her, eyebrows raised.

"Not offhand," Ilen said, and Crise said, "Why?"

"Emris. My brat from Pelegorum. He carries a shadi token, says it was his father's. He says his parents were taken by Riders." She spread her hands. "I thought I'd ask."

The commander frowned. "A shadi cub? I'll ask around; some of the land-barons' shadeen might know. Any idea where he's from?"

"No. Somewhere on the Water Road—he remembers iceboats."

"I'll try," Ilen said. "But don't expect any answers."

"Fair enough." Lyeth yawned again, her jaws creaking, and Crise smiled.

"Get some sleep," she said cheerfully. "I don't plan to."

Elot had added a pouch full of smooth stones to his artillery, hurling them on occasion and with deadly accuracy against his unwilling audience; twenty-seven years of teaching Jentesi Castle's unruly children had given him more than a passing acquaintance with the management of fractious listeners, and neither thrust nor fling marred his shouted iambs. Nor did the glittering high-mark Lyeth threw to him; he snatched it from the air without missing a beat, whacked an attacking shadi smartly across the shoulders, and bellowed his refrain. Lyeth headed for the cloak room.

"But you can't leave." Laret came into the room behind her, his eyes sparkling. "It's early still; the Gate is barely risen. And you owe for that trick with the snake."

"It's late," Lyeth replied, settling the talma across her shoulders. "The Gate has been up for hours, and I owe you nothing for the snake. Besides, stripling, it's past your bedtime."

"I'm not a stripling." He laid one long, delicate hand on her arm. "And it's only past my bedtime if I share it." His smile was rich and full. "Come with me, Rider? I know Trapper magic; I can make your body span the mountains and your soul fly. I promise."

"You've been in Cherek long enough to learn that, at least," Lyeth said dryly. "My body wishes to span sleep, and my soul with it." She shook her arm free. "Good night, shadi."

"I'll play you for it," he said, producing the gaming bones from his pocket. He was, Lyeth thought with exasperation, most annoyingly pretty. "Winner takes me. Two out of three. Yes?"

"No!" She headed out the door. Laret immediately grabbed his own cloak and followed her.

"It's a pity," he said, catching up with her. "I gamble almost as well as I make love. I can tell you why I'm in Jentesi. Do you want to know that?"

She was tempted to say no, but her curiosity got the better of her. She pulled her hood up around her ears. "Will you tell the truth?"

"I always tell the truth," Laret declared. "And Korth really is south of the border. This week. My father is the headman, and he's in Joria right now, talking to Lady Elea's counselors about a treaty."

"Between Korth and Alanti? That's a generous offer, for a bunch of town Trappers."

Laret bristled. "We're not town Trappers. We just have a village we like and don't want to leave it. And it's not Korth, it's all the Trapper tribes. And when the lady heard that your Lord Gambin was dying, she said she had to come and I wanted to come with her, so my father said I could and Lady Elea said I could be one of her shadeen." Laret flung one arm around her shoulders. "There, and all of it the truth. Do you believe me?"

"Why should I?" She slipped away. "The tribes haven't agreed on anything since Constain's day, and if Lady Elea let you come along without a nursemaid, she's less intelligent than I thought."

"Ah." Laret was, momentarily, sad. "Lord Constain was a hero, and we lost much when his dynasty floundered." The grin broke out again. "Doesn't that sound good? My father said it in Joria, but the counselors didn't appreciate it. And I don't need a nursemaid. I'm a full man."

"Not between your ears." She stopped and faced him. "Laret of Korth, you've lived in Cherek or near Cherek long enough—you know what any of those shadeen back there would do if they knew you were a Trapper. You know what anyone in Jentesi would do. You go shouting Trapper cries and telling strangers about your father the headman and this wonderful treaty, and you'll be dead within the hour."

"But Rider." Laret spread his hands. *"You're* a—"

"I am not," she said flatly. "I spent some time in the outlands; I learned the language and some other things. That's all."

"How silently you walk," Laret said. "But you were not taught how Trappers make love, Rider. I can teach you that."

"Stripling," Lyeth said dangerously, "go away, or I'll teach you such about Riders as you'll wish you never learned."

"Sweet flower," Laret said mournfully. "I could make your breasts sing."

Lyeth closed her eyes. "Laret," she began, but when she opened her eyes again he was gone, the ward empty, the snow undisturbed. A laugh ran across the moonlight. She spun around; Laret stood in the Neck and waved cheerfully at her, disappeared, called her name from the top of the Lords Stables, blew a kiss, and the next instant was beside her again.

"You see," he said triumphantly, "I *do* know Trapper magic." He kissed her and laughed again, this time from the pitched gable above the shadeen barracks. She gasped, staring, and felt his arm around her waist.

"I'm a member of the Circle," he whispered in her ear. "They initiated me last fall. See?"

Something bright and complicated flashed in his hand, then he and it disappeared. She whirled, staring suspiciously around the ward, but this time Laret had gone for good. Lyeth shivered, drew her talma close, and unthinkingly made the sign against evil.

Emris was clean and damp and asleep, hair spread over a towel carefully layered across his pillow. Lyeth let the curtain drop into place and, skirting a pile of packing crates, went into her own room, struggled into a heavy nightshirt, and crept under the blankets. After a moment she rose again and made sure the window was securely shuttered. The Circle was a myth, she told herself uneasily. Something Cherans used to scare each other—something Trapper children used to scare each other, these unfounded rumors of a secret society, of magic, of invisibility and swiftness and death. She hadn't believed in the Circle since her eighth birthday and would not, she thought emphatically, believe in it now. She turned from side to side uncomfortably and dislodged the heating brick at the foot of the bed. It fell to the floor, a muffled clunk which left her bolt upright and wide awake. Cursing, she dove all the way under the covers and pulled them over her head, then stuck her head out again and peered around the dark corners of the room. Superstitious nonsense. She'd find an explanation for it tomorrow, in the clear, reasonable light of a winter morning. She turned again, and eventually fell into a light, uncomfortable sleep.

She woke to the faint sound of Emris' sobs, quiet, mechanical, and unceasing. She lit a lamp, shoved her feet into slippers, and padded to his room, looking warily at the shadows around her. He was buried in the quilt; when she pulled it away he turned from the light but didn't waken. His shoulders jerked as he sobbed.

"Emris, wake up."

He didn't respond. She pressed her lips together, then blew out the lamp, picked him up, and carried him through the dark suite to her own bed. When she climbed in beside him he curled quickly against her, sighed, and stopped crying.

Idiot, she thought impatiently. He'll just get used to it—the last thing I need is a kid in my bed. But her eyelids felt heavy, the shadows in the room became only shadows again, and eventually she tucked her body around his.

I must, she thought fuzzily, be very, very drunk. Then she put her arm across the boy's shoulders and slept.

# FOUR

# ELEA

"WHAT's that?" Bedwyn, head cook and far too irritable to be afraid of anyone, scowled fiercely. "Another apprentice thief, is it? Get him out of here—I've nothing for either of you. Scat! And if I catch you in my kitchens again, by the Father's armpits I swear I'll have you turning spits for a week! Out! Fast!" He waved his cleaver threateningly, advancing across the room. "Useless thieving scum! Here, take them and get out! And don't let me see you here again, understand?"

Lyeth and Emris grabbed the muffins he thrust at them and made a hasty retreat from the kitchens, stopping in the passageway outside the Great Hall to eat them. Lyeth used the kitchens only as a short-cut between her rooms and the Great Hall but Bedwyn insisted on seeing her quick visits as food raids, and never let her leave without curses, threats, and something warm to eat. Lyeth brushed a crumb from the corner of Emris' mouth. Her head hurt, and she refused to think about the previous night.

"That was the good part," she told him. "It's downhill from now on. Keep your mouth shut. If I bow, you bow lower. If I go to one knee, you go to both. And save your questions for later." She paused. Emris' hazel eyes looked enormous. "You're supposed to be in ward to me, so try to act like it. All right?"

He nodded, subdued, and followed a pace behind her.

Despite the number of people in it, the immense hall seemed uncrowded. Maranta held court at one end, her thin, querulous voice rising and falling over the discreet cadences of her minstrel. Gambin's minstrel Forne sat by the center fireplace and played in competition, beat heavy and voice raucous. Culdyn himself sat in deep consultation with a group of out-province lords and two men from the Merchants Guild; his manicured hands gestured as he talked. He glanced at Lyeth as she passed and she nodded curtly. That he let himself be seen, in public, talking with members of a non-ranking guild was unexpected; she filed the sight away for contemplation later and lengthened her pace. Her back prickled.

"Rider!"

Lyeth turned reluctantly, walked to Maranta, and dropped to one knee. Like a puppet, Emris copied her. Maranta put her jeweled hands on the arms of her chair and looked at Lyeth with benign confusion and a bare hint of lugubrious playfulness. Lyeth raised her head, expression smooth. The only surviving child of Gambin's older sister, and not much younger than Gambin himself, Maranta lived in her mother's castle at Tormea, near the banks of the Klime, spending her time in study with her endless collection of astrologers or increasing her collection of jewel-encrusted absurdities. Fascinated by the tiny mechanical oddities of the Riando Artisans Guild, she had her jewelers enhance them such that, it was rumored, it became impossible to guess their original function. It was also said that she was terrified of nightmares, believed in ghosts, was still a virgin, and, at sixty-three, likely to remain so. Only she and her pet astrologers took her claim to the sword seriously, and they argued the cosmic validity of such claim vociferously and at every opportunity. They were probably being well paid, Lyeth thought, to do it. Maranta's minstrel had a false eye made of emerald, replacement for an earlier clockwork eye which spun its iris every quarter hour and made everyone save Maranta herself ill. Lyeth stood smoothly and clasped her hands behind her back.

"Lady. May I serve you?"

"Why, no, no, thank you. I am adequately served already." She smiled and her attendants tittered. Lyeth tightened her fingers behind her back. "The lord my uncle, Rider. Is he keeping?"

Resisting the temptation to joke, Lyeth said, "I don't know, Lady. I've yet to check with Master Durn for my master's orders."

"Of course! Naturally!"

"I can inquire, Lady, and send word if you wish."

"No, that won't be necessary. I can send myself. I mean, I can send someone myself." Maranta smiled again. Her teeth were small and neat and even, and looked as though she never used them. "You must be quite lonely, all by yourself. I mean, with no other Riders here. Are you lonely, Rider? It must be quite lonely, I'd imagine."

"On the contrary, Lady."

"Indeed! Well! Yes, I see. And who is the charming little boy? A servant, perhaps?"

"No, Lady. He's in ward to me, under my oath until I can ship him down to Vantua."

"In ward!" Maranta's hands fluttered madly about her mouth. "My! I don't think I've ever seen a sold child. Let me look at him."

At Lyeth's gesture, Emris stepped around her and knelt again. Lyeth clasped her hands behind her back, her fingers rigid.

"A handsome child," the lady said. "A very handsome child. Where are you from, boy?"

"Pelegorum, Lady." Emris' voice was clear and respectful. When Maranta didn't reply, he said, "It's in the Tobrin range, Lady. We raise sheep there. It's under the Mother."

"How interesting!" The lady's smile was a marvel of heavy-handed condescension. "And why were you sold, boy? Were you very naughty?"

Emris glanced obliquely at Lyeth, who held her breath. "No, Lady. My master died, Lady, and my mistress remarried. He's a very hard, mean man, and he beat me whenever he wanted to. I was going to run away, but the Rider came through and my mistress sold me to her. I was happy to get away from my new master, Lady, but I don't like Riders very much." He smiled quickly. "Would you like to see my scars, Lady?"

Mother, Lyeth thought, astonished. She'll offer to buy him.

"Scars!" Maranta said. "You poor child!"

"Yes, Lady. He beat me when I spilled the milk and he beat me when I accidentally set fire to the table, but it *was* an accident, Lady. Even my mistress said so. But he beat me worst of all when I stepped on the cat, Lady, and all the crockery fell and broke. I didn't know the cat was there, Lady, I really didn't."

Maranta, eyes wide, looked at Lyeth. "He breaks things, Rider?"

"Compulsively, Lady."

"I see." She drew her skirts back nervously. "Yes, I see. Tell me, boy, have you had your stars read?"

"I don't know, Lady." He glanced at Lyeth again. "I don't know what that is."

"Not know! Incredible! He doesn't know! Why, child, we figure the stars from the date of your birth on my Circles of Infinity and—no, perhaps it's better to do it alone. Yes. My astrologer will call." She turned to look over her shoulder. Her astrologer stood by curtains screening a niche; Lyeth heard bells tinkling faintly behind him. "Homan, you'll be delighted to read the boy's stars, won't you? Homan!" The astrologer bowed morosely. "Not know!" Maranta continued. "Oh, he must certainly be read. We wouldn't want to have a Budding Princeling here and not know it, would we?"

She smiled, and her attendants tittered again. Lyeth touched Emris' shoulder and they backed away, turned, and left the Great Hall. Emris looked at her, eyes guileless.

"Sweet Mother of Lies," Lyeth said. "How did you dream that up?"

"You're the one who says I'm in ward," he replied. "I had to tell her something. Rider? Can I find my family here?"

Lyeth glanced beyond him. The hall was empty. "I've been asking," she said quietly. "It won't be easy, but we can try. Emris, it might be easier if you give me your token."

The boy shook his head vehemently, his hand clutching the token under his jacket. "Please, Rider. It's all I have."

"It's all right, Emris. We won't need it yet." She shook her head. "Broken crockery," she muttered, leading the way to Durn's chamber. The steam heater hissed and spit and muttered to itself. The crowd avoided it and one smith, on loan from the armory, did ineffectual things to it with a number of grimy tools. Emris, fascinated, stared at the heater and its gaudy tentacles. A woman in Bec's livery stood by the door to the telegraph room, waiting to go in. Durn, with a window open behind him, looked neat and cool and glanced at Emris disapprovingly.

"I await my master's orders," Lyeth said to him, the old formula ready on her lips. "Is there message or request?"

"No. Not today or tomorrow." He leaned back, smoothing the heavy velvet of his tunic. "We can forgo the formalities, under the circumstances. If Lord Gambin needs you, you'll be called."

Lyeth bowed stiffly and turned to go.

"Rider!" She paused to look at him again. "I've tallied your accounts from the last ride. Menwyn has the money for you."

Menwyn smirked and handed her a leather bag. She shoved it into her pocket, sure that Durn had shorted her again, and left the room. The steam heater shrieked indignantly, a dense buzzing of voices emanated from the Great Hall, and Lyeth put her shoulders back, feeling stifled. She pushed open a door at the base of the tower staircase and Emris followed her into the cold of Horda's Garden. The shadows of naked trees etched stark black lines across the snow, over the single cleared path. Lyeth started along it, breath puffing in the cold, slamming doors in her mind until the muscles in her shoulders relaxed. Another door slammed, this one in the castle wall.

"Rider!"

She turned, her shoulders tensing again, to see Culdyn Gambini stride into the garden, adjusting the sit of his white fur cloak. He smiled gorgeously at her.

"Please, don't kneel," he said. "It's far too cold for that. I trust you're well?"

She crossed her arms. "It's far too cold to stand around and chatter, too," she said. "What do you want?"

Culdyn's smile didn't falter. "A lovely morning anyway," he said. "I want to talk with you. Alone." He glanced significantly toward Emris. The boy immediately bowed quickly and walked to the far side of the garden, where he developed a consuming interest in, Lyeth saw, the place where Crise had delved for winter roses the night before. She looked back at Culdyn.

"Well, I suppose there's no point in small talk, is there?" he said with disarming candor. "My father's weakening, Rider. I doubt he'll last much longer." She didn't reply and he smoothed a gloved finger over his moustache. His gloves were set with jewels. "I know my father spoke to you about your support," he continued. "It means much to both of us. A symbol of continuity. That's always important, continuity. The people expect it."

Lyeth raised her eyebrows.

"Well. To be honest, my father is not the most appreciative of lords. He's never adequately compensated you for your good services to him, or to us all. That should certainly be remedied."

"Lord Culdyn, you surprise me."

"Great Father, Rider, I wasn't speaking of money!" He grinned engagingly. "Expenses, a stipend, and knowledge for the guild— everyone knows the Riders are the least greedy guild in Cherek. But surely a lord's Rider shouldn't be quartered above the stables."

"It makes it easy to reach my horse," she said blandly.

"Rider. And to have only one horse, that's ridiculous. You need two at least, a snowhorse and a speeder. A good lord rewards good service," he said seriously. She wondered where he'd borrowed the aphorism but didn't respond, and after a brief moment he continued, somewhat less cordially. "A larger staff, if you like. One servant is not adequate, I agree. A higher place at the banquets." Another pause and more of the cordiality disappeared. "A larger stipend, of course. That goes without saying." Her silence continued and the cordiality disappeared entirely. "A fief—a Rider needs income, naturally, to do her lord's bidding." With an effort, the smile returned. It didn't reach his eyes. "Some might call this overly generous, but I'm not one to ignore loyalty. I'm sure you understand."

"I'm sure I do," she said. "But generous or not, your offer is irrelevant. I will ride your father's death to Vantua; it is my duty and I can't evade it. Neither can you. And once in Vantua I intend to remain." She smiled briefly. "So these offers are a bit tardy, aren't they?"

"Ah, but your oath—"

"Was of personal service to Gambin. It ends at his death."

"And if he commands you?" Culdyn said.

"He cannot command me beyond his death, and you, my Lord Culdyn, cannot command me at all."

Culdyn gestured sharply, jeweled gloves flashing. "You make it hard on yourself, Rider. You can accept or you can be forced, but the results will be the same."

"Ah. If I accept you shower me with riches and if I refuse you shower me with riches. Generosity indeed." She stepped back. "Culdyn, this bores me and you bore me. Your father made his offer, you've made yours, and I've turned them both down. Go back to your games and leave me alone." She began walking toward Emris.

"Rider! You wanted to see the sealed records."

She stopped and looked over her shoulder at him.

"I can arrange it," he said. "Any time you want."

She hesitated, then said, "No. It was just a passing fancy."

"Rider!" he called again as she resumed walking. "You'll regret this."

"I doubt it."

As she reached Emris the door slammed again. He looked up and was quiet while she contained her anger.

"Rider?"

"It's all right, boykin. Just the Gambini trying to run the world again. Did you find the winter roses?"

"These?" His boot tip touched a gnarled mass of branches and buds. "Are they really roses?"

"No, but this time of year they are the next best thing." She started down the path away from the castle and he trailed her.

"Rider?"

"Um?"

"Who was that lady in the hall? The one with the funny voice and all the rings?"

Lyeth smiled and waited for him to come up to her. "Funny voice and rings, boykin? You speak of the Lady Maranta, an heir to the sword. I told you about her yesterday, on the ferry."

Emris looked astounded. *"That* was Maranta?"

"The very same. Stars and jewels and clocks and omens—Budding Princeling, hah."

"Princeling?"

"Mother's sake, Emris, it's just blather." She pushed her hood back; black fur brushed her cheeks. "The astrologer figures out where the stars were when you were born, then they stuff you into some category or another. It doesn't have anything to do with anything, of course, but you get your stars read and they're not going to tell you you're a drudge, are they? No, you'll be a Prince or a Creator or something equally fine, and get yourself all puffed up with it." She snorted, a stream of white mist. "And, of course, they get well paid for it. Come on, it's cold out here."

Emris skipped to keep pace with her. "And the man with the pigtail in the hot room?"

"Master Durn, Gambin's chamberlain."

"Oh. Why did he give you money?"

She put her hand to the gate. "A lord reimburses a Rider for journeys. When Gambin sends me out I have to pay my own way. When I get back I give an accounting to Durn, and if he approves it, he pays me back."

Emris frowned, his lips moving as they left the garden. "That's not enough to—don't you run out of money?"

"Gambin also pays me a stipend."

"Oh."

Emris' bootheels made sharp, syncopated sounds on the cobbles;

Lyeth, as usual, moved with effortless silence. The Snake, like its namesake, twisted sinuously, bordered by the garden wall on one side and the nobles' apartments on the other. An entire morning free —she thought about possibilities, then regretfully decided her time was better spent putting the notes from her last trip in order. They came out of the Snake and sunlight bathed the yard.

"Besides," Emris said suddenly, "I don't know when I was born."

"What?" She frowned. "Oh, that. Not at all?"

"Welfred said my birthday was in the spring because that's when I came to Pelegorum. And she said, my last birthday, that I was ten." He paused. "So the astrologer couldn't do anything for me anyway, could he?"

"No." And, hearing the small sadness in his tone, she added, "Or for me, Emris. I don't know my birthday either." Delivery carts trundled toward the kitchens. "Jandi gave me a birthday, the first day of the year. But I don't know when my real birthday is."

Emris stopped and stared up at her. "Were your parents taken by Riders, too?" he said, incredulous.

For a moment her breath caught in her throat.

"No," she said curtly, and strode off. Emris hurried to catch up with her.

Ilen stood at the barracks door, arms folded across his chest, watching the turmoil of cooks, wagoneers, and shadeen milling around the kitchen door. Bedwyn howled and flapped his apron furiously and the shadeen skipped up and back, stuffing things into their pockets. Horses plunged through the melee, their riders thieving from other riders; the noise was unbelievable. Lyeth walked around the edge of the ward to the commander.

"They have to blow off tension somehow," he said in answer to her raised brows. "And it's either that or risk a repeat of last night's performance. Who's this?"

"My ward. I told you about him last night."

"Indeed you did." Ilen hunkered down, balancing on his toes, and looked at Emris curiously. "Good morning. Sold to a Rider, were you? What for?"

Emris pressed his lips together.

"Tell him," Lyeth said. "The truth, this time."

"I put a burr under Darkness' shoe and she caught me," he muttered.

"I see. And are you properly repentant?"

Emris shot Lyeth a quick, defiant glance and Ilen, laughing, stood. "He'll like Tibbi," he said. His young daughter had a reputation for mischief. "I had early mess with some out-castle shadeen this morning," he told Lyeth over the boy's head.

"Yes?" She bit her lips. "Tell us about it."

"Do you want the boy to hear?"

Lyeth said, "Oh," and put her hand on Emris' shoulder. "Emris, I asked Commander Ilen about your parents," she said quietly. "Hush, don't talk yet. He has something to tell us, but it's not something that you can talk about, do you understand? It's a secret, among the three of us."

"I understand," he said. "I don't have anyone to talk with anyway." He looked at the shadi. "Did you know them? Do you know who they are, or what happened to them, or—"

"Hush, boy." Ilen looked across the yard. "About six years ago one of the land-barons called on Gambin and complained about his commander."

Lyeth hesitated, then said flatly, "Who?"

"Rive, up river. According to this shadi, Rive and Gambin were quarreling and he wanted some way of proving his loyalty. So he bought it with shadeen blood." Ilen gestured sharply and Emris, barely breathing, stared at him. "His commander and her husband weren't happy—his family lived in the country and Rive's taxes, on top of Gambin's, were beggaring them. There was some loose talk around the barracks but nothing the guild couldn't handle alone. The shadi said there may have been something more, but no one talks about it much. You want me to keep asking?"

"Yes," Emris said. "What happened to them?"

Ilen spat. "Rive complained to Gambin instead of to the guild. Gambin sent a Rider, the commander and her husband disappeared, that's all anyone knows."

Into the silence that followed, Lyeth said, "They had a child?"

"A son. Four years old. He was sent away and that's all anyone knows about him, too. Hey, you, Grims! Not so rough, hear me?" He looked at Lyeth again. "I'll keep asking. Damn it, Grims, I've told you once already—" Ilen strode into the melee, yelling. Lyeth stared at Emris, her chest tight.

"A shadeen commander," the boy said slowly.

"It's not positive, Emris. And it doesn't help find your family, not yet."

"But it's a start, it's better than nothing." He threw his arms around her waist and hugged her.

Lyeth, on the verge of hugging him back, stopped.

"Do you have that token, the one I gave you yesterday? Good. Go check on Darkness and Myla. And be back in my rooms in an hour —no more, understand?"

Emris squeezed her again, grinned, and danced away through the horses. Lyeth leaned against the barracks, watching him go, and realized why her chest felt so tight. She'd been waiting for some weeping relative to materialize in the yard. To take him away.

Her apprehension muted into a formless anxiety, the same groundless tension she sometimes felt in dreams. Emris, on his belly by the woodstove, pondered a curling sea of maps; Janya sat in a corner mending one of Lyeth's shirts. Two servants clattered and banged and joked in the bedroom, packing. Lyeth looked back at the contents of her travel box, spread on the table before her. Broken pen nibs, a messy pile of notes and maps and rough sketches, the stoppered jar of ink. She stirred the nibs with her finger, thinking about Emris and Rive's shadeen commander. The boy's father had family in the country. She forced the thought away firmly and contemplated Culdyn instead. Awkward, obvious, infantile—but he implied that he could open Durn's sealed records for her. Not, she thought hastily, that she wanted to see them; she could discover the information in other ways, even if it was sure to take longer. Perhaps Joleda would track it down, after Gambin's death. Damn, she thought angrily, and forced this thought, too, into a small room. One of the nibs stuck in her finger, the packers dropped something heavy, a log hissed in the firebox, and when someone knocked on the door she jumped from her chair, upsetting the table. Janya jumped, too, and at Lyeth's impatient wave went to the door.

A thin young man, hardly out of boyhood, came into the room, smiled sunnily, and bowed.

"Rider, I'm Robin. Do you remember me?"

"No. Should I?" She dumped the last of the scattered nibs back in the box.

His smile widened. "I guess not. I was still in the apprentice dorms when you left. I'm Master Jandi's apprentice, just as you were."

"Fascinating," she said dryly. "Is that all?"

"Oh, no, Rider. My master wants to visit the shops in the holders' village and wonders if you'd like to come with him."

"A shopping trip?" Lyeth said. "Jandi wants to make a—Sweet Mother of Light, the man's . . ." She spread her hands. "Hell. It's better than sitting here with this idiocy. Where's Jandi?"

"In the main ward, Rider. Shall I tell him you're coming?"

She waved and Robin smiled and bowed and skipped from the room. Lyeth turned to find her talma and saw Emris crosslegged by the maps, his expression almost painfully beseeching.

"Oh, Mother," she said sourly. "All right, get your jacket. We might as well make a parade of it. Janya, pick up this mess. Are Emris' clothes clean yet?"

"No, mistress. The laundry was busy—"

"Wonderful." She threw the talma over her shoulders and marched out. Emris ran to catch up.

"You like Jandi, do you?" Lyeth said as they skirted prancing horses in the yard. Emris nodded. "You think he's funny and understanding and a little sweet, right?"

"Isn't he?"

Lyeth stopped in the Neck. "Yes. He's also Rider Guildmaster, Emris. He didn't tell you that yesterday."

If she had said that Jandi was Lord of Vantua, or a warthog, Emris could not have looked more astounded. Lyeth reached down, put her fingers under his chin, and closed his mouth for him.

The boy swallowed hard. "I was rude to him," he said uneasily. "I made fun of his—of his stomach. And I made jokes and interrupted him and—"

"Don't worry about it, boykin. He's still funny and understanding and a little sweet." She put her hands in her pockets. "Just don't be too rude to him in public. In private, you can say whatever you want."

"And he's your friend." Emris' jaw threatened to drop again. "A guildmaster is your friend."

"This guildmaster is also sometimes an exalted pain in the ass. Come on."

The melee in the shadeen yard had ended. Crise, coming off watch, waved to them and went into the barracks, slapping her hands together. Jandi, deep in conversation with a shadi by the guardhouse, rocked back and forth on the balls of his feet, looking in his black talma like a huge, tamed bear. Beside him, Robin grinned and waved.

"Lyeth, my dear." Jandi kissed her. "This gentleman tells me that while we can find some rough goods in the village, the better shops are all in the city."

"You should have thought about it earlier," she said. "It's too late now."

"Another time, then." Jandi bowed to the shadi, who bowed almost to the ground, uncomfortably reverential. Lyeth wondered if he thought Jandi walked on air—or dined on infants nightly. Jandi took her hand, tucking it securely between his arm and his paunch.

"You do want me to ride into the city, don't you? In aid of some abstruse point, I believe. Perhaps tomorrow—no, tomorrow I'm busy. The day after that, then. What's to see in the village, Lyeth? Anything of interest? Anything of worth?"

She pulled her hand back and put it in her pocket. "Hardly. There's a blacksmith, a tinker, a tavern, a goods shop, a cobbler, a tailor, three produce shops, a fishmonger, a bake shop, a butcher, a seminarian, a potter, a weaver, an apothecary, and two whores. One lost his last tooth this past summer, the other will cost you two marks for the laying and another seven to the bush doctor when you go to be cured of her."

Jandi laughed. "My dear, you are a mine of bad-tempered information. Less acidity, Rider. Your guildmaster demands it."

Lyeth didn't reply. They crossed the stretch of barrens between the inner curtain and the fields, and entered the village. Shops lined the main road and a few holders came in and out of them. They stepped aside when they saw the two talmas, and when they saw Jandi's badge of office they bowed, often making the sign against evil at the same time. Lyeth poked Jandi, nodding to them. He waved it aside.

"Small village superstition," he said loftily. "They're warding their evil away from me."

"They're warding your evil away from them," Lyeth said.

"I won't argue, Lyeth. What's in here, do you think? The apothecary? The apothecary."

Jandi went inside and Lyeth waited at the door. The shopkeeper went goggle-eyed and clutched the edge of his crowded counter.

"Here," Jandi said. "Is that criswort you have there? Let me take a look. It's hard to get fresh criswort in Vantua. I sometimes have to wait months for it. Where is it from?"

"Down Tobrin, master." The apothecary came around the counter, bowing as low as he could. "Fresh as it can be found, master. I see to the picking myself."

"Do you? Good! Stop all that bowing and lift it down. That's what we lack in Vantua, some personal touch. Herbs are shipped in bulk and bought in bulk; the 'pothecaries never know what they're selling. Of course, they don't tell you that. Do you gather it in bud or in leaf? I think leaf's more effective, but I've heard good arguments otherwise."

"Well, master, there's good to both and bad to both. If you're treating for a rash, say . . ."

They disappeared into a labyrinth of herbal conversation. Lyeth leaned against the door and crossed her arms. The apothecary had Gambin's eyes and cheekbones, Culdyn's thin hands. She wondered if the shopkeeper hid when his lord came through the village, and decided that he probably didn't—Gambin's by-blows were no secret. The apothecary, Torwyn's steward Heron, a hundred others; she wished them all to perdition. It wasn't their faults, true—they did not engineer a mother's willingness or a mother's rape. But still, but still . . . Across the street, Emris and Robin looked into the open window of a bakery. Robin towered over the younger boy. She wondered how tall Emris would be when he grew up, wondered how tall his parents had been. Robin felt about in his pocket, produced a coin, and went into the shop. He came out munching a stuffed bun and handed one to Emris. Lyeth watched them distantly, feeling the tension still lurking through the back of her mind. Jandi came from the apothecary shop, his pockets bulging.

"A fine shop," he told Lyeth loudly. "The equal of anything in Vantua, and better than most." The apothecary beamed, said he'd be honored to supply any of the guildmaster's needs, and backed into his shop. Lyeth shook her head.

"You could charm a seminarian into a contradiction," she said.

"That would not be hard, but to charm one into a consistency— What's this here? A potter's. Excellent—I need something for all these new herbs."

He dove into another shop. Lyeth leaned against this new door and crossed her arms while Jandi took on another Rider-hating holder and had her eager as a puppy within three minutes. The arched walkways overhead threw shadows over the outer ward, crosshatching the snow. Across the street the two boys licked crumbs from their fingers and talked, voices young and clear. She looked away from them to the rising bulk of the castle, picking out the windows of Gambin's Tower. They seemed small and tight, more suited for keeping the world out than for letting in the light. You'll help my son. The guild can't help a dead Rider. A Rider needs income, naturally—a good lord rewards good service. She glanced away, seeing three riders emerge from the gate and canter toward the village. A small, light-haired woman rode in front, followed by two larger riders in blue. Lyeth squinted and rubbed at her patch, wondering who they were.

Jandi popped from the shop, two glazed jars in his hands.

"The blue or the yellow?" he demanded. "The glaze is perfect on both." He looked over Lyeth's shoulder toward the castle. "Ah! The blue it is, then."

A minute later he re-emerged, cheerfully contemplating the jar, turning it this way and that to catch the sun. "The very shade of summer, isn't it?" he said with satisfaction as the three riders halted before them. The tiny woman leaned from her saddle, grabbed one of Jandi's braids, and tugged it sharply. Laret, mounted behind her, winked lecherously at the Rider. She frowned back, uneasy.

"There you are," the woman said. "I've been looking all over the castle for you."

"But you did find me," Jandi said placidly.

"Of course." The woman dismounted. "I simply asked after a garrulous fat man in a talma. You're remarkably easy to spot."

Jandi kissed her forehead affectionately. "Elea, my dear, this is Rider Lyeth—she's grown since you saw her last. Lyeth, Lady Elea, Lord of Alanti."

Lyeth bowed deeply. "Lady. I didn't recognize you."

Elea smiled. "Not surprising, Rider. We last met—what is it, eleven years ago? When Jandi brought you out of the Clenyafyds. You've improved. Robin—it *is* Robin, isn't it? Get off your knees, child, the dirt's not good for your breeches. Who is the child?"

"Emris," Lyeth replied. "In ward to me."

"Indeed." Elea's large blue eyes looked at him curiously. "History repeats itself. He's a handsome boy."

To Lyeth's surprise, Emris blushed to the roots of his hair. She stared at him while Elea handed her reins up to Laret's companion.

"Take the horses back. I'll be up later."

"Mistress, is it wise to be alone—"

"Nonsense, I'm with friends. Scat."

"Here," Laret said eagerly. "Take mine, too." He swung one leg over his horse.

"Oh, no." Elea said firmly. "You go right back up with him, and no arguments."

"But Lady—"

"No arguments, or I tell your father."

Laret, pouting, sat back and put one hand over his heart. "My soul weeps," he said to Lyeth, sighed heavily, and turned his horse toward the castle. Lady Elea glanced at the Rider.

"Is that how you control him?" Lyeth murmured. "I wish I'd known."

"You've met my—shadi?" Elea slipped her arm through Jandi's. "There is a tavern in this village, isn't there? Then let's go to it. I need something warm and alcoholic. When?"

"Last night, in the shadeen barracks." Lyeth tucked her hands behind her back under the talma. "I thought perhaps he had no bed of his own, he was so eager to share mine."

Elea groaned. "Was he drunk and loquacious?"

Lyeth smiled. "Perhaps, and only in private, Lady. No public trusts were broken."

"Indeed." The lady looked at her sharply. "I am much relieved. Here we are. I hope they don't have a minstrel, too. Master Forne is a bit . . . specific, isn't he?"

"Yes, Lady. He reserves the innocent songs for daylight and descends to obscenity only after dark."

"Innocent! Dear Mother Above."

Robin scurried to open the door for her. The inn had seen its share of out-province visitors and was not impressed by them, but Elea's title earned them a table by the fire and their own servant. The girl brought jugs of warm wine and a basket of rolls, and retreated to stand by the wall with her colleagues and stare, giggling with awe, at Elea. The Lord of Alanti smiled back at them. She had taken the sword at thirteen when her father died in a Trapper raid, organized her own shadeen, and armed them with the deadly but unreliable firearms the Vantua Council had banned almost eighty years before, after the Smiths-Alchemists War. Then, leading her troops herself, she pursued the Trappers summer and winter until she had destroyed the main tribes and left the rest in such ragged confusion that Trapper raids ceased almost entirely throughout her province. That done, she took the Water Road to Vantua and demanded that the ban against firearms be lifted for the outlands, implying that if it wasn't, she'd simply release her shadeen and leave the Trappers a clear route down the Clenyafyd Mountains and into the heartland of Cherek. The council hastily agreed. Jandi had been her personal Rider from the time she took the sword to a year after her appearance in Vantua; he returned from the council with her, was present at her wedding, rode one last raid into the outlands, and returned to Vantua with sullen, silent Lyeth at his side. Watching Elea now, Lyeth thought the legend more formidable than the woman. Elea sat neatly and comfortably, her pale hair braided and pulled back from her face, small hands gesturing as she spoke. Trapper blood, and lots of it, but Lyeth doubted that anyone mentioned it in Elea's presence. Fine-boned, beautiful Laret and his lord could be brother and sister. She had called him snowbrother—she took a sip of wine and turned her attention to the conversation.

"It's a hornet's nest," Elea was saying, her voice low. "Don't you feel it? If Gambin would name someone, anyone . . ." She gestured. "I suppose he's enjoying the chaos."

Lyeth looked at her hands, and when Elea caught her glance she shrugged. "I'm Gambin's personal Rider, Lady. I can't talk about that."

"Of course not. I apologize. Jandi, I've almost secured my borders, but there's a stretch above the Solanti fork that's still giving me some trouble, and I don't have enough shadeen to cover it."

Jandi lowered his cup. "You're thinking of mercenaries?"

"I don't have much choice. Perhaps Petras and his group. Their bond is up with Gambin's death—you've seen them work, Rider. Are they good?"

Lyeth's fingers tightened around her cup. "In some ways," she said slowly. "But . . . they're not battle shadeen. At least, Gambin hasn't used them in battle."

"I see. They are an honor guard, then. Is that all?"

"Please, Lady. My oath."

"Mother," Jandi said, disgusted. "Is everything in this province under your oath, Lyeth?"

"Perhaps," Lyeth said curtly.

"Jandi, leave her be." Elea gestured and the servant scurried over to pour out more wine. "In any event, I hear that Lady Syne is interested in the group, so perhaps she'll keep them on. Or hire them herself, if she doesn't take the sword."

"Truly?" Lyeth sat back. "Could I ask, Lady, where you heard this?"

"From Captain Petras himself," Elea said. "He asked me to wait until after Gambin's death for his decision, and told me why. It seemed a fair enough request." She looked at Lyeth. "You don't approve?"

"No, Lady," the Rider said unhappily. "And I cannot tell you why."

Jandi snorted. "If it's not against your oath," he said with heavy sarcasm, "perhaps you could tell me where the crapper is. You can whisper it—I won't say a word."

Lyeth glared at him. "No, I can't. Because I don't know. Ask the innkeeper."

Jandi summoned the innkeeper, asked his question, and lumbered out of the room. Elea shook her head, smiling, and leaned across the table.

"Rider. About Laret," she said quietly. "What did he say last night? To whom?"

"Many things, Lady, and most of them to me," Lyeth said as quietly. "I don't think we were overheard. He told me about his father the headman and some treaty." She tilted her head. "Is that true, Lady?"

"True enough." Elea swirled the wine in her cup. "It's one of the reasons I'm in Jentesi, to gather support for it."

Lyeth shook her head. "Lady, send him home. He's going to get himself killed." She hesitated and leaned closer. "He spoke Trapper to me. He even said he was part of the Circle, and I was so drunk that for a moment I believed in it, and him. You know what will happen to him if he's discovered."

"His father asked it of me," Elea said. "And I need his favor."

"A dangerous way to seek it," Lyeth said. "If he's found out, you'll have no credit in Jentesi, or Cherek, at all."

"What do you mean, no credit?" Jandi demanded, settling onto the bench again. "*I'm* not going to pay for the wine. I'm just a poor guildmaster, and a thirsty one."

Lyeth sat back, letting Jandi take the conversation. Culdyn Gambini's voice echoed in her mind, and Laret's brilliantly self-confident smile, and Gambin's deathbed threats, and laughter ringing across an empty ward. She pushed it all away, cramming it into small rooms behind heavy doors. It would be over soon, Gambin dead, she on her way to Vantua with Darkness beneath her and Emris at her side. All she had to do was last it out. And try not to get drunk again. Emris and Robin stared at Lady Elea with identical, awestruck expressions, and she was grateful when Elea, glancing at the sun, suggested they start back.

The publican came over as they rose and refused their money, telling Elea that the honor of serving her was payment enough.

Lyeth, holding the door open, smiled. "You must have made quite an impression on him, Lady. Generally he won't let a talma in the door."

"That again," Jandi said. "I haven't seen a shred of evidence for it, not one. Suspicious nonsense." He jerked his hood down and marched ahead to walk with the boys. Elea sighed.

"He doesn't change, does he?" she said. "Still fat and blustery and opinionated. And often wrong." Lyeth's eyebrows rose. "I know about Jentesi," the lady continued. Jandi and the boys drew further ahead. "Most of us do. Poderi, Dorne, Riando, Efet—all the others; we're not here just to see a sword pass. Gambin's set up something unique in Jentesi, and we've come to see if the structure survives him, to see whether the new lord can control it."

Lyeth thought about that. "To what end, Lady?"

Elea clasped her hands behind her back and stared at the path. "Jandi doesn't see a world of people, not really," she said. "He sees a mapmaker's world, graticules and latitudes, legends and symbols, contour lines and the perfect compass rose." She paused. The watch was changing near the barbican, accompanied by the slap of hands on spear butts and the staccato syncopation of boots. "The Merchants Guild sent out a fleet two years ago. Do you remember?" Lyeth nodded, waiting patiently for whatever convoluted point Elea wanted to make. "I heard this morning that one of them just returned to Mayne."

"The rest of the fleet was lost?"

Elea smiled. "Oh, no, Rider. The rest of the fleet is found. *Skaith* came into Mayne with a cargo even the Merchants couldn't have dreamed of, and news of a country beyond Mother Sea. A country of fine cloth and delicate jewelry, of maps and books and a strange, warbling music. But no steam engines, no rail lines, no telegraphs, no clocks. They want to trade with Cherek, Rider. They've even sent an ambassador to meet with Vantua Council. *Skaith*'s sister ships leave for Cherek next spring, all their cargoes sold and their holds filled with wonders." Elea walked on in silence.

"This other country," Lyeth said finally. "It has a name?"

"Merinam," Elea said absently. "Where the beaches are white and fine, and it never snows."

Lyeth grimaced. "Sounds dreadful," she said.

"Perhaps. They are too far away to attack us, or to be attacked by us, but they're close enough for trade." Elea glanced up at Lyeth quickly. "We thought Cherek changed after Constain's defeat, after the guilds founded Lymon. Compared to what Merinam and its trade will bring us, the past two centuries will look as quiet as a pond in summer."

They walked on in silence for a while. Jandi's voice floated back to them and Lyeth shoved her fists deep in her pockets, watching shadows lengthen across the road.

"If we cannot make peace with the Trappers," Elea said, "how can we expect to deal with strangers from Merinam? We may have to learn to accept the known and different before we can accept the unknown and different, and at worst we will use our energy and resources battling the Trappers, while Merinam slips through our hands." She touched the white fur of her collar. "And if Gambin's power passes intact to his heir, half the lords in Cherek will be planning to copy his rule and his province. And the rest of us will be making plans to defend against it."

Lyeth stared at Jandi's distant figure. "And Merinam?"

"Merinam is the door to the future. Gambin is the door to the past. Whatever happens, Cherek will change. It remains to be seen whether Cherek changes for good or ill, whether we regress to fear and torture and distrust, or grow."

"Grow to what, Lady?"

Elea smiled. "Who knows, Rider? Something brighter, and stronger, and surely something with a larger world. But I don't know the details, Rider. And I don't want to know them, not yet."

"You have an explorer's soul," Lyeth murmured. "And Jandi, Lady? Graticules and the perfect compass rose?"

"Like Cherek, like all of us, Jandi sees the details and misses their implications. He takes his loves and hates and various beliefs and thinks them permanent and unchanging, and when they do change, he resents them for it."

"Ah. He needs to be loved and managed."

"He needs to be loved."

Shadeen hung lanterns along the curtain wall; the sun rested on the horizon. Jandi and the boys disappeared into the yard and Elea put her hand on Lyeth's shoulder, stopping her.

"Rider, I don't know what's going on in this castle," she said seriously. "And I honor your oath enough not to ask you. But if you need help, if you need anything, come to me."

Lyeth looked into the woman's wide blue eyes. "Lady. You know who I am."

Elea touched her own pale hair. "And should I, of anyone, object?"

Lyeth took a deep breath. "Yes, then, Lady, to the extent I can, within my oath. I thank you for it."

Elea smiled and turned toward the Great Hall, calling to Jandi as she went. He waved at Lyeth and lumbered toward Elea, Robin at his heels. And Emris looked at Lyeth with shining eyes.

"You talked with Lady Elea," he said. "All the way back from the village, all by yourself."

Lyeth stared at him, then reached out abruptly and ruffled his golden hair.


Stars decorated the rim of the horizon, a thick beading of light cut off abruptly by the dark overhang of rock. Lyeth paused at the broad stone plaza's edge and leaned against the parapet, staring at the bulk of Jentesi Castle. It curved away to her right, layer upon layer bound together by the stone tracery of staircases and occasional splashes of light from lamplit chambers. Moonlight and starlight caught in angles of clean snow; watchfires glowed from the bastions along the inner curtain, all the way to the perilous stones of Lords Walk. Below, moonlight picked out the pale glow of the gravemarkers in the Garden of the Lady and a light breeze stirred the windchimes in the bare limbs of the trees. No silent, racing shadeen decorated the garden tonight.

She bunched her talma closed with her fists and walked toward the Crescent Bathhouse. It lay along the plaza like a lazy half-moon, prongs pointed toward the cold Tobrin. Torwyn said it had been built almost two centuries before by Gambin's aunt's grandfather's granduncle's cousin, Lord Horda, who led his armies against Jentesi's Trappers, who collected fine wines and exotic plants and fears. Lord Horda created the burgeoning, mountain-meadow loveliness of Horda's Garden at the tower's foot and designed the overwhelming tropical beauty of the hothouse plantings in the bathhouse. Torwyn said the lord had spent his final decade locked in the tower, staring down at his fine garden and finer bathhouse and convinced that, some dark and evil night, his plants would eat him. The lord retreated, first refusing to see any of his land-barons and later refusing to see anyone save his personal staff; it was said the lord believed his friends, barons, servants, and children had been taken over by the plants and were walking vegetables themselves. He ate only meat and would not let vegetables or flowers into his room; toward the end he spoke only through a specially constructed, screened opening in the chamber door, and when he died it wasn't known for two days, for it was believed he'd simply decided that even speaking through a screen would contaminate him. He died of malnutrition. Torwyn claimed this proved Horda right after all; Lyeth maintained it proved only that the Lords of Jentesi were, by heredity, insane.

Horda's hunting trophies occupied little space on the stair wall in the tower but his real trophies were here, growing and flowering and keeping their own alien counsel. Generations of gardeners made the bathhouse their especial care; generations of lords, enthusiastically or lackadaisically, approved the purchase of new and stranger flora. Lyeth hesitated, looking at the ornately carved outer door of the bathhouse. If Culdyn takes the sword . . . She shook the thought away, feeling the weary stiffness of her shoulders and back. Tonight she wanted heat and water and the slim comforts of Torwyn's ginger body. Horda's descendants could amuse themselves this evening without her speculations.

A soft pillow of heat greeted her as she pushed through the outer door; when she opened the inner door fog bloomed and swirled where the damp air within met the colder air of the entry. The bath keeper rose sleepily from her chair and came forward, rubbing at her face with the heels of her palms.

"Not catching, is it?" she said suspiciously, peering at Lyeth's eyepatch. Fog danced about their knees.

"No. Is there room tonight?"

"Room!" The bath keeper hobbled down a lamplit corridor. Lyeth paced after, watching the flicker of light on deeply colored frescoes. "Lucky to get three a week up here. It's a good thing I like to sleep. You're almost alone tonight, Rider."

"Lord Torwyn—"

"Is in the pools." The keeper plucked a lamp from a hall bracket and pushed through the curtained doorway of a robing room. She put the lamp on a low table. "He's brought supper; just mind you don't get it in the water. You'll be wanting a scrub?"

Lyeth nodded, draping her talma over a hook. "A good one, please. I've been three weeks on the road with only a quick bath at an inn. And my hair."

The keeper wrinkled her nose and accepted piece after piece of Lyeth's clothing. She took them away. Lyeth pulled on a soft woolen robe and went into the scrub room; the dark blue cloth brushed at her ankles. When she took the robe off again, the scented air was warm on her skin; she scrubbed, standing in the marble drain tub, and the keeper poured warm water over her shoulders. When she took the pins from her hair it fell past her waist, sticky and dull with dirt. The keeper made an exasperated noise and took the hair in her hands while Lyeth knelt by a tub and covered her eyepatch. Three bouts with shampoo and the keeper's strong fingers finally washed the dirt away. Lyeth bound her head in a towel, dismissed the bath keeper with a coin, and walked to the steam pools.

She paused at the entrance and a small, azure bird rose from the tree by her and flew calling across the room. The pools, screened each from the other by tubs of flowering plants, were dark save for one in a distant corner. The fragrance of blossoms filled the warm, moist air and starlight shone dimly through the angled glass overhead. She reached to touch the fleshy leaves of a plant, cool and slippery between her fingers; lianas bearded with moss, studded with blossoms like rich jewels, swung from the high tiled ceiling; an orchid rioted by her hip; a thousand different scents mingled in sweetness and spice. She dropped her hand from the leaf and the azure bird, settled hidden in a distant bough, released a tumbling rill of song.

"Lyeth?"

Her feet were silent on the wooden path; the robe brushed her clean skin. Sliding through a loose screen of vines, she found Torwyn lolling in a small pool, his long body stretched through the water. A crystal lamp, suspended by chain from the invisible ceiling, lit a napkin-covered basket, a flask, and two glasses resting on a marble slab behind his shoulder. Copper hair touched with grey glimmered in the small light; when he smiled creases deepened, bracketing his long mouth. Lyeth turned her head from the smile and, dropping the robe, stepped into the pool. Steam swirled upward, the heat of water beat against her skin.

"Quite raffish," Torwyn said. "Towel and patch and nothing more save a tattoo."

She ignored him, sliding down on the bench until water lapped at her chin. She rested her head against the rim of the pool and closed her eyes.

"Don't spoil it," she murmured, bracing her feet against the far bench beside Torwyn's thighs. "We'll be interrupted soon enough anyway."

"We won't. I bribed the bath keeper to admit no one else."

She opened her eyes, smiling. "Such a generous man."

He shrugged. "It's Syne's money."

Her smile fled. "I don't want to hear about it. Let me take my bath in peace, and wait until the old man dies, and get out of here."

He didn't reply. Lamplight flickered on dark leaves and gem-colored petals, steam rose in ghosts to the darkness overhead. Torwyn's foot brushed her thigh. Sensation claimed her, a universe of warmth and touch and smell and sight, thought banished. She put her hand out, admiring the gleam of water along her forearm, and Torwyn put a glass, precise crystal, between her fingers. Rich amber wine, dry and cool and smooth along her throat.

"Better," she whispered. The words floated. "Much better."

He leaned forward, flask in hand; steam rose along the line of his body from shoulder to waist. She considered him, smiling slightly. She loved him no more than he, she thought, loved her; no messy emotions intruded on the sensual, very private magic they made together. She slid her foot against his hip and he put his hand around it.

"Come back now."

"No."

"Come back, Lyeth. We have to talk."

She put the wineglass down on the rim of the pool and cocked her head. The towel loosened. "I don't want to." Muscles slid beneath his smooth skin, along his shoulders, under the copper hair of his chest, across his flat belly. Her hands remembered the curve of his hips. "Why?"

"Because of three attempts on Syne's life, and two on Coreon's. One at least on Maranta, and maybe more." He pressed his thumb along her instep. "There may be attempts on your life, too. And soon."

She laughed quietly. "Me, Torwyn? I'm only Gambin's Rider. I hold no power in Jentesi Province."

"You're wrong."

She looked at his eyes and her laughter faded. A bird called in the thick plantings beyond.

"Are we secure in here?"

"Yes," he said.

She sat back against the side of the pool. Water lapped at her nipples. The towel slipped out of place and she took it off, twisted her hair, and knotted it behind her neck. Tendrils drifted from her temples to float in the water, rich brown and auburn; as she watched them the sense of unreality took her again. She shook her head gently.

"Tell me."

Steam wreathed his face as he leaned back and reached for his wineglass. "Gambin knew he was dying long before he let it be announced. He sent for Culdyn privately and told him. The old man wants his son to succeed him and Culdyn finds the idea enchanting. Gambin's not stupid, and he knows that if he chooses Culdyn publicly, his enemies will see that Culdyn never takes the sword."

Lyeth turned her face away, bound to silence by her oath. Water moved as Torwyn shifted on the bench.

"Gambin thinks he knows a way around that," Torwyn continued. "He wants you made to pledge to oath to Culdyn, either before Gambin's death or immediately after." He paused. "I assume that's what Gambin wanted to tell you, that you were to support his son."

Lyeth picked up her wineglass. Expensive, imported, delicate, rare, like the wine in it, like much of Torwyn's life. "Spies?" she said.

"Of course."

"Because Syne's back?"

"Lyeth. I serve my Lady in her presence and in her absence."

Of course he would, she thought. She was an idiot to feel surprised. "Assuming you're right," she said carefully, "what good would it do? I hold no power save through my guild; the Riders will serve the Jentesi Lord exactly as they serve any other provincial lord." She paused. "It makes no sense."

"On the surface. But consider: Gambin's power, now, rests on control of the network, of the ferrets. No one knows who they are, where they are—an invisible terror. They report, Gambin studies, and when he wishes sends a Rider." Torwyn leaned forward. "The Rider, Lyeth, is the visible terror, the symbol of Gambin's power—and all perfectly within the rulings of your guild—"

"Not in spirit—"

"Which has nothing to do with it." Impatience edged his voice. "If you pledge to oath to Culdyn Gambini, it will indicate conclusively that Culdyn has inherited the entire network. It makes for a very simple choice. Support Culdyn, or spend the rest of your life waiting for a Rider to knock on your door." He smiled. "Brilliant, isn't it? It cuts right through all the politicking, the bribing, suborning, everything. The delegates will vote for Culdyn as soon as they know about the pledge, and the other possible heirs will withdraw because"—he leaned closer to tap her shoulder—"because with the ferrets and the Riders behind him, no one is safe. No one. Not Syne, not Coreon, not Maranta."

"Not you," she said.

He nodded. She held her wineglass out silently and when he refilled it she leaned back, watching him. He regarded her calmly, blue eyes steady over the worked silver rim of the glass.

"If I refuse . . ." she said slowly.

"Culdyn will try to force you."

"Culdyn and not Gambin?"

"Culdyn, I think. Gambin can't take an active hand in it, not now. Or perhaps he doesn't want to."

"A test," she murmured. "The old man's testing him. On me."

"On you," Torwyn agreed. "If he fails Gambin will repudiate him, but he's not likely to fail. Not with his father and Durn behind him."

"Durn too?" She sipped her wine. "Of course. Durn because he knows the network. He can do the work while Culdyn plays." She paused. "Culdyn spoke to me today."

Torwyn leaned back, watching her. "And?"

She smiled briefly. "He offered me better quarters. More horses. More servants. A larger stipend. A fief. He wasn't happy when I turned him down."

"As you turned Gambin down?" When she didn't reply, he shook his head gently. "That doesn't end it, Lyeth. You know Gambin, and you know his son. If you can't be ordered and can't be bribed, perhaps you can be forced. You're the only Rider on the Rock, or in the city. Culdyn and Durn made sure of that. Durn sent out messages over Gambin's signature, suggesting that visiting land-barons and lords leave their Riders home. They want you isolated, alone, and powerless. If they have to hurt you, they don't want some other Rider trying to help."

"And Master Jandi?"

"Jandi's a guildmaster. They won't touch him," Torwyn said. "And he's kept busy. He might never even know."

Lyeth put her glass down and drew up her legs, one arm around them while the other held her steady on the bench. Steam condensed on heavy leaves overhead and dripped onto her shoulders, small touches of cold.

"Culdyn won't kill me," she said finally. "I'm no use to him dead. But the others might, to keep me from pledging to him. It would end Culdyn's plans, wouldn't it?"

"Unless Gambin lingered, and they could import another Rider. It wouldn't have the same impact, but it would do. And Culdyn wouldn't hesitate to kill you if he thought you would stand in his way, or go back on your pledge—or pledge to someone else instead of him. Every minute you're in Jentesi Castle without having pledged, your life is in danger," he said calmly. "And if you do pledge, Coreon or Maranta will try to stop you." He put his hands to the side of the pool and lifted himself from it; water sheeted down his long thighs. The basket contained meat dumplings, smoked fish on thin slices of dark bread, ripe imported fruit, a round of cheese, a wrapped cloth filled with pastries. Lyeth watched him spread this feast on the marble slab, but her appetite was gone.

"Accidents can be arranged," he said as he worked. "Rider Lyeth vanished without notice, simply abandoned her post. It's happened before, in Jentesi."

"The guild would look into it. They'd find out eventually, and when they did they'd call back all Jentesi's Riders."

"Surely. Coreon or Maranta might worry about that but Culdyn won't. The Riders Guild has no power over the telegraph net, or over the Artisans, or Smiths, or Merchants. If Jentesi shows the Riders Guild obsolete, Culdyn will not grieve." He licked sauce from his fingers. "And if the Riders no longer carry the news, no longer tie

Cherek together, they become what Gambin has always wanted them to be. The executioner's errand boys." He looked at her shrewdly. "You don't seem surprised."

She pulled herself from the pool, fumbled in the pocket of the robe for a comb, and sat with her feet in the water, running the comb through her tangled hair. Torwyn, across from her, watched her silently as he ate.

"What do you suggest?" she said finally, letting the comb drop in her lap.

He came around the side of the pool and sat behind her.

"As your lover? Go to Vantua immediately. Leave tonight." He took the comb. "As Syne's steward, I suggest you stay, talk to Syne. There are ways and there are ways."

"I'm oathed to Gambin," she said as he took her hair in his hands. "I can't leave before he dies. And why would Syne wish to help me?"

"Say that she's interested in hindering her brother." He untangled her hair gently, combing the locks forward to lie over her shoulders and across her breasts. She relaxed into the familiar ritual, eyes closed; a scented silence fell. His hand brushed her neck and she wondered distantly if he combed Syne's hair this way, during those times he spent in Vantua reporting to his lady, or now that she was back on the Rock. She pushed the thought away.

"Why?" she murmured. "Why tell me all this?"

"I care for you," he said calmly.

"You care for Syne," she said, regretting it immediately.

Torwyn chuckled deep in his throat. "A note of jealousy, Rider? Syne and I were lovers a long time ago, and little of it lingers. I am her steward only, and she my lady."

"And I am . . . ?"

"A thick-headed Rider who sees only what she wants to see." He bent swiftly to kiss the nape of her neck. She smiled briefly. The comb ran smoothly through her hair, and Torwyn put it aside. She leaned back to rest against his body. Water dripped from leaves to pool, the only sound in the moist quiet aside from his soft breathing near her ear.

"Remember," she said softly. "Long time back, we promised not to speak of anything outside? Not Syne or Gambin, not your work or mine?" She paused. "Damn."

His fingertips traced the yellow and black guildmark on her right shoulder. "We knew it was foolish."

She turned on hands and knees to face him. "Let's be foolish again, then. Just for a little time, a few hours. Can we do that, Torwyn? Is there somewhere we can go?"

He smiled, putting his hand to her cheek. "We have the entire Crescent Bathhouse, Rider. And we can make the time."

She sighed and leaned forward into his kiss.

# FIVE

# CERDIC

S HE slept uneasily, woke to the sound of birds, and lay for a time beneath the thick quilts listening to the predawn music pouring through her window. They had moved last night, as always, supple and trained, resisting and releasing, teasing and satiating, to settle finally, briefly, in a shared warmth before they rose and dressed and went their separate ways in the darkness. Now Janya moved through the outer room, felt slippers flapping against stone and rug, the chink of metal on metal, the splash of water into a kettle. She pushed aside the covers and sat. The wooden floor chilled her feet. She peeled off the patch, splashed water on her face and arms, and put salve in her eye before replacing the patch. Her body seemed distant, the stuff of fantasy; when Janya stuck her head through the curtained doorway, Lyeth looked at her as though she were an illusion.

"Do you need help, mistress?"

"No. Breakfast?"

"In a minute." Janya went away. Lyeth pulled on clean clothes and paused, her hands on the buttons, before walking barefoot to the door.

"Janya."

The servant looked up from a teapot. "Mistress?"

"The boy's clothes, are they clean?"

"Yes, mistress, but not dry yet."

"See to it, please. And wake him."

She went back to her room and pulled her boots on. Emris could continue wearing her clothes until his own dried. She blinked, wiped salve from her cheeks, and stood before the mirror, unbraiding her hair. Her image peered at her fuzzily. She touched the glass with her fingertips, tentatively.

"Mistress?"

"Um," she said without turning.

"The boy, mistress. He's not there."

Lyeth spun around. Janya stood in the doorway, her hands clasped over her swollen belly. "He's not in his bed, or in his room. Or in any of the rooms, mistress. I checked."

Lyeth, already through the door, didn't reply. Emris' bed was mussed and the pillows dented; the clothes he'd worn the day before were gone, as was his jacket. She jerked open the wardrobe doors, peered around packing crates, and marched into the parlor.

"Was he here when you came in?"

Janya shook her head. "I don't know, mistress. I started the fire, prepared breakfast, went into your room—I didn't check."

Culdyn, Lyeth thought. Emris imprisoned, Emris hurt, Emris used to force her to obedience—she rubbed angrily at her good eye, put the terrible images in a small mental room, and slammed doors on them. They persisted anyway.

"Mistress?"

"Hush. I need to think."

If he'd been snatched they wouldn't harm him, not immediately. She'd be told, and a price named. If not snatched, then he'd probably wandered off to explore on his own. Or tried to escape. Her stomach knotted coldly. One small boy, alone without papers, and Gambin dying—

"Janya! You stay here. If anyone comes with a message, hold it for me. And not a word about the boy, understand?"

"But the laundry—"

"Fuck the laundry," Lyeth shouted over her shoulder. She grabbed her talma, riding a tide of anger and so many other emotions she couldn't begin to distinguish them, and sped from the room.

Crise was breakfasting in the shadeen mess, her hair intricately braided and her uniform crisp. She listened to Lyeth between mouthfuls of eggs, and nodded.

"I'll tell the watch and the duty officers. If he's spotted, he'll be brought back here."

Lyeth, already nodding her thanks, was halfway out of the room. In the ward she stopped suddenly, thinking, then spun about and raced across the snow. Visitors were quartered in the wing behind the Great Hall; Lyeth rushed through the kitchen and paced the corridors, her talma billowing and her unbound hair floating loose. Servants scuttled out of her way or pressed themselves and their morning burdens against the wall. She collared one at the foot of the main staircase.

"The Rider Guildmaster, which room?"

The servant nodded up the stairs, mouth working soundlessly. Lyeth let him go and took the stairs two at a time, her boot heels ringing angrily against stone. Guest flags hung over the doors in the upper corridors. She squinted at them, cursing the salve, and when she saw the stirrups and dagger she pushed the door open without knocking. Jandi, sitting by the fireplace with a plate balanced on his knees, looked at her and raised his eyebrows.

"Where's Emris?" she demanded.

His eyebrows rose further. "I've no idea, my dear. He's your tid-bit, not mine."

Glaring at him, she went into his bedroom. Robin stood by the bed, arms full of linen. He wore the plain black tunic of an apprentice Rider and smiled sunnily at her.

"Rider, good morning."

"Did you sleep with Jandi last night?"

"Rider!" Robin flushed.

"Mother's sake, boy, I was his apprentice before you were. Did you?"

Robin nodded, his teeth sunk in his lip.

"Were you alone?"

If possible, Robin looked even more horrified. Lyeth swung back to the parlor.

"Such melodramatics—"

"He's not been with you? At all? You swear it?"

"I don't dine on infants either," Jandi said curtly. "Lyeth, what is—"

"He's not in my rooms. He wasn't to leave without permission."

"Annoying, but surely not a capital crime—"

"Jandi! You don't know this place. He may be in danger—I may be in danger."

"Oh, come now. Such a fuss over a small boy."

Cursing, Lyeth ran from the room. Jandi called her, but she ignored him and took the steps quickly. The kitchens, perhaps, if he'd wakened hungry. One of the pantries. Maybe the Scholars Garden. She swung around the bottom step, ducked to the right, and almost upset a string of servants bearing steaming, covered dishes. They sprang out of her way, eyes wide. If not the kitchens, she thought as she ran, if not the garden, then . . . the stables. Of course. She burst into the kitchen, heading for the yard door, and Bedwyn howled angrily. Someone in the shadeen yard outside called to her but she ignored that, too. She skidded up the Neck and bolted into the Lords Stables.

"Rider," a stablehand said.

She grabbed him. "Darkness, and the new grey. Where are they?"

"In the back, mistress. Stall near the tack room."

She pushed him away and sprinted toward the back of the stable. Darkness and Myla stood with their heads companionably together over the wall dividing their stalls. A golden head bobbed into sight and out again behind Myla's flank. Lyeth stopped abruptly, so angry she could barely see. She opened the stall door deliberately and walked around the grey. Emris, comb in hand, looked up. He wore a pair of her breeches, rolled up, and one of her shirts with the sleeves rolled and pushed above his elbows. His face paled.

"Rider, I—"

She grasped his shoulder, dragged him out of the stall, and shook him until his head snapped back and forth.

"Don't you ever," she said through clenched teeth. "Don't you ever, again, for any reason, at any—" And surprised herself by hugging him suddenly against her body. Her eyes stung. Emris stood stiffly in her arms and she caught her breath, conquered her incipient sobs, and stepped back, staring at him.

"That was getting out of line, I guess," Emris said. "And you're going to beat me bloody." His voice shook under the bravery.

"Clean up," she said, turning from him. When he finished she clutched his wrist and marched him through the yard, up the stairs, along the portico, and down the corridor to her rooms. Jandi leaned by the window, eating cheese; Janya stood bulging in a corner, and at Lyeth's curt gesture waddled quickly out of the room. Lyeth slammed the door closed behind her and dropped Emris' arm.

"Good, you found him," Jandi said. "Just off wandering, was he?"

"Shut up." Lyeth flung her talma over a chair. Emris stood by the door, fists in pockets, and looked at her defiantly.

"Well?" she demanded.

"I just wanted to check the horses. I still have your token. I don't see what's—"

*"You* wanted to check the horses. *You* don't see." Her voice shook. "I told you to stay in these rooms. I told you not to leave without permission."

"But—"

*"And I will be obeyed!* Boykin, you do nothing without my permission. If the castle's burning down, you don't leave without my permission. You don't open your eyes or close your eyes without my permission. You don't piss without my permission! *Do you understand?"*

Emris nodded, terrified. Lyeth slammed her fist into the mantelpiece, cursing.

"My dear, congratulations," Jandi said. "I thought you'd achieved the pinnacle of evil temper in Vantua, but you've surpassed yourself." He raised his teacup mockingly. "I salute you."

She put her hand over her eyes. "Oh, Mother, Jandi. Oh, sweet, holy Mother. Listen," she said, dropping her hand and turning to him. She told him of the plans Gambin and Culdyn had made for her, of Culdyn's inept attempt at bribery, and Jandi's expression became one of angry disbelief.

"You're not breaking your oath—"

"Mother forbid," she said mockingly. "I heard it from someone I trust. I know Gambin, Culdyn's already tried to bribe me, I've been here long enough to know—"

"Horseshit." Jandi slammed his cup down on a packing crate. "They'd never try it, never get away with it."

"Jandi, they've already tried it—"

"We're a ranking guild. We connect this land—Cherek and Jentesi couldn't function without us. They know better than to try to suborn a Rider, damn it."

She bit back the urge to say things she'd regret later, and reached for the teapot.

"It doesn't matter. Whatever Gambin and his son think, they won't wait to be convinced otherwise. If they want my cooperation, they'll try for it now." She poured a cup of tea and sat, willing the anger to go away. The bench, stripped of its bright cushions, was hard and cold.

Jandi stared at her a moment before taking another piece of cheese. "So when you woke," he said, sitting in the largest armchair, "and found Emris missing . . ."

"I assumed he'd been snatched." Emris stood behind Jandi's chair, his hands on the chair back. "Foolishly," she continued slowly. "As far as the castle's concerned, he's only in ward. Culdyn wouldn't know enough to use him against me."

"Of course," Jandi said. "And you spent dawn tearing the place apart searching for him, as though he were flesh of your flesh."

Lyeth shrugged uncomfortably. "But who's to know? You, me, Janya, but she won't tell—"

"And the servants, and the stablehands, and the shadeen, and anyone else who saw a Rider racing through the castle with her hair unbound. And not a one of them will speculate." He grunted. "Next time, just hang a sign around his neck saying, 'I love this child as my life.' "

"Now who's being melodramatic?" she said sarcastically.

"You're not famous for self-knowledge, girl. Look at him." He waved a hand over his shoulder at the boy. "The Rider as a brat. Lyeth, you're one of the blindest people I know. Even Joleda could see it."

Emris looked at her, his expression closed and distant. She looked away. "Nonsense. But I am responsible for him, whatever you think I think about him. So what do I do now, guard him night and day?"

"Get him off the Rock." Jandi hauled himself from the chair. "Take him to this shepherd in the city, or have Joleda do it. Send him home. But get him out of here, girl, before he can be used against you." He put his tattooed hand on the boy's forearm. "Before he can be hurt."

"Then you agree that I'm in danger?"

"From stupid people, of course," he said sternly. "But they must be very stupid, if they think to harm a Rider while her guildmaster's on the Rock."

"I wish I had your confidence," she said bitterly.

"I wish you had my brains," he said. "Goodbye, young man. You'd have made a fine Rider, but I don't suppose you want to hear that, do you?"

"Yes, sir," Emris said. "No, sir."

Jandi, chuckling, closed the door behind him. Lyeth closed her eyes and cursed comprehensively, both in Cheran and in the harsher Trapper dialect. Tea slopped out of the cup onto her hand. Jandi was right; she'd have to hide the boy. Ilen and Crise would help but they were castle shadeen and even more vulnerable than she. Nowhere on Jentesi Rock, not even in Lady Elea's care, would Emris be safe—and, probably, nowhere in the city either. She looked at the boy and grimaced ruefully.

"We'll have to leave. Have you eaten?"

Emris shook his head.

"Best do it now. I'll pack. You can have some of my clothes; yours aren't dry yet." She attempted a smile. "I'll forgo the beating this time."

Emris tightened his grip on the chair back, looking stubborn. "I'm not going," he said emphatically.

"What?"

"I'm not going." His chin tilted defiantly. "And I don't care if you beat me."

"Boykin," she said dangerously. He ignored her.

"I don't want to go to the city and I don't want to go to Pelegorum. I'd never find my family there. You brought me here, and you have to take care of me. I won't leave."

"Damnation, Emris, are you deaf? You're not safe here and I'm not safe if you're here. Have you lost your wits?"

"No. And I can live in the stables. Maybe Lady Elea would hide me."

"Mother Night! You'll go to Jentesi-on-River or Pelegorum or hell if I tell you to. Do you comprehend, boykin? Do you understand?"

"But I—"

"Shut up!" She yanked the bellpull viciously and stormed into Emris' room, grabbed his saddlebags, and began stuffing his things into them. Finished, she slung the bags over her shoulder and marched through the parlor. Emris hadn't moved.

"You eat," she commanded. She pushed through the curtains and yanked her wardrobe open.

"Mistress?" Janya stuck her head through the curtains, looking frightened.

"I want the horses saddled immediately." She picked another shirt and crammed it into the saddlebag.

"Yes, mistress." Janya ran out, holding her belly awkwardly.

Lyeth jerked the buckles closed and went into the parlor. Emris sat at the table, unhappily chewing cold meat. Lyeth pressed her lips together and grabbed her talma.

"Put that in your pocket. You can eat on the way."

He opened his mouth, thought better of it, and put the meat into his pocket. His jacket bulged over the rolled shirtsleeves. Lyeth slapped her talma's pockets, making sure her papers were in order and she had some money, and jerked her head toward the saddlebags. Emris picked them up and preceded her to the stables.

The daily supply ferry had already docked; carts clacked up the ratchet road, carrying bales and boxes and baskets piled high with vegetables and fruit. Emris stared at them as the horses picked their way down the path and Lyeth, riding slightly behind him, stared at his golden head and the round profile of his cheek. Her fury, departing, left a host of uncomfortable emotions in its wake; she didn't want to contemplate any of them and turned her face away from the boy so that she looked over the Tobrin to the city. The fortnightly supply boat from down river had arrived and lay at winter anchor amid the fat-bellied merchant barges and the smaller iceboats within the harbor. That explained the fruits and vegetables, then. Bedwyn would be pleased.

The shadi at the quay checked her papers, saluted briskly, and stood aside. Emris put the horses in the corral and leaned against the stern rail, fists in pockets, staring at Jentesi Castle while Lyeth, on impulse, bought two mugs of cider and some meat pies from the concessionaire. Emris took his mug without looking at her. Boatmen shouted, sails snapped, and the ferry moved away from Jentesi Rock, fine arches of splintered ice rising behind. Lyeth ate one of the pies, watching Emris watch the Rock.

"I don't understand," she said finally, shaking crumbs from her fingers. "I've given you no cause to love me—why should you want to stay, Emris? Can you give me one good reason why?"

"My family," he said, not looking at her. "I want to find my family."

"Oh, Emris." She stared into her mug. "Even if we did find them, and that's not too likely but even if we did—it's province policy to move the families of people who've been—taken. Move their wives or husbands, their children. The people who remain behind try to forget, because they're afraid that if they don't, they might be taken, too." She glanced obliquely at him, but he stared resolutely at the

Rock. "If you showed up," she concluded, "they probably wouldn't believe who you are. And if they did believe, they probably wouldn't take you in. They'd be too scared to do it."

"I don't care," he muttered. "I still don't want to leave."

The boat heeled slightly, tacking. The morning sunlight dimmed and she glanced overhead to see high, dark clouds moving up the Tobrin Valley.

"I like it here," Emris said after a while. "It's . . . it's exciting."

"Sure. You could be kidnaped, tortured, killed, locked away for life. I can see how that would spice things up some."

"That's not what I meant," he said angrily, turning to face her. His eyes were bright with tears. "I'm not that stupid. It's that—it's different from Pelegorum, it's like a different world. And I've only seen a little piece of it. I want to see more, I want to see it all. If I have to go back now, it'll be like—be like being promised something and not getting it." He gestured abruptly and cider brimmed over the top of the mug. "Pelegorum's boring. I don't come from there, I don't have anyone there, just Trave Innkeeper and Welfred, and they didn't ask for me, they had to take me." His lips quivered and he spun to face aft again.

Lyeth concentrated on taking a smooth sip from the mug, then said, "And Cerdic, intrepid sheepherder and mountaineer? What about him?"

"He's just around, is all," Emris said raggedly. "But I don't live with him and even if I did—I like it here better. Isn't that enough reason?"

She sighed and shook her head. "Boykin, it may be boring in Pelegorum but at least it's safe. Stay here and you may die—and that's a pretty high price to pay for a little excitement."

He glanced at her. "But you'd protect me, wouldn't you? You're a Rider."

"Oh, Emris. I can barely protect myself. I'm in as much danger as you are."

"But you won't be if I go away." His tone was faintly accusatory. "You told Jandi that."

"No," she said slowly. "I'll still be in danger, just of a different kind." She finished the cider and put the mug down. "If you were a Rider, it would be different. If you were really in ward, or if you were a conscript, then whatever they did to you the guild would avenge. If you were really in ward, then Trave Innkeeper would have to pay me back if I sent you home, and he wouldn't much like that, would he?" Emris refused to answer her smile. "And if you were a conscript I couldn't send you away at all, I'd have to keep you with me no matter what."

He tilted his head back then and looked at her evenly. "Then make me a conscript," he said. "I'll be your apprentice. When you go back to Vantua, you can take me with you."

She breathed in sharply, staring at him. "But you hate the Riders," she said. The boy's gaze didn't waver. "And—and it still wouldn't—you'd still be in danger, Emris. It wouldn't change that —the price is still too high."

"I don't care. I'd rather be in danger here than . . . I'd just rather be with you."

She turned away at that, bracing her arms against the gunwale. Jentesi Rock flew away from them, featureless against the low winter sun; she closed her eyes against it and breathed deeply.

"It's too late, Emris," she said quietly, without emphasis. "No. It's far too late."

Emris didn't reply, and she didn't try to look at him. Wasted in Pelegorum, yes—and dead in Jentesi. Nothing had changed, nothing would change. There wasn't even the pretense of choice. The ferry tacked again; the springs above the runners groaned. He'd be Pelegorum's village hero, she told herself. The traveler, with tales of evil Riders and the wonders of Jentesi Castle. And when he grew up he could travel, could take the Water Road all the way to Lymon, or Mayne on the sea. If he grew up. She put her shoulders back, turned her back to the gunwale, and watched the wharf grow larger.

"Rider," he said. Brake-beams howled against the ice. She looked away from the city and down at him. "You haven't changed your mind, have you?"

She banished the urge to touch his hair. "No," she said shortly, and walked toward the corral. After a moment he followed.

The avenue was busy with horses and carts and walkers, and the shops were crowded. Folk in the costumes of their native villages haggled over delicate cloth from Riando, Alanti carvings, the enchanting miniatures painted on bone and imported from Teneleh, down by the sea. A traveling showman had an electrical display set up under a naked tree; glass bulbs glowed dimly, outlining the cart's shell, and he held a metal rod in his hand, inviting the onlookers to come up and be shocked, for a fee. The city folk, used to such arcane wonders, avoided him, but the provincials crowded around, awed and excited. The city's citizens filled the more prosaic shops, buying bolts of strong Jentesi woolens, worked leather, pots and pans and tools, dried fruits and meats, sacks of grain. Hoarding, Lyeth thought, remembering the fat merchant barges moored in the harbor. A brewer's wagon forced a path through the crowd, all its bells jangling and a handful of urchins clinging to the back bench, gesturing rudely at the walkers and giggling. Three dancers twined about each other to the staccato music of a clay drum; nearby, under a bleached awning, a brazier glowed and the scent of spiced meatsticks appeared and vanished. A dilapidated street magician stood on a corner, making apples disappear and pulling eggs from people's pockets. His apprentice sat at his feet, playing a mouth organ and keeping an eye on the coins in the magician's bowl. Emris stared, fascinated, and Lyeth guided their horses closer.

"Rider," the magician said, bowing. Eggs and apples danced through the air. Lyeth glanced casually over the crowd, rubbing her eyepatch. Children laughed, a thin woman said she'd seen better back home, a man in a knitted blue cap stood on tiptoe to see over people's shoulders. The magician produced a dove from an empty box. He filled the box with water, shook it, and pulled out a jug of cider, a cake, and a patched tablecloth with gravy stains along one side. He spread the cloth over the air and put the jug and cake atop it. The dove flew into his hair, he yelled indignantly and reached for it, and the apprentice stole the cake and ate it. The thin woman snorted. In a tangle of curses and spells and faded sleeves, the magician freed the bird, scolded the apprentice, and upset the cider jug. "Falenka falepa!" he cried, producing the cake from Emris' boot top. The boy laughed with surprise. The crowd shifted, growing and diminishing, but the man in the blue cap stayed. Lyeth dropped a coin into the magician's bowl and he bowed as she urged Darkness and Myla into the traffic again.

In the broad, relatively quiet plaza near City House they hitched the snowhorses to a railing and went up past the lounging shadeen. Lyeth reached the doors first and held them, turning, for Emris to enter. The man in the blue cap stood engrossed before a message board.

The clerk in the registry office produced the delegate roster and

Emris stood by the door while Lyeth went through it. She found Pelegorum sandwiched between Parteen-on-Mountain and Peves Landing; the villagers had indeed sent one Cerdic Shepherd to council and he listed as local residence the Inn of the Boar near Palisade Gate.

"Did you find him?" Emris said as they went down the stairs.

"Yes."

The boy's lips pinched down. The man in the blue cap was gone but showed up two streets later, staring at a display of hoods in a shop window. Lyeth let her gaze pass over him, expressionless. He had to be one of Culdyn's people. Or Coreon's. Or Maranta's. Or, she added viciously, Syne's. Not one of the regulars, though— Gambin's ferrets were usually better shadows.

The stablehand at the Dagger and Plow pocketed a coin and found room for their horses. Joleda, in the common room, wiped her hands on her apron and came across to them.

"I need a jacket," Lyeth said by way of greeting. "And someplace to hide my talma for a few hours."

Joleda raised her eyebrows, gestured, and led them into her private rooms. "Want to tell me why?"

Lyeth sketched Culdyn's plans and Emris' morning absence as she took papers from the talma, looked at them dubiously for a moment, and put them in the jacket's inner pocket. Best to be safe, she thought. Caught with the wrong papers she would die, but caught without any papers she would die more quickly. Listening, Joleda folded the talma and put it on a high shelf in her wardrobe.

"You believe this?" she said when Lyeth finished.

Lyeth shrugged. "I don't want to take chances." She took the fleece cap Joleda offered. "I'll get him back to Pelegorum. Culdyn doesn't have time to find him there." Gritting her teeth, she peeled off her eyepatch and put it in her pocket.

"Ferrets?" Joleda said.

"I think so. The patch is like a signboard." She buttoned the jacket. "That's what you wanted, isn't it? To see Emris sent home?"

The innkeeper looked at him. He sat before the fireplace, his hands between his thighs.

"Well, Master Emris? Pleased to be going home?"

He looked at her defiantly. "I'm the Rider's brat from Pelegorum," he said clearly. "I have to do what she tells me, don't I?"

Joleda raised her eyebrows.

"Later." Lyeth pulled the cap over Emris' bright head. He jerked away and smoothed his hair under the cap with his fingers.

"Ferrets," Joleda said suddenly, and took the talma from the wardrobe. "I'll hang this over the mantel. I can always say you're busy upstairs."

"Tell them," Lyeth said savagely, "that I'm dining on infants. In privacy." She pulled up the jacket collar and led Emris out the back door and into an alley, where they picked their way around arguing cats and piles of garbage. A few citizens in Brassmakers Alley poked among the piles of polished wares; Lyeth and Emris joined them.

"The horses?" Emris said.

"I'll get Myla to you. She'll be safe." Lyeth looked around casually. "Take your time. Keep close by me and stroll, unless I say otherwise. If I tell you to run, get away from me and back to Joleda. And keep your hair covered."

He looked up at her. "We're being followed."

"I think so." They walked around a large, brass washtub filled with kettles. Emris ran his finger along the tub's rim. "A man in a blue knit cap. With luck, he's still waiting for us at Joleda's."

He wasn't. Lyeth saw him come around the corner from Tinkers Lane, obviously intent on the inn's back door; she took Emris' shoulder and pulled him after her into a dimly lit shop. Bells jangled as she closed the door, pots gleamed in the shadows, and the shopkeeper bustled in from the back room, wiping lunch from his blond moustache.

"A chamberpot," Lyeth said regally. "But something solid, hear me? None of this thin stuff you palm off on the provincials."

"Only the best," the shopkeeper said, insulted. "The very best. If you don't know Benele's reputation, you'd best shop elsewhere." He smoothed his starched apron ostentatiously.

"Yes? Show me, then."

"I have a fine selection over here." He crossed to some crowded shelves, looking Lyeth up and down carefully. "I'm sure we can find something within your means."

"My dear man, your entire shop is within my means," she said, looking bored, and glanced out the window as she followed him. The shopkeeper plucked a plain brass pot from the shelf and held it out.

"Ugly," Lyeth said. "I want to see that one, the one with blue stones."

The man followed her glance upward. "Mistress, that's inlay work. I'm sure you'd be just as happy with something more reasonable and—"

"That one, brassmonger. Now." She took Emris' hand.

He grimaced and began climbing shelves, and Lyeth sprinted for the back room, dragging Emris with her. The shopkeeper shouted, bells jangled, and the family jumped up from their meal, startled. The back door opened on a deserted alley. Lyeth glanced along it, pulled Emris diagonally across the muddy track, and boosted him to the top of a wall. She vaulted up after him, inspected the small, snow-covered garden below, and dropped to it. Emris landed beside her and opened his mouth.

"Hush. He spotted us from the street. This way."

A narrow passage connected the garden to Market Square. They strolled through and insinuated themselves into a group of mountain folk headed for Palisade Gate and complaining bitterly about the prices in the shops. Clouds massed overhead. Emris tugged on her sleeve.

"He took his cap off," Emris whispered. "As we were running out."

"Did you see his face?"

"Not much of it. Sort of plain-looking. He's got dark hair, brown, I think."

She frowned and straightened. The mountain folk straggled to a halt before a bakery, arguing about budgets and hunger. Lyeth and the boy kept walking. Brown hair, middling tall, ordinary-looking— any random figure in the city could fit that description and without his cap she had no way of distinguishing him. She paused at a public fountain and bent her head toward the water.

"Take your cap off," she said conversationally. She pulled the eyepatch from her pocket and put it on.

"He'll spot us," Emris said, looking at the patch.

"Exactly."

He looked at her as though doubting her sanity, but put the cap in his pocket. They sauntered along, changing direction aimlessly at intersections. After a few streets, Lyeth smiled.

"Got him," she said with satisfaction. "He has his cap stuck under his belt, plain as day. Idiot. Over by that grey stone house, with the flowerboxes. Don't stare, just glance across. Recognize him?"

"Yes," Emris said, excited. "Now what?"

Lyeth looked down the street and her smile widened. She ruffled his hair, leaving it in wild curls.

"You need a bath, boykin. Can't go another minute without one."

"I do not! Janya made me wash last night. I'm clean."

She rubbed her fingers across the smudged windowsill behind her, then ran them down Emris' cheek. "Not clean enough, sweetling."

Emris opened his mouth, looked at her, and clamped his lips together. The bathhouse down the street was crowded and smelled of wet cloth and used water; the bath keeper slapped Lyeth's coins into his box.

"Boy or girl?" he shouted over the roar of the furnaces.

"Are you blind?" Lyeth shouted back. "Of course my dumpling's a girl. Where are our towels?"

"Fah." The bath keeper produced two tattered, rather grimy towels and gestured toward a door. Lyeth pulled Emris after her.

"Not one damned word, Elena my lass, or I'll skin your bottom."

Emris glared and kept silent as Lyeth pulled him into the stuffy, moist changing room. A gaggle of young women, heads together, giggled as they wrapped towels around their waists and wandered toward the baths. Lyeth made for a pile of gaudy fabric against the wall, stopped beside it, grabbed Emris' hair, and rubbed at his face with a wet towel. He rolled his eyes.

"I need a bath, huh?" he muttered. "Get me clean, right?"

"Shut up, my spongecake," Lyeth crooned. She wrung the towel over the ends of his hair, released him, unrolled the cuffs of his pants, and tucked them into his boot tops until they bloused around his knees, the way the city girls wore their pants. Emris looked at them with disgust. Lyeth deposited him on a bench, wagged an admonitory finger, and swiftly unpinned her hair. One of the young women scampered back in, grabbed a comb, and left. Lyeth braided her hair, put the eyepatch in her pocket, grabbed the two gaudiest cloaks, dropped some coins onto the clothing under them, and marched from the changing room, closing the cloak and pulling up the hood. Emris trotted beside her, pulling at his cape distastefully. The bath keeper didn't even look up as she tossed their towels at him and swept through the room, yelling at Elena to hurry up. Emris clutched the front of his cloak and scurried after.

"This is a disguise?" he said with disbelief. "This? We look like a couple of—of whores, that's what!"

Lyeth grinned at his glaring green cloak. "A fine and honorable profession, my muffin, with a guild of its own and a hall in Vantua filled with extravagances." She twitched his hood more completely over his hair. "There. Don't pout, creampuff, just look servile. I know it's difficult, but you can do it for momma, can't you?" She smoothed the dirty red fabric of her own cloak with satisfaction. Her braid, already coming undone, poked from her collar.

"But I *hate* green," Emris whined loudly. "I told you I hate green, you know I hate green, and you always make me wear it anyway. I want a yellow cloak, like Auntie Welfred's."

"Then you can just ask her to buy you one. You and your blessed Auntie Welfred! I'd like to see *her* support you for a change. Elena! Keep your blessed hem out of the mud! Balls of the Father, don't you ever learn?"

Arguing, they swept by the watcher. He leaned against a wall, twisting the blue cap in his hands, and ignored them. As they reached the corner he thrust the cap under his belt and stalked into the bathhouse. Emris giggled.

"Mind yourself, crumpet, we're not free yet."

"If I have to wear this," Emris said, gloriously mutinous, "at least you could buy me a new dress. Everyone will make fun of me. Everyone always makes fun of me."

"They wouldn't if you'd stop playing the clown all the time. And as long as I'm paying, you'll wear what I give you."

"Just you wait." Emris patted his damp curls complaisantly. "Auntie Welfred says I'm going to grow up to be a beauty."

Lyeth sputtered.

The breeze, threatening to become a wind, blew the cloaks around their legs; Palisade Square, as always, housed a tumultuous crowd. The Rider and the boy moved from booth to booth, discussing the wares; when Lyeth saw the sign of the Boar she nodded with satisfaction and marched inside, pulling Emris after her. Ten or twelve people sat in the smoky public room; Lyeth glared about until she spotted the innkeeper and stormed over to him.

"Where is he?" she howled. "That goatherd, swineherd, whatever he is? I know he lives here—you can't fool me. Where is he?"

"What the—"

"He didn't pay me! Took two hours of my time and didn't even pay me! Bastard! Where is he?"

The patrons tittered. Emris tugged on her cloak.

"That's him, Momma," he said, pointing. "That's the man. I saw him come out of your room."

"You never mind what you saw." She rapped his head and dragged him toward the table. The tall man, looking baffled, stood hurriedly.

"Hah! You! Don't think you can get away this time."

"I wasn't trying to—"

"Cerdic—that's your name, isn't it? Isn't it?" She planted her fists on her hips and glowered at him.

"Yes, but there must be some misunderstanding—"

"Hah! You think you can take advantage of a poor woman with a little child to feed and clothe, an innocent little child, and just swagger away without paying me? And don't tell me," she concluded triumphantly, "that I didn't earn it either!"

Laughter erupted behind them and Cerdic turned red. Lyeth spun around to confront the room. Even the innkeeper had stuffed his cleaning cloth into his apron and leaned against the wall, grinning hugely.

"You," Lyeth shouted with disgust. "Laughing at a poor woman! You should be ashamed of yourselves."

"Take it to the guild, woman," one of the patrons advised, grinning. "Take it to Whores Court."

"I don't need a guild to fight my battles," Lyeth said defiantly, amid more laughter.

"A freelance prostitute," the innkeeper chortled.

"I am not! I told his fortune, that's all. I'm a good woman, trying to raise my poor daughter—"

"A two-hour fortune?"

"Tell us about it, goatherd, it must have been—"

"Did you read his palm or his prick?" another demanded, wiping tears from her cheeks.

"Swine," Lyeth said with tattered dignity. She turned to Cerdic, opening her hands in supplication. "Sir, I beg you. For my child's sake, my innocent little sweetcake . . ." She pulled Emris in front of her. "Just look at that face, sir, you wouldn't want—"

Cerdic rolled his eyes and appealed to the room at large. "Gentlefolk, I swear I've never seen this woman before in my life."

"Bastard!" Lyeth shrieked. "Liar! Thief!"

Emris sniffed. "And he's got a big ugly mole on his backside, too," he remarked loudly. The room roared and Cerdic grabbed at him, but he skipped behind Lyeth's cloak.

"How do you know that, you little bitch?"

Emris simpered. "I peeked."

Under the howls of laughter Lyeth caught the shepherd by his ears and dragged his head down.

"It's Emris, you jackass. Get us up to your room."

Cerdic's jaw dropped. She slapped it closed and stepped back.

"My money?" she demanded. Cerdic nodded and she grabbed his tunic sash. "And we'll go upstairs with you, if you please. I know you country folk—steal a poor woman's money and run out the back door. Hah!" she concluded victoriously, took Emris' hand, and followed Cerdic up the stairs. "Fortune-teller," someone said in the public room. Renewed laughter followed them down the hall.

The little room was cold and smelled of stale beer. Cerdic bolted the door while Lyeth, shaking her hood back, took Emris by the shoulders and kissed his forehead.

"Boykin, you are a wonder. Thank you."

He smiled uneasily and stepped back. "Someone had to get us out of that," he said, pushing the hood from his hair.

Cerdic sat abruptly. "Mother Above, it is you."

Emris shrugged. Lyeth dropped her cloak and kicked it away.

"And you're the Rider who kidnaped Emris."

Lyeth, busy inspecting her jacket, cursed. "Damn. I've probably got lice now. Emris, take that thing off or you'll have lice, too." She sat in the room's one chair and pushed her fingers through her hair, untangling the braid. "I didn't kidnap him, and I'm giving him back."

Cerdic frowned and beckoned Emris over.

"Has she harmed you?" he said. "Are you all right?"

Emris turned away but Cerdic caught his wrist and pulled him back.

"Answer me, Emris. Are you—"

"She treated me all right," Emris muttered. "Let me go."

"I see," the shepherd said. Tanned skin wrinkled around his eyes. "You can't talk before her, is that it?" Emris jerked away and stalked across the room. "What about Trave's horse?"

"She's at an inn," Lyeth said. "Do you want to question her, too? And she's Emris' horse now. I paid the innkeeper for her."

"That's not what Trave says."

"Trave's a pinchpenny and a liar," Emris said. "Myla's *mine* now. Lyeth gave her to me."

"That's a fine trick," Cerdic said sternly. "Buying the child's affection with someone else's horse."

Lyeth gestured sharply, disgusted. "Emris, is he usually this dense, or just on special occasions?" she demanded. "Sheepherder, shut up."

"I just want to know if the boy is—"

"I said, shut up! I may not be in talma but I'm still a Rider and you'd best remember it."

Cerdic clenched his jaw and clenched his fists, glaring.

"Better," Lyeth said. "I'm sorry we came to you this way, but we were being followed." He opened his mouth, she looked at him warningly, and he closed his mouth again. "My name is Lyeth. I'm Lord Gambin's personal Rider. There are some problems up castle, with the sword. You don't need to know about them. Some people think I can help them; it doesn't matter who. They want to guarantee my cooperation and I think they'd use Emris to get to me. He's in danger, and as long as he's anywhere near Jentesi Castle, I'm in danger, too." She sat back. "Now you can talk."

Cerdic, too, sat back. "Why should I believe you?"

"Ask Emris."

"It's true," Emris said. He looked at Lyeth briefly. "That's what you want me to say, isn't it?"

"Emris," she said flatly.

He bit his lower lip. "It really is true. And someone did follow us here, a man with a blue cap. Lyeth fooled him by stealing the cloaks."

"I left money for them. Probably more than they're worth, even counting the livestock."

Emris didn't smile. *"She's* in trouble, so *I've* got to leave. It isn't fair."

"You want to stay with her?" Cerdic said, incredulous.

Emris refused to answer.

Lyeth spread her hands. "He thinks it all exciting and wonderful, he doesn't believe he could be hurt or killed. And he will be, Cerdic Sheepherder, unless he's helped."

"Ah." Cerdic crossed his arms. "You want me to help you."

"I want you to help Emris."

"How?"

"Take him back to Pelegorum," Lyeth said promptly.

"For how long?"

"Forever, damn it. He's not in ward, or a conscript, or an apprentice. I just want him to go home." Cerdic looked at her suspiciously. "I swear it on my oath! I won't come back for him."

The shepherd hesitated. "These people after you, they're important?"

"Very important, shepherd, and we don't have much time. You'll take him?"

"Yes," Cerdic said. "Yes, of course. I've always been fond of Emris. I thought of him—think of him as my own son. We'll leave as soon as the council is done."

"Council! Sweet Mother, haven't you listened at all? He has to leave now, this minute, it can't wait."

"But Rider, be reasonable," Cerdic protested, spreading his hands. "If I go now, Pelegorum won't be represented and they'll cut off our trade. There's no one else here from the village, no one to take my place. I can't do it." He paused. "Unless there's some news from up castle I don't know. Unless Gambin isn't going to die soon. Is he, Rider? Is there time to ride to Pelegorum and back before the lord dies?"

Lyeth put her fingers in her hair and muttered under her breath. "I don't know," she said finally. "I don't think so. Forget it, Cerdic."

"I could hide him here—"

"Impossible, it's one of the first places they'd look. If I can't protect him up castle, you surely can't protect him here."

"From whom?" Cerdic demanded. "If I did drop everything and take him, how could I keep him safe if I don't even know who to keep him safe from?"

"Travel overland," Lyeth said immediately. "Take the route I took, directly over the mountains. Emris knows the way and I can draw you a map—but you're not going, are you? Not until after council." Standing quickly, she scooped her cloak from the floor. "Emris, get into that thing again. It's almost noon; we don't have much time. Shepherd, forget you saw us."

"But I want to help you," Cerdic said, standing. "Just tell me what you want me to do."

"Forget it. You last saw Emris in Pelegorum; that's all you know."

"There must be something—"

"There isn't." She pulled Emris' hood over his hair. The boy glanced at her and returned his gaze to Cerdic; she couldn't read his expression.

"Perhaps I can help *you,* then."

"Good. Tell me where the back stairs are."

"That's not what I meant."

"No, but that's what I need. Emris, hurry up." She braided her hair quickly. "About that stuff downstairs, don't talk about it and they'll assume you're embarrassed. Where are the stairs?"

"Down the hall toward the stable yard. I know," he said urgently. "I can follow you, see if I can spot whoever was following you before and—"

"Don't be an ass." She looked into the hall. "If I see you following me, now or anytime, I'll have you taken. Understand?"

"You should take help when you can get it," Cerdic said.

"I do. I don't need yours."

"I need your help, though."

Emris ducked under her arm and stood in the hall, swathed in the vile green of the cape. Cerdic rubbed his palms against his thighs.

"Rider, you live up castle. You know more about the people there than I do." He spread his hands. "It's important for the village to support whoever might win, important that I vote the right way. Who's going to win, Rider? Who should I vote for?"

She stared at him. "Lady Mother, Cerdic, I don't know. But . . . just don't vote for Culdyn. As you value your life or your village." She looked at him a bit longer, puzzled, shook her head, and followed Emris into the hall. The door closed behind them.

They found the back stairs and descended to the innyard door. Dark clouds filled the sky; wind snatched the door from her hand and slammed it closed. In Palisade Square most of the tents were gone, folded out of the storm's reach, and stallholders hurried to store their goods. Lyeth strode into the square, looking at the last open shops.

"Lyeth?" Emris skipped to keep up with her. "There's something wrong with Cerdic."

"You think so, boykin? I thought he was a hero of yours."

Emris tugged at his collar. "He's everybody's hero, all the kids. But he never paid special attention to me—when he said that thing about me, about how he thought about me like his son? I think he was lying. And he asked too many questions."

"Indeed. I think so, too." She looked down at him. "Was he this way in Pelegorum?"

"Sometimes. He likes to ask questions. I didn't think about it much." He looked desperately unhappy. "Lyeth? It's bad, isn't it?"

"Oh, not as bad as all that," she said lightly. "We almost got our money, didn't we, Elena my lass?"

He looked away. The wind boomed.

She bought two new cloaks from a merchant more concerned with profits than weather; heavy, serviceable woolen ones, the grey cloth cut city style. They discarded the gaudy cloaks behind a deserted tinker's stall while chickens ran back and forth between their legs.

"Falenka falepa," Lyeth said, pulling on Emris' cloak to settle the shoulders. "You're a boy again."

He put his hand on her arm. "If there's no safe way to get me out, I'll *have* to stay with you, won't I?"

She touched his cheek, not trusting her voice, and led the way from the square.

The private room Lyeth hired above the wine shop was quiet and warm and faintly shabby; Emris slouched about it in miserable silence while she scribbled a note, sealed it, and sent it off with the barmaid's younger brother. The boy stared in awe at the coin Lyeth dropped in his dirty palm and scampered out of the room. She watered some wine for Emris, filled her own cup, and stared at it bleakly. Outside, wind muttered around the chimney-pots.

Her wine was still untouched when the door opened and Joleda came in. The old woman's eyebrows rose when she saw Emris; she dropped a large sack on the table, covered it with her cape, and came to sit beside Lyeth at the fire.

"Going to storm tonight," she said conversationally. "Sky's dark, wind's up—it might be a real howler. The shepherd wouldn't take him?"

Lyeth spread her hands helplessly, and told her about Cerdic. Joleda, listening, rubbed her stump absently, and when Lyeth finished she sat back in the chair.

"Asked a lot of questions, didn't he?" Joleda said quietly. Lyeth met her gaze.

"I couldn't prove it," she replied in the same tone.

Joleda nodded. "Proof is always hard. And he knows where you want Emris to go."

Lyeth turned, shrugging. "Once Gambin's dead, he's out of danger. It won't be too much longer."

"We thought that a fortnight back. How long does it take to ride to Pelegorum?"

Lyeth took a deep breath. "Not long enough."

"So." Joleda sipped from Lyeth's winecup. "Horrible stuff; I serve much better. Emris, fetch my bag. I'll take him."

Lyeth looked at her quickly. "Where?"

"You don't need to know that. Or when, or how." Emris put the sack beside her and sat at their feet, facing the fire. "He'll be safe, I promise you."

"Mother's sake, Joleda," she said, looking away. Her glance stopped at Emris' head. Some of his curls were still damp, a darker gold against the curve of one pink ear. "I'll find a safe place in the city," she muttered.

"No."

"The supply boat's due to leave tomorrow. I'll—"

"Nothing will sail in this storm," Joleda said flatly. "And you're the one who said he's in danger *now.*" She pulled Lyeth's talma from the sack and held it in her lap for a moment. "You were willing to send him back to Pelegorum, never see him again. Why is this any different?"

"At least I'd know where he was," Lyeth said unhappily. Emris' shoulders moved abruptly and were still again under the voluminous folds of the borrowed shirt. She looked away, caught Joleda's glance, and looked away from that, too.

"Your horse is stabled next door," the old woman said. "You'll have to pay the stableboy. Don't forget your patch."

"My . . . yes." She transferred her papers from jacket to talma and stuffed the jacket into Joleda's pouch. "He doesn't have his clothes," she said abruptly, remembering.

"Doesn't matter. Who had you followed?"

Lyeth, rising from her chair, hesitated. "Any one of them."

"Good. Don't forget that. Get out."

"Joleda!" she cried, her hands fisted tight in the talma's fur. "Is there no kindness?"

"It's not called for," Joleda said with the same cold calmness.

"This is a surgical procedure, girl. What made you think it could be anything else?"

Lyeth's stomach went abruptly cold, the breath gone from her. Dragging the talma, she spun, looked wildly at Emris, and ran for the door, almost tripping over the dark cloak. The corridor was empty, dimly lit, filled only with the rustle of the talma until, behind her, the door slammed open again and Emris shouted her name. She froze, her back to him, and heard his footsteps approaching, slowing as he neared her. When, finally, she turned he stood a pace away, eyes bright and hands busy under his shirt. He brought them out, staring at her, and closed the small space between them.

"Keep this for me," he said unevenly, "until you come for me."

"Emris, I can't—I won't be—"

"It's not yours," he continued. "It's mine. It's a loan." His voice broke. He pressed something hard into her palm and bolted back into the room, slamming the door. Lyeth opened her fingers and saw the shadi token, still warm from the boy's skin.


Wind howled up the avenue, tugging at bare trees; the magician, dancers, musicians, vendors, and shoppers were all gone, stores closed, windows shuttered tight. The light had turned a nasty yellow-grey and the bell in the town hall, barely audible in the storm's noise, tolled the hour past noon. She hadn't shown him the passage through Jentesi Rock to the lookout niche, or taken him to the Crescent Bathhouse or the menagerie behind it; she hadn't told him about running forfeits; he'd never played with Tibbi.

Darkness fidgeted, objecting to the wind; a gust lifted his mane and she shook her head hard, urging him forward again. She could send him a letter, once all of this was over. Send a message through Joleda. Something. The time was past and more than past; she couldn't endanger him for the sake of a few minor adventures. For the sake of seeing him again. He still had her Rider's token, deep in his pocket or, maybe, dangling about his neck. Instead of comfort, the thought made a tight, hard bolus in her chest.

The shadi at the wharf said the ferrymen would make one last run before they, too, hid from the storm, but she had to wait half an hour for the boat. She spent the time staring at the frozen Tobrin and cursing methodically and monotonously. The gleam from a passing lantern caught at a scrap of cloth, bright as a boy's hair. She turned her head from it and touched the token in her pocket. The shadeen left her alone.

# SIX

# SYNE

THE afternoon filled with the special, murky darkness preceding a storm, and the wind played with her talma, sending unexpected tongues of cold against her skin. She ignored them, letting the talma billow unformed while she fought sorrow into a more manageable shape. At the first curtain the shadi held a lantern to her face, motioned her through, and retreated to the shelter of the gatehouse. Darkness trudged the path between the fields of the outer ward, head down. Storm shutters covered the windows of the village houses, the shops were closed and dark, the castle a looming presence behind them. It, too, retreated behind dark walls as she approached the second curtain. At the inner gate two figures approached, one swinging a lantern. She reined Darkness to a halt.

"Rider." The figure with the lantern threw back his hood; she saw the lined face of Heron, Torwyn's chamberlain, and bit back her instant irritation. Heron was a good man, a plodding, thorough man with no evil to his name or history save that he, too, was one of Gambin's bastards. Not his fault, and because she knew her irritation to be groundless she tried to mask it and hoped, for Torwyn's sake, that her mask succeeded. Now she leaned from the saddle to hear him.

"My lord and his lady desire your presence," Heron shouted politely. "Immediately. Porlon will take your horse."

She dismounted but kept the reins in her fist. "Why?"

"I don't know, Rider. He said it's urgent. Will you come?"

She thought about the bottle of apato sitting in her room and shook her head.

"Rider? The Lady Syne desires it."

"Damn." Syne couldn't command her, but it would not be wise to refuse. She handed the reins to Porlon; Heron pulled his hood up, tucked his chin down, and led her through the Snake. The alley funneled the wind to gale force and she bent her shoulders as a fine, dense hail began to fall. Joleda would take him out of the city; they were probably gone already. South, perhaps. Traveling in the storm.

Heron ducked through an arch and she followed him up a curved, semi-enclosed stone stairway. A bundled servant took torches from their brackets and dunked them in a bucket of water, resetting dead torches in the supports. Night seemed to climb the stairs in his wake. Parts of the castle were still black with soot where, a century earlier, high winds had flung a lit torch at a wooden wall. The fire had destroyed the servants' quarters and many of the storerooms, and care of the castle's lights was now strictly observed. The servant pressed against the wall to let them pass.

The stairs became an angled passageway, the passageway became a corridor where torches burned calmly along the walls. Heron opened his lantern and pinched out the flame as Lyeth dropped the hood of her talma, brushing ice from the fur.

"What time is it?" she said.

"The third hour past noon, mistress."

Her stomach rumbled. She put her hands through the talma and into the pockets of her trousers, tangling her fingers in the token's chain; her thigh muscles flexed against her hands as she walked. Joleda would have found him some warm clothes before they left the city. If they found a solid waystation outside the city, they could ride out the storm in relative comfort, and the storm itself would protect them. It would be cold there.

She had expected to be taken to a new section of the castle but Heron led her to Torwyn's chambers, behind the White Tower and snug against the dark stone of the Rock, at the castle's highest level. Hangings covered the rock walls; the two flanking the door no longer showed Torwyn's complex quartering, but Syne's curving black sigil against russet and blue. The sigils seemed to dance in the torchlight and two shadeen in Syne's colors flanked the door, looking at Lyeth curiously. Heron conferred with them briefly and the carved wooden doors swung open. An entry hall, where servants in Syne's livery took their cloaks; Torwyn's guest hall, where everything had changed. The huge crystal chandelier still hung overhead, all the prisms sparkling, but Torwyn's delicate, comfortable furniture had been replaced by sober chairs and couches ranked before a plain, uncushioned chair at the far end of the room. Fragile porcelain and glass decorated the tabletops, thick Dorne rugs covered the floor, but the precise warmth of the room was gone, replaced by a cool, formal stiffness. The guest hall had become an audience hall, and Lyeth didn't like it. Heron led her to another carved door set behind hangings, and Lyeth took a deep breath as he opened the door, bowed, and gestured her inside. He retreated and the door clicked shut behind him. This room was still, in greater part, Torwyn's.

The steward, facing her, smiled and turned toward the fireplace. "My Lady, the Rider Lyeth." Lyeth dropped to one knee and bent her head.

Syne, like her father, was tall and big-boned, square of hand and face, with heavy lids and thick, sensuous lips. And her eyes, like her father's, were a flat black that gave away nothing. Wings of grey highlighted her thick black hair. Lyeth rose and stood with her hands in her pockets again, feet apart, looking curiously at the woman and prepared to be rude.

"I thank you for coming." Syne's voice was low and smooth. "And coming so promptly. I believe you were off the Rock this morning."

"I just returned. You might have given me time to eat and to change."

Syne smiled. "I don't demand formal attire. Lord Steward, have someone bring in some lunch. The Rider must be hungry."

"And some wine," Lyeth added. "The Rider is also freezing."

Torwyn crossed between them, giving Lyeth a subtle, sober look which she ignored.

"May I sit, Lady?"

"Of course." Syne gestured and Lyeth sank into a chair across the round, inlaid table from the lady. She stretched her legs under the table, crossing her arms.

"The child isn't with you," the lady said. Lyeth glanced at her suspiciously. "Did you leave him in the city?"

"Why do you want to know?"

Torwyn set a silver decanter on the table. "Lyeth. The lady is trying to help you."

She shrugged. "I can take care of myself. Is that the wine?"

Torwyn poured, his lips tight; the translucent porcelain cups yellowed as they filled. Lyeth tasted the dry, delicate wine and put the cup down carefully.

"What's your interest in my ward?" she said. "He is surely beneath your notice, Lady."

"I wonder that you think so." Syne touched the silver-banded lip of her cup gently. "We all have conflicting interests here, Rider. They determine much of what we do. Torwyn wishes to serve me and to help you. And you seem to have an interest in the child you chased all about the castle this morning. I assume you've made arrangements for him in the city. Are you related?"

The pale southern wine became sour. "You know about Torwyn's conflicting interests, Lady. You presume to know about mine. Surely you know the answer to that, too."

Syne's smile barely moved the sharp planes of her face. "There's much information to hand, Rider. Some of it interesting, some important, some useful—and some of no interest, import, or use at all. Your blood relationship to that child, if any, is interesting only in that it may explain your fondness for him. The fondness is important, not the cause." She lifted her cup. "I'm pleased you took him off the Rock. Children should not be a part of this."

"A part of what, Lady?"

"Rider. By all means be rude if you must, but there is no need to pretend stupidity."

Lyeth tightened her lips. A page came in, balancing a platter; the room filled with the scent of roast chicken and fresh bread, and her mouth watered. At Syne's gesture the page put the platter before Lyeth and retreated.

"We've already eaten," the lady said. "Our talk can wait."

Lyeth dined from translucent plates while Syne and Torwyn talked about music and wines and books and sculpture, the lazy, aimless conversation of friends. She wondered whether there wasn't, still, something between the sternly elegant lady and her younger but equally elegant steward. They made a striking couple, Lyeth decided sourly—they'd have handsome children. Torwyn said something light and Syne laughed deep in her throat. Lyeth pulled a wing from the chicken and gnawed it morosely. What did she know of music, or sculpture, or the precise difference between a lile from Saek or a chatifand from Denere? Torwyn kept immaculate order in his lady's accounts, in the running of her lands, the harvesting of her crops, the collection of the relatively minor taxes she imposed on her land-barons and her tenants, minding his absent lady's business during the long years that she minded her father's business in Vantua. Lyeth wondered how Torwyn's life would change if Syne permanently returned to Jentesi, wondered at the relationship that could foster this light, amiable chatter, as though they had spoken together daily for the bulk of both their lives and knew each other as intimately as they knew themselves. She poked at the vegetables, smelling dill and feeling jealous. Torwyn talked about a tapestry he'd seen in Mywen, Syne asked how it compared to one in her hall in Vantua, and Lyeth tried to listen beyond their words to their voices. They were very good at it, this light conversation; she could barely hear the tension below it and wished she knew what they were hiding. She pushed her empty plate away and the page, stepping forward quickly, cleared the table.

"Thank you," she said. Syne turned toward her. "Is Gambin dead?"

Syne's heavy brows drew together. "No. The old bastard lingers and the young bastard waits. You saw my father two days ago—it's an evil death, isn't it?" She paused. "He deserves the pain."

Lyeth raised her eyebrows. "He's your father."

"And your master. It doesn't guarantee affection." She leaned back in her straight chair. "They won't raise monuments to my father after his death. Unless, of course, Culdyn takes the sword."

"Ah." Lyeth laced her fingers around the stem of her cup. "The reason for your hospitality, isn't he?"

"In part. You know of Gambin's plans for Culdyn—do they threaten you?"

Lyeth frowned. "My Lady. I thought we were here to be oblique and subtle."

"I have no time for subtlety. Are you threatened?"

Lyeth hesitated. "I'm not sure," she said finally. "I believe I may be."

"Believe this, too, then," Syne said. "Culdyn, if he takes the sword, will be far more dangerous than Gambin ever was. Wait, let me finish. Gambin could control his greed, could see the value of moderation—"

"The ferrets are moderation?" Lyeth said sarcastically. "The network? The Guard?"

"Yes," Torwyn said quietly. "Gambin sent his Riders against the guilds, rarely against shadeen, never against the land-barons. He put no limit on the taxes the barons could collect, granted them privileges unknown in the rest of Cherek, and they kept the commons quiet for him. As long as commons and land-barons don't join to demand it, a lord can't be deposed. And the barons knew that to topple Gambin would be to topple themselves."

"Stealth and bribery," Lyeth said. "But not moderation."

"Irrelevant," Torwyn said curtly. "Culdyn is too greedy. Once he's firmly in power even Durn won't be able to sway him, and he'll use the nobility as they use the commons. Once they realize it, Culdyn will fall."

"Then it's just a matter of time, isn't it?" Lyeth rose and walked around the table to the fireplace. "Let Culdyn take the sword and he'll dictate his own end. If you're right."

"Of course," Syne agreed. She extended her cup and Torwyn refilled it. "But what price does Jentesi pay in the interim? You know about the Merchants' trading fleet, about Merinam? We're on the brink of a new world, a new universe, but Culdyn would take us into the past; he'd try to re-create a world in Constain's image. Confusion, death, fear, famine—lost crops, declining trade, war. By the time Culdyn's finished with Jentesi there will be nothing left to save."

"Good." Lyeth crossed her arms. "Excellent. You can sell Jentesi to the Trappers, who would probably handle it better than your father did, or your brother would. I think it's a fine idea."

Syne rose abruptly. "Remember, Rider, that this is my home. I may have been away for twenty years, but Jentesi is *my* province."

"Perhaps if you hadn't deserted it, it would be in better shape," Lyeth said maliciously. Syne clenched her fists and stalked across the room. Torwyn looked from his lady to Lyeth and shook his head.

"Rider, you're a fool."

The lady turned angrily. "No, Torwyn. A child, perhaps, but not a fool." She leaned forward, her fists braced on a small table and framed in figurines. "Consider this, Rider. Some of Cherek's lords are good ones, living within the laws, concerned for their provinces and their people. And some look enviously at Gambin and wonder how he did it, whether he can pass it on. If Culdyn takes the sword he won't change this province and they know it. And if Culdyn can handle Gambin's legacy, even in the short term . . ." She gestured eloquently. "You suggest giving Jentesi to the Trappers. Would you give all Cherek to the Trappers? We are the nexus of a choice, Rider. We can look to the sea, to Merinam, and the future, or we can look to Culdyn Gambini and a land that only Trappers would find pleasing. If Culdyn takes the sword—"

"Damn Culdyn, then!" Lyeth grinned suddenly. "Or better yet, kill him. He's obviously dangerous, that he's your half-brother seems to be neither interesting nor important, he's a threat to the entire civilized world—so have him tossed off the curtain wall some stormy night. Today, perhaps; there was a fine storm brewing when I came in." She moved away from the fireplace, smiling in passing at Torwyn's shocked face. "You can't tell me that your conscience prevents you. You are, after all, Gambin's daughter."

In one smooth movement, Syne grabbed a figurine and smashed it against the floor. Lyeth's smile fled.

"I won't kill Culdyn," Syne said deliberately, "because I don't think I could get to him before he gets to me. Is that practical and heartless enough for you?" She straightened abruptly. "And it wouldn't help. Murder only complicates, it never simplifies. We have enough complications already."

"Lady, I believe you." Lyeth picked up her cup, eyeing Syne and the shattered figurine. "But, Lady, I don't care. Gambin will die, I'll ride his death to Vantua, and it will be an evil day that brings me back." She finished the wine. "I thank you for my meal, Lady. May I go?"

Syne clenched her hand around another figurine, then replaced it, looked at Torwyn, and sighed.

"Rider. Once more. For Torwyn's sake. Life in Jentesi must change."

"Surely."

"It will be better, or it will be worse."

"Without doubt."

"Culdyn would make things worse."

"Absolutely. He's the Constain of his generation."

"Lyeth," Torwyn said. She ignored him.

"Rider, I promise that I will change things, Gambin's work be undone, the ferrets abolished. Do you believe that?"

"I will if it pleases you. As I said, I really don't care."

Syne hit the table; figurines bounced and tottered. "Torwyn, I give up. You want her saved, you save her."

"Finally." Lyeth grinned. "My thanks for Your Ladyship's hospitality, but I really must go."

Syne hit the table again and this time glass shattered. Torwyn stalked from the room.

"Has he gone to fetch my talma, do you think?"

"Rider, you're an ass." Syne crossed her arms. "I'm not asking for your life, I'm asking for your support."

"Are you, Lady? What of Coreon, then? Or Maranta?"

"Maranta is negligible, and Coreon only a little less so. The contest is between myself and my brother."

"Yes?" Lyeth cocked her head. "Torwyn warned me, Lady, that Maranta or Coreon might try to kill me, to keep me from oathing to your brother. It would work as well for you, and if you believe this to be between yourself and Culdyn, you'd profit more from my death than they would."

The figurines looked in mortal danger again. "I told you, Rider. Murder complicates." Lyeth raised her eyebrows, disbelieving. Syne gave her a look of unalloyed disgust. "Very well, then. If I can't engineer your support, at least let me engineer your safety. As a token, if you will, of my pure intentions." She walked around the mess of broken glass. "For what you can make of it, take this advice. You're in danger and you will be in danger. Don't hide yourself. Don't be alone. Be conspicuous, move in public places, be observed, be known. Shun solitude, seek out crowds. Never let yourself be in a place where you can be made to disappear."

"Oh? May I shit in private?"

"Not if you wish to shit again," the lady said with tight fury.

"I see. And of what passing use, Lady, is my safety to you?"

"If you disappear from Jentesi this instant, Rider, and I never see you again, I would be more than delighted." She paused. "My steward asks this of me. I told you he has conflicting interests. The primary conflict is you."

"Horseshit," Lyeth said instantly. "I know what he is to me, what I am to him. You're either misled, Lady, or you're lying."

Torwyn came into the room and stood with his back to the door. "Rider," he said, looking at his lady, "have some more wine."

"No. I've some fine apato in my rooms and I want to go there and drink some of it. Now. Alone." She moved purposefully around the table.

"Lyeth—"

"Do you know," she demanded, "what your lady says of you? Tender feelings, Torwyn. Undying devotion. Mother, Torwyn, you might have told her it wouldn't work." Torwyn spread his arms to the door's edges, blocking her, mouth opened to speak. "Get out of my way, *steward,*" she said viciously, slapping his arms aside. He grabbed her wrists, she twisted to throw him, he blocked her, and they balanced precariously, bodies pressed tight, muscles sliding and hardening; Torwyn's breath moved along her cheek and she glanced at him, unable to read his expression through her anger. Then he shifted marginally, seeking a hold, and she seized the instant of his imbalance to break away, her hand falling automatically to her dagger as Torwyn's hand, just as automatically, touched the hilt of his blade. Syne gasped. The door behind them opened abruptly and Heron, eyes widening, looked over Torwyn's shoulder, beyond Lyeth, to Syne.

"The storm's abated, Lady," he said, his glance sliding toward Torwyn and the Rider. "A little bit. It's safe to leave."

Torwyn dropped his hand from his weapon. Lyeth straightened, shoved the dagger deep into its sheath, and wordlessly left the room. Heron hopped out of her way, Torwyn followed at her heels, and Timbli, from a small timber barony on Syne's lands, stood near the door handing her cloak to a servant while another held Lyeth's talma gingerly. Brushing Timbli aside, Lyeth snatched the talma and threw it around her shoulders; Torwyn moved nimbly to step in front of her.

"Leave me alone," she said. "You're no better than she is." She pushed him aside and strode between the shadeen into the corridor. Turning right, she followed a maze of stone hallways that led eventually to the stone bridge over the Snake and Horda's Garden, and once there she leaned against an embrasure, breathing deeply. The storm howled, spitting dense snow and splinters of ice; the bulk of Gambin's Tower had disappeared and even the gardens below were invisible. Emris, she thought, while rage mingled with sorrow and she pounded at the stones with her fist, fighting the urge to scream, or weep. Then, carefully, she put Emris and Syne and Torwyn into mental rooms and closed doors, imagining each of them in detail, studded with brass or iron, heavy with oak or ash, locks chunking and great wooden braces falling secure into their housings. She retreated down the hallways of her mind, slamming, barring, locking, shutting, until her hands were steady and the knots in her chest and stomach loosened. Standing away from the wall, she shook the talma neatly over her shoulders and paced through the convolutions of Jentesi Castle to the Great Hall.

The hall was as full as she'd ever seen it, fires roaring in both huge fireplaces and torches festooning the walls, but the corners of the hall were still dark and cold. She walked further into the room. The heirs were absent and she couldn't spot Jandi, but otherwise every living soul on the Rock seemed present. Forne sat near one of the fireplaces, singing bawdy songs to a clapping crowd; against the far wall wrestlers grappled and fell, bodies stripped and slick with sweat, while spectators shouted advice and wagers. Beyond them a group of castle women sat intent on their spinning, ignoring the snoring drunks piled along the walls under tapestries depicting battles. Lady Elea, neatly dressed in blue and white, shared a flagon of wine and deep conversation with the Lord of Efet; behind her, Laret, looking young and sullen, stood at parade rest and watched the room longingly. Lyeth hunched her shoulders under the talma and went over to him.

"Well, highlander?" she said.

Laret's expression was a wonder of misery and lechery. "I am on duty," he said unhappily. "I think the lady may keep me on duty forever. Unless," he said, brightening, "you ask to borrow me."

"And what would I do with a borrowed shadi?" Lyeth said.

Laret's smile blossomed. "I could show you," he said, "what I can do with my lips and my fingers."

For one wild moment she found herself considering it, then shook her head, grimacing. "No, stripling. Did you offend Elea?"

His smile fled. "A debt of honor," he said stiffly. "Cherans don't understand such things."

"Ah. You gambled again with Coreon, and lost."

"I would have won," Laret said. "It was just a run of bad luck, but it was changing. But my lady made me stop." He shook his head sadly.

"The thing your father gave you?" She said it lightly, and to her surprise Laret's pale face paled further.

"A trinket," he said uncomfortably. "I'll get it back." He ducked his head toward her. "But it was part of my initiation. Into the Circle. If I don't get it back my father will—"

"Mother's sake," Lyeth said. "I'm no stupid peasant, to believe that. The Circle, indeed."

Laret's shoulders went back. "I may not be very good at it yet," he said stiffly, "but that's no reason to make fun of me. I had the—that, and I have this, too." He reached through his doublet to his under-shirt and brought out a bright stone.

"Wait." Lyeth captured his wrist in her hands and looked at the stone. Milky white, shot with gleams of green and blue, carved into a delicacy of sphere within sphere; both stone and stonework looked vaguely familiar. "Oh," she said. She looked at him, keeping his wrist steady in her hands. "Maranta has one of those. In her stupid device." Across the room, something shattered and derisive laughter followed. She reached to touch the stone.

"No!" Laret closed his fingers around it, jerking his hand away. "The lady cannot have one—it is impossible." He hid the stone in his clothes again. "I shouldn't even have showed it to you—if my father ever finds out . . ."

"He'll punish you for telling lies," she said. "Maranta does have one, I'll show you. Lady Elea?"

The Lord of Alanti looked at her. "Rider?"

"Could I borrow your shadi for a moment? There's something I want to show him."

Elea shot Laret a warning glance, nodded to Lyeth, and returned to her conversation. Lyeth took Laret's sleeve and towed him across the room toward a guarded, curtained alcove. A few words with Maranta's shadeen, and a coin, brought them into the presence of the Circles of Infinity.

"Well?" Lyeth said.

Laret stared in alarm through the glittering spheres of the device, at the stone in its heart. "Very bad," he whispered. "Very, very bad, Rider. This should not be here." His voice dropped further. "It breaks the Circle. It is very evil."

"From one circle to another, Laret? No, it's not evil. Just stupid."

Laret didn't bother to reply. Light glittered through the latticed carving on the stone and the outer jewels gleamed richly. Lyeth took Laret's sleeve and tugged him out of the alcove, and to her amuse-ment he made the sign against evil and put one arm firmly around her shoulders.

"I will not be able to sleep," he said. "Rider, it must be returned. It is very much not good—I will take it back to my people. It doesn't belong here."

"Sweet Mother." Lyeth pushed his arm away. "You'll leave it precisely where it is—if I hear even a rumor that it's disturbed, I'll tell Lady Elea. Do you want that?"

Laret glanced uneasily at his lady, wrapped his arms around his middle, and looked unhappy. Lyeth deposited him behind the Lord of Alanti, nodded to Elea, and went across the room. Three loud games of pit dice punctuated the uproar, musicians in the gallery sawed inaudibly at their instruments, and Gambin's acrobats performed in a clear space between the tables. Most of them looked drunk, too, and as they tripped over each other their audience howled appreciatively, waiting for someone to break a bone. Lyeth glanced back at Laret, who stared at the curtained alcove miserably. A lecherous Trapper with sticky fingers and an overactive imagination, inebriated acrobats, inaudible musicians, and more drunken nobility than she had thought existed—this would be the company that, should she take Syne's advice, she would be obliged to keep. The image of her apato beckoned enticingly; the prospect of drinking herself into a stupor in the privacy of her own rooms seemed irresistible. She retreated from the hall and went quickly into the kitchen.

"What do you want?" Bedwyn demanded ritually, waving a ladle. "By the Father's Omnipotent Prick, they're a hungry lot. Where do they expect me to get melons in a storm like this? Fah! Here, take it and go away, I'm busy."

She caught the hot brandycake and bounced it from hand to hand, blowing on it, as she crossed the kitchen.

"And close the door!" Bedwyn yelled after her.

The steeply angled snowroof of the walk between kitchens and storerooms kept the storm at bay; she stood in the shelter eating the cake and watching the blizzard. Pleadings, daggers, wine, demands, the ghost of Constain and a mythical country in the southern sea— she shook her head abruptly. Damn Syne, she thought suddenly, refusing to pursue the thought. Her shoulders ached. She judged angles, brushing crumbs from her gloved hands, pulled the hood of her talma around her face, and sprinted into the storm, heading toward the invisible fastness of her rooms. The wind grabbed at her, shouting; the steps were treacherously icy and she held tight to the railing, fighting her way up. When she gained the corridor she leaned against the wall, catching her breath. All the torches were out and she cursed the darkness.

"Rider?"

Her breath caught; one hand moved to her dagger.

"Sweet Mother, please—Rider?" Fear could be aped. She lifted the dagger free and peered into the darkness. "Rider, please, I'm Robin." And names could be spoken falsely. The storm howled.

"Rider, I saw you on the stairs. I—oh, listen. From the Trapper lands to Mother Sea, I swear to ride the land roads and the Water Road, to undertake as I am ordered by guild and by lord, to hold the confidence of my guild and of my lord as I hold the secrets of the Mother, on whose warm heart I swear this oath, my life and my soul—"

"Enough." Lyeth shifted her grip on the dagger. "Where did you learn that?"

"Please, Rider, Jandi taught me. In the big room in Vantua, in the guildhall, the one with the speeders carved on the lintels and the big windows over the gardens, and—"

"Hush." She moved silently down the corridor. "You're alone?"

"Yes, Rider." His voice trembled.

"You swear it?"

"By the Mother."

She paused, thinking hard. "All right. Go into my rooms and fetch a light."

"I can't. Your servant locked the doors, she won't let me in." The boy's voice caught on a sob. "Rider?"

"Stand by my door, then. Face it, hands flat against it."

Footsteps shuffled down the corridor; she had to concentrate to hear them. When they stopped she followed cautiously, sheathing the dagger, and at the door she reached quickly, grabbed arms, and twisted them expertly. The boy cried out in pain, but she held his wrists firmly with one hand and, with the other, pounded on the door with the dagger's hilt.

"Janya! Damn it, open the door!"

"Mistress?" Janya called fearfully through the door. "How do I know it's you?"

Lyeth cursed loudly and Janya immediately unbolted the door. Bright light spilled into the corridor as Lyeth pushed the boy inside. He was dressed only in light tunic and pants, and when she released him he moaned and wrapped his arms tightly around his torso, shaking.

"Mother Night," Lyeth said, disgusted. She slammed the door hard behind her and Janya immediately bolted it.

"There had better be a good explanation for this," Lyeth said coldly. "Janya, get some hot tea."

"But I'll have to go downstairs—"

"I don't care," Lyeth yelled. "Get it!"

Janya picked up a torch, lit it, and walked from the room, holding the torch like a club. Lyeth threw her talma at the rack, found a blanket, and tossed it over Robin's shoulders. He crouched by the stove, clutching the blanket; the room seemed intolerably hot but his shivering only slowly abated. Lyeth dragged a chair close to the stove and shoved him into it as Janya came in, holding the torch with one hand and, with the other, balancing a tray on her belly. She pushed the door shut with her foot.

"Mistress, if you could bolt it . . ."

Lyeth frowned but bolted the door. She poured a sizeable slug of the apato into a cup and Janya filled it with tea.

"Here," Janya said, handing it to Robin. "I'm sorry, I didn't believe it was you."

He clutched the cup with both hands. "You had—visitors, too?"

Janya looked away. Lyeth made her take a cup of doctored tea and sit beside Robin, and the two looked at Lyeth apprehensively.

"All right," Lyeth said, helping herself to the apato. "Janya, do you by any chance have a reasonable explanation for this?"

Janya licked her lips, obviously debating beginnings.

"A man came by, mistress," she said finally. "Looking for you. The packers had gone and I was clearing up, just a little after you and Master Emris left, and he just came in. I didn't like him very much." The baby started to kick, bouncing the front of her gown. She put her hands over her middle. The man strode through the rooms with Janya lumbering behind him, trying to shoo him out and insisting that she didn't know Lyeth's whereabouts. Eventually, muttering unpleasantly to himself, he left. More indignant than frightened, Janya went about her duties and was standing in the smaller bedroom folding Emris' clothes when the man came back. This time he did more than mutter unpleasantly. Finding the rooms still empty, he forced the servant against a table and bent her backward over it.

"He had a knife," Janya said, her voice breaking. "And he said he'd hurt my—my—" She put her face in her hands and wept.

"So you told him I'd gone into the city. With Emris."

She nodded without looking up, and when Robin put his hand on her arm she clung to it.

"I see. Oh, stop that. There's no harm done. He didn't hurt you, did he?"

Janya shook her head, rubbing her eyes with a corner of her apron and keeping her grip on Robin's hand. "He said he'd come back if I was lying, he said he'd hurt my baby, so I bolted the door. I didn't know it was you," she said to Robin. "I was so scared."

"I know. I was, too."

Lyeth, sipping her apato, looked at them carefully. "The man came by just after I left. And the second time?"

"An hour ago?" Janya hazarded. "Not very long, mistress. I'd just come from the laundry, and that was just after lunch, before the storm got so bad."

Lyeth nodded. "And you, Robin?"

The boy took a deep breath. "It's about the guildmaster, Rider."

She leaned forward abruptly. "Go on."

"About an hour after he came back this morning, after he was here, a man came for him. He said Master Jandi was needed, said you'd sent for him. He said it was urgent. So Jandi went with him, and he told me to stay in the rooms and not to leave."

Lyeth raised her hand. "You've taken Memory? Good. Tell me about the man, Robin."

The boy closed his eyes. "A head taller than Master Jandi, and very thin. A fur cap pulled low, with some brown hair sticking out the sides. Dark brown. Very light eyes, maybe green. A small moustache and a beard, clipped, darker than his hair. He wore dark gloves, worn ones. No sigil. Dark brown cloak, shiny around the hems. His boots had mud on them." He opened his eyes.

"That's him," Janya said positively, bobbing her head. "That's the man."

"Good, Robin. Go on." She put her cup down carefully.

"He came back later, alone. Maybe an hour later. He gave me this and said not to open it, but to give it to you." Robin fumbled under the blanket and produced a small, cloth-wrapped package. Lyeth turned it over; the wax seal, intact, bore no stamp.

"I told him I couldn't leave and he said it came from Master

Jandi. And he said to tell you that—that . . ." He screwed his eyes closed. " 'She'll know what to do. And if she has sense, she'll do it before she gets another present. Something less easily spared.' " He shivered quickly. "It didn't make sense, Rider. So I came here but nobody was home and the man said I was to give this into your hands, so I didn't think I could just leave it. I went back to the guildmaster's rooms, and after a while the man came again and gave me another thing for you. And he said not to come back until I put it in your hands; he'd kill me if I didn't. I believed him, Rider. He didn't even let me take my cloak. So I came here again and Janya wouldn't let me in so I waited for you," he concluded in a rush. Now he clutched Janya's hand as fervently as she had clutched his.

Lyeth took the second package from him and leaned back in her chair. "No message with this one?"

"No, Rider. He said you'd know what it meant."

She put the second package aside and lay the point of her dagger against the wax seal of the first one. It opened easily. Within the cloth was a twist of paper, and within the paper, its chain tangled, lay Jandi's guild token. She put it on the table and looked at it, her stomach cramped and cold; Jandi's name and the date of his first oathing were incised clearly on the worn metal.

"Is it—" Robin whispered.

Ignoring him, Lyeth took up the second packet and broke the seal. The opened cloth revealed a small wooden box, its top closed by a little catch. She flicked the catch with her dagger's tip and raised the lid. In the box, nestled in blood-soaked cotton, was a little finger, intricately and artistically covered with blue tattoos.

She was halfway down the treacherous stairs when Robin, clutching her new grey cloak about his shoulders, caught up with her and together they flung themselves into the cold wildness of the yard. Within four steps the castle disappeared. Lyeth angled toward the wall surrounding Scholars Garden and followed it along the garden to the base of the steps. The wind caught at them again halfway up and Robin slipped; she grabbed his cloak and pushed him ahead of her into an open corridor and thence out of the storm and into a crowded classroom. Children gaped and scampered out of their way and Elot, shouting, took aim with a pen; the sharp nib stuck in the door, quivering, as Lyeth wrenched it open and rushed into the dark, angled passageway beyond. Two old women in an alcove stared at them, bottles of apato between their knees; beyond them birds shrieked in the aviary and a tailor, alerted by the sound of Robin's boots, popped his head from a doorway and as quickly popped back in again. She turned right and fled down a flight of stairs into a room crowded with footmen and valets in the colors of a handful of provinces. The servants barely had time to move out of her way.

"Rider!" someone shouted. "Is it Gambin?"

Down another flight of stairs and into the broad corridor behind the Great Hall, Robin's breathing harsh behind her and the guest flags still against the walls. Jandi's door stood open. She stopped abruptly and sidestepped to let Robin skid into the room ahead of her, almost into Master Durn's arms. Durn looked distressed; behind him Torwyn and the land-baron Heath Ebek, from far up the Clenyafyds, turned from the fireplace where a bedraggled man in a gardener's apron knelt by the dead fire. Lyeth stared at them, her breath ragged, and Durn pushed Robin aside and came to her, hands extended.

"Rider, we're all so sorry," he said, voice concerned and eyes cold. "We're doing everything we can, but there's not much hope."

She jerked away from him. "Where is he?" she said to Torwyn. The steward looked away.

"I'm sorry," Durn repeated. "We assumed you knew."

"Torwyn," she said flatly, and he came forward quickly, brushing Durn aside, to lay his hands on her shoulders.

"This gardener saw Master Jandi on Lord's Walk, Lyeth. And saw him fall."

She stared at him. "Fall," she said finally, stepping back. "Fall down, or over?" She turned her gaze to the gardener, who blanched and twisted his hands together.

"Mistress, I was staking trees in the Lady, I saw a talma on the Walk, mistress—it was like he couldn't see, hitting things, falling down, and I ran out there shouting, mistress, but he turned and slipped and fell, and I couldn't see him anymore. I ran to Lord Torwyn's, he was closest, and he sent to Lord Heath, and—"

"My climbers will find him, Rider," Heath Ebek said, tangling his fingers in his beard. "They're used to mountain work, to storms and hard climbs. If he can be found—"

"They're on the Walk now?" she demanded, and was gone before he'd finished his nod.

The corridor was already crowded with nobility and servants and guests, eager for any break in the storm's monotony. If Robin tried to follow her she didn't know it, and certainly gave him no time to catch up. She bolted down the broad stairs and ducked through the door at the base of the tower into Horda's Garden, clinging to the lee side of the wall until she came to a service door. A moment's work popped it open; a service door on the other side of the Snake yielded as easily and she was in the dark supply channels below the apartments of the nobility, running silently through the old, damp stone lanes. Cry forfeit, she thought with wild irrelevance as she ducked into a new hallway. A bone, a blow, a boon, a breath, a dusk, a dawn, a doom, a death. *Jandi!* A door resisted her, not with locks but with the pressure of wind. She forced it open and the storm took her, fighting her every step through the Garden of the Lady, over the snow that covered tombstones. Gargoyles leered from stone walls; Lords Walk loomed. She paused to reel in her talma, slapping the seams together while she peered ahead; dark figures moved obliquely at the far end of the Walk. She made her way toward them, cursing the uneven footing, while the wind tried to plaster her against rocks and then tried to rip her from them, and the broken pavement seemed to dance under her boots.

Heath Ebek's climbers had spun a web of lines and pulleys; Lyeth grabbed a line and leaned over the precipice, unable to tell rock from human in the snow. Someone grabbed her arm and dragged her back.

"Rider, it's not safe here," the woman yelled over the storm. "Go back."

"There's been no sign of him? I'll stay. I'll stay until he's found."

Someone shouted. The woman produced a safety line and hurried away while Lyeth bound herself to the guideline. The snowfall lightened marginally, but not the wind. It shrieked and moaned and sang seductions in her ears. A dusk, a dawn, a doom, a death. Wind scrubbed at her soul and the snow moved in curtains across the broken rock; cold crept into her veins. Nothing seemed real save the wind and the cold and the snow, and they were immutable, ceaseless, time an abstraction of no form and less meaning, she herself a figment of the storm. She watched the climbers and no longer remembered who they were or why she watched them or where she was; the voices in her head disappeared. Storm magic, the Trappers called it, one of the terrifying gifts from Death their god.

"Rider!" The woman shook her roughly. "Rider, we've found him."

It took a moment for her meaning to be clear. "Where?" Lyeth said slowly.

"The bottom." The woman looked away.

Lyeth didn't bother to ask if he was alive.

Another cold infinity passed before they brought Jandi up, wrapped in his talma and bound with ropes. Lyeth rested her hand on the dark bundle and searched the echoing coldness within for some hint of grief. Storm magic. The climbers staggered under Jandi's weight as they carried him from Lord's Walk and into the covered labyrinth of corridors above the Crescent Bathhouse and behind the White Tower, over the stone bridge above Horda's Garden, down the corridors of the main wing to his rooms. The parlor was thick with people; they shied back as the climbers carried Jandi through it to his own bed. Lyeth dropped the curtains, closing them out.

"Rider, we tried—"

"I know," she told the woman flatly. "The guild is grateful. You will be remembered." The words came to her by rote and she barely paid attention to them. "I'll commend you to your lord. Please, go now."

They filed out silently, the last one holding the curtain open for Torwyn. He stood just inside the doorway and looked at her uncertainly.

"Yes," she said calmly. "I'll need a witness." Voices murmured in the outer room as she cut the ropes with her dagger and pulled the talma open.

What remained did not look much like Jandi, or any human thing. The face was battered away, one eye missing and the other hidden under a caul of frozen blood, the teeth broken, much of the hair gone. Torwyn choked and turned away.

"Ah, no," she said quietly. " 'It was like he couldn't see,' " she quoted, " 'hitting things, falling down.' A man blinded, in the blizzard on Lords Walk. Turn again, Lord Steward. Witness this."

He clenched his fists and looked to the bed again. Lyeth peeled the talma from the body, exposing the tatters of clothes, the rips and cuts, skin flayed, bones broken. She put her hands under Jandi's right shoulder and turned the body marginally; the guildmark was intact, including the mole just below the dagger's point, the mole

Jandi, laughing, had called his drop of blood. She traced the tattoo with her fingertip and let the body roll to its back again.

"Lyeth, by the Mother—"

"Look."

She moved the body again to reach Jandi's left hand, wedged between his thigh and the bed. The fingers were broken, palms slashed and gaping, little finger gone. She laid the hand over Jandi's belly and reached into her talma for the wooden box. When she laid the severed finger gently in Jandi's palm, Torwyn stepped back abruptly.

"Not a bad job," she said evenly. "The storm and the fall hid what damage they did to him, except for this." She looked across Jandi's body at her lover, her mind still cold and clear. "In the second year of the Dancing Plague, Raedon of the Alchemists killed his lover Gaen, Alchemist Guildmaster. Of all things these two are sacred in Cherek, the life of a lord and the life of a guildmaster, and when they carried sentence out on Raedon the commons cheered, gathered in the Square of the City in Vantua, come with beer and picnics. It took him seven days to die, the picnics gone, beer gone, cheering gone, and in its place a silent horror. Raedon had the Dancing Plague, but it didn't excuse him. And no guildmaster has died of violence since." She paused, her fingers resting on Jandi's shoulder. "Until now. How much of this did you know? That he'd been taken, yes, or you'd not have summoned me to Syne's rooms. That I could save him, and would if you'd not kept me there? Yes, all of that, I think. What else, Torwyn? This, perhaps? Or this?" She touched Jandi's forehead, took the severed finger, and put it away. Torwyn only shook his head.

She turned from the bed, still lost in storm magic, and lifted the curtain. Faces turned to her, curious, avid, horrified.

"The guildmaster is dead," she told them. "You must notify Vantua."

"The wires are down," someone said apologetically. "When the storm has gone . . ."

She nodded. "The apprentice?"

"Asleep, Rider. He was given a draught."

"I want hot water and cloths." She paused. "Go away. All of you. Now."

They left quickly, jostling each other at the doors. Someone would tell Gambin, if the old man was awake or rational. If he needed to be told. Lyeth went back into Jandi's room and stared at Torwyn.

"Get out."

"Lyeth . . ."

She held the curtain open. He walked slowly around the bed and out of the room, but as he passed her he put his finger to her cheek, then to her lips. She couldn't understand why she tasted salt.


They hadn't let her do this for her father, years ago in that high, cold valley beyond Alanti's borders. The raid had been swift and brutal, Lady Elea's retaliation for a Trapper raid the month before in an outlying village. A different tribe of Trappers, a different squad of shadeen, a different part of the outlands, but it didn't matter. The random attacks and counterattacks were part of a struggle ancient long before Lyeth's birth, and would continue, tribe for village and life for life, long after her death.

She knew they were not yet Trappers, her father and herself. Their tent was pitched always at the edge of camp, their places farthest from the fire, but she tumbled in the deep snow with the Trapper cubs, equal in their games and in their learning, while he hunted with their parents and struggled with the dialect, his smooth, lowland voice never at ease with the harsh consonants and long vowels of the mountains. She spoke both tongues with ease and could not remember a time when she knew one only. She knew they had come up from Cherek, that she had been born there and her mother had died there, and felt no need to learn more. Her history extended no further back than the seasons of the past year, and it seemed sufficient.

The hunting was good that winter. They feasted and sang through the night, praising Death the Giver for their pelts and their food. The men who would carry the pelts to market in Cherek boasted of their success as traders, boasted of the fine food and eager women they would find beyond the Clenyafyds, and the others laughed at them. Her father, flushed with krath and laughter, sat for the first time amid the hunters; he had taken a cave tiger that afternoon, working alone amid the tumbled seracs in the low cirque east of the camp. The tiger's immense, deep black pelt lay in the curing tent, one of the winter's finest gifts; its pungent meat enriched their dinner and they ate it reverently, hoping for a transmigration of the cat's fierce, swift soul. Lyeth, sitting with the cubs, watched her father proudly; he caught her glance and winked at her across the circle of firelight. Tomorrow, it was understood, they would move their tent out of the ring of supply tents and curing tents and into the inner circles of the camp, and in the spring he would marry and become, at last, fully a Trapper, honored at the fires and part of the tribe. And spring would come soon now, these lower valleys turned to slush and wildflowers, but by then the tribe would be far to the north, chasing death and the cold on the mountains at the edge of the world, far from Alanti's dangerous borders. Already she could catch more rabbits than any of her peers, but in the summer her real apprenticeship would begin, high in the mountains for weeks at a time learning to stalk, to trap, to kill. She yearned for it, but even more she yearned to see the most distant peaks and beyond even them. The Trappers said that beyond the Clenyafyds the land tumbled into a great sea the color of a cold green dawn. She dreamed of tasting its water. Now she finished her krath, listening to the jokes. The white-haired Trappers told outrageous stories of the stupidity of the lowlanders and her dark father laughed and topped their tales. The drowsy heat of krath and fire eased her into sleep.

When her father woke her the fire had burned to embers and he smelled of smoke and krath and sex. She held his hand as they walked through the sleeping camp and he hummed under his breath, as he always did when he'd been with a woman.

"Here, mouseling," he said in Cheran, gesturing toward an open space between tents. "Our tent will face the fire and you'll be a Trapper princess with tens of tiger pelts at your feet."

She snorted. "I'll be a hunter," she said in the Trapper tongue. "And I'll catch whales in the northern sea."

He laughed and held their tent flap open for her.

The shadeen came the next morning, as they were breaking camp. It was over swiftly, the harsh crackling of hackbut fire and a rain of bullets through the dawn light, followed by screams and the battle shouts of the shadeen. Her father took a bullet in the chest, a fast kill, dying before he could defend himself, before he saw the yelling shadeen, before he could say goodbye. She stood frozen, unable to believe him dead, while the shadeen screamed into the camp, snowhorses skidding in plumes of snow, swords raised and plunging; one thundered over the side of their collapsed tent and the rage of the god overcame her; she grabbed her father's spear and stood over his body, shouting and jabbing at the shadeen. She wounded two before they overpowered her and dragged her away, still fighting. Someone hit her, hard, and she doubled over, unable to breathe, while they bound her and a huge man took her onto his saddle and turned his horse abruptly from the fight.

"You're lucky you curse in a civilized tongue," he said. "Where did they take you from, child?"

She clamped her lips tight and refused to open them, save to eat, for the next three months. Jandi was patient, Elea amused, and the Master of Apprentices in Vantua Guildhall rolled his eyes and set about civilizing her. And her father lay dead in a cold mountain meadow with a bullet in his chest.

The Trappers would have seen to her father, cleaning his wounds and leaving him in peace on a high rock, silent witness to Death their god. Now Lyeth moved around Jandi's body, tending to him in compliance with Cherek's customs, praying over him to the Trapper god. She stripped him and washed him, remembering panniers of maps and food, his patience only partially disguised by his temper, his ribald jokes, his stubbornness, his warmth. The splintered bones of his face moved under her fingers as she molded them into features that looked, almost, like Jandi. Second father, second teacher, first lover. She dressed him in his best tunic, found his spare talma in the travel chest and spread it over his ruined body, and, lastly, took the patch from her own face and covered his missing eye. His face seemed to float above the black fur. She brushed her fingers across her dry lips and laid them on his, pulled the hood of the talma over his face, put away the wet and bloody cloths, and left the room.

A small fire burned in the parlor grate and Lady Elea sat before it, her hands folded motionless in her lap. Alanti shadeen stood against the walls, hands on sword hilts.

"Lady," Lyeth said, inclining her head.

Elea rose. "They spoke of an accident."

"No accident."

The lady looked at her sharply through eyes rimmed with red. "May I see him?"

Lyeth raised the curtain and stepped back. Elea walked into Jandi's room and stood by the bed while her shadeen crowded the door behind her. Lyeth put her hands in her sleeves; her fingers felt cold against her elbows. Elea moved the talma's hood from Jandi's face and looked at him silently.

"There's no doubt. . . ."

"I saw the guildmark, Lady."

"Ah." She traced the curve of eyebrow above the patch. "In the arms of the Mother," she murmured and bent swiftly to kiss the ruined lips. The shadeen rustled behind her, rising on tiptoe to see. Elea straightened. "Tell me," she said.

Lyeth told her about Syne and Torwyn, about Robin and Janya, about the wind and cold on Lords Walk. She showed Elea Jandi's token, his mutilated hand, the finger resting in its bloody box.

"Who?" Elea said when she was done.

"I don't know, Lady. I'll learn."

"And then?"

Lyeth closed the wooden box and put it back in her talma. "What did you do, Lady, when your father died?"

The lady nodded and pulled the hood gently over Jandi's face.


The storm magic cradled her as she led Elea and Robin up the stairs of Gambin's Tower. The guards at the far door watched them coming and dropped their spears, crossed, to bar the way. Lyeth opened her talma, revealing the full uniform of her guild, the deep black of tunic and breeches hemmed by crimson piping, high supple black boots, the guildmark in gold glowing on her left breast. A guard surreptitiously banged his heel against the door as they approached. Lyeth halted as the door opened and Petras emerged. He closed the door and rested his large hands on his hips, regarding Lyeth calmly.

"Lyeth of the Riders on business of the province to my master, the Lord of Jentesi," she said formally.

Petras frowned and bowed quickly to Elea, standing slightly behind the Rider.

"My Lady. Rider. Lord Gambin's health—"

"Guildright." Lyeth wondered distantly if Petras' hands had touched Jandi's blood; the blunt fingers and square palms seemed tinged with pink light. "Let me in," she said.

Petras' frown deepened. He went inside, returning a moment later with Master Durn. The end of the chamberlain's pigtail was frayed and a stain decorated the collar of his usually immaculate shirt; his hands rose unconsciously to give his pigtail a mighty tug. They, too, were tinged with pink.

"Guildright," Lyeth said before he could protest. "I have it as long as Gambin lives. Shall I make it formal?"

Durn glanced obliquely at Lady Elea. "Guildright doesn't cover you."

Elea inclined her head. "True. I come as witness."

Durn pinched his lips together, shrugged, and flung his pigtail over his shoulder. "I don't like it," he said, opening the door. The guards raised their spears. "The boy stays outside."

"No." They followed him in.

The antechamber was warm and stuffy and no physicians huddled here now. Instead the advisors and retainers of the four heirs crowded the rooms, strictly kept spaces separating each group from the others. Their buzzing conversation halted; some bowed or knelt to Lady Elea, who ignored them. The massive inner doors opened and Lyeth paced through them as though traversing a tunnel in the world, part of but separated from the faces, the smells, the busy undertone of muttered talk. Gambin's bed filled the tunnel's end, his heirs grouped around it; Culdyn Gambini, near his father's pillow, crossed his arms and clasped his elbows with pink-tinged fingers. Syne turned away from him to look at Lyeth; Coreon, leaning against a bedpost, framed his amused expression with a pink hand; Maranta's rings glinted against pink fingers. Then Syne took her hands from her sleeves and it seemed that even she stood bathed in bloody light.

Culdyn jammed his fists against his hips. "Lady Elea." He directed his bow beyond Lyeth. "We're honored, of course, but you have no business here."

"I stand witness for the Rider, and the Rider claims Guildright," Elea replied evenly.

"Guildright!" Maranta almost squeaked the word. "Witness!"

"Quiet," Gambin said sharply from his nest of pillows. "I'm not dead yet. Little bitch, come here."

She stepped around to the head of the bed. Gambin, propped amid white linen, looked pale and sharp-eyed and very much alive. Lyeth dropped to one knee. "My Lord."

Gambin looked over her, beyond Robin's kneeling form, to the Lady Elea, who nodded, the greeting of equal to equal. The old man's lips tilted.

"As witness, Lady?" he said. "Why should my Rider need a witness?"

Lyeth rose. "She is not here to speak, Lord. She is here to listen, and remember."

Gambin's smile broadened. "Little bitch. Are you joining my circus? Do you want my sword?" He paused. "I am sorry about your guildmaster, Rider. The storm eats of its choosing."

"This storm, Lord, was fed." She raised her voice to fill the crowded room. "I come to beg justice for the murder of Jandi, Rider Guildmaster."

"Murder!" Culdyn snorted. "The woman's ranting."

"I have proof," Lyeth said calmly.

"What proof could you—"

"Shut up!" Gambin coughed harshly and Tobi held a white cloth to his lips. He glared at his son before turning to Lyeth. "Tell me, little bitch. Make me believe you."

She told him, her voice flat and clear. She took the small packages from her talma and opened them, laying their contents on the coverlet. The old man touched the guild token and stared distastefully into the bloody box, Maranta stuffed all her fingers into her mouth, Coreon stared at the box, and Syne stared at Culdyn, who looked resolutely across the room, lips tight. She stopped talking; silence and pale pink light filled the room.

"She's making it up," Culdyn said suddenly. "Who would want to kill a guildmaster?"

"I have asked your quiet twice," Gambin said coldly. "I will not ask it again. Get those things away from me."

Lyeth closed the packages and returned them to her pocket.

"You have witnesses?" Gambin said. Lyeth nodded. "Durn," he said, still looking at the Rider. She couldn't read his expression under the mask of his illness. "Durn, this death is not resolved. Begin an investigation—once I am well again."

"My Lord!" Lyeth said. "This is not a game."

"Am I gaming, then? I can't do justice with one foot on the mountain, little bitch. And this is justice for a lord to do, not an underling." His expression resolved to one of malicious amusement. "This lord or the next, it makes little difference."

"This won't sit well in Vantua," Lyeth said angrily, but Maranta jerked away from the wall, hands flying.

"In blood and a blizzard," she cried. "The Circles predicted this, the stars told of this. No! No, the Circles won't accept murder, a guildmaster's murder. I'll have no part of this, I won't condone it. I'll consult—I don't want the sword, do you all hear me? I don't want the sword. I'll leave for Tormea immediately, tomorrow, as soon as the Circles allow, and I—" She stopped, distressed. "Take the sword, blood and all. I deny my claim, do you hear me? In blood and blizzard, why didn't I— I deny this claim. I'm going home." She turned quickly to face Elea. "You heard that, Lady? You'll remember that?"

Elea nodded. Maranta pushed her way from the room; her pet astrologer, looking even more distressed than she, led the rest of her suite after her and the door closed behind them. Coreon raised his face from his hands and let his smothered giggles become laughter.

"Priceless," he said, and laughed again. "The old frog hasn't been that upset in years."

"Shut up." Culdyn glowered at him. "I'll remember that, Coreon."

"And so," said Elea, "will I." Coreon stopped laughing and Lyeth looked away from them to Gambin, barely able to contain her anger.

"A lord will sit justice on this, little bitch," Gambin said. "Swear it, all three of you. Whoever takes the sword sits justice on this guildmaster's death. Swear it to me now."

They gave their oaths, Syne calmly, Coreon as though it were part of the game, Culdyn Gambini with exaggerated formality. Lyeth turned away abruptly.

"Rider! Did I give you permission to leave?"

Lyeth clenched her fists and turned back, too furious to speak. Lord Gambin leaned against his pillows, grinning.

"Go then, little bitch. Go and go and go."

She tapped Robin's shoulder. He scrambled to his feet and followed, Elea behind him, as Lyeth stalked from the room; the crowd in the antechamber shied away and, in the hall, one guard wheeled sharply to stand in her path.

"Rider." His spear dipped. "Captain Petras would speak to you."

"I would not speak to him." She made to go around him.

"But you can't refuse the captain—"

"Watch me." She walked around him and he stepped back to let Elea and Robin pass. The huge wooden doors banged shut behind them.

"Rider," Robin said weakly. "There's someone else."

She turned. Two shadeen stepped from an embrasure and halted a few paces away; Syne's sigil decorated their short cloaks. Elea stepped back, crossing her arms.

"What do you want?" Lyeth demanded.

"Pardon, Rider," the male shadi said apologetically. "Lord Torwyn ordered it. We are to guard you until relieved by our mates."

"We can't disobey," his companion added.

"Elea?"

The Lord of Alanti shrugged. Lyeth pressed her lips together and went swiftly down the stairs.


By midnight Jandi's trunks rested in Lyeth's locked storeroom, the shadeen sat in her parlor on either side of the door, and Robin lay in Emris' bed, having cried himself to sleep. Lyeth cradled a glass of apato between her palms, her mind still swept clean and clear, until her eyes felt gritty and, rising, she nodded to the shadeen and went into her room. The salve stung her eyes and the wrapped brick in her bed had long since cooled; she put on her heavy nightshirt and stood frozen by the bed, listening to the storm, then took Jandi's old token and Emris' mysterious one and hung them around her neck. They felt cold on the skin between her breasts, and the shutters banged and banged again. She thought of wind knocking against the castle walls, battering the fallen stones of Lords Walk, howling outside the room where Jandi lay in state. The images came with a cold clarity, storm victorious and stone tumbling under its assault, cracking and groaning and sliding down to cover her eternally. She put her hand to the bedpost, shuddered, and went into the parlor.

The shadeen looked at her, surprised, and she stared at them until she remembered who they were.

"Rider?" one said uncertainly.

"It's all right," she muttered, lifting the curtain to Emris' room. Robin lay curled into a tight, fetal lump under the quilts. Lyeth remembered who he was, too, and turned to the wardrobe. Emris' clean, dry clothes were piled neatly; she filled her arms with them and carried them back to her room.

A patched tunic, a pair of breeches, leggings tied together in their middles to keep the pairs straight. She sat before her shuttered window, running her hands over the cloth as though between them her fingers and the clothes could rekindle memories, as though a shirt could sing under her touch. She should have taken the extra ten minutes, gone back to the wine shop, told him that she loved him. She should have loved Jandi more, and less critically. She should be able to remember her father's face. Something cracked sharply, wood or stone succumbing to the storm. She shivered, touching the clothes. Emris patted his golden curls and grinned, mincing behind her through the city's streets. Jandi put his arms around the apothecary's shoulders, laughing over some herbal joke. Her father hummed with quiet content, breath puffing white in the cold moonlight of the Trapper camp. The dense, insulating storm magic turned and resettled itself, filling her mind and numbing her emotions, leaving her awake and dry-eyed in a room populated by ghosts.

# SEVEN

# TORWYN

B Y the next morning the wind had shed its erratic wildness and become a steady roar, prying under doors and around windows, heaping snow against walls, talking to itself in shrill, ceaseless voices. Lyeth woke in the dark and listened to it; no supplies from the city would crawl up the ratchet road, no iceboats skim the Tobrin, no shadows float on ground or walls. "Death has eaten the sun," the Trappers would say, spilling krath on the tent floor, a liquid appeasement. Sometimes it even seemed to work.

Someone in the corridor banged on the door and shouted; the two shadeen responded, a clatter of steel on steel and a cacophony of voices. Cursing, she rolled from the bed, wrapped the quilt around her shoulders, and went over the cold rugs into the parlor. The guard must have changed during the night, for these two shadeen were unfamiliar. A woman, the taller of the two, looked over her shoulder at Lyeth, her sword pointed unwaveringly at the door.

"Pardon, Rider," she said. "We're not to admit anyone we don't know—"

"Iceheads," Janya shouted from outside. "I suppose *you* are going to make breakfast, and fill the stove, and—"

"Put your swords up," Lyeth said curtly. "It's my servant." She reached between the shadeen and opened the door. Janya planted her hands on her hips and stared belligerently, her belly filling the doorway.

"Mistress, who are these pigheads? It's past sunup—don't you want breakfast?"

"Mother's sake." Lyeth turned to go back to bed. "What sort of mischief could a woman that pregnant make? And I suppose it's not within your duties to fill the stove, is it?"

"I'll fix that." Janya waddled majestically into the room, glancing at the shadeen scornfully. She had probably spent the night recounting her adventures to a hall full of breathless servants, and looked no worse for wear. Lyeth clambered into the bed, still wrapped in her quilt, and pulled the rest of the bedclothes over her face.

A minute later Janya stormed in.

"Mistress, am I to feed those two also? They want tea and cakes and beer, and I'm not going to fetch it just on *their* say-so."

"Feed them," Lyeth mumbled. She pulled the pillow over her head and the bedclothes over the pillow. Two minutes later Janya was back again.

"Mistress!" She pulled the covers away from Lyeth's head. "They want porridge, too. With butter and honey. And eggs, and meat, and—"

"All right!" Lyeth sat up abruptly, scattering pillows. "Mother Night, there's no sleeping around here, is there? By all means, feed them whatever they want. Feed Robin, too, while you're at it. You might even remember to feed me. Feed the whole fucking castle!" She fought her way free of the quilt. "Did you bring my hot water? Good. And get this icefield warmed up, fast."

Janya, content with her orders, lumbered from the room while Lyeth hopped about pulling on her clothes and cursing the cold. The salve had jelled; she tucked the jar into her pocket to warm it and slapped the already cool water on her face. When she looked in the mirror something was wrong. The patch, of course. She pushed away the image of Jandi's blinded face and found the patch Emris had made for her . . . when? She counted rapidly, her feet on the cold rugs. Six days ago, on that high ledge with the pass behind them and the Tobrin Valley filling with night. She shook her head quickly, not believing it, and took her boots into the parlor to warm by the stove. A shadi stood by the door; another sat on a crate by the fire with a mug of tea in one hand and a cake in the other. Lyeth sat, drawing her feet up, and rubbed at them to warm them.

"Do either of you have names?" she said after a moment's silence.

"I'm Maev of Syne's shadeen," the woman said, and gestured with the cake. "That's Hivis, my partner." Hivis, short, fair, balding, and muscular, tipped his spear.

Robin came in, rubbing his eyes, and held his hands to the woodstove. Janya yelled in the corridor and Hivis opened the door.

"I had to send to Bedwyn for more," Janya announced. "He wasn't happy about it." She took bowls from the cupboard and served porridge. Lyeth looked away. The room seemed to grow smaller each time she looked at it; too damned many people and not enough space. Her neck prickled. Janya offered her the first bowl of porridge but Hivis, moving quickly, lifted it from her hands.

"Pardon, Rider." He took the bowl and, while Lyeth stared, stirred the porridge thoroughly and took a bite. "Lord Torwyn's orders," he said apologetically, his mouth full. He swallowed, paused for a moment as though listening to his body, and gave the bowl to Lyeth. "Quite good."

Lyeth stared at him. "Am I confined here?" she said, dangerously quiet. "Are those Lord Torwyn's orders, to lock me up and drive me crazy?"

The shadeen looked at each other and spread their hands. "No, Rider," Maev said. "We're just to protect you, not let you out of our sight. That's why one of us is a woman, Rider. So one of us will be with you everywhere."

Lyeth stared at her coldly. "Mother forbid that I should be snatched while pissing." She picked up her bowl. "I think we should talk, Lord Torwyn and I." She forced herself to eat the porridge. Hivis, done with breakfast, traded places with Maev, Robin gulped his food, and Janya, glaring at the shadeen, collected the empty bowls and plates, piled them together, and marched toward the door, her hands full.

"Open that up," she demanded of Hivis. He did so, with a look of beleaguered patience. Janya sailed through, dropped the dishes, and screamed. Lyeth rushed to the door, just ahead of Maev.

On the wooden wall across the corridor, pinned to it by a long dagger through its belly, a black cat twitched feebly. Hivis swiftly jerked the dagger free and slit the animal's throat, then turned to the Rider, the dead cat in his hands. Around its neck someone had tied a red ribbon, and from the ribbon dangled a crude drawing of the Riders' guildmark. Lyeth's stomach clenched. Behind her, Robin moaned.

"Get rid of that," Lyeth said curtly, and strode to the woodstove.

Sitting on a packing crate, she began to pull on her boots. Janya, forgetting the shattered crockery, rushed to her and grabbed her arm.

"Mistress, you're going out? You can't leave me here, mistress; they might come again. That's what the cat means—they *are* going to come again."

Robin, pale, stood behind her. "Please, Rider. You can't leave us here alone."

Lyeth, on the verge of sarcasm, saw the fear in their eyes and sighed with exasperation. "All right. You, Hivis, get rid of that thing and stay with them. Maev can come with me—"

"Pardon, Rider," Maev said immediately. "Lord Torwyn ordered us both to guard you, together. We can't split up." She gestured apologetically. "We have our orders."

Hivis, back from disposing of the cat, rubbed his palms against his breeches and nodded. Lyeth frowned at him, her lower lip between her teeth; Janya and Robin huddled together, Robin's arms barely able to reach around Janya's middle. Lyeth's frown smoothed.

"Fine," she said to Maev. "Torwyn orders you, but you're Syne's shadeen, right?"

Maev nodded and Lyeth smiled quickly.

"Good. Robin, fetch your talma. Janya, there's a grey cloak in my room—it should be big enough. Where are your boots?"

"We're going out?" Janya said, alarmed. "Into the storm?"

"Indeed we are." Lyeth pulled the talma over her shoulders. "Go on, woman, fetch your boots. *Now.*"

Janya scuttled from the room while Lyeth checked the pockets of her talma, smiling tightly, and slapped its seams closed.

"Rider, this is going to make things very difficult," Hivis said.

"Too bad. You're to protect me and I'm to protect them. You have orders and I have responsibilities. Robin, stop snuffling and put up your hood. Janya! Hurry up!"

She marched them through the corridor, along the portico, and down the steps. Maev had to support Janya over the slippery steps and the wind launched a determined, steady assault against them, blowing them toward the walls of Scholars Garden. Lyeth angled against it, ducked into the covered pantry walk, and led her cortege into the kitchen, where Bedwyn spun to face them and tossed a cleaver over his shoulder, shrieking. His undercooks scattered.

"By the Father's Mighty Asshole, it's a fucking parade," he

howled. "Get out, get out, there's no damned end to you, is there? Is it any wonder I drink? Out, *out,* damn it, or I'll—I'll—" His arms windmilled as he tried to come up with a sufficiently terrible threat. They hurried from the kitchen.

"Sweet Mother," Janya whispered. "Bedwyn himself, no less. He'll never feed us again."

Lyeth glanced over her shoulder at her parade and stifled the urge to laugh: Hivis' spear towered over his head, Robin's nose was the color of cherries, Maev leaned to one side under Janya's weight, and Janya herself, in her best blue tent and Lyeth's grey cloak, looked like nothing so much as an iceboat under full sail, pregnant with the wind. On impulse, she led them down a narrow access corridor, turned sharply, and drew the parade up the middle of the Great Hall. Forne, in a messy pile of cloth and furs near the fireplace, raised his head from his lute, said, "I knew I was dreaming," and closed his eyes again; someone snickered and one out-province shadi, standing weary guard over a huddle of drunken nobility, laughed outright. Servants fled before them as they climbed the steps beyond the Great Hall. Lyeth paused at the door of Jandi's rooms and looked in.

"Any problems?" she asked the shadeen.

"All quiet, Rider." The shadi captain was one she had met in the barracks hall, one of Elea's white-haired, pale-eyed minions. Lyeth nodded, looking at the covered doorway to Jandi's bedroom, and turned away. The motley parade continued through the maze of corridors behind the Great Hall, past the cattery and the aviary, through the mouldering Hall of Tapestries and up a broad staircase flanked with ancient statues and pots of ceramic trees filled with tiny mechanical birds. Janya stared as though she'd never been here before, and probably, Lyeth thought, hadn't; statues and trees and mechanical birds were not considered stylish by Jentesi's dying lord. The staircase led to a hall lined with shelves and cases, each one loaded with the accumulated knickknackery of generations of Jentesi Lords, and here Lyeth found the three delegates from the Merchants Guild standing before a case of intricately woven ceremonial baskets and talking quietly among themselves. She stopped abruptly, staring at them, and they turned toward her.

"Rider," one said, bowing formally.

"Our sympathy," another said. "We grieve for your loss."

Lyeth turned away rudely and led her parade out of the hall and

onto the covered stone bridge. Janya begged a halt halfway across
and leaned against a wall, panting slightly, her hands pressed to her
belly.

"Robin, hold her other arm. We're almost there."

"Mistress, I think—"

"Save your breath for walking. And next time don't get so fat."
She set off again.

The shadeen at Torwyn's door regarded them with confusion.
Maev and Hivis conferred with them *sotto voce* and with many gestures until Janya grabbed her stomach and groaned loudly; a minute
later they were ushered into the audience chamber. Janya staggered
and Lyeth pressed her firmly onto a small divan.

"Mistress—"

"I know. Don't worry about it."

Robin knelt beside the divan and stared at the collection of sparkling porcelain, mouth agape; a couple of Syne's shadeen smiled
broadly until Maev muttered threats under her breath. Lyeth fumbled the salve jar from her pocket and, ignoring the curious shadeen,
put some in her eyes and wiped her cheeks with her sleeve, settling
Emris' patch over her face. When Syne swept into the room Robin
gasped and Janya tried to rise, but Lyeth put a hand on her shoulder,
stilling her, and didn't bother to bow.

"It's all rather simple, Lady," she said before Syne could speak.
"Torwyn ordered your shadeen to guard me—I presume you know
about that? They're to protect me, it seems, from unspecified evils.
But I have these two to protect, and this morning someone made me
a present of a spitted cat. With my guildmark hanging around its
neck. It makes these two understandably nervous, and I can't leave
them but I won't trail a parade around the castle." She smiled innocently. "So I've brought them here to you. *You* can keep an eye on
them—I already know how good you are at keeping people where
you want them."

Syne put her hands in her sleeves and looked at Lyeth's companions. "Why not dump them on my lord steward?" she said lightly,
her voice on the edge of amusement. "He seems to be behind this,
not me."

"They're your shadeen."

"Ah. Young man," she said to Robin. He scrambled to his feet.
"You were the guildmaster's apprentice, I think."

"Yes, Lady." His eyes started to water. Syne looked beyond him to the miserable, sprawling Janya.

"And this?"

"My servant Janya." Lyeth kept the woman firmly on the divan. "She and Robin were given messages for me yesterday. The ones you kept me from receiving until it was too late."

"And this qualifies them for your protection? I see no danger to them."

"But there is, Lady," Robin interrupted, made bold by fear. "They came yesterday and they threatened us, and they could come again today, Lady, they could hurt us, and if the Rider doesn't help us, we'll be—" He started to cry. "We'll be—"

"Robin, hush." Lyeth fumbled in her talma and gave him a linen handkerchief; it had Torwyn's crest embroidered in a corner. "So you see, Lady, how murder complicates. Will you protect them?"

Syne pursed her lips. "Very well. I'll detail another two to go back and stay with them. Would that, Rider, be acceptable?"

"I'm afraid not, Lady," Lyeth said, and Syne's tiny smile disappeared. "Janya's in labor, and you wouldn't send a laboring woman back through that storm."

"You brought her here—"

"She wasn't in labor when we left," Lyeth said. "And the boy petrifies at the very thought of being alone. Would you send them, Lady, the way of his master?"

"Would you argue morality with me?" Syne said coldly.

"Is that still possible?"

The lady's jaw tightened. "There is an end to my patience, Rider."

"Then treasure it, Lady, for I have gone beyond the end of mine."

Janya groaned with pain and fear.

"Get her out of here," Syne commanded, staring at Lyeth. "Put her in one of the small rooms and find a midwife."

"Mistress," Janya said, pleading.

"You'll be all right." Lyeth didn't look away from Syne. "Robin, stay with her."

Two shadeen gently helped Janya from the room, Robin close behind them. Syne and Lyeth stared hard at each other and the remaining shadeen watched silently.

"I'm not an easy enemy, Rider," the lady said with quiet fury. "I saved your life yesterday."

"Oh, no, Lady. Yesterday you helped kill a guildmaster, but no lives were saved. Today I've put two into your keeping, soon three. See if you can do better by them."

"By Death and hell!" Syne grabbed a vase and smashed it to the floor. "Must I bear this?"

"May I leave?"

The lady stalked into the inner chamber, and Lyeth, as rapidly, left the audience hall. Maev and Hivis hurried to keep up with her.

"An impressive entourage," Elea said, looking around Lyeth's shoulder at the shadeen. "Lady Syne's doing?"

"Torwyn. Syne and I are no longer on speaking terms." Various Alanti shadeen stood or sat around the room, but Laret wasn't among them.

"Yes?" Elea beckoned to a page. "Give them tea and seat them in a corner," she said. "And tell them that I have no designs on the Rider's life or virtue, would you?"

The page took the teapot across the room. Maev and Hivis refused the tea and sat, watching Lyeth and the room warily; even sitting, Maev towered over her stocky companion. Lyeth leaned against the wall by a window and refused tea.

"If I do, the short one will come flying over and drink it for me," she said sourly. "Someone left me a warning this morning. A cat, alive, pinned to my wall with a dagger. And the guild's mark around its neck."

Elea, in the act of seating herself on a bench by the window, paused. "Rather obvious, don't you think? Who did it?"

"Whoever murdered Jandi." She pounded at the wall by her side. *"Why,* Elea? Why murder a guildmaster? It couldn't have been—it's stupid. It's suicidal."

"People do stupid things when they panic." The lady folded her hands in her lap. "I told you that I wouldn't ask what's happening in this castle, and I still mean it. I respect your oath. But if there is anything that you can tell me . . ."

Lyeth pressed her lips together, then sat abruptly beside Elea. "This is not from my lord," she said, quickly and quietly. "I break no trusts." She paused while Elea nodded. "Gambin wants me to pledge to oath to his son Culdyn. Culdyn has tried to bribe me. Neither of them succeeded. I think they snatched Jandi instead of me, that they thought to use him as hostage to my pledge." She beat at her thigh gently with one fist. "Stupid, stupid—even if it worked, they'd have had to kill us both. They couldn't afford to let either of us go."

"As I said, people do stupid things when they panic."

But Lyeth, staring at her fist, pursued a different line of thought. "They snatched Jandi as I was leaving the Rock yesterday. Then they sent someone to my rooms, but I was gone. Janya didn't tell them I was off the Rock—either they have no spies, or their spies are inadequate, or something prevented them from learning where I'd gone. So they sent the guild token to Robin. When I still didn't respond, they sent Jandi's finger. And then they sent again to my rooms, and this time forced Janya to tell them I was off the Rock. And the storm was rising." She looked up at Elea. "They must have thought I wasn't coming back. And they were left with a mutilated guildmaster. So they killed him, because they couldn't think of anything else to do. Because they panicked."

"It's plausible." Elea poured herself a cup of tea; across the room Hivis shifted and sharpened his attention. "Whatever the means, the end remains the same." She made an elaborate show of sipping the tea, and offered the cup to Lyeth. Hivis was halfway across the room when Lyeth shook her head, and the shadi settled into his chair again suspiciously. "Remarkable," Elea murmured. "Do you think I could hire him?"

"Better him than Petras," Lyeth replied. "But you can't hire Petras, can you? Syne wants him." She unclenched her hands. "Lady, you promised once to help me."

"I keep my promises," the Lord of Alanti said calmly. "Rumors spread quickly in this place—I've had four sets of visitors already, come to whisper of a guildmaster's murder." She hesitated. "I don't know if all of them really believe it. It would help if they did."

Lyeth, rising to pace, looked at her. "Who came?"

"Orlsky from Bec, the woman from the Artisans, Riando's observer, and the assistant guildmaster from the Merchants. I fed them all cakes and tea. They seemed to be making the rounds."

"I saw the three merchants," Lyeth said. "In a display hall, just after dawn. They tried to offer condolences."

"Tried?"

"I didn't speak to them. I was in a hurry." She paced away, catching Maev and Hivis staring at her. "They shouldn't be here. It's not right."

"You sound like Jandi," Elea said quietly. "They represent change, and that's what bothers you." She folded her hands in her lap again. "We talked of Merinam the other day, and the treaty with the Trappers, and the trading fleet. If they are all part of our future, then the Merchants are equally part of our future. And," she said firmly, stilling Lyeth's protest, "they may not be a ranking guild now, but they will be one soon."

"We haven't had a new guild in almost a hundred years, when Havister created the Clockmakers. And they were never a ranking guild."

"Neither were the Smiths, until after the war with the Alchemists."

"The Smiths replaced the Alchemists in Vantua Council," Lyeth said curtly. "Who will the Merchants replace?"

The question hung between them for a moment, then Lyeth herself dismissed it, waving her hand sharply. "Seventy years since the murder of a guildmaster, one hundred since a new guild attained rank. Syne said Merinam and the Merchants could lead Cherek into the future. I wonder if, instead, they are just leading us into the past."

Elea canted her head slightly. "You see a connection between them, then? Alchemists and Smiths, Merchants and Merinam and peace with the Trappers?"

"I don't know what I see," Lyeth said angrily. "Every time I seek answers, I'm blocked by more questions. I don't give a damn about Merchants or fleets or Trappers or the future. I want to find Jandi's murderers, I want Gambin to die, I want to get out of Jentesi Province. I want—" She stopped abruptly and turned away from the memory of Emris' face. Wind sang in the silence.

"I think," Elea said slowly, "that I'll instruct my shadeen to expose Jandi's hand. There will be visitors today, come through curiosity or boredom. Jandi's hand should cause talk and speculation, and from that we may learn something." She looked up at the Rider. "Do you have it with you?"

Lyeth reluctantly dipped into her pocket and produced the wooden box. Elea took it from her.

"We are going to drown," Lyeth said bitterly, "of talk and speculation."

"We must begin somewhere. I'll spend the day in the Great Hall, I think. A little warmth, a little companionship, some gossip. Perhaps someone saw Jandi yesterday, perhaps someone heard tell. It would be interesting to learn that."

Lyeth resisted the urge to touch the guild tokens around her neck. "With our highland friend to guard you? I don't see him here."

Elea's lips thinned angrily. "Our highland friend slipped away last night, probably to go gambling again. Or find another bed to share." She rose. "I intend to let his father know about it in detail. And his father can deal with him—after *I've* dealt with him."

"He's not in the shadeen barracks?" Lyeth said, walking beside her toward the door.

"I've not sent to check. I want to give him a chance to come back on his own, first. Then I'll only half-thrash him. But if I have to send to find him, I'll have his hide."

A tiny smile tugged at Lyeth's lips. "I want to go to the barracks anyway. I'll keep an eye out for him."

"It's not funny," Elea said sharply. "If anything happens to that boy, my treaty with the Trappers will disintegrate. Worse, it may start a new round of warfare, and neither I nor they nor Cherek can afford that." She put her hand to the door. "If you see him, Rider . . ."

"I'll grab him by the ear and drag him home." Maev and Hivis, in a quiet clatter of weapons, stood and joined them. "And I'll ask the shadeen. About Jandi. They tend to hear things."

Elea put her hand on the Rider's arm. "Lyeth, don't think of the questions as blocks—they're all important. Any one of the heirs could have killed Jandi. Anyone in this castle. He may have died for reasons we can't begin to know yet." Elea nodded, her pale head almost pure white in the lamplight. "Watch everything, Rider. We don't know yet what we may need."

Lyeth looked down at her a moment, in silence, before gathering her shadeen and walking out.

"I've barred the door," Bedwyn said with satisfaction. The kitchen was warm and humid and smelled of fresh bread. "No more thieves traipsing mud and snow through *my* kitchen. Go out the main doors, like everyone else."

Lyeth turned to go.

"Rider!" Bedwyn pressed something into her hand. "I'm sorry about your guildmaster," he said gruffly. "Get out of here." He marched away, yelling at a pastry chef. Once in the corridor again, Lyeth took the sweet roll from her pocket and gave it to Hivis.

"I suppose you want to taste this, too," she said, walking away before he could reply. Forne was still asleep by the fire. A servant replaced old torches with new ones, another pushed benches into place, cleaning and settling things in expectation of the new day's assault against boredom. Voices murmured behind the curtain guarding the Circles of Infinity. The drunken nobles had disappeared. Lyeth stepped into the yard and the cold made her gasp; wind tossed ice and snow against the castle and no shadeen stood watch now. Guide ropes laced the yard, stiff with cold; Lyeth found one and fought her way along it to the shadeen barracks and into the cloak room, which was stuffed with damp winter gear and smelled vile. While she shook snow from her talma and hung it up, Hivis produced the sweet roll and gave it to her. A bite was missing from the side.

"Oh, hell." She broke the roll in two and handed one piece to each of them. "I'm not hungry anyway."

A Jentesi shadi at the door of the crowded hall told her that Crise was taking reports but would be free soon, and looked at Lyeth's escort curiously.

"How soon?" Lyeth said.

"A few minutes, no more."

As Lyeth nodded her thanks and turned away, the shadi cleared her throat. "Rider? My sympathy . . . about the guildmaster."

It happened often as she made her way down the length of the hall, one shadi or another stopping her with a word of sympathy or condolence, and behind each face a barely hidden well of curiosity. Her hands felt cold and she tucked them into her armpits. Dice rattled sharply in bowls, voices sang or argued, someone by the far window demonstrated holds and escapes, other shadeen mended armor or uniforms. The scent of mulled cider filled the air; Ilen rationed wine during castle-bound times, and only the out-province shadeen muttered complaints. The hall was not cold, but one shadi sat before the fire, huddled in a cloak, the hood pulled far forward. A familiar, delicate hand held a mug of cider. Lyeth stopped behind the figure.

"Why don't you bring me a cup of that," she said conversationally, "and tell me how you plan to avoid being flayed."

Laret jumped up, spilling his cider, and faced her.

"Did she send you?" he said. "Does she know where I am? Is she —is she very angry?"

"She's livid." Lyeth sat on the bench and stretched her boots toward the fire. "She says she'll tell your father, after she's done with you. She says if you come back on your own she'll only half-kill you, but if she has to find you she'll make you very miserable indeed. No, she didn't send me."

Laret moaned and sat beside her. "I *had* to leave, Rider. It was a . . . a debt of honor. Rider, you understand, don't you? I *had* to do it. I didn't have a choice."

"You'll get no sympathy from me, stripling. Hivis, go taste the kettle and bring me some cider. Why didn't you go right back afterward? You must have known that staying away would only make it worse."

Laret, his face miserable, didn't reply. Shaking her head, Lyeth accepted a cup of cider from Hivis and, turning her back to Laret and the fire, blew into the cup and faced the room.

"She'll kill me," Laret muttered.

"She'll kill you permanently if you don't go back," Lyeth replied. Crise made her way across the room toward the fire, looking determined.

"Rider." She dragged a stool forward and sat on it, lacing her fingers together. The shadeen around them fell silent. "They tell me your guildmaster was murdered," she said bluntly. "Is it true?"

Lyeth put her cup down on the bench. "It's true." Silence grew around them.

"They tell me Lord Gambin has refused to investigate it," Crise continued.

"Lord Gambin has ordered an investigation," Lyeth replied. "Once he's well. And he's made his heirs swear to an investigation, once he's dead."

Crise spat into the fire. Lyeth could hear wind prying at the shutters. "Tell me about it," Crise said.

Lyeth's stomach knotted. "To what end, second?"

Crise put her shoulders back. "The lord may play with a guildmaster's death," she said. "But I won't and Ilen won't. This is our castle and our command, and we will do our duty by it."

Lyeth took a deep breath, the knot gone, and nodded. "Will you hear the news?" she said, as she had said countless times before in countless villages and towns and local guildhalls and the manors of land-barons. Into the silence of assent she told the story plainly, as though reciting news of a distant province, layering fact upon event upon action with all emotion pared away. And, in that silence, spread her hands in conclusion and dropped them to her thighs. Laret stirred on the bench beside her.

"No one has left the Rock," Prena said eventually, breaking the quiet. "Not in this storm."

"Maranta says that peace and knowledge will come together," a shadi reported quietly. "She says that death moves through stones, and Jentesi's heir will not be found until the murderers are revealed."

"Maranta's a fool," Crise said, but some of the shadeen made the sign against evil, and Laret twitched again.

"There's a thousand places to hide," a shadi said from the back of the room. "The castle, the holdings—someone could hide in the warrens and not be found for years."

"The Geese have been asking into it," Crise said. "Quietly, but nonetheless . . ."

"What geese?" Laret said. "What warrens?"

Lyeth ignored him. "And you?"

Crise shrugged and raised her voice. "We are not investigating," she said. "Our lord has not ordered it and we can take no action without his consent. Therefore, we do not investigate this death. Openly." She looked around the room. "But we do listen, and we do ask. And we share what we learn."

Lyeth closed her eyes briefly and Hivis refilled her cup.

"Rider?" Grims touched her knee. "We had a death last night. A gardener."

Crise looked at him sharply. "Why wasn't I told?"

"Ilen took the report," Grims said. "The man's wife found him at dawn. He might have been dead for hours." He turned to the Rider. "My captain couldn't tell what killed him. Neither could I. You don't remember the gardener's name, do you?"

"I never learned it," Lyeth said. "But I remember his face. Where is he?"

"In the coldrooms."

Lyeth and Crise exchanged glances, and Crise nodded. "Grims, you'll take us there. The rest of you stay quiet, listen, and do nothing without my consent or Ilen's. Understood?"

The shadeen murmured as the group by the fire rose, Laret with them. Lyeth raised her eyebrows.

"You're coming with us?"

"No." Laret attempted a smile. "You're all discussing murders and I'm worried about a gaming debt. I'll go back to my lady. Before she kills me permanently." He rested his fingers on Lyeth's hand for a moment before turning away.

Crise finished issuing a string of instructions and looked beyond Lyeth to her guards.

"Your nursemaids," she said. "I don't suppose I could order you to stay here, could I? I thought not. All right, then. Lyeth?"

The Rider nodded and followed Crise through the cloak room and into the storm. The world had disappeared save for an icy cable knotted to a ring in the wall. Grims put his hand around the cable and moved forward, a shadow in the blizzard; darker shadows loomed on either side of the Neck and retreated as they fought their way into and through the second yard, past the invisible quarters of the Guards, and into the relatively protected confines of the Scholars Garden, changing guide cables as needed, fighting to stay upright in the ice and moving snow. Three of them had to force open a wooden door in the castle wall; once within the deserted hallway, three had to force it closed again. Maev and Hivis crowded close to her while Grims lit torches; just beyond the hallway, steps spiraled into darkness. Lyeth shoved her hands into her pockets. Surely the storms of her childhood had been as bad or worse than this one, and not left her shivering. Hivis took one of the torches and Grims led the way down, followed by Crise, then Lyeth and Maev, Hivis in the rear. Lyeth clenched her teeth, feeling as though, in a portion of a second, she had stepped from the real world to one much older, much darker, and totally strange.

Their breath puffed clouds against the damp moss on the stone walls; rock seemed to move in torchlight, crouched and turned and shifted, a malevolent presence sprung from the roots of the world. Reptiles, Lyeth thought, burrowing, tunneling, fixing space in stone long before the first human reached Jentesi Rock. Crise cleared her throat, and Lyeth, startled, almost missed the next step.

"An outer warren," Crise said quietly. "There's another entrance near the Great Hall, for the physicians' use."

"And a third one for bodies," said Grims. "There are other warrens and other ways into them. The Geese know about them."

Lyeth glanced at Crise's head below her. "Whose bodies?"

"Castle dead." After a moment she added, "The Geese have their own coldrooms."

Silence, stones, and reptiles; stairs curled into darkness below and darkness above, a stone serpent, a fist curled loosely but ready to clench. People found bones in rock, old bones, bones turned to rock themselves. Shoulders tensed, belly tensed, she forgot the painful chill in her hands. Jentesi's noble dead lay under a thin mantle of soil in the Garden of the Lady, filling niches hacked in the rock, bones in rock, silence, stones, and reptiles. Coffined in the rock. She forced herself to breathe.

Pale yellow light appeared on the steps below and Grims led them into a dimly lit corridor; some of Lyeth's tension dissipated. Grims and Hivis tucked their torches into wall brackets and Maev, hands moving under the protection of her cloak, signed against evil.

The coldroom lay deep in rock where even the heat of summer could not touch it; stone slabs protruded from the rock, leaving narrow corridors between the rows. Lyeth looked at the two covered slabs with interest as Grims walked to one and, touching the cloth gingerly with his gloved fingertips, pulled it back. Lyeth looked at the gardener who had knelt, cringing, in Jandi's room the day before, and took a deep breath. Here was only simple, mortal death, free of stone and reptile. She pulled the cloth aside and tossed it to the floor.

"Is it . . . ?" Crise said.

"Yes."

All four shadeen retreated hastily as she took off her gloves and put her hands on the body. No obvious injuries, no obvious wounds; she turned the body over. No bruises on back or spine; the intense cold of the room had kept the gardener's blood from settling completely and his skin was relatively free of marks. An old scar along the shin, another on the right shoulder, his hands calloused and decorated with the evidence of battles with thornbushes and roses. His face was peaceful. She took his head in her hands and, following a hunch, examined his neck, finding what she looked for under his left ear, very tiny and very clear. In sleep, done quickly, it was a merciful death. She stood back, rubbing her hands against the sides of her breeches, feeling the cold again. A debt of honor, Laret had said. And he'd been gambling with Coreon. It didn't make sense. She traced the sign of Death on the gardener's chest and covered him again.

"Can we leave now?" Hivis said unhappily. "This isn't a good place to be."

Lyeth silently and fervently agreed with him. She pulled her gloves on and masked her expression. "Grims, who is the other one?"

"A laundress, died last night." Grims was already moving down the corridor. "The wasting sickness, I think. She'll be buried when the storm lets up—she'll have more company by then." He led them away from the spiral stairs, further up the lit corridor. Maev and Hivis dropped behind and Crise, at Lyeth's side, looked at her quizzically.

"What killed him?" she said.

Lyeth shook herself out of thought and, glancing at the shadi, considered. If she told the truth it would be the equivalent of saying a plague was loose in Jentesi Castle—and what of Elea's treaty then? Too much to consider, between one step and the next in a subterranean corridor. She shrugged and said, "I don't think the Geese killed him; assassination isn't their style. But he was killed. What's this?"

Crise stared at her a moment before following her gesture. "Physician's waiting area." Within the room, benches and tables rested on faded rugs. "Lyeth—"

"And these?" She nodded toward a row of closed doors.

"Old rooms, old corridors. Some are blocked, some lead to earthfalls, old warrens, other stuff."

Lyeth put her hand to a door and pushed. It opened with an unholy protest of rusty hinges; dank air spilled into the corridor, making the torches waver. Hivis, Maev, and Grims signed themselves fervently but only Grims moved back. Beyond the door a slanting corridor reached into darkness, its floor covered with dust. Lyeth tugged the door closed. "Where do they lead?"

"Dungeons, storage rooms, one part of the castle or another. They're not used anymore." She paused, hands buried deep in her cloak. "They may look evil, but they're probably not."

"Probably?" Lyeth echoed.

"I'm second in command," Crise replied. "I sign myself so others can't see it." The corridor turned and they followed it. "Lyeth. The gardener—"

"Crise. Don't." They both stopped, facing each other. Lyeth chewed on her lip. "When I know positively, I'll tell you. But I can't now, Crise."

The shadi's expression darkened. "You can't afford to throw away my help," she said finally. "Or Ilen's."

Lyeth nodded, acknowledging the threat. Ahead and behind them the shadeen fidgeted against the cold. Lyeth touched the guild tokens through her shirt. "I need your trust," she said finally. "And I have no coin for it yet. If I'm wrong, Crise, if I'm even a little bit wrong—" She put her hand on the second's shoulder. "Give me a day, Crise. But don't ask me to risk this now. Please."

"It's truly that important?"

"I swear it," Lyeth said. They stared at each other a moment longer, then turned together and walked toward Grims. He looked relieved.

"One day," Crise said. "But one day only." They ascended a flight of steps in silence. The faint sound of voices and music came from the far end of the corridor.

"Lyeth? Where's the boy?"

"I took him into Jentesi-on-River yesterday." Lyeth stared at the wooden door ahead. "I should have taken the guildmaster and left the boy."

"You should have taken them both. At least the child is safe." She paused. "Ilen thinks there may be something else about his parents, but hasn't been able to find out. He's still asking."

"It's probably not important," Lyeth said bitterly. "People live and people die, and in this province it's hard to tell why." She put her hand to the door, thinking about Emris and Joleda and the storm while Crise muttered something in farewell and took Grims with her down a separate corridor.

"Rider," Maev said. Lyeth nodded and went through the door, slamming her own mental doors on the image of a boy and an old woman in the snow.

The Great Hall boomed with talk and movement, with the cacophony of competing musicians and the glaring heat of the fireplaces. Lyeth loosened her talma. Extra trestle tables had been set along one wall and Bedwyn's staff fussed around them, laying out platters of meat, baskets of fruit, great quivering masses of jellies, loaves of hot bread, huge pots filled with soups and stews and sauces. The scent reached deliciously through the room. Lyeth saw Elea moving toward the tables and stopped, suddenly uncertain.

"Lunch," Hivis said with feeling.

Lyeth settled her shoulders. "Lunch, indeed," she replied, making her way forward. A meal would serve as well as anything else to buy her time to think. "Do you propose to taste all that?" She grabbed a trencher. "Taste my food here and you'll just look foolish."

"It might not be a bad idea." Elea smiled placidly at her. "If nothing else, it would let people know what not to try."

"How thoughtful of us." Lyeth made room and Maev handed Lady Elea a plate. She took it and inspected the table.

"What's this?"

"One of Master Bedwyn's specialties," Lyeth told her. "Filleted mutton wrapped about an herbed stuffing, covered with egg pastry, and baked. Or you might try this, Lady. Raw marinated fish. Bedwyn spent a year of his apprenticeship in Teneleh, where they taught him to do various ignoble things to uncooked seafood. The first time he made this Gambin almost had him cooked in his own ovens. It's quite good, though. I intend to eat a lot of it." Hivis looked distressed and she smiled maliciously. "Ah, rye noodles in green sauce, and very spicy. Some of that, certainly, and you might want to try these, Lady. Pickled lizards, cleaned and boned, in pepper sauce and bitter cream. And snails in oil, and raw greens in vinegar, and sweetbreads stuffed with tongue." She looked at her trencher with satisfaction. "Enough for the first pass. Perhaps I can find some rat's milk to wash it down with."

Elea shook her head. "Rider, you should be ashamed. Pickled lizards, indeed."

"It's true, Lady," Hivis said miserably. "The raw fish and snails, too. But the rat's milk is a damned lie."

Lyeth looked indignant. "Are you in Master Bedwyn's confidence? Do you know what the supply boats bring? Are you asked to procure delicacies here and there around the province? Rat's milk cheese is a delicacy from Lorat, where they have rat ranches and breed them specially, and small children milk them every day. The cream, I'm told, is heavenly." She turned away, looking for a place to sit.

"Lady," Hivis said, pleading, "she is making it up, isn't she?"

"How should I know?" Elea replied serenely. "I'm not in Master Bedwyn's confidence either." She sat beside Lyeth, and Hivis, looking pained, handed his own plate to Maev and took Lyeth's from her.

"Mother's sake!" Lyeth grabbed it back.

"Please, Rider. Believe me, I don't want to do this either, but Lord Torwyn ordered it." He took the plate again.

Lyeth cursed and watched as Hivis took one careful bite each of fish, noodles (they made his eyes water), lizard, snails, sweetbreads, and greens. He then gulped from Lyeth's cup, blessedly free of rat's milk, and sat quite still, clutching the plate in his broad, freckled hands.

"The problem is," he complained, "that if I do get sick I won't know whether it's from poison or all this—this horrible stuff you've put on your plate."

Maev, contentedly eating raw fish, took the plate from him. "If it doesn't come from a cow and isn't overcooked," she said, handing the plate to Lyeth, "he won't eat it."

"And we won't be relieved until after supper," he mourned. He took his own plate from Maev and began eating morosely.

Lyeth ate a snail and looked at Elea and beyond her. No one lounged nearby and the uproar effectively masked their voices. The lady ate neatly with knife and fingers, blue eyes gazing around the room, and said, "Was your morning fruitful?"

Lyeth stared at the empty minstrel's gallery, remembering Crise's words. She couldn't afford to throw away Elea's help either, despite Laret and the small, clear mark on the gardener's neck. And by the same token, she could not afford to solicit it. She swallowed and told the lady about her visit to the barracks, omitting any mention of the young Trapper, and told of her visit to the coldroom. "Definitely the same man who saw Jandi," she concluded. "And just as definitely dead."

"Ah. And what killed him?"

"I don't know," Lyeth said. Elea glanced at her sharply. "Yet. The shadeen are investigating Jandi's death, but only informally. They can't do anything else without the lord's consent." She speared a pickled lizard with her dagger. "And you, Lady? What news?"

Elea sipped her wine, looking at Lyeth over the gilded rim of the cup. "I've spent the day sitting and listening," she said finally. "An interesting, if somewhat tiring, exercise. And Forne is unbearable. I've heard every conceivable theory, including one that the guildmaster simply got drunk and wandered off in the storm, and you're being uncommonly stupid in claiming he was murdered. I think the word 'hysterical' was used." She paused but Lyeth remained silent. "That seems to be Culdyn's official position," Elea continued. "With Coreon indicating that he believes it but declining to say so openly. No one finds the theory credible, especially if they've seen Jandi's body. Syne has yet to be heard from, or seen. It does her little good, this absence. Maranta has spent the morning with her astrologer and her device, consulting the heavens. You'll be happy to know that the cosmos is entirely on her side and promises her a long life and respect if she returns to Tormea as soon as possible. And the Circles say," Elea added, "that Jandi's murderer will be found before Lord Gambin dies."

"The stars say?"

"The stars. The weather seers say the storm may blow past by tomorrow but nobody believes them. No one admits to seeing Jandi yesterday. Gambin's condition worsened during the night; they say he slides in and out of coma and has trouble remembering who people are."

"That I don't believe. The old bastard's corpse will be alert and evil, and planning to take over the mountain from Death."

Elea finished her wine. "Torwyn was here for a few hours this morning." She hesitated. "I didn't speak to him. Your guard and who orders them seem common knowledge. Forne says the steward is thinking with his prick."

"I don't care what Forne says," Lyeth said. "If Torwyn makes a fool of himself it is no care of mine. What else?"

Elea looked at the Rider speculatively. "Captain Petras has been seeking you."

Lyeth put her cup down. "Why?"

"I don't know. You might want to let him find you."

Lyeth shook her head. "And Jandi?"

"Has had a number of visitors this morning, all inquisitive," Elea said grimly. "My captain has become quite adept at pulling Jandi's finger from the air. I don't know whether it has done any good, but I intend to let it continue. No one has asked me to stop yet."

"Oh? You expect that?"

"Perhaps. It will be interesting to see who makes the request." The Lord of Alanti stood, brushing small creases from her tunic.

"Lady." Lyeth handed her empty plate to Maev. "How goes your treaty?"

Elea moved her shoulders. "It's difficult to tell. Maranta likes the idea, but she's relinquished her claim to the sword. Coreon treats it as a joke. Syne refuses to discuss it, and Culdyn thinks it a fine idea."

"Culdyn would be bugger-boy to Death if he thought it would help him," Lyeth said viciously. She finished her wine. "And our highland friend?"

"Still missing." Lyeth looked surprised. "I've left instructions in my rooms that he's to be sent to me. So far he hasn't appeared. He wasn't in the barracks, I take it."

Lyeth shrugged. Elea gestured and went across the hall. The Rider signaled a passing servant for more wine and, having obtained it and watched Hivis take his obligatory sip, sat back and watched Elea speculatively. She stood talking with the second son of Lord Dorne and a thin, dark woman from Koyae, down by the shores of Mother Ocean; the representative from the Captains Guild in Vantua came to join them. Come to watch the passing of the sword, to watch power thrive or power collapse. Come to eat Gambin's food and drink Gambin's wine and watch the antics of Gambin's fat minstrel. How much, Lyeth wondered, did the Lord of Alanti want her treaty with the Trappers? Enough to come, and talk, and persuade. Enough to support whoever would support her. Enough to murder a guildmaster? She dismissed the thought quickly. Not Elea. Not Jandi. Across the room, a tinkle of bells announced the workings of Maranta's device; people nearby turned to watch it. Besides, she thought, only Culdyn offered his support, and Laret had not gamed with Culdyn, but with Coreon. She searched the room for him, finding him standing with the young Lord of Poderi, watching the spinning of the Circles of Infinity. He said something to the Lord and she giggled, her gaze resting adoringly on Coreon's laughing face. It would make a good match, Lyeth thought distantly. He handsome, she rich, Poderi a great, flat, wealthy province near enough to Vantua to keep Coreon entertained. But he had gambled with Laret and a gardener was dead; Syne thought the contest between her brother and herself, but Coreon's plans could not be that easily dismissed. His baronies lay through the Clenyafyd foothills, poor holdings of small farms, woodlots, some hunting, some fishing. Meager tax revenues, even if he bled them dry. His mother murdered, his father dead these twelve years of the wasting sickness, he himself growing up in the shadow of his richer cousins, knowing that his claim to Jentesi's sword, through his mother, was just as good as theirs through Gambin. If his ambition were to govern Jentesi, she thought, he could concoct some scheme to assure it. He was not a stupid man. And he had gambled with a Trapper.

Maranta's minstrel began a love song, voice pure and ethereal above the noise; servants cleared plates from tables and laid down wrestling mats. Lyeth stared at them abstractedly as men stripped off their shirts. Laret had killed the gardener. Her conviction was as strong as though she'd seen it herself, as strong as her conviction that the young Trapper had nothing to do with the guildmaster's death. Laret had lost at dice and paid his debt with silence and a shayka, the evil little Trapper weapon that killed with only the smallest of marks, invisible if one didn't know where to look. Only one man in her tribe had had one, and showed it to her father one night when they both thought her asleep. A rare weapon even in the outlands. Trapper magic. Laret's brilliant smile appeared before her and she turned her head from it.

Hivis, sitting on the floor at her feet, took a block from the wood-box and began whittling. People grew louder as their boredom increased, singing, playing knife-throwing games against the walls— they had taken the tapestries down for the purpose—yelling encouragement at the wrestlers, arguing over dice. Gowns and tunics swirled across the hall, eddied, reformed. The group before Maranta's device murmured and multicolored points of light decorated the ceiling and walls above them, turning in time to the singing of tiny bells. Hivis' block of wood took on the features of the Father under his knife; Maev, lounging against the bench on Lyeth's other side, stared at the far end of the room. They both seemed abstracted and at ease, but when Lyeth moved they swiveled quickly to face her.

"The air is turning sour," she muttered. "Come be my nursemaids somewhere else."

Hivis sheathed his knife and, regretfully, tossed his carving into the fire. It glared at them as they rose, its hawk nose and large almond eyes picked out in light before the flames devoured it. Lyeth entertained a vision of Laret poking his way back to Elea's quarters, dawdling like a child, hoping to put off his lord's wrath, hoping that the payment of his gaming debt would remain a secret. She offered a quick prayer that the vision was true; she would give him another hour to arrive, then go in search of him herself. And if he didn't come . . . She pushed the thought away as they left the Great Hall. One of Maranta's portable clocks clanged, announcing the hour. Unruffled and impeccable, Menwyn paced down the stairs from Gambin's Tower and along the corridor to Durn's chamber. Lyeth stood back to let him pass.

The aviary, above and behind the Great Hall, was dark and silent, the windows shuttered tight against the storm. The cattery, in contrast, seethed with cats plain and dappled, calico and striped, presided over by one teal-blue patriarch who lay atop a lintel, chin on paws, and watched the progress of Lyeth and her guards with unwinking yellow eyes. Lyeth found the keeper and asked, but he had seen no one come that morning, and certainly had seen no one, cat in hand, leave again. Hivis sneezed, apologized, sneezed again, apologized again, then sneezed continuously until they left the suite and, cat hair floating behind them, climbed another set of stairs, and yet another, to emerge on a broad stoa doubly protected by the rock overhang, barely a man's length overhead, and its own stout ceiling and triple row of columns. Cold and wind snatched at their breaths and there was nothing to see save the dark storm, so they left after a short time, the two shadeen obediently trailing Lyeth as she walked through the castle, counting minutes in her mind.

Below the stone bridge, Horda's Garden was a blanket of grey snow visible briefly as the storm lifted and settled itself again. The shadeen at Torwyn's door admitted her readily and told her that their lady was at supper. She gestured, dismissing it.

"My servant Janya?"

Maev and the shadi captain spoke for a moment, and Maev led the Rider into the servants' quarters. Iron and glass lanterns burned along the carpeted hallway and the air was warm, decorated with distant voices raised in cheerful argument. Maev opened a door, nodded toward the bed, and retreated.

Janya lay in a nest of blankets and pillows, deeply asleep. The skin under her eyes was dark and her uncombed hair straggled across her shoulders and along the bright coverlet. Lyeth touched the coverlet and stepped back. A large basket rested on a table by the fireplace and within, swathed in clean linen, two wrinkled red infants slept. No wonder she got so fat, Lyeth thought, and touched a small hand gently. The baby made sucking noises in its sleep.

"Mistress?"

She turned. The midwife stood in the doorway, her arms full of clothes. "You're the Rider, then," the woman said, dumping the clothes on a settle. "She called for you a few times."

"Is she all right? Was it hard?"

"Hard? Humph. Like spitting out apple seeds. Five hours from start to finish. Had a bit of trouble with the boy, though, had to blow into him some, but he came around and no worse for it." She flipped the covers back and turned the babies over with professional competence. A boy, a girl. "Never lost one yet," she said with pride.

"They're lovely," Lyeth said, for politeness' sake. She'd never found newborns particularly appealing. Fumbling in her pocket, she pulled out a handful of coins from which she abstracted four gold high-marks and gave them to the midwife. "Thank you."

"Thank *you,* mistress." The coins disappeared into the woman's capacious skirts. "Do you want me to wake her?"

"No. Do you know where Robin is, the boy?"

"Asleep next door." The midwife sniffed, covering the children again. "You'd think him the father, pacing and worrying and lurking at the door, for all he's too young to father anything. Wore himself out more than she did."

"Let them both sleep, then." She looked at the infants again and left, the midwife bobbing a curtsey behind her. In the audience chamber Hivis turned from a group of grinning shadeen and came over to her. His shoulders drooped.

"We're to stay with you until nightfall," he said. "We'll be relieved at bedtime."

"Wonderful. I'll have eels for supper. Where's Maev?"

"Outside, talking with—"

"Good." Lyeth moved quickly toward the door, unwilling to chance a meeting with Syne. Hivis trailed after her.

"Good night, nanny," one of his companions whispered loudly. Hivis ignored it.

It's time, Lyeth thought, and stood momentarily paralyzed outside Syne's door. Maev, joining them, looked at her strangely and Lyeth turned, pursued by need and resisted by fear, to lead the way to Elea's rooms.

The lord's chamber servant, a man with greying hair and a thick Northern accent, at first didn't understand what she wanted and then shook his head, his expression disapproving.

"Not since dawn," he said. "Comes in, he goes right to Lady Elea." He nodded, crossing his arms. "Wastrel," he said. "Scapmullion. He'll see, when he comes. Not right to disobey the lady."

"Scapmullion?" Lyeth said blankly. The chamber servant, scowling, closed the door. She stared at it, arms wrapped around her middle. Tell Elea? Elea wanted a treaty. Ilen, Crise? That a Trapper was loose on the Rock? Petras? No. Syne, Culdyn, Coreon, Maranta. She shivered. A thousand places to hide. Laret's smile. A child, just a child. You'll stay for my son. Turn the witch-hunters loose to look for him, they'd tear that slight body to rags. You'll regret this. Of no interest or import. Smoke and krath and sex. Keep this until you come for me. A surgical procedure. The apato's excellent. Trapper magic. Not so easily spared. After my death. Little bitch. And go and go and go—

*"Rider!"* Hands shook her again. She focused suddenly on Maev's face. "Rider, are you all right?"

Storm magic. She turned quickly and almost ran down the hallway, the shadeen close behind, voices raging in her head. You can't leave us here. When you come for me. The storm would clean her, take her, scrub her soul again. Her talma billowed as she ran, and the shadeen, saving their breaths, strove to keep up with her. Dispense with the formalities. How silently you walk. Enclosed stairs curved along the outer wall of the White Tower; she plunged down them, hesitated at the covered archway, and ran into the storm.

The image floating in her mind was of Lords Walk, distant and malevolent, where the wind could take her and clean her mind. But the storm itself rejected her, battering and pushing and almost lifting her from her feet, shoving her back toward the castle. Then Hivis grabbed her left arm and Maev her right, and thus linked the three stumbled and slid between the pointed arms of the Crescent Bathhouse. The outer doors opened and they fell into the antechamber. She leaned against the wall, panting, to discover that the voices in her head had gone away, leaving an echoing silence in their wake.

"Lord Torwyn said," Maev told her when she'd caught her breath, "we were to keep other people from killing you. He didn't say anything about you killing yourself."

Lyeth closed her eyes. "I wasn't planning to." She straightened and pushed through the inner doors. Steam billowed wildly around them and around the four shadeen by the bath keeper's cuddy. They wore Torwyn's colors and one of them, at a gesture from his captain, walked rapidly down the hallway.

"Mistress?" the captain said, stepping forward.

"There's a tunnel," Lyeth said. "Back to the castle. Do you know where it is?"

"No, mistress. You'd best ask the bath keeper. She'll be back soon."

Lyeth nodded and faced the mosaics, thinking that the storm could have killed her, and thinking that she didn't know if she cared. She clasped her elbows in her palms and pushed her arms hard against her breasts. The guild tokens bit into her skin.

"Rider."

She turned to face the captain. "Lord Torwyn bathes," he explained. "He requests your company." When she didn't answer, he said, "Your shadeen can wait with us."

It couldn't make a difference, she thought, releasing her arms. "All right. Hivis, do you want to come taste the bathwater?"

Hivis turned red. Maev settled herself against a wall, already deep in conversation with a colleague, and Lyeth walked silently down the hall, by habit shedding her clothes, bathing, wrapping herself in a red robe. It was too large by far; she belted it tightly and tucked some of its front under the belt. The bath keeper stuck her head in briefly, grunted, and padded away again. The pool room was lit only in one corner, the birds silent, and the storm sounded as though it blew through a different universe. She put her hands to the leaves and, pushing them aside, stepped through them to the pool.

He sat on the marble slab, a flagon at his feet and a stemmed glass between his fingers, and didn't look up as she sat across from him.

"You wanted to see me?"

He shook his head without looking up. "It's quiet in here. And private. I thought you might need that." When she didn't reply he said without moving, "I'll find another pool."

"Keep your pool. And call off your shadeen."

"No." The wineglass glittered between his fingers. "You hate it and Syne hates it," he said. "But I would not see you dead."

She let the words fall into silence, and when he still didn't look at her, she said, "Who made Jandi die?"

Torwyn looked up. "I don't know. Not positively."

"Tell me about it."

The glass moved; he watched pale wine slide from side to side. "Syne had someone watching his rooms. The watcher saw Jandi and the messenger leave, and she followed them to one of the old doors near the coldrooms. They went inside and the door was locked. She waited for a while, then went back to her post. The first messenger came to Jandi's boy. The watcher reported to Syne. That's when we decided to . . . snatch you."

"And keep me until Jandi was dead?"

"Gods, Lyeth, we never expected— When we realized what was happening, we thought they'd just keep him for a while and then let him go. They could blindfold him; he'd never know who they were, and when you gave them what they wanted they'd release him. Even if you didn't give them what they wanted—I swear it, Lyeth, we never expected that they'd harm a guildmaster. We didn't think anyone would be that insane."

"We, or you?" He didn't answer. "Where is the watcher?"

"I don't know. She never came back."

"The gardener was one of Syne's people?"

"No," Torwyn said bitterly. "The gardener was accidental; his coming to my rooms was accidental. Syne's watchers learned nothing at all."

"He's dead," she said. "The gardener. He was killed last night, or perhaps early this morning." Torwyn looked at her as she said, "And I know who killed him, and I think I know who arranged to have him killed. And there's not a soul on this Rock that I trust to tell it to."

He met her gaze across the water. "No one?"

"Do you ever tire of it?" she said. "One death after another, just so someone can play at God in Jentesi Province. Syne, Culdyn, Coreon." She closed her eyes, watching the red darkness behind her lids. "Have you thought," she said quietly, "that it might even be Syne?"

"Is it?"

She didn't answer, and after a moment of silence she looked at him. He sat with his elbows braced against his knees, forehead in the palms of his hands.

"She wants power," he said finally. "She's a Gambini. But not enough to kill for it, Lyeth."

"You believe that?"

"Yes," he said simply. "What else is there to believe in?" He braced his shoulders. "Who is it? Lyeth, can't you even trust *me?*"

She looked at him and beyond him to a pale yellow flower. Its petals curved extravagantly over themselves, exposing the flower's deep scarlet heart. "I hardly know you anymore," she said. "You used to be one of my answers, and now you're another part of the problem, a part I don't understand. No."

He spread his hands. "What choice do you leave me? I can tell you that I love you. And I do. And you'll see it as a bribe. I could repudiate my lady, and you'd see it as a lie. You would be right. I could walk away, abandon you, but I can't do that. I could dismiss your guard; you would like that and Syne would like that, and I wouldn't be able to breathe for fear." He picked up the glass and flagon and stood. "Keep your confidence, then. If I can only earn your trust by not asking for it, then I will not ask for it. And you may see that as you please." He put his hand to the screen of leaves.

"Torwyn." She wet her lips, watching his back. "Give me some wine."

He came around to her slowly, holding out the glass. She took it and watched as he filled it with wine. He didn't look at her and kept his face stiffly expressionless. She wet her lips again.

"There's a shadi," she said unevenly. "In Alanti's retinue. His name is Laret. He's very young and very fair. I need to talk to him. But he's disappeared."

Torwyn watched her silently. A little of the wine slopped out of the glass.

"I didn't ask for this confidence," he said.

"What choice," she said bitterly, "do you leave me?"

"Lyeth." He opened his arms as though to gesture and she went into them immediately, holding tight to his shoulders, and began helplessly to cry.

# EIGHT

# GAMBIN

SILENCE woke her, a profound quiet that seemed to fill the world. Torwyn mumbled in his sleep as she rolled from the bed and padded across the large chamber to the window. The fire in the grate had burned to a bed of sullen orange embers. She pulled back the heavy curtains and pushed the shutters open. New snow lay over the castle, gleaming in the moonlight, black with shadows; beyond the lip of the overhang a skyful of stars stretched to the horizon. She closed the window and went back to bed. Torwyn mumbled again, wrapping himself around her, and she settled into his warmth.

When she next woke it was to the almost-darkness before dawn and the sound of quiet footsteps in the outer room. Torwyn slept with his temple pressed to her shoulder; she traced the lines of his mouth and eyes with her fingertip and, waking, he put his arms around her.

"You're not going yet," he said sleepily.

"I have to." She laid her finger over his mouth. "The storm's over. I need fresh clothes. It's dawn."

"No." He pressed his palm over her body. "Stay with me. How will I find you, if we catch this Alanti shadi of yours?"

Lyeth smiled and kissed his ear. Last night, after they left the bathhouse, he had quietly set his own small network of spies and his own shadeen, not Syne's, to find the missing shadi. Reports had come in through the evening as she sat with Torwyn in his private chambers, safe from both Syne and the storm. By the time they went to bed the boy was still not found and Torwyn, true to his word, did not press her for details, merely filled the evening with anecdote and music and a quiet, undemanding attention which she finally recognized for what it was and accepted, wearily, without comment. Now, in the blessed silence of the morning and the clarity of her mind, she laughed and said, "If your spies can find one missing shadi in Jentesi Castle, surely they'll be able to find me." She turned to look down at him, leaning on one elbow. "Torwyn? What will you do when I leave?"

"Go back to sleep?" He took a hank of her hair and made a moustache with it, layering it over his own copper beard.

"Be serious. When Gambin dies I take the Water Road to Vantua. Today perhaps, or tomorrow. What you said last night—"

"Doesn't change." He put his hands under his head. "I don't know. I suppose it depends on you."

She moved her head, her hair slipping away from his face. "I won't come back to Jentesi," she said.

"Not even as my Rider?" he said lightly, but his expression was not light at all.

"No."

"Or as my lady?"

She let the question fall into silence. A bird called from the Garden of the Lady and when its echoes, too, were gone she said carefully, "It would not be a good alliance, my Lord. Your family has better hopes than marriage to a Rider without land, without wealth, without standing. I would bring you nothing but myself."

"It is sufficient."

"For you, perhaps. But not for your baronies. And I am a Rider, Torwyn. I need distances and mountains and new places to go." She put her head on his chest. "I wouldn't do well locked to a castle or a barony. Especially in Jentesi Province."

The clatter from the neighboring room increased and died again, and Torwyn said, "You can't say it to me, can you?"

"No," she said quickly. "What good would it do? I won't come back to Jentesi and you won't follow me."

"Have you asked Maranta's stars," he said, "that you can tell the future? I want to know, Lyeth."

"Why? Look what has happened to the other people I love." She started to roll away but he put his arms around her, turning them both so that he lay half atop her.

"Then give me one more hour, Lady Rider," he said. "Since you leave today, perhaps. Or tomorrow. And we can make a promise not to speak of Syne or Gambin, of your work or mine." A smile touched the corners of his mouth. "Will you be foolish with me, Rider?"

"Yes."

"This way, perhaps? Or this?"

"Oh, yes," she said, catching her breath, and pulled him down to her.


Maev and Hivis, sharing a pot of tea, stood as she entered, and Hivis smiled.

"Looks like we lived through another one," he said, gesturing toward the window. "Where do we find breakfast?"

"I thought you would be relieved," she said, making sure her tunic was buttoned.

"Hivis asked for the duty again," Maev said, following her from the room. "Seems he's developed a taste for sauteed worms."

"Hah," Hivis said.

Voices sounded from the audience chamber, Syne's clear among them, and without instruction Maev led them away from that room and through the servants' quarters toward another exit. Janya proved to be bathing and Robin, a manservant said, had grown enough courage to be outside looking at the morning. Satisfied, Lyeth ventured out.

Sunlight bathed Horda's Garden and lay in rich bars over wooden floors and tapestried walls. Servants paused with their hands full of plates or linen to stare from the windows at other servants shoveling snow in the main yard. The Snake was already clear, the cobblestones shiny with ice. Three men with a barrow scattered sand over the stones and down the steps; it grated under Lyeth's boots. The Neck, too, was clear. Bedwyn stood at the kitchen door shouting at the wagoneers; the first ferry had arrived but the wagoneers refused to trust their carts to the ratchet road until it, too, was cleared and sanded. There was much shouting about broken legs and shattered carts on the one side, about ravenous loudmouths and the private anatomy of the Father on the other; eventually the carts moved slowly from the yard and toward the gate in the inner curtain. Lyeth, catching the wagonmaster in a foul mood, nonetheless secured his services in taking her things, and Jandi's, to the quay. He would do it, he grumbled, when that fool cook's supplies were delivered, and hoped the cook would choke on them. Lyeth nodded her thanks and gave him a high-mark.

Militent, Janya's flirtatious kitchen helper, had a fire roaring in the woodstove and platters of food in the pantry. She set out plates, chattering about Janya and her two babies, while Hivis watched her swaying blue skirts appreciatively and Maev scowled at him.

Clean linen, clean clothes, clean boots. She brushed her hair and braided it, wrapping the braids around the top of her head and pinning them in place. The storm, departing, had taken with it her dense apprehensions and the clouding of her mind. Report to Durn, check with Elea, talk to Crise. One step at a time, one thing after another, and everything would fall into place, the puzzle become its own answer. She tucked the two guild tokens under her shirt, told Militent where she might be, and returned to the morning.

Equerries and mounts filled the yard before the Lords Stables, the hands shouting and the horses eager for exercise after their confinement. She grabbed a passing stablehand and sent him to tell Danae to have Darkness ready to go. Children tumbled in the drifts against the castle walls, burrowing tunnels and piling snow into the walls and turrets of a mock castle, a cheerful anarchy of snowballs and shouts. One small boy lost his balance atop a high drift and cartwheeled, howling, to the yard, where Hivis caught him, swung him, and set him on his feet again. The boy ducked into the snow castle and pelted the shadi with snowballs and Hivis, laughing, retaliated. More shadeen, attracted by the noise, spilled from their barracks to join the fight. The children shrieked with excitement. None of them had Emris' golden hair and Lyeth turned toward the main yard, wondering whether Durn would be holding high audience in his overheated chamber or hovering solicitously about his master's bed. One step at a time.

"Rider! Lyeth! Wait!"

She stopped and Petras, deftly threading his way through horses, children, and shadeen, called her name again. She put her hands on her hips and her guards, glancing from the Rider to the captain, rested their hands on sword hilts, flanking her. Petras stopped a length away and looked at them.

"I need to talk to you," he told Lyeth. "Privately." Something about his face looked different, but she couldn't pin it down.

"This is private enough."

He shook his head, raising a hand to brush hair from his forehead. Maev shifted balance. "I don't want to harm you," he said. "I just want to talk."

He's wearing his city face, Lyeth thought suddenly. Not the hard mask he habitually wore on the Rock. It jarred.

"Talk here," she said.

He grimaced, acceding. "I'm sorry about the guildmaster."

"Yes? Do you have anything to be sorry about?"

"Rider, this is difficult enough." He stepped closer and both shadeen shifted. "I have some things to tell you. One of them is that we didn't do it. The Guard had nothing to do with his death."

"Of course." She spat. "Not a single person on the Rock did, I understand. He managed to kidnap himself, torture himself, and throw himself from Lords Walk without any help whatever. A monument of human tenacity. It's a pity we had to lose him." She glared. "Don't mouth at me, Petras. Don't tell me anything. Prove it." She turned abruptly. Petras stepped toward her, hands open, and Maev lifted her sword.

"No farther, Captain," the shadi said.

"I don't want to fight," Petras said coldly. "Rider, I said I had some things to tell you. That was one. How can I prove it to you?"

"Find the ones who did," Lyeth said, turning back. "You have to. Because if you don't, you and the Guard will take the blame for it." She paused, a little surprised, and nodded quickly. "Of course. The leader of an oathed mercenary company under a dead lord—as good a scapegoat as Jentesi is likely to get."

"I know that," Petras said. "You're not the first to tell me." He flexed his hands at his sides. "I have another thing to tell you, and something to show you. Will you come?"

"Why should I?" Behind Petras, one of the snowball-fighting shadeen went down under a barrage of snow and children. The captain ignored them.

"I can't prove I didn't kill your guildmaster, not yet. But I can prove my goodwill. At least give me the chance to do that."

*You can't afford to throw away my help,* Crise had said. True of her, and of Elea. And possibly of the Captain of the Guard. She narrowed her eyes, considering, and nodded decisively. "All right. But my shadeen come with me."

"You don't trust me, Rider?"

"Petras. Of course not."

To her surprise, Petras grinned openly and executed an elaborate bow. She followed him to the Guards' quarters and inside, Maev and Hivis close behind her. These rooms had improved considerably since her last, unwilling, visit to them, and compared to the shadeen barracks they were luxurious. Rugs instead of reeds covered the floor, thick woolen hangings hid the stone walls, a woodstove burned moderately in the corner. The few guards present studiously ignored them as Petras led them through a doorway and down a flight of steps. Stone again, cool and dry and malevolent, treads worn smooth and bathed in the yellow light of lanterns. Lyeth tried to ignore her tight midriff.

"You were here once before," Petras said over his shoulder.

"On Gambin's orders."

"Aye. I didn't like that either, Rider. I don't like the warrens and I don't like what's done here, but I'm oathed, as you are. We're not that dissimilar, you and I."

She refused to reply. Petras glanced back at her, not breaking the rhythm of his steps. "I won't argue it, but it's true. And, like you, there are orders that I will not follow. I would not obey an order to kill a guildmaster. None of my people would obey that order."

"Were you asked?"

This time, Petras didn't reply. Lyeth wondered distantly when her fear of the rock would overcome her curiosity, or her promise.

"Heron, Lord Torwyn's chamberlain," Petras said suddenly. "He looks much like his father, don't you think? But I've seen others who don't resemble Gambin at all. You'd think that face would stamp itself forever, but it's just a face, like any other. Eventually the body's memory fades."

"I don't need your chatter," Lyeth said through clenched teeth. The steps seemed interminable.

"I had a woman here once," Petras continued. "A lovely young woman and her husband. Gambin had ordered the full treatment for them both, but I tried to make it easy on her. The second day, she told me she was Gambin's daughter. She didn't do it to help herself, she obviously hated it, but I thought it might help. I mentioned it to Gambin."

"I don't care."

"He laughed," Petras said. "Said he couldn't be bothered by it. Said she was more important to him dead, that her corpse, her husband's corpse, would bind a lord to him. It was his only interest in her."

Under the protection of her talma, Lyeth pressed her clenched fists against her stomach. "Don't these steps ever end? Should my interest be any greater?"

Petras shrugged. "She was a shadi. And a commander."

Lyeth stopped so abruptly that Maev bumped into her. Petras, too, halted and turned. His round face looked quiet now, and sad. "Oh, Lyeth, you may be the only one on the Rock without spies," he said. "I heard Ilen asking and I remembered. You never guessed, did you?"

"I—I don't believe you."

"It's immaterial, isn't it? It's all immaterial. The boy's ancestors are not his fault. And even if it were common knowledge, even if he stood at Gambin's bedside and called him Grandfather, do you think it would matter? Gambin doesn't care. Why should you?" He moved down the stairs again. "That's the other thing I had to tell you. There is still something left to see."

Numbly, Lyeth followed. Petras reached a landing, opened a door, and ushered them into a wide hallway punctuated by heavy wooden doors. He stopped by one, his hand to the bolt.

"I said I wanted your goodwill, and I'm willing to give you something in earnest of my own," he said, looking hard at her. "This is my choice, Rider. Remember that. This giving gives no benefit to me."

She nodded, her hands still tight against her stomach. He shot back the bolt and pushed the door open as Maev planted herself before it so it could not be closed, and Hivis, a torch in one hand and his sword in the other, entered quickly. Lyeth, pausing in the doorway behind him, heard the rustle of movement and a weary sigh.

"Dark Mother, it's more of you. Can't you leave us alone?"

Her heart skipped. Hivis moved aside. Emris stood before her, dirty, tired, and very angry, his left arm bound in a makeshift sling. Joleda lay on a pallet against the wall, her face bruised and her wooden leg gone. Emris, looking beyond Hivis to the Rider, stared.

"They're yours, aren't they?" Petras said.

"Yes. Yes, they're mine."

He produced Joleda's wooden leg from the corridor and handed it to her. "Then take them. They haven't been harmed."

Lyeth took the leg and, kneeling, untangled the straps. Joleda stared at her. "Is that true?" Lyeth said.

"No. Not by him." Joleda brushed the Rider's hands aside and saw to the strapping herself as Lyeth turned, still on her knees, to face the boy.

"Are you . . . are you all right?"

"Of course I'm not all right," he said angrily, but his voice cracked in the middle of it. "I thought you'd never come get me. They broke my arm." He started shaking. Lyeth pulled him close and covered him with her talma; his good arm locked around her neck.

"Rider. Do you believe me now?"

She looked at him, not trusting her voice.

"A ferret brought them this morning," Petras said. "Do you want him?"

"You want him," Joleda said flatly. "It's your blessed Cerdic. He said he was working for the next Lord of Jentesi." She smoothed her breeches over her wooden leg. "He said so at length, in the waysta-tion where he caught up with us. After he'd jumped us and tied us, and before the storm ended. And he kept saying it on the towpath back to Jentesi, in the night. Probably to keep his spirits up. It's a wonder he didn't slip and kill us all." She let Maev help her up and even let the shadi support her. "He stopped saying it on the iceboat he stole, after Emris tried to jump out and Cerdic broke his arm for him. He was too busy to talk, trying to haul an iceboat by hand along the towlines—he didn't even wait for the lanes to be cleared. What he didn't say," she concluded sourly, "was who he thought the next Lord of Jentesi was to be."

Emris' shoulders stilled and Lyeth rose slowly, keeping him tight against her under the talma. "How would he know?"

Emris pulled the talma from his face. "The man in the blue cap, the one who followed us. He went back to City House after the baths and found out who we were looking for, and then he went to Cerdic. Cerdic rented a horse and went to Palisade Gate." Emris scrubbed his face against her talma. "There weren't too many people leaving the city just before the storm. The shadeen remembered us. Cerdic told us all about it."

A cool subterranean breeze moved through the chamber. "Petras," Lyeth said slowly, "who has he asked to see?"

"He hasn't had a chance to ask for anyone. I recognized the boy and locked them all up until I could find you. And they came in early, with the first holders. I don't think anyone noticed them." He paused. "Certainly no one has asked for him."

"Then perhaps, Captain," Lyeth said, "you should go talk to him."

Petras tilted his head to one side. "And in return, Rider?"

"You asked my help. You'll have it."

She put her right hand out and he covered it with his own and was gone. A door opened down the hall.

"Help with what?" Joleda said. "Can we go someplace warm?"

Lyeth stared at her. "You don't know. Dark Lady, how could you know?" Voices sounded down the hall. "Hush. I'll tell you later."

Petras' voice, reassuring and conciliatory, sounded counterpoint to Cerdic's shrill indignation. The words were indistinct. A door slammed.

"Tell me now," Joleda insisted.

"It's not a story for a place like this." She tightened her grip on the boy as Petras, frowning, appeared in the doorway. He looked from Lyeth to his own clenched fist and shook his head.

"He was given a scrap, a token, to identify himself," the captain said, loosening his fingers to reveal a strip of cloth sewn thick with gold embroidery. "I told him I'd deliver it myself."

Lyeth stared at the scrap, still crumpled in the captain's palm. "To whom?"

Petras smoothed the scrap with his fingers, revealing the design.

"Syne Gambini," he said.


She carried Emris up the stairs and through the shadeen quarters, while Maev and Hivis walked ahead, Joleda between them. She stopped at the door, looking at the snow fight, remembering Emris' dignity.

"Do you want to walk?" she said, looking down at him.

"Do you want me to?"

"No. I mean, if you want to. . . ."

He moved in her arms and she set him down gently. He ignored the other children, the exercising horses, the shadeen, and looked at Lyeth with determined, tired eyes.

"I thought I was never going to see you again," he said. "And when Cerdic started taking us back, I was glad, because it meant I was going back to you." His lips trembled. "I don't want to go away again. Not even if you send me away."

She knelt, ignoring the cold snow, and held his shoulders. "But— your father's family—I thought you wanted to find—"

Emris shook his head. Tears clung to his lashes. "I have a—I mean, I think I found my family. I don't need another."

She forced her hands to relax on his shoulders. "Emris, wait. I've —I've found your family. Your mother's family. I know who they are. Before you make any promises, you ought to know that. And then you can make whatever decision you want."

He raised his chin. "You don't want me?"

"Holy Mother, Emris, don't do this to me." She took a deep breath. "Lord Gambin is your grandfather; your mother was his illegitimate daughter. Syne is your aunt, and Culdyn's your uncle."

He stared at her. "Lord Gambin? But Ilen said Gambin killed my parents. Both of them."

Lyeth nodded.

"No," Emris said. "If it's true, I don't care. No."

"But there's still your father's family," she said carefully. "We could still find them, and—"

"No." He braced his shoulders. "I don't know them and I don't love them. I love you. I want to stay with you."

"But I'm a Rider, and you hate—"

"That doesn't matter," he said angrily. "You dragged me out of Pelegorum, whether you bought me or not. And you dragged me to Jentesi Castle, and you dragged me to the city, and you sent me away and we almost got killed and then we got hurt and then Cerdic broke my arm and that captain threw us in the warrens and I think you owe me something for all of that."

"Damn it, boykin—"

"There," he said, and smiled. "I knew you'd take me."

"You little brat, I ought to—" she said furiously, then grabbed him and hugged him tightly. "I do love you, Emris. Mother help me, I do."

"And you'll never send me away again?" he said into her ear. "I can stay with you always—you'll never leave?"

"I swear it," she said, and he put his good arm around her neck and kissed her. She swept him into her arms again and held him close as she crossed the yard.

The wagonmaster's men had come and gone, leaving nothing in her rooms but Gambin's hard furniture and her packed saddlebags. Hivis took the saddlebags, Maev supported Joleda, and Lyeth carried Emris secure in her arms to the shadeen barracks, where Crise summoned a shadi physician and took them all into the small apartment she shared with Ilen.

"Great Father, get them checked first and talk later," Crise said, but Joleda, stubbornly clinging to a windowsill, shook her head.

"Tell me," she demanded of Lyeth. "Gambin isn't dead yet, is he? And we have almost been killed. Tell me."

Lyeth, sitting on a bench with Emris on her lap, looked at the faces in the room and sighed as it came to her that the next step was both the simplest and the hardest. Sending an unspoken apology to Torwyn, she opened herself to trust.

The story, as she told it, seemed neat and clean, from Syne's watcher following them into Jentesi to the messenger that Jandi, despite that morning's disparaging comments, believed enough to follow immediately. Once Jandi was secure, the messenger went to Janya, finding Lyeth gone but still, presumably, on the Rock. Then the guild token to Robin; the boy would vouch for Jandi's absence, but Robin could not find the Rider and returned alone to wait in Jandi's rooms. While Lyeth and Emris eluded Syne's watcher in the city, someone waited for the Rider to appear; while Cerdic asked questions at the Inn of the Boar, someone cut off Jandi's little finger and sent it to Robin in a wooden box. The messenger had gone directly from the boy to Janya, so that while Lyeth waited on the last ferry to the Rock, Robin beat on Lyeth's locked door and someone realized that Jandi would have to die. They must have waited until the last ferry docked at the quay, and when Lyeth, spirited away by Syne and Torwyn, still did not appear, they took the broken, blinded guildmaster to Lords Walk and let him loose in the storm. Someone knocked at the door and Lyeth, staring at Emris' hair, stopped talking while Crise admitted the physician.

"Be quick about it and be gone," she said brusquely. The physician looked at them all curiously and unbound Emris' arm.

"He's dead, then," Joleda said.

Lyeth nodded, seeing the glimmer of tears in the old woman's eyes.

"A clean break and a good set," the physician said. "But the boy needs rest."

"I set it myself," Joleda snapped, ignoring the tears on her cheeks. "Keep your hands off me. I can tend as well as you."

The physician snorted and backed from the room. Crise closed the door. It reopened immediately and Ilen came in.

"News?" Crise said.

"No. I was told there were strangers in my rooms. I didn't expect a platoon of them."

"We arrived during the second act," Joleda explained. "We're simply being told the plot. Go on, girl. You haven't finished, have you?"

Lyeth moved abruptly, as certain doors sprang open in her mind. "I have finished," she said, putting Emris down. "For now. Crise will tell you about the gardener. I have to go."

"What gardener?" Joleda demanded as Lyeth stood and dropped a kiss on Emris' hair. "Lyeth, you can't leave now."

"Watch them for me," she said to Ilen. "Emris, I'll be back." And ran out of the room with her guards at her heels. She snatched her talma from the cloak room and flung it around her shoulders as she came into the yard. Hivis was still struggling with his as she rounded a corner of the armory and came, skidding, to a halt. The two shadeen faced her, looking perplexed.

"We come to a crossroads here," Lyeth said, her talma open and one hand on her dagger. "You're under Torwyn's orders, and you're Syne's shadeen. You heard what Petras said back in the warrens. What I do next may damage your lady. So either you leave me now, or you kill me now." She looked from one to the other. Maev and Hivis consulted with their eyes.

"Tell her," Maev said. Hivis frowned and she prodded him. "Tell her, or I will."

"Rider." He glanced at his mate and she nodded. "Rider, we never thought we'd do this. We're sworn to Lady Syne; we bonded to her even before our apprenticeship. But . . . but someone killed a guildmaster, and that's a sin. I don't believe our lady had a hand in it —we don't believe it." He took a deep breath. "But Maev says the sin of murdering a guildmaster is greater than the sin of breaking an oath. So," he concluded, rushing it, "if you'll take us, we'll oath to you. Not forever, just until the murderer is caught. If you'll take us."

Startled, she dropped her hand from her dagger. "Why?"

"You sheltered a shadi cub," Maev said. "And you cared about a shadeen commander."

Lyeth shook her head. "Your loyalty is so easily bought?"

"No, Rider. But I think you've bought our trust."

"Well, then," Lyeth said after a moment, and raised her hands. First Hivis, then Maev knelt before her, hands steepled to be clasped in hers, and made a simple, limited oath. When they stood again she looked at their stern faces and took a silent oath of trust herself.

"I need your silence and your speed," she said. "You remember the Alanti shadi who sat beside me yesterday in the shadeen hall? The one wrapped tightly in a cloak? He killed the gardener and he disappeared. But I know where he is."

"Rider?" Maev said as she led them at a run around the armory and into the main yard. "Rider, where?"

"Lords Walk," Lyeth said. "Hurry, we may not have much time."

The walk between the Garden of the Lady and the inner curtain was not yet cleared. They slogged through it, Lyeth cursing the absence of snowshoes, and floundered up the stairs onto the Walk. Here the storm's residue was entirely untouched, drifts heaped about the broken pavement or swept free, and the cold breeze blew unmolested. Maev shuddered and pulled her cloak close.

"Rider, there's nothing here. Nothing alive."

"There may be. Pray that there is." She closed her eyes, visualizing how the Walk looked under a clear summer sky, and nodded firmly. "Stay here. I'll call you when I've found him."

She knew exactly what he'd look for: a place where the jumbled blocks created a lee from the winds, a place where snow would pile to make a small cave that his body could warm with its own heat, and thus take him through the storm. That would have to be near the broken ledge above the Tobrin; the wreckage closer in was not great enough. It would have been a terrifying search.

It was not that pleasant a search on a clear winter day either. The first three places were untenanted; the fourth, nearer the edge, had fallen to the rocks below. She found herself making the sign against evil, stopped it halfway through, and grimly continued her quest, stopping occasionally to close her eyes and consult her memory again.

She found him in the seventh place, where her foot went through the snow and hit something neither frozen nor rock. She dug quickly, calling to her shadeen. When they reached her she was murmuring rapidly, delving into Laret's clothes to find a heartbeat.

"Is he—"

"Hush." His heart beat slowly but steadily against her fingers; a lump pressed against the back of her hand and she drew it out of his clothes, feeling the ridges of carving. She slid it into her pocket as Laret groaned and stirred.

"Don't." She put her hand over his mouth. "You're weak; you're not to talk. Maev, Hivis, help me get him out of here." She wrapped her talma around him and they carried him from the Walk.

"Sweet angel," he said, grinning at her with pale lips, "will you share my cave?"

"If you don't shut up," she said impatiently, "I'll stake you to your cave and leave you there. Naked."

"Rider, where do we take him?" Hivis said as they gained the parapet above the Garden of the Lady. "He'll need a doctor. It's a wonder he's alive at all."

Lyeth frowned. Not Torwyn's chambers; Syne might be there. And it would be foolish to carry him through the castle's yards, wrapped like a package in her talma. She raised her head suddenly and smiled.

"The bathhouse," she said. "Close and private, and all that hot water. Hurry up."

"A bath?" Laret said with weak alarm. She flipped the talma over his face.

The bath keeper squawked indignantly as they marched Laret through the hallway and into one of the changing rooms, and Lyeth filled her palm with coins and sent her away. The shadeen deposited Laret on a couch and Lyeth immediately began stripping him. He squirmed ineffectually.

"Maev, find Torwyn and bring him here. Make sure he comes without Syne's noticing. Hivis, you bring Crise, Ilen, and Petras. Maev, you'd better find Elea and bring her, too." She pinned one of Laret's hands to the couch with her knee. "Go on. No one's going to bother me here."

"Rider, no," Laret said, alarmed, as the shadeen left. "You can't do this. You can't bring them here. I—they'll—"

"They'll be told that you killed the gardener," she said, pulling off his boots. "No frostbite. Good. Where's your shayka?"

Laret stared at her. "The snake wouldn't give it back to me," he said. "How did you know?"

"About the gardener? Simple. I saw the body." She started to take his breeches off.

"No!" He fumbled wildly at his shirt. "I'll leave, I'll go to—where is it?" he yelped. "Where is it?"

"This?" Lyeth held up the carved, milk-white stone. "I borrowed it."

"Give it to me." He tried to sit up. "Give it to me. I can't move without it."

"It's a pity you can't speak without it, too. If it's such a magical thing, why didn't you use it last night?" She pushed him down and went for his breeches again.

"I was weak," he said. "They hit me on the head. Besides, I told you I'm not very good at it yet."

"I'd imagine. Stop that, it won't do you any good."

"Don't take those off! It's not proper!"

"You were eager enough to take them off yourself not so long ago. So you couldn't use your wonderful magical charm, and you got into trouble. You didn't go back to Lady Elea after I saw you in the barracks, so you must have gone to whoever made you kill the gardener. And whoever made you do that probably killed the guildmaster." She paused, her hands on his shirt. "Your lady said that people do stupid things when they panic. They also tend to do the things they did before. So they promised to help you, and took you to Lords Walk, and left you there." She jerked the shirt away. "They just didn't count on who you are, stripling."

He immediately covered his genitals with his hands. She snorted, grabbed him under the arms, and dragged him, protesting, into the pools.

"We have a much better way of doing this," he said indignantly as she forced him into the water. "Two people take off all their clothes and get into bed with you. We should try that; it works much better."

"Perhaps." She pushed him down until water lapped at his chin. "But there's only one of me and one of you, and this is the best you'll get."

He was still complaining about it when Torwyn entered, calling her name. Laret stopped talking and plunged his hands under the water to cover himself, and Torwyn, coming through the plants, saw him and froze.

"Who's that?" Torwyn said, bewildered.

"The shadi we've been looking for." She came around the pool quickly and took his arm. "Come here. I have to speak to you. Alone."

"You can't leave me like this!" Laret called.

"Move and I'll tell your father," she said over her shoulder. She stopped beside the neighboring pool and turned to Torwyn urgently. "Don't say anything yet. You have a decision to make, and you'll have to make it quickly. I told you that I took Emris, the boy, into the city, and that we were followed. I left him with Joleda and they tried to leave the city. A ferret caught them in a waystation and brought them back after the storm. Petras found them and kept them for me, and the ferret. He said he was working for the next Lord of Jentesi. And he had a token to prove it."

His face went very still. "Who?"

She pulled the crumpled cloth from her breeches pocket. "There are others coming. Elea, Petras, Crise, Ilen. You'll have to make up your mind before they arrive." She put the cloth in his palm and closed his fingers around it, holding them there with her hands. "Torwyn, you asked me to trust you. I trust you enough to give you this. And to tell you that, after you've seen it, if you want to leave us you're free to go. But quickly, Torwyn. There's very little time." She started to add something else, then pressed his hands and went back through the plants, leaving him alone with Syne's sigil.

He still hadn't emerged when Petras arrived with Elea close behind him. She saw Laret and stalked toward him, her neat little hands tightly fisted.

"You sneak," she said furiously. "You misbegotten little cretin—"

"Leave him be," Lyeth said. "He's spent a day in the blizzard on Lords Walk, and he's not in the pool because he wants to be. A few minutes, Lady, and you'll learn about it."

She turned on Lyeth. "My treaty—"

"Patience, Lady. Just a little while."

"Rider, *please,*" Laret begged. With both hands covering his genitals, his legs and bottom tended to rise and let him float around the pool. "At least a robe."

She thought a moment and shook her head, smiling. "I think not, highlander. You're far more likely to stay put just the way you are."

The Trapper lapsed into a miserable silence, broken only when Hivis, Crise, Ilen, and Maev appeared in quick succession. Then he moaned and tried to turn his back on all of them, but they surrounded the pool. The leaves parted again to admit Joleda, leaning heavily on Emris' shoulder.

"I made them bring me," Emris said quickly. "I almost got killed. I think I have a right to be here."

"Don't argue," Joleda said wearily, lowering herself to a marble bench. "I already tried. We both have a right to be here, Lyeth. We didn't want this, but it seems to be our battle, too."

"You sent me away once already," Emris said. "And look what happened then."

"Mother Night." Lyeth went around the pool and put her hands on Emris' shoulders. "All right, boykin. And I suppose it involves you more than you know."

"I sent someone for Robin," Ilen said, looking distrustfully across the pool at Petras.

"I know," Maev said. "I saw them in the chambers. Rider, I left someone guarding your servant. One of Lord Torwyn's shadeen. I told him it was on my lord's orders." She looked over as Torwyn, the cloth held loosely in his fingers, stepped through the plants. "I apologize, Lord, for the liberty."

"It's all right," he said without inflection. "Rider. I'll stay."

Lyeth closed her eyes briefly. She turned, Emris in her arms, to face the pool. "Joleda, they told you about the gardener?"

The old woman nodded, her hands unconsciously massaging her stump.

"Good. You all know parts of the story, and most of you know almost everything. But there is one part that only this boy knows." Laret, one hand between his legs and the other gripping the side of the pool, looked at her beseechingly. She shook her head at him. "I think it's probably the most important part. But there's a price for it." She looked at the assembled faces. "That price will not sit well, especially for you," she said to Crise and Ilen. "But too much rides on this, and I don't think we have a choice. In return for his part of the story, he goes free. Someone takes him across the river to Dorne and leaves him in a safe place, where he can wait for Lady Elea to pick him up. Anything he has done is forgiven, and anything he says goes no further than this room. To the rest of Jentesi, the boy died on Lords Walk, as he was intended to die."

"Rider," Petras said, "is it worth the price?"

"I think so." She moved her fingers on Emris' shoulders. "I think we'll learn the name of Jandi's murderer. Tell me, Captain, is that worth the price?"

"Yes," he said immediately. "I'll meet that price."

"He's to go entirely unpunished?" Crise said. "No matter what he did?"

"Not entirely, no," Elea said. "He'll be returned to his father. And that, I think, will be punishment enough. I'll pay."

Crise, assessing Laret's expression, nodded. "And I."

They agreed, one by one around the pool, until only Torwyn remained. He gestured with the hand that held the cloth. "I think my world has changed in any case," he said slowly. "Yes, Rider. For no return or a bad return, I'll pay."

"Rider," Elea said. "Thank you."

Lyeth gestured it aside. "Listen, then. This is Laret, who comes from Korth, which is south of the Alanti–outlands border. This week. He's young and boastful and a Trapper. And he loves to gamble. That's what he's going to tell us about."


When he finished, a silence settled around the pool, and into it Petras said thoughtfully, "Coreon sold him to Culdyn, then. A debt for a favor."

"He did not sell me," Laret said hotly. Throughout his entire recitation, no matter how extravagant his gestures, he had never once removed one hand from its modest task, and as a result he was wet all over and, as he muttered, half-drowned in addition. "He sold my gambling debt. A debt for a favor, as you said. But he didn't sell me. I don't know," he added sulkily, "what the favor was."

"Why should you care?" Elea said prosaically. "First you gambled away your shayka, and when you tried to get it back you lost a service. It didn't seem much at the time, did it?"

"He promised to give my shayka back," Laret said.

"You should learn," the lady said, "that the simplest debts are the hardest to pay. Your father, I'm sure, will teach you that when you get back. Rider, what now?"

"They'll be worried, I think." She glanced at the skylight overhead. Light slanted obliquely into the room, gilding the leaves and flowers. "Both shadeen commanders, the Captain of the Guard, Lady Elea, Lord Torwyn—and me, the target. We've all been away, at the same time, for at least two hours. Petras, you saw Gambin most recently. How long does he have to live?"

Petras chewed on the ends of his beard. "He's worse, Rider. Tobi said an hour, maybe four or five. They've not rung the bells; he's not dead yet."

"And they'll want to be in at that. I suppose they're all with Gambin."

"Even Maranta," Petras said. "The roads to Tormea aren't clear yet, but the stars said she could stay a little longer." He spat the ends of his beard from his mouth. "They'll all be sitting around the death-bed, playing with their fingers or staring at each other or staring at the walls, and every time the old man twitches it's heads up and noses to the fore, like dogs sniffing a badger." Lyeth raised her eye-brows at the bitterness of his tone. "Maranta making lists—the woman makes lists of everything from buttonholes to benefices, and when she's done with them she starts right at the beginning and does them over again. And Coreon winks. At Culdyn, who pulls his lips out, or at Maranta, who puts him on her lists, or at Syne, who stares at him. Wouldn't that make a lovely marriage, then, our Coreon and the Lady Syne? By the Father!" He glared at them, his round bear-face red with anger. "By the Father! Four hours a day I spend in that stench and fury, listening to Gambin rasp and bait them, and they never say a word to him; they nod and agree and grin when he savages someone else. Some days ago, Lady," he said, turning to Elea, "you asked my service and I told you to wait on an answer. Aye, Syne wants me, and for all her wanting she can go to the mountain and take this province with her. If you'll have it, Lady, my guard is yours. And myself, and my woman, and my children. If this is a Trapper, Lady, I'll find your province boring. But I'll come."

Lyeth and Torwyn shared a glance across the pool.

"Syne wants you?" Torwyn said.

"She didn't tell you, Steward? Aye, me and my guard, and every day she sends to tell me so again." He planted his fists together, knuckle to knuckle, across his belly. "Generally she sends my fair Lord Coreon—but I don't suppose she's told you about that either."

"No." Torwyn looked at the scrap of cloth in his hand. "Nor that either." He let the scrap flutter to the ground and turned away. After a moment Crise picked it up and smoothed it with her fingers.

"Culdyn and Coreon, Coreon and Syne," Joleda murmured.

"Snake and snake friends," Laret retorted. "May I leave this pool now? I'll be filled with water and round as a bladder."

"And cleaner than you've been since the midwife bathed you," Lyeth said. "Lady Elea, you should leave him here. Let the lords see this Trapper in a pool and you'll have your treaty in a week."

"Get him off the Rock, or I won't have a treaty at all," the Lord of Alanti said. "Captain Petras, the warrens seem to be your fief. Can you find the place this idiot told you about?"

"I know the place," the captain said. "It's not been used in twenty years, but I know the place." He looked at Torwyn, who stood with his back to them. "Gambin's children used to play there." Torwyn didn't move.

"Culdyn and Coreon, Coreon and Syne, Syne and Culdyn," Ilen said. "Rider, I think we have a trap to spring."

"Yes." Lyeth looked away from Torwyn's still shoulders. "Lady Elea, this is castle business. It would not sit well were you a part of it."

Elea, nodding, rose. "I agree. I think I'll pay my last respects to Lord Gambin. And perhaps complain about my missing shadi. Or is he dead yet?"

"I don't know," Lyeth said. "But first he leaves the Rock. Hivis, Maev?"

"Right." The stocky shadi effortlessly dragged Laret from the pool. "We can spend the time learning to survive in blizzards. Stop howling, boy. They're not that impressive and we've seen the like before."

"Rider, my—"

"He'll need fresh clothes," Maev said critically. "Some of mine, I think. He's more my size."

"And tie him to you," Lyeth said. "He has a tendency to disappear."

"My Lady!" Laret yelled in protest. "Rider!"

"Ah!" Lyeth reached into her shirt and took out the carved stone. "Lady, perhaps you'll keep this in trust for him until you pick him up. He seems to think it's marvelously important."

Elea, her eyebrows raised, took the stone and looked at it somberly. "As indeed it is, Rider. Yes. Keep a list," she said to Hivis, "of his transgressions. His father will want to know."

Laret groaned and the shadeen hustled him from the room. Lyeth

looked at the bench, where Emris sat leaning wearily against Joleda.
A bird called distantly across the room.

"Lady Elea," she said, "I think you should ask Coreon about your
missing shadi. Demand a search from him. In Culdyn's presence."
Elea nodded. "Petras?"

"Aye. I'll deliver a message from a ferret." He took the scrap from
Crise and tucked it under his belt.

"But first you show us to this playroom," Ilen said. "Lord
Torwyn, do you come with us?"

Torwyn gestured without turning. Lyeth, watching him, said,
"And me? Tower or playroom, where do I do the most good?"

"In the tower," Torwyn said, turning at last to face them. "Someone's going to leave that room and someone will have to follow. And
Lyeth, you move so silently."

She raised her chin. "And you, my Lord?"

"In the playroom, of course. With the other Gambini toys."

She would have gone to him then, but Crise touched her arm and
said, "Rider? The boy, and Joleda?"

"You can't send me away," Emris said immediately, sitting up.
"I'm part of this, too."

Lyeth considered them both, Emris red-eyed and defiant, Joleda's
eyes weary and mouth determined as she nodded.

"In the tower," Lyeth said, making up her mind. "I don't think
anyone would dare snatch them there. Petras, could you order your
guard—"

"Of course," Petras said, just as Joleda said, "Will Syne be there?"

Petras looked at her. "They're all there, innkeeper. All four of
them. What difference does it make?"

Joleda straightened her shoulders. "I lost my leg because of Syne
Gambini," she said, without expression. "I was her Rider for a little
while. We were ice-flying and I fell beneath a runner." She paused.
"The lady pushed me, and swore it was an accident. By the time I
recovered she had left Jentesi, and who was I to challenge her? I was
a crippled Rider, and she an heir to the sword." She looked at all of
them, but most particularly at Torwyn. "Do you believe me, Lord?"

"I don't know what I believe," Torwyn said. "You're supposed to
be in the warrens still, with Emris."

"They can stay in the antechamber," Lyeth said. "Syne won't see
them unless she leaves, and she'll have heard Petras' message by
then. They have a right to be there. Emris especially."

The boy looked at her, eyebrows raised. "Are you going to tell them?" he demanded.

"Yes. I think they need to know."

The corners of his mouth turned down. "They won't take me away from you," he said vehemently, grabbing her hand.

"No. I swore I'd never leave you, Emris. I meant it."

He nodded then and moved within the circle of her arms. "Then tell them," he said. "It doesn't matter. Let them know."

Lyeth looked over the boy's head at the others. "We tried to find Emris' kin, and so, my friends, we have. His family lies all around us —he's Lord Gambin's grandson."

Durn's audience chamber was hot and stuffy and deserted, the little machine in the telegraph room silent. The wires would not be up for a while yet, and she made a mental note to stop at the next station down the Water Road and send word of Gambin's death, and Jandi's, to Vantua. Tradition aiding progress, she thought wryly, and climbed the curving steps of Gambin's Tower. Emris clung to her hand; they walked slowly so that Joleda would not drop too far behind. Pausing by a window, she showed Emris the snow sweeps already half-finished on the Tobrin, great brushes and plows forming high-walled roads between the Rock and the city. Towlines webbed the snow and already the supply boat from down river moved laboriously along the lines, headed south toward the sea. Joleda reached them and they climbed higher, under the dusty hunting trophies of dead lords.

A guard readily admitted them to the antechamber, and another, face impassive, gestured Joleda and the boy to a padded bench and sent a servant for wine. The room was unchanged, still littered with plates and winter gear, still presided over by the ragged tapestries of Death. The two seminarians dozed with their boxes on their laps, woke to stare blearily at her, and nodded their heads again. The guard at the inner chamber let her in.

Stench and murmur. Petras, at the foot of Gambin's bed, looked at her and away again, expressionless; Syne stared thoughtfully at him and, in a corner, Elea stood in quiet but animated discussion with Coreon. Culdyn, she noted, had edged close enough to overhear them. She came around the bed, dropped to one knee, and rose again.

Gambin was asleep, his head back and his mouth open. His body barely ridged the coverlet. Tobi came to stand beside her and she said, "How much longer?"

The physician shrugged. "The sleep's a blessing. He's coherent when he wakes." He stared down at his master's face. "He'll see the mountain when he goes, fighting every step of the way. The Mother grant I die in my sleep."

"And swiftly," Lyeth said, agreeing. She went around to find Master Durn. Coreon, smiling indulgently, murmured something that made Culdyn frown; Elea prodded his chest with one finger, whispering angrily.

Durn was not pleased that she'd already transferred her trunks, and Jandi's, to the quay, and was even less pleased when she told him that Jandi's body, coffined, waited with them under guard. Timbli, one of Syne's land-barons, bent her head to listen to her mistress, then made her way around to Culdyn. Durn flatly refused Lyeth his permission to book passage on an iceboat or engage one of her own. Lyeth shrugged.

"I need your leave only until Gambin dies. This will cost me a little time, but nothing else."

Durn fingered his pigtail. "Your master desired one last service of you," he said. "You know what it is. Discharge it now and I'll see that you go to Vantua in Gambin's own iceboat, with all the crew and servants that you need."

Lyeth smiled. "I shit," she said evenly, "in Gambin's iceboat." Elea crossed her arms and Coreon, with a word to one of his retainers, left the room. "And I shit, Master Chamberlain, on you." She turned away.

Timbli, her task accomplished, returned to Syne as Culdyn bowed quickly to his father's bed and made his way toward the door, stopping once or twice to address a brief word to a supporter. Lyeth met Petras' blank gaze, gave Culdyn a minute's grace, and slipped out after him. One of the captain's guards had already stepped around the edge of the room, the note that was Petras' excuse for leaving folded in his hand.

As the captain had predicted, Culdyn went down the stairs leading to the coldrooms and, in the dimly lit hallway, took a torch from a bracket and opened one of the heavy, dusty doors. It swung silently open and closed again; Lyeth put her hand to it, breathed a quick prayer, and followed. Culdyn's torch cast light around a distant corner and his footsteps hurried over stone and dirt.

The cold intensified, as though the stones hoarded an eternity of winters. Lyeth pulled the talma close about her, keeping well behind the wavering pool of light from Culdyn's torch. The darkness helped, she decided firmly. The watch niche was just behind her and in a minute she would step into the sunlight, ride through the pass to the plateau above the Tobrin, emerge into the day. Culdyn breathed harshly ahead of her, gasping in time to his running footsteps.

"Coreon!" he shouted suddenly. Lyeth froze. "Damn you, wait for me!"

Coreon's voice shouted back indistinctly, and Culdyn tore after it. Lyeth shuddered, following. Petras would take a different route to the playroom; for now, she was alone with two murderers in the hungry stones. They must be under Horda's Garden by now, deeper than the crypts in the Garden of the Lady. She pushed the thought away and ran.

Ahead, voices shouted and someone screamed. The corridor turned abruptly and light flooded into it from a door halfway down; Lyeth pressed herself to the wall as Culdyn stopped suddenly in the light and stared. The same voice screamed again.

"You idiot," Culdyn said hysterically. "What are you doing?"

A grunt, the sound of something falling. Then Coreon said, breathing harshly, "What you would be doing if you had the brains. Cleaning up."

Culdyn went into the lit room and Lyeth crept down the corridor.

"Did you want," Coreon continued, "to leave him alive? So that he could testify about this? Death and hell, Culdyn, put that away and help me get him out of here."

"Why?" Culdyn said, to the sound of something heavy being dragged. "Leave him here. He's the one who killed the fat man." Culdyn giggled and Lyeth slid closer to the door. "He certainly can't say otherwise now, can he?"

"Brainless," Coreon said. "Who will believe that a cashiered boatman concocted all of this? If they find him, they'll trace him and discover that you hired him, and then where will you be? Here, take his shoulders. We haven't got much time."

Lyeth loosened her dagger in its sheath, trying to imagine the layout of the room, trying to decide where Torwyn and the shadeen were hiding. Culdyn was not the only one running out of time.

"They're heavier when they're dead," Culdyn said, gasping a little. "Are you going to take his feet?"

"No." Coreon laughed. "I think I'm going to take you instead." The hiss of metal drawn from metal, a thud, another hiss. Lyeth held her dagger ready, desperate to see inside the room, and Corcon laughed again. "By the Father, you're a stupid man," he said. "Put that down before you cut your own foot off. And let's go up tower, shall we, to tell your father how the fat man died."

"Who paid you to do this?" Culdyn demanded. "You're to be my minister, don't you remember? You're to run this damned province for me. I even promised to make you my heir—damn you, Coreon, you'll throw it all away!"

Steel clanged against steel, almost tentatively.

"Take me up tower and you're dead, too," Culdyn said. "You won't dare indict me. I can prove that you were part of this."

"Who will believe you, princeling? I have a witness."

*"Who?"*

She felt a movement in the corridor and saw Petras arriving at last, his sword held ready in his hand. And in that minute, unable to restrain herself, she peered in through the doorway in time to see Coreon feint, thrust, step back and, glancing over Culdyn's shoulder, see her and hesitate. It was all the opening Culdyn needed; he plunged his sword through Coreon's body and by the time he withdrew it, shouting with triumph, Petras was upon him and the reddened sword clattered to the floor. The room filled quickly with movement and voices, Ilen catching Coreon and lowering him to the floor, Torwyn kicking the swords into a corner, Crise kneeling beside the body of a brown-haired man.

"You saw it!" Culdyn shrieked. "I killed him, the guildmaster's murderer! I found him—the credit's mine!"

" 'Leave him here. He's the one who killed the fat man,' " Lyeth said with disgust. " 'You're to be my minister, don't you remember?' "

"Your word against mine," Culdyn said venomously from Petras' embrace. "You're all in league with Syne—that's why her steward's here. You're all in league to blacken me, but it won't work. You know nothing, and Coreon is dead."

Coreon pushed Crise's hands away and slowly lifted his head. "Not yet, Culdyn. Soon, I think, but not quite yet." He looked at

Lyeth. "You like to take your chances, don't you, Rider? Who sent you here?"

Lyeth opened her mouth to reply, and a final door opened in her head. "Syne, my Lord. Not directly, but you know she does nothing directly. But we were sent, I think, by Lady Syne."

Coreon's mouth set around his pain. "Then I think we should talk about this, Rider," he said, and gasped, and clenched his hands. "Upstairs."


Gambin, propped against a white mountain of pillows, was awake and, as Tobi had predicted, coherent. He blinked as Lyeth went to one knee and rose again.

"Bitch," he said.

"Aye, my Lord," she agreed. "How goes your circus?"

"Strangely. Have you come to watch me die?"

"I've come to make your dying easier, Lord. Can you hear me?"

"An easier death." He sounded weakly amused. "By all means, Rider. Bring me an easier death."

She smiled at him, fully and openly, and bowed. "I bring you the man who murdered my guildmaster, Lord. That will surely smooth your passage to the mountain."

The humor left his face. "Prove it, Rider."

"Nothing easier, my Lord. Here is the closing of your circus, with all the performers come to take a bow." She met Syne's calm stare and raised her hand. Petras opened the far doors. Culdyn came in first, bound, framed by Crise and Ilen, and behind him a thin, bedraggled woman leaning on Torwyn's shoulder. Emris and Joleda followed; Emris came around immediately to stand at Lyeth's side and Syne stared at Joleda, her face impassive. Coreon came last, on a stretcher, pale and bandaged, with a smile resting at the corners of his mouth. Maranta gasped. Syne's face was as clear as a pool of still water. Gambin stared at his son.

"I am betrayed by liars," Culdyn said. "Ignore them, Father. They're in Syne's pay."

"A pleasant fantasy," the lady said, "but fantasy nonetheless."

"Prove it, Rider," Gambin said again.

Lyeth bowed again. "The story, Lord, is Coreon's."

And Coreon told it with pained good humor, as though laughing at all of them. Culdyn, he said, had solicited his help in attaining the sword and had told him of the plot to entangle the Rider. It would have worked, Coreon said, had the Rider been less stubborn and Culdyn less stupid. He and a hired assistant, whose corpse was now in Petras' custody, snatched the guildmaster, and one of Syne's spies, standing there now looking much the worse for wear, had found them torturing the guildmaster and been captured by Coreon for her pains. He kept her as his insurance, he admitted cheerfully, against the day that Culdyn was unmasked, but did not expect to be dying at the time. When Lyeth did not respond to the grisly little tokens Culdyn sent to her, and when she did not appear to have returned to the castle before the storm, Culdyn panicked: he and his assistant took the dying guildmaster to the Walk and left him there, with known results.

"So you see," Coreon said, smiling, "that Culdyn can't be accused of killing the guildmaster himself, not actually, not with his own hands. But then, nobody in this castle does anything with his own hands. Or hers."

Syne stirred but did not speak, and after a moment Coreon continued.

Culdyn had not expected the guildmaster's death to be overseen, and when he heard about the unfortunate gardener, he panicked again. He tended, Coreon said judiciously, to panic far too often for his own good. So Coreon had traded him a gaming debt, the services of a young Alanti shadi who lived close to the outlands border and knew a number of interesting tricks. Culdyn sent the shadi to kill the gardener.

"With a shayka," Lyeth said, taking the instrument from her pocket. "It was in Culdyn's clothes, my Lord." She raised the thin bone rod. "It's a merciful death, done in sleep. Insert the point below the ear, into the brain, and—" She twisted the bottom of the rod and three slender, resilient bone blades slid from the top. She spun them quickly, drew them into the rod, and mimed drawing the tube from a body. "It leaves a tiny wound under the ear, my Lord. A Trapper weapon."

Gambin stared at her with loathing, and she smiled.

"And when the shadi thought he might be discovered," Coreon continued, "he went to Culdyn for protection. My lord Culdyn, not being very smart, tapped him on the head and took him to Lords Walk. You'll find his body there, if you look. Unless the storm ate it."

"We found it," Elea said grimly. "I will want a blood-price for this."

"But not from me." Coreon tapped his soaked bandages and grinned, showing clenched teeth. "I've only a little left, and that going fast enough. So you see, my Lord," he said to Gambin, "your son is guilty, directly, of one death only. My own." He pushed Tobi's hands away. "Go play with someone else—this fussing won't make it happen any slower. Well, my Lord?"

"Well, my Lord?" Syne echoed, coming to stand by the bed. "Will you sit judgment on this, or shall it wait until I take the sword?"

"How neatly it happens," Gambin whispered. "How easily it falls into place for you. Is it luck, daughter? Gambini luck?"

"Hardly, my Lord," Coreon said, and Syne turned quickly to look at him. He smiled at her maliciously. "Or only the luck the Gambini have always manufactured. It was her idea."

"He's dying," the lady said scornfully. "He'll try to take as many of us with him as he can."

"What?" Coreon said in mock protest. "Do all your promises mean so little? Marriage, Lady Syne? Protection, my love? A joint rule, share and share alike, in this fine province? And in return for so very little—a word dropped in your stupid brother's ear, an idea planted in your stupid brother's mind, a fine hand on the sword to help him cut himself?" He moved too sharply and grunted with pain. "Do you think, Lady, that I trusted you any more than you trusted me? I bought insurance against this betrayal, Lady. The messages you sent to Captain Petras that I delivered myself, the servants who overheard your fond avowals, the shadi, hiding, who saw you creep to my bed at night."

"I never entered your bed," Syne said furiously.

"Prove it, Lady. Lord, your children are tainted. Both of them. And I, my Lord, am all but dead. Who will take your precious province now?"

Lyeth looked up from him to Torwyn's face, in the moment that the lord steward said, with flat finality, "Maranta."

"No," the lady said immediately, pushing forward. "No. I relinquished my claims; I want none of it. This sword is tainted, there is blood, the stars would cry for justice. This sword needs clean hands —and who will be heir to Jentesi now?" she cried, her hands clutched together, knuckles white. "The murderer is found, Gambin can die. The murderers are revealed, the heir can stand revealed. Who will take Jentesi now?"

The land-barons and retainers and advisors shifted, whispering. Torwyn looked across Gambin's bed at them, then down at the lord.

"Will you say a choice, Lord?" Torwyn said. "Otherwise you leave the province to war—every land-baron will fight for the sword."

"No," Gambin said, voice rough. "No. If no Gambini takes the sword, why should I care?"

"'Gambini blood but not of Gambin's body,'" Maranta said shrilly. "The stars predicted it—who—"

"I don't care." Gambin choked and coughed, then caught his breath. "Carrion," he muttered.

Lyeth looked away from him, sickened. The land-barons talked openly now, angrily; Emris shifted between her hands. Syne stood with two guards at her elbows, their hands on her sleeves; she stared at Torwyn. Torwyn, in turn, stared at Emris. Lyeth's stomach went cold.

"No," she said.

"Durn could prove it," he said, still gazing at the boy. "He can unseal the records. He's of the blood."

Gambin batted angrily at the air, and Elea said, "He's your grandson, Gambin. You murdered his mother, your daughter. You probably don't remember."

Maranta gasped and whipped around to stare at Emris as Syne said coldly, "You would leave this province to a child? Not even a legitimate heir, only a child?"

"Does it work?" Maranta demanded. "Is he of Gambin's body, too?" She was ignored.

"There's no demand for legitimacy," Torwyn said. "He's of the blood. Durn's records will prove it."

"No," Lyeth said, her hands white on Emris' shoulders. "No, he's mine."

"He was never yours," Joleda said. "Emris, do you understand this?"

"Yes, I think so." The boy stepped to the bed, still clutching Lyeth's hand. "You're my grandfather," he said to Gambin. The lord, staring at him, didn't reply. "You killed my parents. And you don't care what happens after you die."

"Yes," Gambin said. "Exactly."

The corners of the boy's mouth moved down. Gambin looked

away, and Emris came back to Lyeth's side, holding her with both hands. "You won't leave me," he said. She put her arms around him.

"You're sure?" Maranta demanded of them all. "He is of Gambini blood?"

Syne said, "Gambin, this is madness."

"She's right." One of the land-barons shouldered forward. "You can't leave this province to a child."

"I leave this province to no one."

"He'll have regents," Torwyn said. "Maranta, perhaps myself. You think you could do a better job?"

"Yes! I—" His voice drowned in shouting. Two of the land-barons had their daggers out, and the guards efficiently disarmed them and shoved them against walls. The room filled with angry voices.

Lyeth looked at Emris, who stared at his grandfather's bed. She looked beyond him to Joleda, who crossed her arms: Joleda was born in Jentesi; she would die in Jentesi. At the Lord of Alanti: Merinam, Trappers, and the sea; a future Jentesi would forfeit to a civil war. Torwyn looked grim, and Coreon, from the stretcher, giggled. Culdyn wept, and Syne looked over the chaos of the room with cool triumph. Emris moved in her arms and she held him tighter. I can't lose him, she thought wildly. I won't let them have him. He's all I have. Torwyn, Elea, Joleda, Crise, Ilen—the eyes of all her friends, centered on one Rider and one small boy. Lyeth bent from them abruptly.

"Emris," she whispered with despair, "I don't know what to do."

He stared past her at the shouting barons. "You promised that you'd never leave me. That's all that matters. That you'll never leave me."

She touched his cheek. "Do you know what they want of you?"

"Yes. I am to be owned again. I am to be what they want me to be. Lyeth," he cried suddenly, "don't make me do it by myself."

She straightened abruptly and, almost without volition, grabbed her dagger from its sheath and held it aloft, point down. Someone called her name and the noise ebbed to silence.

"Little bitch," Gambin said.

She put both hands to the dagger's hilt and knelt before the boy, watching his eyes.

"On this I swear," she said, and stopped, and cleared her throat. "On this I swear, by my guild and by my honor, that I will serve you when this oath is done, that I will ride for you as my only lord and my only master, protecting your trust and cherishing your secrets as I would those of the Mother, on whose warm breast I swear this oath. Take my dagger as you take my trust."

Emris reached hesitantly for the dagger's hilt. She nodded.

"Rider," Gambin said.

The boy cupped his hands around the Rider's fingers and Joleda stooped to whisper in his ear. His clear voice rose over the room.

"I will take you as my Rider, when your oath is done, to ride for me within the bounds of your oath and of your guild. Take your dagger as you take my trust."

Petras came around the bed to rest his hand on Emris' shoulder, and Lyeth closed her eyes. In the hush that followed a wheezing came from the bed. Tobi rushed forward, hands extended, and the two seminarians crowded close, already opening their boxes. Gambin gasped and wheezed and gasped again, gesturing them away. He looked at Lyeth, eyes streaming, and she realized with horror that the old man was laughing.

"You'll stay after I'm dead, Rider," he said, coughing. "You'll oath to my son. Gambini blood. I won, Rider. I won." Then the laughter choked him and he died.

She left before midnight. Three horses stood in the corral amidships; Jandi in his coffin rested in the hold of the Gambini iceboat, and Robin, wrapped in cloaks and blankets, slept uneasily in the cabin beside him. Lyeth stood at the stern, looking up the dark face of the Rock to the castle. The Deathnote, carefully lettered by Maranta's favorite astrologer, rested in the pouch at her hip. In the second hold, guards stood over Culdyn Gambini and his sister Syne, bound for the council's justice in Vantua. Coreon was dead.

"Set, mistress?" the captain called.

"Set."

Emris and Torwyn, on the quay, watched silently. Lyeth touched the guild tokens around her neck. Deckhands slid the gangplank onto the boat and pushed away from the quay; wind slapped into the sails.

"A month," Emris called suddenly. "Lyeth, no more than a month."

"A month, my Lord," she called back. Torwyn put his hand on the boy's shoulder and the boat heeled. Jentesi Rock rushed away from her, black and white and grey under the bright moonlight. Walls of snow loomed along the cleared path; as the iceboat moved into them she turned her face and saw the Crescent Bathhouse lit from within, a bauble of incandescence quickly glimpsed before the iceboat tacked sharply and raced down the frozen Tobrin toward the sea.

# Epilogue

**B**Y the time Lyeth returned from Vantua the season of storms had passed, winter roses bloomed through the snow of Horda's Garden, and the Lady Maranta, now firmly ensconced as co-regent along with Lord Torwyn, had delved through Master Durn's records and unearthed Emris' history, including, to her vast and longwinded delight, his birthdate. Lyeth heard about this on her way up castle, and it did not please her. Neither did the absence of both Emris and Torwyn at the quay, and the unpacking job Janya and Militent had done in her new rooms behind the Great Hall, and the court's whole-hearted adoption of astrology as its favored pastime. Natal signs cropped up on personal banners, jewelry, tinware, cups; some of the gaudier courtiers wore their charts, done in embroidery and set with gems, on tabards and cloaks. Emris would not be able to see her until the next morning. Crise and Ilen were both on duty. Torwyn was not in his rooms. Muttering under her breath, Lyeth strode into the kitchen to be cursed by Bedwyn Cook.

Maranta had caused the new lord's chart to be set in deep crystal on a little clockwork base that, once properly wound, turned grace-fully and emitted a cheerful, tinkling tune. Lyeth watched it suspi-ciously as Emris, combed and cleaned and dressed in satins, set the toy in motion. Clear winter sunlight fell through the windows; in the next room, a minstrel picked out melodies in a minor key that clashed faintly with the music of the chart.

"I'm governed by the Moon," Emris explained gravely. "And since I was born at dawn, the Sun is my Ascendant. That's Ice and Fire, and Maranta says that's very good."

Lyeth grunted noncommittally. They had greeted each other tentatively, as though searching for signs of change, and she now tucked her hands behind her back and tried not to feel bereft.

"The Minstrel governs my Natal House; that's an Earth sign to balance the Fire and Water, and it's ruled by Teben and Teben is another Fire sign. That's good, too, but Maranta says it means I tend to be hotheaded."

"I could have told you that," Lyeth muttered. "My Lord."

The boy ignored her. "Teben is also in my House of Strength, along with Ice Palace and the influence of Garth. Two Air signs and one Fire sign. But Albyn rules my House of Progress, and Albyn is a Time sign and that's probably the reason it took so long for me to get here. Garth—that's Air, and that's here, in my House of the Soul. And over here, that's Thed in my House of Intelligence. Thed's a Water sign. But my Earth signs balance that, especially with the Mill in my House of Progress. Of course, I've got Fire signs in my Houses of Soul and Intelligence—Maranta says that means I'll govern wisely but I have to watch my temper. And everything I do will last a long time, because none of my Fire signs are washed out by Water signs. Do you understand?"

Lyeth crossed her arms. "Not a damned word."

"Oh." Emris put his finger to the clockwork chart, stopping it in midtinkle. "You should make an effort."

"My Lord."

"It's really very useful."

"My Lord."

"It's taught me quite a lot already."

"My Lord?"

"For example," Emris said, releasing the chart, "it taught me to be patient with Lady Maranta." A smile tugged at the corners of his mouth. "Besides, whenever she gets too awful, I just command someone to have a chart drawn up and it keeps her busy for a while."

"Not me, Emris," Lyeth said, alarmed. "My Lord. I don't have a birthday, remember?"

"You can share mine," Emris said grandly.

"You don't . . . you don't believe any of that stuff, do you?" Lyeth said uneasily. "My Lord?"

In answer, Emris shouted with laughter, rushed around the table, and flung himself into her arms. She hugged him tightly and carried him from the room, golden head next to her brown one, while he earnestly tried to talk her into running forfeits through the castle halls.

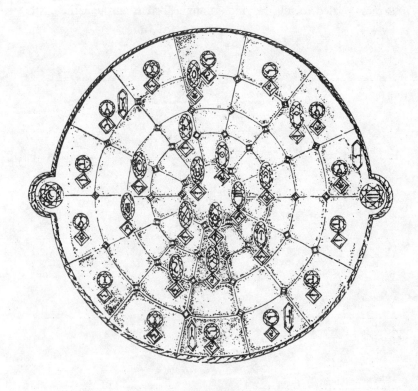

MARANTA'S HOROSCOPE
FOR EMRIS

# THE HOUSES

## First Circle

 The Loom
Water
Thed

 The Mill
Earth
Garth

 The Plow
Earth
Albyn

 The Wheel
Fire
Garth

 The Bucket
Time
Teben

## Second Circle

 Ice Palace
Air
Garth

 The Tree
Water
Albyn

 The Horse
Fire
Teben

 The Oxen
Time
Thed

## Third Circle

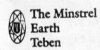 The Minstrel
Earth
Teben

 The Scarf
Water
Thed

 The Child
Time
Albyn

## Fourth Circle

 The Eye
Time
Teben

 The Lady
Fire
Garth

# THE PLANETS

 Moon    Sun    Albyn
Time    Thed
Water    Teben
Air   Garth
Air

# PLANETARY INFLUENCES

 Albyn    Thed    Teben    Garth

# THE ELEMENTS

 Time   Earth    Water   Fire   Air

M. M. Roessner-Herman

# ABOUT THE AUTHOR

Marta Randall was born in Mexico but has lived most of her life in Northern California in the San Francisco Bay area. She attended college in San Francisco, married and had a son, and has worked for many years for a patent attorney, an experience which she finds very useful when negotiating publishing contracts for her books.

She began publishing short stories in the early 1970s, and her work appeared regularly in *New Dimensions* while Robert Silverberg was editing it. With Volume 11 she became coeditor with Silverberg, and with Volume 13 she took over all editorial responsibility for the series.

Her first novel, *Islands,* was one of five nominees for the Nebula Award. Since then she has published *A City in the North, Journey,* and *Dangerous Games,* all of which take place against the same background of future history.

Randall was toastmaster at the World Science Fiction Convention in Chicago over Labor Day weekend in 1982. She has served for several years as an executive officer in the Science Fiction Writers of America and is currently president of the organization. She lives in a house in the Oakland hills with her son, two cats, a dog, and an electric typewriter.